ACT OF FATE

Also by John Bishop

ACT OF MURDER

ACT OF DECEPTION

ACT OF REVENGE

ACT OF NEGLIGENCE

ACT OF FATE

A DOC BRADY MYSTERY

John Bishop, MD

MANTID PRESS

CONTENTS

THE SHOOTER

Wednesday, April 4, 2001

Meredith Brown James stepped into the shower, reached for the polished brass knobs inlaid with the onyx letters *H* and *C*, turned them until the temperature was just shy of steaming, and put her head under the customized matching brass spigot. Hundreds of tiny jets of hot water pummeled her scalp like needle pricks. Painful, but . . . it hurts so good, she often said. As did the massage she received an hour earlier, when Manny, the Polynesian masseuse, kneaded her spasmodic muscles after her daily strenuous one-hour aerobics work-out. The young, energetic female instructor at Body Rock had taken the class into a frenzied communal endorphin high, while the state-of-the-art sound system blared a medley of Doobie Brothers tunes, like "Long Train Running," "Jesus is Just All Right With Me," and "China Grove."

But Meredith had grown to love the daily pain of an hour of frenzied high-impact aerobics to deafening dance music, followed by a thirty-minute muscle "melt-down" by a man who could have been a Sumo wrestler in another life. And now, a near-boiling shower. But so what? No pain, no gain. A woman can't be too rich, or in too good of shape at forty-five years of age, especially at this very important point in her life.

Meredith opened her eyes, faced away from the steaming, prickling spray, and leaned her head back. She ran her long, delicate, manicured fingers through her shoulder-length auburn hair, allowing the water to deeply penetrate the follicles. As she massaged her scalp, she admired, through squinting eyes, her private bath. The black marble whirlpool tub built for two, the glassed-in black marble shower in which she stood, the customized pink and black tiles on the spotless, gleaming floor. Smaller pink and black square tiles bordered the black marble sink and built-in dressing table. Custom brass fixtures adorned the sink and blended artfully with the shower and tub fixtures. When she and her husband were building the house, they had decided to spare no expense, especially in the bathroom.

Her husband. Dr. Frank James. This special lunch was about their marriage, their future together. Frank was scheduled to arrive promptly at two o'clock. One moment Meredith considered making him wait, but the next, meeting him at the door with a drink. She smiled, relishing the fact that Frank would not be able to open the front door to his own home. She doubted he would dare try to open the door with his now-defunct key, not that he has a clue the locks have been changed. She hoped that perhaps the wayward Frank James had finally evolved, had become an honorable man, and that he'd ring the doorbell, like a proper suitor.

Meredith smiled and continued to lather her lithe five-foot-four body. Her breasts were full but did not sag, because her pectoral muscles were tight. Hard work had conditioned those chest muscles to hold her breasts high, giving her the appearance of a much younger woman when wearing a dress with a plunging neckline. No breast enhancements or breast lifts for this girl, she had repeated time and time again. Meredith's motto was simple: take care of your body's muscles, and they will take care of you.

She massaged her muscular thighs and calves and checked her fingernail and toenail polish, ensuring there were no chips or scratches that needed to be repaired before *his* arrival. Then she methodically shampooed her thick, reddish-brown hair, rinsed it, chased it with conditioner, then rinsed again thoroughly. She wanted her hair to have body and to shine radiantly during the afternoon's festivities. She wanted to be perfect. Perfect hair, perfect nails, perfect body, perfect makeup, perfect dress. A perfect ten.

Meredith sat at her dressing table in the pink and black bathroom and carefully applied several layers of cosmetics under the revealing lights of the built-in Hollywood mirror centered precisely between the two marbled his-and-hers sinks. Just the right amount of powder, makeup base, rouge, eyeliner, and eye shadow. She was beautiful without the beauty aids but even more stunning with it. She applied a good deal of lipstick for her large, pouting lips. Regardless of what the current New York and Paris magazines said about fashion in general, she believed them to be absolutely correct about one thing: that lips were pure sex. That the mouth was a woman's most erotic feature. And Meredith made absolutely sure that Frank would notice hers. She puckered her thick lips and read the label on the cap. Ruby Red. Is this bright enough for you, baby?

She stood, dried her hair, teased it into a "yes, I'm wild, and I'll do anything" look, and gently sprayed it into position. She stepped into her closet and selected a pair of black three-inch pumps and a very short black cocktail dress. The dress was cut too low for a bra, and God forbid Frank should notice a dreaded panty line under the sleek, tight outline of what he had once referred to as "that spray-on dress." So, forget the underwear. She wanted Frank salivating in his pasta. She wanted him to want her more than anyone else he'd ever wanted in the history of their marriage. More than those bimbos that worked at the hospital, the ones Frank had been intermittently bedding for years. She thought all nurses were continuously trying to snare a married surgeon for their own husband. But Meredith could play that game as good as anyone. Maybe better.

She decided to make a pitcher of Bombay gin martinis to get them both loosened up a little. They'd have a drink, make small talk, sort of get to know one another again. They'd discuss their relationship, agree to put all others aside, and concentrate on their marriage. Then, she would serve Frank his favorite tagliarini pasta from Grotto Ristorante, which she picked up on the way home from Body Rock. And when the time was right, and Frank was putty in her hands, she'd make all the moves necessary to get him back, which was all she'd ever wanted in the first place. But now, it was finally possible for Meredith to cement their relationship.

Sure, Meredith had had several affairs of her own, more out of self-defense than physical desire. She never truly wanted to have an extramarital relationship, but Frank had started it first, years before, about halfway through their fifteen-year marriage. It had all started with late nights, allegedly at work. Then came the out-of-town medical meetings, after which he would return home with a strange woman's scent on his clothes. Like she wouldn't know. Women can tell when their mate has been intimate with another; it's sort of a built-in sixth sense.

So, to allay her fears about being unattractive and undesirable—not that she truly believed that of herself—she had a fling or two. The men meant nothing to her but were simply a temporary diversion. Meredith felt the need to be wanted, to be desired, to be held. Is that a sin?

After the separation, she had a series of male relationships, some sexual, most just dates for dinner, a movie, or a play. Only one of the affairs could be categorized as torrid, probably because it was essentially a two-month sexual romp. The man was adamant about continuing to see her and did not want to take a hike as he was instructed. He became a little belligerent and even tried to get physically abusive. Meredith had simply dismissed him with a wave of her hand and an uplifting of her nose. He pestered her for a while, then finally gave up when she refused to see him, answer his letters, or return his phone calls. She had another agenda, one much more important than anything physical pleasure could provide.

But all that was over, "Thank God," Meredith whispered. Frank was coming home, and the two of them could work it out. She would see to it. And after a blissful and intense sexual reunion, Frank would drive her over to University Hospital to see her father, who was undergoing an operation to rid himself of a nasty bone cancer. She wondered what the survival rate was, then quickly put the irrelevant and disrespectful thought out of her mind. Not very kind, Meredith, to think about the amount of your inheritance when your father was in surgery. Besides, there could be no kinder or more generous parents than Melvin and Sarah Brown.

She checked the clasp of her Rolex watch with the diamond bezel, the one Frank gave her for a previous birthday. She admired it, rotating her wrist from side to side, watching the stones sparkle as they caught the ceiling lights in the closet.

Meredith decided she needed something else, an exquisite piece, perhaps an item from Frank, appropriate for this, the perfect occasion. She reopened her jewelry box, searched, then smiled. She stepped back in front of the mirror, fastening the 18-karat-gold necklace holding a three-carat white diamond solitaire in an 18-karat-gold heart-shaped setting, at the nape of her neck. She stared for a moment, deciding this piece was . . . perfect. She had been surprised with it two months before, on the eve of her birthday, during her nightly love affair with the man she now found repulsive. It had been delivered to her front door in a blue box with a white ribbon, accompanied by a red rose. The card that accompanied the gift stated simply, "From one who cares." Meredith assumed at the time that Frank had remembered her birthday in spite of their marital difficulties, and the separation. She would wear it today, monitor Frank's reaction, and only hope he had been the one to send it.

Meredith experienced a sudden twinge of guilt for not being in the hospital waiting room, holding her mother's hand during Daddy's operation. She regretted her parents were upset about this "special" lunch being scheduled at the same time as her father's surgery, but this was more important. Once this afternoon had passed, her troubles would be over, and she and Frank would be together again. Forever.

Meredith stood in front of the full-length mirror, turned from side to side, and admired her reflection. You've got a great body, kid, she told herself. You will be irresistible. Frank will do anything to get in your panties. Laughing aloud, she considered the irony. She didn't have any on.

She fluffed her long, gorgeous hair one more time and turned completely around, facing away from the mirror. She then rotated her head back toward the mirror to check for threads hanging from the hem of her black minidress. Once again assuring herself that she was as perfect as possible, she turned around once more and started to exit the closet.

The shooter carefully stepped along the boardwalk and over Buffalo Bayou, the ravine that begins in downtown Houston as the western tributary of the Houston Ship Channel. The old boardwalk, half-hidden by thick underbrush, was once used by the staff of Memorial Bend, formerly a massive family-owned property on the west side of town, to cross from their employer's mansion to the servants' quarters on the south side of the bayou. The property had been sold and subdivided many times over the years, and the ancient and rickety hand-constructed walkway had long been forgotten.

The shooter tromped through the tangle of moss-covered pines and willows, giant oaks and elms, and thick ground ferns, toward the rear gate of the home. The shooter walked along a newly constructed asphalt path, which ran east to west behind the homes, making sure of the correct home. This was not a time for mistakes.

Now certain of being in the right place, the shooter opened the eight-foot redwood gate and peered into the small backyard.

Wednesday was trash day, and all the residents were required to keep the back gate unlocked if they wanted to be delivered from the unpleasant stench of waste products from their respective homes. How convenient that the residents thoughtfully pooled a minute portion of their vast collective fortunes in order to build the gray-black walkway behind the ten bayou-front homes, in order that employees of the private refuse collection company wouldn't have to muss their work boots in case of rain.

The figure quietly walked along the flagstone deck, stopping to view the sparkle of the bright April sun as it reflected off the kidney-shaped pool. The shooter dodged a stream of chlorine-tainted spray from the pool sweep, then stepped a few more yards to the glass doors that led into the sunroom. Pausing under the green and white canopy, an extension of the roof overhang, the shooter gently pulled the wooden handle to the right, in order to slide the door open. Locked, as it should be. Homeowners in this enclave are highly paranoid about robberies. They all have a lot to steal.

The shooter opened a leather case, pulled out two small metal picks, and opened the customized burglar-resistant door lock in eight seconds. The shooter carefully slid open the door and listened closely for the familiar sounds of an alarm, electronic or canine. Nothing.

The shooter crept into the Mexican-tiled sunroom, slid the entry door closed, then carefully checked the alarm panel to the right of the glass doors for assurance that the security system was, in fact, disarmed. A silent alarm system would make this adventure very unpleasant.

The shooter looked around the living room. Such order, such opulence. Impressive. Carefully and quietly, the shooter stepped toward the staircase in the entry hall. The athletic shoes made progress virtually soundless.

After removing the sneakers, the shooter quietly walked up the carpeted stairs, paused at the landing on the second floor, and listened. There was the sound of a hair dryer and tinny background music coming from a radio. The shooter raised the right pants leg of the jogging suit and unfastened a 9-mm Beretta automatic from its Velcro straps. The shooter chambered a round, then waited a second to make sure the hair dryer had not stopped. The slide needed to be oiled; it made too much noise.

But the hair dryer was still going, just like the Eveready pink rabbit. The shooter carefully detached the silencer from its Velcro binder on the same leg and screwed it into place.

The shooter waited, waited for the precise moment when it would be time to—

The shooter heard laughter and panicked, thinking the target might not be alone. For a split second, changing course was a consideration. Turn back, get out, forget about it, before it's too late. But time had run out. It was too late to retreat, the shooter decided, and ran up the second flight of stairs, through the master bedroom, into the pink and black bathroom, and met her as she was turning to walk out of her closet.

She was dressed to the nines and looked absolutely gorgeous. The shooter watched her mouth sag, then the shooter stared at the full, red lips as they parted to form a scream. The shooter stepped toward her, brought the pistol to her forehead, and fired.

The impact of the bullet propelled Meredith Brown James backward against her full-length mirror, instantly scattering globules of blood, brain tissue, and bone fragments, forming bright-red rivulets against the reflective surface. The human quagmire smeared vertically, following Meredith as she slid down the mirror and onto the floor.

The shooter leaned over her body, counted down from her thin neck to the fifth rib with the end of the silencer, and fired again, directly into her failing heart.

The shooter stared at Meredith's dead body and noticed the diamond pendant. The shooter leaned down and pulled it free, snapping the soft, 18-karat gold necklace precisely at the clasp. Standing erect, the shooter pocketed the diamond and chain.

The shooter looked at the body one last time and smiled at the private joke. She *had been* drop-dead gorgeous.

The shooter flew down the stairs and sat only long enough to tie the athletic shoes, but hesitated at the bottom step as it spilled into the foyer. A figure was standing outside the front door. Fortunately, the solid oak entry door was composed of reinforced leaded stained glass from the waist up. The person at the door would see only a shadow, and a distorted one at that.

The shooter heard the doorbell ring and watched the person on the front steps wave. The shooter smiled again, pointed the Beretta at the figure, and said, "Bang."

The shooter quickly left through the rear door, trotted past the pool, and left the back yard through the rear gate. Picking up speed, the shooter ran along the asphalt pathway behind the complex, abruptly veered down the incline through the underbrush, and ran over the boardwalk to the north side of the bayou and to safety.

The shooter reached the car, unscrewed the silencer from the weapon, and reattached each component to its proper position in the Velcro of the holster. The engine turned over and revved, and the shooter took off.

While driving, the shooter removed the cap and glasses and threw them in the rear seat. The timing was as it should have been, perfect, in fact. The mission was . . . a perfect ten.

PART 1

MISSED LUNCH

Wednesday, April 4, 2001

I glanced at the clock hanging slightly askew in Operating Room 26 of University Hospital in the University Medical Center in Houston, Texas. It was Wednesday afternoon and already three thirty, and I was still wrestling with Mr. Melvin Brown's log of a leg. "Dr. James Robert Brady, you have to be half crazy to still be working this hard!" I yelled into my helmet. Such dedication. Such loyalty. Such horse manure.

Earlier that morning, I made arrangements to meet Mary Louise, my wife, at Paco's, a new restaurant on the west side of town. She was to arrive at one o'clock. I, perennially late, was to have been there no later than two. Unfortunately, my surgical schedule burgeoned as the day progressed, and operations took longer than expected. After all, you can't open up the human body, replace a joint with an artificial substance, and just leave the premises to go have lunch with your wife. The patient has to be identified, an operative permit has to be signed, and the patient counseled for any last-minute questions that might arise. The operation has to be completed as perfectly as humanly possible, the wound has to be closed, the operative report dictated, post-op orders written, and the family spoken to. That is not a process that I or any other surgeon can, or would, ever rush. Always try to do the right thing and do your best to take the best possible care of your patients, surgically and emotionally. That is the Creed. The Hippocratic Oath. That was my job.

I was a doctor, an orthopedic surgeon, a hip and knee joint replacement specialist. I was a native Texan and stood a little over six feet tall, although I would swear, after a single-malt scotch or two, that I used to be six two. My brown hair was graying behind a steadily expanding widow's peak, and my similarly discoloring mustache was, and always had been, and probably always would be, unruly. I never seemed to remember to trim the damn thing until someone like Mary Louise, or my secretary Fran, or my nurse Rae, or, on occasion, a long-term patient, reminded me that I'd left a remnant of breakfast or lunch in the weed patch. I enjoy a readily available snack, I liked to retort, gross as that seems.

And although I suffered a few other signs of aging, such as a waistline that had gradually expanded from a size 32 to a size 40, and visible crow's feet to each side of my hazel eyes—or so the driver's license read, even though they looked more brown to me—my wife still said that I was a handsome man.

And, if that weren't enough, Mary Louise said—and she knew me better than anyone—I had a loving, caring personality. Which, I suppose, was designed to partially compensate for the physical and mental toll that the practice of medicine had bestowed upon me over these previous twenty-two-or-so years. As far as I was concerned, however, a "warm and fuzzy" personality didn't come close to making up for wrinkles, a soft body, and a bald head.

I got along with most everybody: patients, the nursing and ancillary personnel, my colleagues. I could even abide other surgeons, though they were for the most part a jealous, competitive, and cynical lot. Most importantly, though, I got along with my wife of thirty years. She was my best friend, which made the fact that I was standing her up for our Wednesday lunch date that much more regrettable. And I felt especially bad that I was forced to have my old friend, orthopedic nursing supervisor Loretta Birdwell, make the "regrets" call to Mary Louise's cell phone while she was sitting at the restaurant, patiently waiting for me, the tardy husband. As usual, she was understanding, and through Loretta's side of the conversation with her, I learned that Mary Louise's plan was to order her lunch and sample the cappuccino—she was a connoisseur, after all—and that she would deal with me later, at home. And that could be good, or otherwise.

Despite those ruminations, I continued working on the difficult surgical procedure, relieved that, as always, Mary Louise was sympathetic. She never made me feel guilty when work took me away from our scheduled time together, which made me love her that much more. While she was the most important thing in my life, right above J. J., our grown son, work did come first.

I contemplated that irony while mixing cement in my space suit.

The patient was suffering from a giant-cell tumor of bone, specifically of the femur, the large thigh bone that ends in a trumpet-shaped flange that forms the top half of the knee joint. I was in the process of resecting the tumor and replacing the ruined knee joint with a stainless steel and plastic substitute.

During surgery, I usually reflected quite a bit about various subjects. It's not that I didn't pay attention to my work, but times existed during a case when the procedure was so routine and had been embedded in my brain so many times, that I allowed my consciousness to drift. Sometimes I shared these thoughts with my fellow operators, and sometimes I did not. On that day, I was reminiscing about that patient's first visit to my office.

He was a very important man, that Melvin Brown. He was a member of the board of directors of both University Hospital and University Medical School, as well as numerous other prominent institutions in Houston, such as Houston Lighting and Power, Exxon, and the University of Houston. And, being a very wealthy man and a philanthropist, and therefore a patron of the arts, he had funded numerous events to benefit the Houston Grand Opera, the Houston Ballet, and the Houston Symphony.

He also happened to be the father-in-law of one of my colleagues, Dr. Frank James, a neurosurgeon at University. All that added up to extra pressure, not that we surgeons didn't feel some degree of pressure during each and every procedure. But there was more than usual with this man, probably because the chief of orthopedics stopped by in the pre-op area, as did the CEO of the hospital, and several board members.

That probably explains why, as I was holding the new knee-joint components in position while the cement hardened, there was some extra angst if they didn't fit properly. They were, of course, perfect, so my worry was needless. However, none of us doctors and health-care professionals were immune to the terrible trials and tribulations that could befall anyone in that pressure-cooker business of ours, especially when the patient was a mucky-muck of some note. And it was not that Mr. Brown was any more important than any other patient. I firmly believed that all patients had been created equal. The difference was that if his result wasn't as good as anticipated, he knew a lot more people to tell about my shoddy work than, say, Aunt Mimoo from Possum, Texas.

CHAPTER 2

BONE CANCER

Wednesday, April 4, 2001

Mr. Brown had presented himself to my office two weeks earlier, complaining of pain and swelling in the knee. He had rushed right in to see me about his knee problem, three months after the symptoms had become almost unbearable for the average mortal. His friends, over golf and cocktails at an exclusive Houston country club, told him repeatedly that guys his age get arthritis, torn cartilages, that sort of thing, and that he should take some Advil, or Motrin, or have an extra martini. And to work on his swing, which apparently was worse than ever, but which was never that good, according to the patient.

But nothing he tried had worked to alleviate the pain. Melvin Brown's knee pain became so severe that he could not even play golf, not even when he used a cart. He wasn't able to swing through the ball due to the pain, and his golf scores went to hell in a handbasket. And that wouldn't do, he told me during the initial office visit, since he and his friends placed wagers on every game, from $100 to $1000 *per hole*, depending on the day, and the competition . . . and the blood-alcohol levels of the individuals involved. He said he was losing a lot of money, and that was not something he enjoyed or intended to continue doing. He needed fixing, and quick, so he could get back on the golf course and recoup his losses.

At a cursory glance, Mr. Brown was an ideal candidate for arthritis. He was sixty-seven, with a height of over six feet, and a weight in excess of 250 pounds. However, when I reviewed his X-rays, much to his and my chagrin, I found the patient had a massive destructive lesion in the distal femur. The cortex of the bone was expanded on both the right and left sides of his thigh and had extended down into the knee joint itself. The tumor looked like a large, multiloculated cyst, which had fractured through the protective covering of the bone, called cartilage, and spilled its toxic contents into his knee joint cavity. That explained the intense swelling and pain, the poor golf scores, and the disastrous capital contributions to his friends.

Looking at his films, it seemed to me that a lesser man could not have withstood the pain as long as Melvin Brown had, but that was part of his countenance. A self-made billionaire, he had repeatedly lost, then regained, untold fortunes in the risky business of wildcatting in the oil fields. Oil. Black gold. Texas tea. Houston was built with profits made in the oil business by tough risk-takers like Melvin Brown who, with a roll of the dice, made or lost all they had on one hole in the ground.

I explained to Mr. Brown that he had a bone tumor, that it might be malignant, and that it needed to be biopsied right away. He balked, told me that I was crazy as hell, and demanded a second opinion. He checked out his X-rays and went to another orthopedic surgeon the next day. He received the same diagnosis and the same treatment recommendations. And he saw yet another surgeon the following day and again heard the same story I had given him.

So Mr. Brown came back to see me and told me to go ahead and do what I had to do. He said that I had come highly recommended by his internist, by some of his friends whom I had operated on, and by his son-in-law, my doctor-colleague Frank James. He also intimated that if he had to have an operation, he preferred to have a doctor with a name like Jim Bob Brady, who wore cowboy boots. He wanted his surgeon to be a Texan, not, in his words, "some East Coast infiltrator."

Perhaps that concept was a little corny to some, but I'd lived here all my life, and I could attest to the local flavor of our conversations. It was just down-home trash talk about other regions, not unlike what we did at sporting events.

I performed a needle biopsy of the tumor the following day, under local anesthesia with some intravenous sedation, in a minor-procedure room in the outpatient center of University Hospital. A pathologist required seven days to report accurate results of a specimen such as Melvin Brown's and to make the decision whether a tumor of bone is malignant or not. The specimen had to decalcify, so that the calcium, phosphorus, and other minerals could be leeched out. This allowed the pathologist to properly interpret the slides by studying the intrinsics of the marrow, with its blood cells and protein matter. It was this substance of the bone, the microscopic collagen, the very essence of the body's often-fragile existence, that would seal the fate of my patient.

And so it came to pass, armed with a printout of the soft tissue and bony pathology reports, that I again saw Melvin Brown, his lovely wife Sarah, and their only daughter, Meredith Brown James, Frank's wife, in the University Orthopedic Clinic the following week.

"Mr. Brown, you have what we call a giant-cell tumor. It's growing in the bone just above your knee but has extended into the joint, which explains all that swelling and pain you've had there. Problem is, there are some cells in the tissue specimen that seem to have undergone malignant change."

Sarah Brown rose from a chair adjacent to Melvin Brown, who was sitting on the examination table fully dressed and entering a state of emotional shock. She sidled up to her husband, put her arm around his shoulders, and stood beside him. She was a short woman, and despite the fact that she elected to stand, her head still didn't quite reach his eye level. She wore a denim dress that day, with red ropers, lots of turquoise jewelry on both wrists, and a large Navajo sterling-silver pendant hammered into the shape of a huge cross. Her silver hair was coiffured into a short pageboy style, which blended pleasantly with her blue eyes.

Meredith, on the other hand, was exceptionally striking, as always, but in a different way from her mother. She wore a cream-colored Chanel suit, a red silk blouse, and red satin high heels. Her long auburn hair was pulled fashionably behind her head and held with a silk scarf that matched her outfit. When her mother rose to stand with Melvin Brown, she rose as well and flanked her father on the opposite side. The three stared at me like I was Lucifer unleashed from the gates of Hades.

"So what does that mean, Doc? You have to cut the leg off?" Melvin Brown asked incredulously.

"Well, sir, that is one option. I hate to be blunt, but you should know that the one surefire way to cure this tumor is to do an amputation. But the level would have to be well above the tumor."

I stepped forward from my spot against the opposite wall, placed a hand halfway up his thigh, and drew an invisible line.

Sarah Brown stared at me, a total stranger of a doctor—it was her first visit to my office—giving her and her husband some of the worst news of their lives.

"Above all else, Dr. Brady, I want my husband to live, whatever it takes. If he lost a leg, an arm, or both eyes, it makes no nevermind to me. But I want this man to live. We've only been married forty-three years, and we got a lotta good years ahead of us. We've got Meredith here to look after, and we still hope someday to have grandchildren. Whatever you have to do, you make sure he survives. I don't want you to take any chances with some newfangled kind of treatment. I want the surest thing you know how to do to be done. Our daughter says you'll do the right thing. And so does her husband."

Meredith had married Dr. Frank James, one of my medical school classmates who had become a very prominent neurosurgical colleague. Frank, like me, grew up in humble beginnings in West Texas, and had scraped through college and medical school in order to make something of himself. When it came time for marriage, Frank's philosophy was simple: it's just as easy to love a rich girl as it is to love a poor girl. Thus, he had married the beautiful socialite Meredith Brown.

"Mama, Daddy, just listen to what Jim here has to say," Meredith said, in a sexy alto voice. "He's going to do the right thing, like Frank and I told you. Now don't interrupt him. Please."

Melvin Brown hung his head, like a child being scolded for eating cookies before supper. I studied him for a moment before continuing. This wealthy scion of a Houston oil fortune wore wrinkled and faded khakis with scattered black spots, which looked like old, dried crankcase oil. The sleeves of his plaid flannel shirt were rolled up irregularly to the elbows, the right pocket stuffed with reading glasses, folded papers, and two Bic pens. He had on scuffed, once-tan bull-hide cowboy boots, with one leg of his khakis tucked down inside the right boot. Although there are exceptions to every rule, Melvin Brown confirmed that day the inverse relationship here in Texas between how much money a man has, and his concern over appearances.

My patient kneaded his gnarled, calloused hands, so rough they sounded like sandpaper as he wrung them together. As I studied the ruddy, leathery face of one of Houston's richest and most generous men, partially hidden under the faded felt Western hat like the one country singer Don Williams wore, I noticed a tear roll gently down his cheek. Sarah reached over, picked up her purse, withdrew a white handkerchief, and wiped his eye. Melvin Brown continued to hang his head low under the brim of his hat and avoid my eyes.

"We do have another option, folks. Do you want to hear about it?" I said, as positively as I could. I wanted to cry as well at that point in the conversation as I watched this couple, still in love after forty years of marriage, trying to cope with the problem of bone cancer. Whatever I may be, and the verdict's still out on that, I am ultra-sensitive to my patients' maladies, especially those that can result in death.

Melvin Brown looked up at me, then at his wife, then at Meredith. "Sure, Doc. What you gotta say?"

"If we run some tests—total-body bone scan, CAT scan, MRI, abdominal ultrasound, blood tests—and find there has been no spread of the cancer into any other part of your body, I may suggest to you, and to your wife and daughter, of course, that you consider a removal of the tumor and the insertion of an artificial knee joint, which would in essence be a cure."

"How can you remove the tumor if, as you've shown us on the X-rays, the end of the thigh bone has been destroyed?" Sarah Brown asked. "Take the whole thing out?"

"Yes, ma'am. You see—"

"Wait a minute, Doc," interjected Mr. Brown, "how can you just take my bone out? What would hold up my weight?"

I had, the day before, retrieved some photographs of a custom-made total knee replacement, along with similar X-rays of a previous patient who had received this state-of-the-art treatment.

"What we do, folks, is to go in and remove the top part of the tibia, that's the lower leg bone that makes up the bottom half of the knee joint, just like we do when we replace a knee joint for arthritis. Then, instead of removing just the end of the thigh bone, like we would for arthritis, we take out all of the bone that's involved by tumor," illustrating on the X-rays just how far up the femur the tumor extended.

"In your case, Mr. Brown, that's about eight inches." I paused and waited for questions. None were forthcoming, so I proceeded.

"Then, we cement a custom prosthesis into position, which replaces the knee joint, and then, with wires and cement, we weld the top of the stem of the femur side of the prosthesis to the rest of your thigh bone."

"Doctor," Mrs. Brown asked, "how would he walk? Normal?"

"No, ma'am, not normal. But better than he would with an above-the-knee amputation, especially a man in his late sixties. Not that you're old, Mr. Brown," I said, and smiled my most optimistic smile.

Melvin Brown and his wife gazed at each other, sharing a silent communion they had developed during forty or so years of togetherness.

"What about survival rates, Dr. Brady? Can you comment on that?" Sarah asked.

"Well, Mrs. Brown, that all depends on the extent of metastases, which imply spread of the cancer, that is. If the tests are clear, the five-year survival rate is the same, whether you go with removal of the leg or with removal of the tumor and prosthetic replacement."

Melvin Brown looked up from underneath his tattered, worn hat, a hat that had probably seen millions of barrels of oil rushing out of the ground at breakneck speed. He stared deeply into my eyes, then right through them, it seemed at the time, after which I appreciated his publicized technique for finding oil. He would simply look right through the ground, into a 5,000-foot-deep pool of fossil fuel. Drill here, boys, he would say. His geologists would ask, But what about the seismic? Drill here, he would answer, and point at a mound of South Texas dirt and clay that couldn't grow a blade of green grass if it wanted to. And sure enough, that dilapidated earth would soon be spewing forth 500 barrels of crude a day. In a rare interview for *Texas Monthly*, my patient had been referred to as "Diviner" Brown.

"What would you do if you were in my shoes, Doc?"

I smiled, nodded, gave him my straightest answer. "Go for the replacement. In a New York minute."

One side of his mouth upturned, in a sort of half smile. "Mama?"

"It's up to you, Papa."

"Daughter?"

"Jim's already told you what to do, Daddy. Go ahead," she said, and placed a brightly polished and manicured hand around his shoulder.

Mr. Houston, Mr. Wildcatter, member of the Board of Directors of University Hospital—my employer, more or less—perked up.

That positive look he was known for, the one that for decades had preempted the science of geological formations, the one that had allowed him to discover a record number of virgin oil fields throughout South Texas, came over his face. "I'm in your hands, Doc. Do what you think is right. But do me one favor?"

"Yes, sir?"

"Don't care much for that New York City. Boys up on Wall Street have just about ruined the oil business. Let's leave them fellows out of my problem. Deal?"

"Sure, Mr. Brown, that was just an expression. Sorry. A minute down here in Texas . . . well, things move pretty slow, sometimes, and I'd like to move a little faster with this tumor treatment."

"There you go, Doc. We're in your hands, right Mama?"

"Yessireebob."

CHAPTER 3

SURGERY

Wednesday, April 4, 2001

After almost a week of puncturing, probing, radiating, and phlebotomizing, Melvin Brown was found to be clean of any obvious cancerous lesions, other than the one in his femur. Bone scans showed his skeletal system to be free of disease, except for a little arthritis in his spine, the weight-bearing joints, and his fingers. This was confirmed by CAT scanning of his entire body.

MRIs and ultrasounds revealed no spread to the lungs, liver, pancreas, spleen, brain, or any other vital organ. His calcium and phosphorus metabolism, often totally out of whack with bone metastases, was normal. His alkaline phosphatase levels were normal, indicating the absence of destructive bony lesions that usually caused that enzyme to be elevated in the bloodstream.

His system was clean. He was a good candidate for tumor resection and prosthetic replacement. He signed on the dotted line. The procedure was a go.

✦ ✦ ✦

I started Melvin Brown's surgery late, shortly after noon. And I was still struggling with the finishing touches, making sure the prosthesis was stabilized by the methyl methacrylate—bone cement—and making sure the cerclage wires used to join the long-stemmed metal flange of the femur side of the prosthesis to the relatively normal upper thigh bone were strong enough to hold the patient's weight. The stem spanned over a foot-long section of femur bone. The stresses and strains on the prosthesis would be great, especially in an active sixty-seven-year-old overweight man who made his living trudging around excavation areas, drilling rig sites, and golf courses.

Mr. Brown would have appreciated the technique. I used what cattlemen and oil men would have called "baling wire" to wrap around the leg bone to secure the underlying prosthesis. Cement alone often wasn't quite strong enough to hold the parts together, especially for a man Melvin Brown's size.

I was drenched in sweat, as were my two assistants, Rae Harris, my nurse of fifteen years, and Dr. Jeb Long, the fourth-year orthopedic resident assigned to the Hip and Knee Replacement service for a three-month rotation. One of the luxuries of being a professor of orthopedic surgery at University Medical School was having house staff available twenty-four hours a day. Dr. Long's job was to assist me in surgery, to make rounds with me, to see patients in the emergency room (which is usually at three o'clock in the morning), and to help with one of the diseases orthopedic surgeons can't cure: paperwork.

I had always enjoyed teaching up-and-coming young surgeons my techniques, innovative or otherwise, and I relished the intellectual challenge. Those young doctors questioned everything I did. But what bound the attending staff, which was me, and the house staff, which was Jeb, was the shared love of doing carpentry work. That's what orthopedic surgeons essentially do: carpentry. Plastic surgeons? Sculpting. Internists? Computer analysis. Ophthalmologists? Camera repair. Neurosurgeons? Electronic circuit repair. Heart surgeons? Wellhead pump repair. Radiologists? Golf.

All four of us operating personnel—those of us actually participating in the operation, including the scrub nurse—were dressed in space suits, customary attire for a joint replacement of this magnitude. Postoperative infection was a disastrous complication, and every precaution had to be taken to avoid bacterial contamination in the wound. The custom-ventilated suits provided the most sterile environment, when combined with an operating suite with laminar air flow. And although air was continually pumped through the large, bulky suits, complete with hoods just like the astronauts wore, it was still hot. Very hot.

And what with all that air blowing through constantly, we could hardly hear each other. So, as usual, we communicated with hand signals or by ineffectively yelling at each other through the sealed helmets, which was a waste of time but an unbreakable habit. The loudness of the pumped-in air, which reminded me of the howling winds that used to continually blow through my hometown in West Texas during the winter, prevented me from hearing the orthopedic surgical nursing supervisor, Loretta Birdwell, call my name. I realized there was something amiss when she started pulling on the air hose attached to my space suit and almost toppled me over onto the waxed green tile floor, slippery with blood and debris from Melvin Brown's surgery.

"What the—?!" I turned my head to see Loretta staring at me. She always wore a large, flowered bonnet and a flowered cloth face mask, revealing nothing but the ebony skin around her orbits, her high cheekbones, and her coal-black eyes. I'd known her a long time, so I knew when she was upset, and I knew when there was a problem. I couldn't help but notice her eyelids were wide open, as though her irises and pupils were about to bulge out of her head.

"What's the matter?" I yelled, still trying to hear her soft voice over the roar of the desert storm in the helmet.

She mouthed words that I hoped I heard incorrectly, words that I hoped I had misunderstood. But there was no mistake, as she urgently screamed into the space suit's baffle over my right ear.

"Your wife's been involved in an automobile accident. They've Life Flighted her into the emergency room. You need to get over there right away!"

CHAPTER 4

MARY LOUISE

Wednesday, April 4, 2001

I was so distraught by the news of my wife's accident that I could no longer function. Dr. Long walked around the operating table to my normal place as Rae and Loretta each took an arm and backed me out of the operating field. Jeb wedged his lanky six-foot-four frame against the operating table, assumed the position, and began to work confidently.

"Don't worry, Dr. Brady," he yelled through his helmet. "I can finish up here. You did a beautiful job. I'll complete the cerclage wiring, get hemostasis, and close. And I won't forget the Hemovac drains. You go and check on you wife. I hope she's okay."

At least that's probably what he said. I couldn't hear him. I tried to speak, but the words weren't there.

"It's fine, Doc," Loretta yelled encouragingly. "Jeb's a good surgeon. He only has three months to go before he's finished up with his residency. He'll take care of it. No problem. You come along now, with Rae and me. Come on, help me with the spacesuit."

Once we were out of the operating room, Loretta and Rae struggled to get me out of the suit by first disconnecting the inflow and outflow tubes. I just stood there in a trance while the two nurses detached my insulated boots, then completed the removal of the cumbersome but lightweight asbestos suit like I was some sort of incompetent child.

I couldn't think, and I was afraid. Scared to death, in fact. I didn't know if I could find the strength to make the long walk to the emergency room, and I couldn't stand the thought of what I might find. Oh, God! Why Mary Louise? Why not me? She's the strong one. She could survive without me, but I would be lost without her. And it's my fault, because I was too damn busy to meet her for lunch. This would never have happened if I had been on time for our midweek date, like I was supposed to be.

In my daze, I recalled a summer in Colorado on a trout-fishing trip when J. J. was only eight or nine years old. He unexpectedly walked behind me while I was casting the fly rod, and I snagged the tiny hook into his right eyelid. Mr. Surgeon was shaking so badly that our fishing guide had to remove the hook and get him to the hospital. Fortunately, there was no permanent damage to J. J.'s vision. But Mary Louise knew how I was. She knew I was worthless when it came to emergencies involving the people I love. All that quick responsiveness, rapid-fire decision-making, and spectacular emergency surgery I did was just an act for the strangers who were counting on me.

I managed to stumble across the elevated sky bridge that led from the University Hospital orthopedic operating suite into the main structure of University Hospital, while Rae and Loretta each held onto an arm. Physicians, administrators, and ancillary hospital personnel stopped and stared, and I vaguely heard them from what seemed a far distance, asking my two companions, and each other, what was wrong with Dr. Brady. He was usually so neat—hair combed, freshly pressed scrubs, clean white knee-length clinic jacket. He was so predictable, so consistent. Was he sick? Was this yet another stressed-out surgeon having a heart attack? Or a nervous breakdown?

But that Wednesday afternoon, I was stumbling because I was in shock. Emotional shock, perhaps, but still functionless. My operating greens were drenched in sweat. People who passed me obviously didn't know I had been in a hot spacesuit for the past three hours, so they must have thought I was diaphoretic from some sort of disease. My hair was probably tousled, and I was undoubtedly white as a sheet.

Patients, nurses, and doctors who passed us must have thought I had lost my mind. For once, I did not care about my image.

✚ ✚ ✚

"I can't go in. I can't do it. It's Mary Louise, for God's sake."

I stood outside Shock Room 3 of the University emergency room, clinging as best I could to the dull lime-green walls, and tried to remain erect.

"Dr. Brady, you've got to help me," said Dr. Stan Berry, after he introduced himself as a fifth-year cardiovascular surgical resident and the current ER chief resident. "Your wife's been badly injured. We need to run some tests, and fast. We've got to get your permission to treat her any further, and to do that, you have to walk in there and make sure . . . well, make sure that's your wife lying on that table."

"You mean there's some doubt?"

"Well, sir, maybe somebody stole her purse, then had an accident, which could mean the woman in there is not really your wife. After nine years in this institution, Dr. Brady, I'm convinced of only one thing, and that's anything can happen. Point is, you have to go into the shock room and identify her. Please. We need you to help us, so that we can help her. These next few minutes are critical. She's unconscious and nonresponsive. We know she's sustained a severe cerebral trauma. She has an open skull fracture. But she could also have a compartmentalized subdural or epidural hematoma. Or maybe we're seeing the results of a God-awful extracranial bleed. But, if she has an internal bleed, or has bone debris embedded into her brain, we need to get her to surgery and decompress the pressure right away, to avoid . . .

"But then, you know all this, Doc. Surely you've been through situations like this a thousand times with when your own patients. So, please? Help us out here. We don't want to lose her. Just make sure the woman in there is your wife before we go any further."

I continued to stare at the floor. I felt the tears well up in my eyes. All the years of treating patients and operating on a myriad of fractures, dislocations, deformities, and cancers had not prepared me for that situation. It was my own wife now who was the victim, and when she needed me the most, when she would be counting on me to help her, suddenly I was physically and mentally paralyzed. I was helpless and worthless.

"I just don't think . . ." I started to say, but felt myself falling into an oblivion.

"Jim Bob Brady, you listen to me, and you listen good!" I heard Loretta speak sternly in my direction. She grabbed hold of me and started to shake me into a state of feeble awareness.

"I've known you since you were a snot-nosed medical student. You're just about the best doctor I've ever seen, and I've seen plenty. And I love you with all of my heart. But you've got to get a grip on yourself. That's probably your wife in there, and if there's anything those of us who know you well know for sure about you, it's how much you love that woman."

She held onto me tightly, pulled my head into her face, and squeezed me.

"I can't breathe, Loretta."

"Good," she said. She stepped back and placed her hands gently on each of my cheeks. "Rae and I'll help you, won't we, Rae?"

"That's right, Boss. We're right here with you," Rae said, and put my left arm over her shoulders. Loretta did the same with my right arm, and the two of them gently pulled me away from the tile wall. They slowly walked in a semicircle and led me into Shock Room 3.

CHAPTER 5

INJURIES

Wednesday, April 4, 2001

The scene was a blur. The combination of bright fluorescent ceiling lighting and high-beam operating lights gave the shock room a surreal glow, like the graveyard scene in *Easy Rider*. I felt unsteady, like a Dennis Hopper under the influence. I could not fathom that the woman on the trauma table was, in fact, my wife. But one quick head-to-toe glance, and I knew.

I began again, slowly the second time. I noticed the burnt-orange nail polish and the familiar manicured toes. My eyes slowly scanned Mary Louise's uncovered legs. I appreciated a large bruise on her left thigh, overlying an angular deformity. Possible hematoma, probable broken femur. She needed an orthopedic surgeon, but not me. That was progress. I was being more clinical. She needed me to be clear-headed, so I had to at least try and do this for her.

I observed the Foley catheter tubing draped over her right thigh. Her urine was reddish-brown, representative of possible bladder or kidney contusion or laceration. She needed a urologist. I kept moving.

Her pubic area was open for everyone to see. My first thought was to get a blanket and cover her. I scanned her abdomen, then her ample breasts. She was totally uncovered except for the EKG leads and plastic tubing. Shock-room trauma patients were always exposed like this, to minimize the risk of a missed injury. It seemed a disgrace, and I was ashamed—embarrassed—for her. Mary Louise would die if she knew how her body was exposed for all the world's viewing.

But she might die, so I kept moving.

It was necessary, critical, even, to check every square inch of her battered body for signs of injury. There was bruising on her left rib cage. Fracture? Possible hemothorax? Or a pneumothorax? She might need a chest tube to drain blood or air from her lung cavity, to let the lung expand. For sure, she needed a STAT chest X-ray. Or had they done that? What was the resident's name? Berry.

I walked closer to the gurney, shook loose of Rae and Loretta. They realized I had taken control over my emotions and they stepped back. I began to focus on people I had not noticed before as my peripheral vision kicked in. I had not appreciated the presence of anyone else during those first few moments in the shock room. It was just me and Mary Louise. I began to see nurses, technicians, and doctors, working to try and save her.

I tried to refocus on her injuries, on her, and her alone.

There were IV lines in both wrists, an arm board taped to each to keep the lines from kinking. I noticed an arterial line in the right radial artery, and my eyes darted to the pulse oximeter above her head. Her oxygen saturation was only 80%. Not a good sign.

She needed blood work and an MRI of the abdomen and chest. She had lost quite a bit of blood. Was it from internal bleeding? Or was there an open wound somewhere? I didn't want there to be one, but Berry said something about her head. I knew I had to look at her face, and therefore her skull. But Mary Louise was unresponsive. That was a very bad sign, so I did not want to look further. I wanted to stop then and leave, maybe go home and play with my dog, and have my wife meet me at the door with a cocktail, and awaken from this nightmare.

I backed up, but the arms of Loretta and Rae pushed me forward. Keep going, they said.

Take care of me. Save me. That's what I heard Mary Louise say.

I moved forward, toward the shock-room table.

Her pulse was 120, according to the digital LED numerals above her head. I heard the beeping of the portable EKG machine. The heart rate was rapid, but I didn't see any skipped beats on the scanner. That was a good sign, a fast but steady heartbeat.

I gazed at the sphygmomanometer readout. Her systolic blood pressure was only 70, and the diastolic was too low to register.

Rapid pulse and low blood pressure implied shock. She needed fluids, maybe blood.

I moved up to her left arm, noted another angular deformity in the humerus, the bone between the elbow and the shoulder. That was obviously a displaced fracture. I leaned over her exposed body and noted that the right elbow and upper arm were clean. Her extremity injuries appeared to be only on the left side, so she must have been struck on the driver's side. Her left arm and leg were crushed by the car door. Who did this to my wife? Where is he? Or she? I hoped that miserable person was injured and suffering as much as Mary Louise. Better yet, I hoped whoever did this to my wife was dead.

Sorry, God, I said in my mind, and I admitted I was the merest of mortals.

Reluctantly, I moved up to her face and head. There was severe bruising on the left side of her face and temple. Her facial features were swollen and distorted. Her left eye was ecchymotic—purple—and swollen shut. I touched her face gently, trying valiantly to hold back my tears. I noticed several broken teeth, upper and lower, and lip and tongue lacerations. I could not assess the extent of the damage because of the white plastic endotracheal tube in her throat.

I became aware of the rhythmic hiss of the respirator and up to then had chosen to block out its meaning. I looked at the portable breathing machine and noticed it was set to AUTO, not MANUAL. Mary Louise wasn't triggering her own respirations, but then Berry had already told me that.

There was a long gaping laceration over the left side of her forehead and temple. It oozed blood through the loose temporary tape probably applied by the EMTs that picked her up at the scene. She needed a plastic surgeon, a gifted expert. She could have an orbital fracture, or a mandible fracture, or both. She needed an oral surgeon, and maybe an ENT surgeon.

At last, I let my eyes drift up to her hair. That beautiful, thick blond hair was dirty, blood-stained, and tangled like an abandoned bird's nest.

The left side of Mary Louise's cranial vault was a bloody pulp. I gently touched the area, which had been hastily shaved in order to inspect the wound. She had a severe open skull fracture, probably involving the temporal lobe, possibly the parietal lobe as well. I wondered how severely the delicate brain cells underneath the fractured bones were damaged. Was there a secondary, contralateral injury to the white and gray matter of the brain on the opposite side of the fractures? There was no doubt she had brain damage. The question was, how badly was her brain damaged?

I tried to gently lift the right eyelid, since the left was too swollen. That pupil had a slow slight reaction to light, but it definitely constricted. Mary Louise's brain was alive, so she had a chance.

DON'T GIVE UP. SAVE ME, I felt her say.

I gently patted her forehead, touched her lower lip, and placed my hand ever so slightly onto her left wrist, taking care to avoid constricting an IV line.

"Berry? Where are you?"

"Right behind you, Dr. Brady."

I stepped back from Mary Louise's bedside, looked carefully around the shock room as though for the first time, and was again cognizant and appreciative of the fact that there were other people in there trying to save Mary Louise's life.

The respiratory therapist was standing next to his ventilator, which was breathing for my comatose wife, and carefully checking the attachments to the endotracheal tube to ensure there was a satisfactory air flow. The EKG technician was running continuous rhythm strips of her heart beats. The phlebotomist was standing by, waiting on further instructions to draw blood. Three nurses were in attendance and began simultaneously checking her pressure, monitoring her pulse, and hanging bags of Ringer's lactate IV solution as I moved out of the way. There were two interns, a medical student, and Berry, all there working hard to try and save Mary Louise's life.

"You need to splint her left arm. The humerus is fractured. Her left femur probably is, too. She needs a splint, and some traction on the foot to decrease the muscle spasm."

"Yes, sir, we were in the process of doing that when—"

"We need a plastic surgeon, an ENT, and an oral surgeon to tend to her facial injuries and lacerations. I want a urologist to evaluate what appears to be blood in her urine, and I want a general surgeon to check her belly. Once you get her into X-ray, I'll see which bones are broken, then call in specialists from my orthopedic group.

"But, most of all, Stan, she needs the best brain surgeon at this hospital!"

"Yes, sir. I've already called for a Neuro consult. The resident is on his way down from surgery. And I've called in all the other services you requested as well. Everybody is either here or should be here in a few minutes. I've ordered STAT chest films, belly films, an abdominal MRI, and a CAT scan of her brain and cervical spine. Radiology has an open room, and I'd like to get her in there ASAP. I just had to make sure you were informed of the situation, and that this patient is in fact Mrs. Brady. You understand, sir."

I nodded, scanned the room, looked at each individual face.

"Thank you all for what you've done so far. I can't tell you how much it means . . ." and I began to cry.

Rae and Loretta grabbed hold and managed to gently lead me out of Shock Room 3 and into the hallway before I made a complete fool out of myself.

I stood by and watched as Mary Louise's stretcher was immediately transported out of the shock room. The respiratory technician continued to breathe for her with an Ambu bag while four other emergency personnel swiftly pushed the gurney toward Radiology.

As I began to try and compose myself, I felt my mind racing into overdrive. "Rae, we need to talk to the family of Melvin Brown. His wife Sarah will be in the waiting room. And I would think that Meredith James is with her mother, although I didn't see her when I identified Mr. Brown in pre-op. Run over there, check on Jeb, make sure he's completed the surgery, and then see if by any remote chance Frank James is with his wife and mother-in-law.

"I'll get over there as soon—"

"And I need to call J. J. He and his mother are extremely close. He is not a fan of hospitals, but I'm sure he'll want to get over here right away. I can't imagine breaking the news to him."

I paused for a minute, thought as hard as I could, considering the circumstances, and tried to remember who all needed to be notified about Mary Louise's condition. Our parents were deceased, so . . .

"Oh. And call Susan Beeson please. She's a detective with HPD, and one of Mary Louise's closest friends. She'll want to be notified. And maybe she can shed some light on what happened, with the accident and all. Surely there's been some kind of report—"

"Dr. Brady?" Dr. Stan Berry asked as he exited Shock Room 3. "I'm going to stay with your wife in Radiology, just in case she—well, as a precaution."

"I appreciate it, Stan. Really. I'll be along shortly. I've got to tie up a few loose ends. Just keep her alive until we can get her up to the OR."

"That's something . . . no problem, sir. Listen, as you said, she needs the best neurosurgeon . . ."

"Say no more, Stan. There is only one man I trust implicitly to take care of my wife. He'll tell me the truth about her condition, and he'll do the right thing, regardless. Besides, in my opinion, he's the best damn brain surgeon at this hospital.

"My nurse has gone to see if he's in the orthopedic surgery waiting room. I operated on his father-in-law this afternoon, so he could be there, waiting for a report from me. At any rate, to keep the bases covered, and to avoid any needless delays, put in a STAT call for my friend Dr. Frank James. And tell his office it's an emergency!"

CHAPTER 6

SUSAN BEESON

Wednesday, April 4, 2001

I stayed in Radiology as long as I could stand the waiting, and I watched the technicians first run Mary Louise's head and neck through the CAT scanner, then begin the process of MRI scanning her chest and abdomen. She was still on the portable respirator, attended to by Dr. Berry, a respiratory therapist, and two ER nursing personnel. Two radiologists were present in the reading room and attempting to quickly and efficiently interpret the films as they were developed.

No one said much to me, which was customary when a doctor's wife was undergoing tests and the husband was hovering over the testers. This was particularly true in an emergency situation, when doctor husbands were best left out of the loop. After a half hour or so, I stepped out of the X-ray suite and walked back through the cacophony of the busy ER. Babies were crying, and I heard the dissonant sounds of patients in pain, requesting immediate assistance at the registration desk. There were the hushed murmurs of visitors' voices, waiting for words of comfort about a loved one.

I was not accustomed to being on this side of the patient–doctor fence. I did not want to be *here*, on the patient side, behaving erratically and incompetently. I wanted to be *there*, on the doctor side, where I was logical and capable.

University Hospital was a trauma center, as a city–county hospital might be. It had a Level I classification as an emergency center, complete with helipad. Life Flight had brought Mary Louise here rather than to County General, also a Level I trauma center and known as the Houston Knife and Gun Club by the staff. Normally, a patient injured as badly as she was would have been shipped immediately to County. Maybe there had been some identification in her purse that told the paramedics she was a physician's wife, not that under routine circumstances it would make a difference. But then, we each have a University Hospital Gold Card, and maybe the paramedics noted it and brought Mary Louise here. I never would have dreamed the card would be of any use. Most gold cards just cost you money. This one had possibly saved a life.

I told one of the nurses I would be outside smoking a cigarette, and to come and get me if there was a problem, or if the radiologist had anything to report. Or if Dr. Frank James showed up. She said fine, and that I should quit smoking. I told her it was not a good day for me to make a decision like that.

It was almost five o'clock. Cocktail hour. And I could have used one. Any kind of single-malt scotch would do. Macallan on the rocks, please, hold the ice, hold the glass.

Instead, I lit up, inhaled deeply, and held the nicotine-laced smoke in. I immediately became dizzy and sat on a concrete bench outside the ER, marked Smokers Only, and watched as the reflected shadows of high-rise medical office buildings and hospitals in the University Medical Center changed shape in the descending sunlight.

My son was probably on his way by now. When Rae Harris returned to the emergency room after completing errands and calls for me, she told me she had fortunately found J. J. at his office in Greenway Plaza. For once, he wasn't out and about on some crazy investigation.

He and his college roommate, Brad Broussard, began the work that was to be their livelihood while still in Austin, at the University of Texas. Now, they owned B&B Investigations, a firm that hired out to corporations, insurance companies, and private individuals who needed investigative work. Neither of the boys had done stellar work in college but had discovered their niche with computer wizardry. They could find out just about anything about anybody, financial or otherwise, and never leave their respective terminals. It was a changing world, I guessed. Brad and J. J. spent their lives cooped up in an office on monitors all day. I was happy for J. J.'s success, but that wouldn't matter to him that day. He'd only be able to deal with one issue. His mother's injury.

I felt deep dread with the prospect of having to explain Mary Louise's injuries to him. The two of them were so close, much closer than he and I were.

Rae also told me that Dr. Jeb Long had finished my operation, and that Melvin Brown was in the recovery room and doing well. She had kindly gone over to talk to Sarah Brown, telling her that her husband was recovering satisfactorily, and that surgery had been a success. Rae relayed that we wouldn't know for a week or ten days if I had been able to resect all the cancer, since that critical information would come with the final pathology report, once the bone had decalcified and the slides had been prepared, but that I was optimistic about Mr. Brown's prognosis.

About my wife's prognosis, though, that was another matter.

I thought it odd that Meredith Brown James, Sarah's daughter, had been absent from the waiting room, or so Rae said when she returned from her mission. As the Brown's only child, I couldn't imagine what would keep her away from the hospital on the day her father was having surgery for bone cancer. Apparently, Dr. Frank James wasn't present either, and he had yet to return the page from the emergency room, even though I knew it had been issued STAT.

Neither had I heard from Lt. Susan Beeson, but her presence wasn't nearly as critical as Frank's. I knew she would return my call, talk to Fran, my secretary, and get to the hospital as soon as she could.

A homicide detective never was short of work in Houston. I knew she was extremely busy, probably tied up with the investigation of yet another serial murder. Unfortunately, the crime wave in this country had now hit home.

I heard the screeching of tires and a tremulous siren, which came from just around the corner to the ER, where I was still sitting on a bench at curbside, smoking a second cigarette. I assumed it was a fire department emergency vehicle, and I stood up and walked behind the bench in order to give the EMTs a wide berth. But it was no ambulance.

An unmarked black Ford LTD spun into an EMERGENCY VEHICLES ONLY parking spot in front of the ER, siren blaring and portable red light flashing from the roof.

Susan Beeson jumped from her vehicle, slammed the car door, and leapt up the steps to the ER entrance two at a time.

"Susan. Susan!"

She stopped, turned. "Jim Bob? Oh, my God! What happened?"

We met each other halfway, in the middle of the driveway entrance to the ER, embraced, and cried together.

"Your office said Mary Louise was in a terrible accident and had a severe head injury. I got here as fast as I could. Can you tell me anything?"

I wiped the tears from my eyes with my fingertips. "Not much. All I know is that we were supposed to meet for lunch at Paco's, that new Cuban restaurant at Woodway and Post Oak."

She nodded.

"Anyway, I got tied up in surgery. My cases ran late, and my last surgery was a real bear. So, I had one of the nurses call her, tell her it didn't look like I was going to make lunch. The message she sent back was that if I had not joined her by the time she had finished her cappuccino and dessert, she'd see me at home."

Tough Detective Lieutenant Susan Beeson, impartial solver of heinous crimes, promulgator of law and order, reached into that massive black bag of hers, pulled out a few sheets of facial tissue, and wiped her eyes. I admired this short, spunky policewoman. Even though she was the police chief's daughter and one helluva detective, it had been my observation over the years that she somehow was able, despite the job, to maintain her humanity. With her blond hair and easy-to-maintain pixie cut, and her fair complexion dotted with light brown freckles over her nose and forehead, she was cute. Deceptively cute. She wore a nicely tailored beige jacket, tan pants, a white collared shirt, and comfortable walking shoes. I ignored the brown and green stains around the knees of her slacks.

"So, I'm finishing up this case, it was about three forty-five, when I get a call from your office saying that Mary Louise had been in an accident, that a Life Flight helicopter had brought her in, and to get over there right away. Where is she?"

"In X-ray, getting an MRI of her chest and abdomen, a CAT scan of her head and neck, and extremity X-rays to see what the fractures look like."

"Shouldn't you be in there with her, Jim Bob?"

"Susan . . ." I had to stop for a moment and gather myself together. "It's bad, Susan. She's comatose and basically unresponsive, except for a few vital functions. Her heart is beating, and she's maintaining a decent pulse and blood pressure. But she's on a ventilator, since she's not triggering spontaneous respirations, probably because she has an open skull fracture and brain damage. How extensive, the doctors don't know. Her left leg and left arm are broken—at least, I think they're broken, because they're crooked and the overlying skin is tented—and she may have internal bleeding from a ruptured spleen, maybe a lacerated liver. Her urine has blood in it, and her belly is distended, so they're checking out all her internal organs. And she looks like she has some broken ribs, and maybe a collapsed lung. The chief ER resident, a young man named Berry, has already called in consults for all the appropriate specialists. Mainly, though, we're waiting to see what she has wrong inside her head, to know what to do next. I called in a STAT consult to a neurosurgeon friend of mine, but he hasn't called back yet. So, I'm out here smoking, waiting for test results, and waiting for Frank to get here."

Susan blew her nose, a kind of honking sound. How such a cute girl could make a sound like that, I never would figure.

"Frank? Frank who?"

"You probably don't know him. Dr. Frank James, a classmate of mine and a top neurosurgeon. He and his wife Meredith have been acquaintances of ours for years. In fact, coincidentally, the case I was doing when the ER called me away was Meredith's father, Melvin Brown. You've probably heard of him. The oil man and philanthropist?"

Susan stared at me, a horrified look on her face.

"What? What, Susan?"

"I think you'd better sit down, Jim Bob. You're not going to believe this."

"I can't take any more bad news today, Susan."

"Just sit and listen. I was out at Lake Houston, investigating the sexual assault and murder of that twelve-year-old Smithson girl, the one whose body was found by the boaters last Sunday? That's why I'm filthy. Anyway, I'm trudging around the marsh looking for clues when I answer an emergency call on my pager from Sam Polk. You remember Sam. He was my partner for the past five years, taught me just about everything I know about police work."

"Sure. The one you call 'Yosemite Sam.'"

She smiles. "That's the one. Well, a few weeks ago, Dad promoted him to Chief of Detectives of the Southwest Homicide Division. He's a captain now, and no one deserves that promotion more than Sam Polk. He's been with the department longer than I have and is just about the best detective in the business. When the department decentralized, Dad thought the timing was right to promote him.

"Well, I was scheduled to get a new partner last week, a kid who has been on the force for five years, and who recently blew the top out of the detective's exam. He is someone I could teach the detective business to, and share all the knowledge and experience that Sam imparted to me over the years.

"But then last week, he was one of the patrolmen who got caught in the crossfire of that gang war over the in the Fifth Ward. He, along with three others, were critically wounded. He's still in the hospital, and I'm without a partner.

"Anyway, the Detective Division is very shorthanded, which means that Sam, even though he's now our chief of detectives, had to personally respond to a call at Memorial Bend. A security guard at the complex called 911 shortly after two o'clock this afternoon and reported a murder. I hate to be the one to tell you, but the dead woman is Meredith James."

CHAPTER 7

MURDER

Wednesday, April 4, 2001

I was dumbfounded. Words could not express my shock over the death—murder, yet—of Meredith James.

"Do you have any idea what happened, Susan?"

"I'll tell you what I know. Lee Perkins, the initial patrolman on the scene, was the first to talk to the husband. Dr. James apparently showed up at the house about two, for a late lunch date with his wife. They've been separated, but I guess you knew that?"

"No. Well, I heard mention of it through the hospital grapevine. I mean we're friends, but we're not intimate. Frank and I trained together and have shared patients over the years, but we're only casual social friends."

"Well, the story is that Dr. James arrived at the house, and while he's standing on the front porch, waiting for his estranged wife to answer the doorbell, he sees someone inside the house leaving the back way. He used his key and tried to get in, but the locks have been changed. He panicked, called 911 from his car—or has security call 911, I'm not sure which. The doctor, Lee Perkins, and the paramedics break down the door and find the wife upstairs in her dressing room, shot twice. Sam Polk, of course, thinks Dr. James did it."

"What?!"

She raised a hand. "Just let me finish. Once Lee Perkins starts talking to the doctor, he picks up that the deceased is the daughter of *the* Melvin Brown. Lee called Sam, and Sam called Dad. Our politically aware chief of police realized this will be a high-profile case, and he told Sam to get his butt over there, so to speak.

"So, once Sam got there and evaluated the crime scene, he immediately called me, told me to drop what I'm doing, and to get *my* butt over there. 'Gonna be a tough one,' he said. Anyway, I left Lake Houston and drove like a bat out of hell over to the west side of town and hauled my tired, overworked ass into the house. I hadn't been there five minutes when your office called me."

"Why does Sam Polk think Frank killed Meredith? From what you just told me, it sounds like Frank is the person responsible for discovering her body."

"Preliminary gut-level response from Sam. That's typical, though. The Gospel According to Sam is: The Husband Did It Until Proven Otherwise. I left him there to check out the scene. He wasn't too happy about it, but he knows how close Mary Louise and I are. When I left, he was out in the back yard, talking to the husband. It wasn't a pretty sight. Dr. James looked pretty upset. Kind of like you look, old boy," she said, and patted my arm.

My bad dream was becoming a nightmare. The one man I trusted to take care of my injured and comatose wife was at home at that moment, grieving over the murder of his own wife and, according to Susan, entertaining questions about his possible involvement in her murder.

But I knew in my heart that there was no way Frank James could have had anything to do with it. Of course, he and Meredith had their share of problems. I had heard that he and Meredith separated, because Mary Louise overheard a conversation about it at lunch at Maxim's restaurant some months ago. As far as I knew, at least from the Jameses' past marital history, their problems centered around Frank and his reputation as a ladies' man. That was no secret around University Hospital. But murder? No way.

The fact that Frank didn't answer my call was now understandable. He either didn't get my message, or he did but couldn't deal with it. It seemed like he and I were sailing in the same ship, with one major difference. Mary Louise was still hanging on to her life preserver.

I didn't envy Frank's responsibility of breaking the news of their daughter's death to Sarah and Melvin Brown. That was probably where he would go, as soon as the investigating officer finished with him. Susan left the crime scene before she actually got started, once she got the message from my office. That meant that Capt. Sam Polk, her former partner and new superior officer, would complete the initial questioning. I'd met Sam, even had some dealings with him in an unrelated matter involving another doctor. I felt sorry for Frank James. Sam Polk could be . . . intense.

Then I began to wonder if Frank even knew that it was Mary Louise who had been injured when the ER called his office. Would that have made a difference to him? Or had he simply called his office and told his secretary to have one of his colleagues handle the STAT call?

I felt the need to speak to him and tell him it was Mary Louise that needed his help. I was sure he didn't know. He probably couldn't even think or speak coherently, if he'd felt the way I did. But on second thought, would I even *want* him to take care of Mary Louise, given the circumstances of the afternoon?

And more importantly, who would he send in his place? Or would he even have any input in the matter? Did a nurse or secretary decide who responded to an emergency room STAT call? There were very few neurosurgeons that I liked. Most were quite competent, but as a general rule, their bedside manner left much to be desired. I would have to see which attending neurosurgeon responded, evaluate them, and decide whether or not I want to take a chance with them, or try to talk Frank James into operating on Mary Louise. I needed to see what condition he was in. Which meant I had to get over to the floor—the Browns should be in their suite before too long—and try and speak with Frank. I needed to offer my condolences to Meredith's parents and then evaluate Frank's mental and physical condition. But I had to make a decision quickly. And then I wondered if perhaps I shouldn't even have been making decisions, considering my own mental state.

These and a million other thoughts went through my confused mind as Susan and I walked over to the smoker's bench and I lit yet another cigarette. "I've got to call Frank's office and find out who's coming over to evaluate Mary Louise. Do you have your cellular with you?"

Susan nodded, extracted it from her bag, and handed it to me. "As soon as you're finished, I'll make some calls, see what I can find out about the accident she was involved in. Surely one of the uniforms at the scene followed the fire department ambulance over here. That's usual and customary. Has anybody talked to you?"

"I don't think so, Susan, but even if they had, I'm not sure I would remember it, considering my state of mind."

Before I could dial Frank's number, one of the young emergency room nurses, wearing white standard-issue scrubs, came running through the automatic sliding doors and looked around until she saw me, then she bounded down the steps and ran across the asphalt entrance ramp to the smoker's bench where Susan and I were sitting.

I stood, scared to death that she had something terrible to tell me. "What's wrong?"

"Dr. Flanagan's here. He's in X-ray, looking at the CAT scan. And there's a policeman at the desk. Said he needs to speak with you."

"Flanagan? You mean George Flanagan? The neurosurgeon?"

"Yes, sir. In fact, there's a whole group of doctors who want to see you."

"And Mary Louise?"

"No change, Dr. Brady. She's on the respirator, and still in the scanner."

"Thanks. I'll be right in."

She stayed put, bounced on her white high-top athletic shoes with the black and red stripes. "I can't believe you're smoking. It's gross."

"Thank you for your comments. Desperate times call for desperate measures. Now run along. It's probably time for your nap."

She stared at me, saying nothing for a moment. "I'm twenty-two years old, Doctor, and old enough to know better than to destroy my health with those cancer sticks, and you should as well. After all, you've been around a lot longer than I have."

Ouch. And with that, the energetic nurse ran back across the driveway, dodged an oncoming emergency vehicle, bounded back up the steps, and flew inside.

"I wonder if I ever had that much energy, Susan."

"I wonder if I did, and I'm twenty years younger than you. At least you were holding your own in the insult department. I don't know why these kids think they can get by with talking to people like—What is it?"

"George Flanagan. Of all the damn people. I don't know if I can deal with him."

"What? You have a problem with the neurosurgeon?"

"Oh, he's one of Frank's partners. He's a superb technician, but with the bedside manner of a roach."

"Didn't know roaches had a bedside manner."

"That's the point, Susan. We've had a few run-ins over the years about the way he's treated some of my patients. I can't stand the man, and I don't know if I can let him take care of Mary Louise. I just don't know."

"You might better take whoever's here right now, Jim Bob. If he's a good surgeon, and she needs immediate attention . . ."

"Maybe you're right. I'd better go in," I said, then stood, stretched my aching muscles and bones. "How's the baby? And Gene?"

"You know, Jim, I told myself after my son was born that I should retire, or transfer to the White Collar Crime Division, so that I could have better hours, and a safer job, and more time to spend with Gene Jr. I wonder how many times I have repeated that mantra to myself in the last two years. So, the $64,000 question is, why do I keep doing it?

"No offense, Jim—wild horses couldn't keep me away from Mary Louise—but what I would like to do right now is to pick up Gene Jr. from the babysitter's, give him a bottle of apple juice, and watch him play with the new childproof, non-toxic, baby-sensitive stuffed polar bear I have in the Toys"R"Us sack in the backseat. I picked it up this morning on the way out to Lake Houston. To be honest, that's the reason I was somewhat late to that juvenile homicide assignment, not that I can share that with anyone but my husband. And you."

That brought a smile to my otherwise distraught countenance.

"But instead, I find myself at two additional tragic crime scenes, two more seemingly senseless murders, in a city teeming with hundreds of senseless murders. Before Gene Jr., it was exciting, Jim. I admit it, it was a quest. I had to prove to myself, and to my father, that I could handle the job. You know, it's not easy being the daughter of the chief of police in the country's fourth largest city. But now, it has become a grind.

"So, you may ask, why do I still do it? I guess, because in some sick way, I still love it, although I'm reluctant to admit that, especially to myself. It's much easier admitting it to you.

"But in answer to your question, and sorry for the diversion, Gene Jr.'s great. Light of my life. And Gene is fine, but, poor guy, he's putting in twenty-hour days, getting ready for tax time. I had to call him on the way here to get him to go pick up the munchkin. What with the child found in the lake, Mrs. James's homicide, and now Mary Louise . . . anyway, I'm way behind today. He is too, but he understands. Mary Louise is dear to my heart. I couldn't stand it if anything happened to her. Gene knows that."

"I know how you feel about your job. Most of us professionals have a love–hate relationship with our work. And our families bear the brunt of the conflict and the stress. So, I give you an especially sincere Thank You Very Much for coming. I appreciate it, more than you know."

"Can I see Mary Louise?"

"I don't know, Susan. Probably a bad time. I doubt the staff will let visitors in right now."

"I understand."

She put her arm around me and hugged me tight.

"C'mon. You go speak to this Dr. Flanagan, and I'll speak to the HPD representative. He's either the investigating officer at the scene of Mary Louise's accident, or one of the detectives from Traffic."

We walked together, arm in arm, into the ER.

"I'd like to say something sympathetic to Sarah Brown about Meredith, but I want to make sure that Frank gets there first. Do you think he's on his way to the hospital by now?"

"As I said, Sam was questioning him when I ran out of there. It was just a preliminary interrogation, so he shouldn't be too long. It will take a few days to study the crime scene, gets prints, collect blood and hair and nail specimens from the victim, look for clothing samples, go over the property inside and out, and get the autopsy results. We'll have to talk to everybody that knew Meredith James, including the family dog. Plus, we'll have to contend with the media and the press. Meredith James is Melvin and Sarah Brown's daughter, after all, so I doubt even Sam Polk will be too eager to act on his theory without some hard evidence. This investigation won't be like TV, or the movies, or a really good Robert Parker book. We can't solve it in a few hours."

I nodded, stopped just inside the emergency room entrance. "Try to find out what happened to Mary Louise, Susan, and, if possible, check on the status of the driver of the other car, and see if there were any other people injured in the accident. And if you can, try to determine the circumstances of the wreck. It's bad enough that Mary Louise has sustained potentially fatal injuries, but if she was the cause of—"

"Don't you worry, Jim Bob," she said, and patted my arm. "I'll make Mary Louise my number-one priority."

CHAPTER 8

DIAGNOSTICS

Wednesday, April 4, 2001

I found J. J. at the ER registration desk, looking lost and in a panic. He was alone, in his normal business attire of timberland hiking boots, wrinkled khakis, and plaid shirt . . . a very thin, blond version of Al on *Home Improvement.* As usual, his sun-bleached, tousled hair was kept in control by his ever-present baseball cap turned backward.

I caught his eye. He nodded, walked over, and hugged me. No tears are apparent through his thick, round, frameless glasses, which distort his large blue eyes.

"What's the story, Dad?"

I brought him up to date on the situation and asked if wanted to come into the bowels of the ER with me to talk to the doctors about his mother's condition.

"Sure, but I want to see Mom first."

"Well, I don't know. She's probably still in the scanner, and you know how you are in situations like—"

"Dad. I want to see Mom. She'll know I'm here."

"J. J. Your mother is comatose, and—"

"Dad?" he said, insistently.

They had a special relationship. Who was I to say that what he felt, and what his mother might have felt, didn't have emotional significance. Perhaps there existed some type of unexplainable, synergistic biorhythm between a mother and her child.

"Fine. Come on," I said.

We walked past the registration desk and through the double doors that lead to the patient examination rooms. We continued past the shock rooms—they were still cleaning up the mess from Mary Louise's presence in #3—down the fluorescent-lit, hospital-green tiled hallway, and into the Radiology suite. The place was packed with men and women in short and long white clinic jackets and in an array of colored surgical scrubs.

There was a pecking order at that time, detectable by scrub-suit color and length of white coat. White scrubs represented hospital staff uniforms: nurses, phlebotomists, EKG and radiologic technicians. The lowest of the low were the medical students, all wearing dull-gray scrubs with short polyester white coats. Med students could also be detected by jacket pockets full of their particular necessities: otoscope, ophthalmoscope, stethoscope, and *The Merck Manual of Diagnosis and Therapy*. Residents and fellows wore green, with or without a thigh-length white lab coat. The attending staff doctors, at the apex of the medical food chain, wore bright-blue scrubs with a knee-length starched white coat. Some of the most important physicians wore a sport coat and tie to signify their elevation to Higher Status, such as impending beatification. I was still in the same sweaty, wrinkled blue scrubs I wore all day in surgery, and in my dazed journey to this place, my traditional white coat was inadvertently left behind in my locker. My uniform bespoke of a disheveled member of the housekeeping staff.

Most of the doctors present there were colleagues, men and women with whom I had worked on countless patients over the past twenty-two years of my orthopedic practice. When J. J. and I entered, all levity and conversation stopped, and the group became somber. I found it strange how we medical folk could do that. One minute we were laughing, joking, and giddy, then suddenly cold, factual, and rigidly clinical the next. Switching gears, I believe it's called.

The only sounds I heard were the somewhat distant, muted emergency room noises, and the staccato tap-tap-tap of the MRI, still housing my precious wife's inert, ventilator-assisted body.

Dr. Gary White, urologist, stepped up first, shook my hand, and introduced himself to my son. He was shorter than me, rotund, bald, pale, and normally, a very jovial man.

"Jim, it looks like she's got a severe contusion and interstitial laceration of the left kidney, which is where the urinary blood is originating. The ureters and bladder look okay, but while her abdomen is open, I'll take a look. It may require repair, maybe some ductal work, but I don't think she'll lose the kidney. That's the good news."

"What do you mean, while her abdomen is open? Have you decided to do an exploratory laparotomy on her?"

"Oh, sorry. We're getting ahead of ourselves. Mike, you should have gone first."

"Jim," said Dr. Michael O'Reilly, general and thoracic surgeon. He was my height, slim build, with brown hair protruding under his surgeon's cap. He also shook my hand and greeted J. J., who was beginning to turn a light shade of green. The boy never had the stomach for medicine.

"Get him a chair, please," I said, holding on to J. J.'s right arm, while one of the residents—I guessed he was a resident, since I didn't recognize him, and he didn't look much older than my son, plus he had on green scrubs—grabbed a metal folding chair. We sat J. J. down just before he passed out. I pushed his head between his legs. He was light-headed and probably wouldn't remember any of these details.

Mike O'Reilly continued. "Your wife has had quite a bit of abdominal trauma. Looks like her liver is lacerated, and her spleen is ruptured. We'll have to do a splenectomy and repair the liver. Unfortunately, she has four broken ribs on the left side of her chest. By the time I got down here, her left lung had completely collapsed— it wasn't, when the EMTs at the scene of the accident first intubated her—so I had to put in a chest tube while she was in the scanner.

Her lung seems to be expanding satisfactorily, though, and that is a good sign. I don't think she'll remember the discomfort of inserting the chest tube without anesthesia, Jim Bob. Sorry I had to put her through that, but I had no choice.

"Good news is that there's no evidence of cardiac contusion, or a hemopericardium—in case you've forgotten, that's a collection of blood in the sac that surrounds the heart, which—"

"I know what it is, Mike."

"Sure. Anyway, we'll open her abdomen, and Gary can take a look at her kidney once I get the spleen out and fix the liver. Questions?"

"When is all this going to be done?"

Mike stared at me for a moment, then stepped back. One of my partners, Jeff Kosar, parted the crowd and gave me a bear hug. A giant of a man with a black beard and short black curly hair going to gray, he looked like an offensive lineman with a good sense of humor. He represented the medical professions' stereotyped view of an orthopedic surgeon.

"Sorry about all this, my man. Just want you to know I'm with you," he said, and fortunately relinquished his grip before he squeezed the life out of me.

"Mary Louise has a fractured left tibia, and a badly broken left femur. Both need to be fixed. I can rod the tibia, but the femur needs a plate. It carries a higher risk of infection, I know, but there's no way to get a rod down that thigh bone because there is too much comminution. The humerus is broken, too, but circulation is good in the hand. She'll need a plate there as well. Important thing is, I can fix all the fractures at the same time the other docs are working."

"Everybody's talking about fixing everything, but nobody's saying—"

"Brady," I heard, from a basso profundo voice. "That's because I've saved the best for last. Your friends and colleagues are waiting on me to decide what to do, and when to do it, since I am the neurosurgeon, and the brain is, well, the most important part of our anatomy.

The center of the universe, so to speak. So as usual, no one does anything until I say it's okay. I am in charge."

George Flanagan. The Little Napoleon. He was about five foot eight, with penetrating green eyes and a hairless face. He had a full head of thick red hair combed straight back. I noticed for the first time that a few freckles dotted his hooked nose and forehead. He had a very muscular build, his biceps, triceps, and pectorals stretching the fabric of his dark-blue scrub shirt. His legs were obviously muscular as well—word is he worked out all the time—and I noticed that his scrub pants clung to him just as tightly as the shirt. He wore Wellington boots, enabling him to disguise his true height of no more than five foot six, or so it was rumored.

Some of the nurses thought he was a hunk because of his body building. I thought his personality negated whatever physical charm he might have possessed, but then I knew him all too well, and I could hardly stand to look at the man.

"You're probably not too happy that I'm your wife's neurosurgeon, but with Frank, shall we say, indisposed, I'm your man of the hour. We need to put our differences aside, Brady, and take care of the problem at hand. Come along, and let me show you her CAT scan, so you can understand what I'm dealing with here," he said, and turned and into the main X-ray reading room, which was not the kind Mary Baker Eddy was famous for, although I would have gladly accepted help from her or anyone else possessing any special healing powers at that point. Even a shaman would have been a welcome sight compared to George Flanagan.

The sea of surgeons parted, and Flanagan strolled through the crowd, playing the role of Moses. I followed him, and the gap closed behind me.

We gathered at a far corner in the darkened room. All four walls were covered with floor-to-ceiling X-ray boxes, lit by fluorescent bulbs from within. Everyone turned their attention to the particular wall covered with pictures of Mary Louise.

"Here is the point of impact," he said, pointing to the left side of multiple sections of images which revealed the dissected interior of my wife's cerebrum and skull. Through the magic of computerized axial tomography scanning—the CAT scan—Mary Louise's brain and cervical spine had been photographed and projected in intricate detail onto silver-impregnated film.

"Your wife has a depressed skull fracture, unfortunately open, which has damaged the temporal and parietal sections of the brain. You can see on these sections, here, and here, where there has been internal damage."

He pointed to white areas, in contrast to the delicate outlines of dark, normal-appearing, convoluted brain tissue. He had used the word "internal," suggesting that Flanagan was softening the blow. This was an unexpected and uncharacteristic kindness.

"Now, if you look at the right side of her brain, here and here, there are also indications of contrecoup injury—contralateral tissue injury—from the impact. An indirect blow, so to speak. Fortunately, the fracturing of the cranial vault allowed blood that might normally have accumulated in the epidural or subdural space, to leak out, so I probably don't have to drain the brain of clot that might compress otherwise-normal gray and white matter. Although I do plan to drill a burr hole over the parietal lobe opposite her injury, just to make sure I'm correct. Her entire head has to be shaved, so what's one more scar, huh?" he says, and attempted a smile.

He turned toward me, away from the massive array of films. "I'll elevate the depressed fractures, explore the temporal and parietal lobes, debride—remove, rather—any obviously damaged, nonviable brain tissue, and try and piece the skull back together as best I can. She'll still have a large depression externally with the best case scenario. Later, and I mean much later, if cosmetics is a problem, I can fashion a methyl methacrylate plate—that's like the cement you use for hip and knee replacement—and replace the damaged portions of the cranium. But not now. The heat from the cement's curing process might damage more tissue. That's about it. Any questions, Brady?"

"Any idea on prognosis?"

He hesitated for a moment and attempted to twist his lips into what he probably considered a kindly smile, but which to me appeared to be a leer.

"She could come out of this perfectly normal, although with an injury this severe, that's unlikely. Residuals we normally see with this type of injury vary. Speech defects, visual defects, partial paralysis, and seizures are common, especially temporal-lobe epilepsy. In fact, she's already had one seizure during the CAT scan. Could have been from brain swelling, or tissue damage, I don't know. We pushed some IV Dilantin, and of course, we have a rapid mannitol drip going, to try to reduce the brain swelling before I open her skull. Another problem she might have is amnesia, which can be mild to severe. And Brady, be aware that a prolonged comatose state is not unusual, either. We just don't know yet, and probably won't for a while.

"The most important issue, now that we have a handle on all the injuries, is to get her into the OR quickly and get to work. I've told the other surgeons that I don't want to risk further potential brain damage with multiple anesthetics, so we're going to do everything we can tonight. It could take anywhere from eight to twelve hours before we're finished. It's five thirty now; by the time we get her upstairs, prepped, and draped, I figure it will be six thirty. I'd say we won't be through until, oh, three or four in the morning, and that's with some of us working simultaneously."

He backed away, as several other doctors quickly paraded in front of me, explaining Mary Louise's seemingly endless list of injuries. Most of it was a blur after Flanagan's speech.

An otorhinolaryngologist—an ENT specialist—said Mary Louise had a broken nose and fractured ethmoid and maxillary sinuses on the left side of her face. He would set the nasal bones in surgery and elevate the imploded sinus cavities. His surgery should heal fine, he said, and patted my shoulder.

An oral surgeon described Mary Louise's broken mandible and numerous broken teeth. He'd remove all the broken teeth, and later, much later, major dental reconstruction would be needed. He'd also have to rig up an external fixator through small pins on each side of the break in her jawbone. Seemed it was in too many pieces for some type of internal fixation to be of much use.

Lastly, an ophthalmologist said Mary Louise had significant damage to the left eye. The retina was detached. The only female surgeon in the group would line the eyeball with a silicone rubber band to repair the tear, called a scleral buckle procedure. Otherwise, Mary Louise would lose her sight. The eye surgeon couldn't promise she could save the eye, though, or that Mary Louise would see out of it. Another physician-optimist with the ultimate bullshit disclaimer.

When all was said and done, I lifted J. J. from his chair. He was still pale, tinged with green, but able to walk. We made our way into the scanning room as the person who was nearest and dearest to our hearts was being slowly fed automatically out of the magnetic resonance imager after completion of her chest and abdominal studies.

Just at that moment, her legs and arms spasmed and extended outward to their full length. As her back arched violently, the normal rhythmic ventilator hiss stopped and the alarm bell rang. The areas of skin overlying the fractures in her left leg and left arm tented almost to the point of ripping the skin and were held only by the flimsy temporary splints applied in the ER. I instinctively grabbed Mary Louise's broken left arm just as the skin split and her arm bone pushed through.

"Somebody grab her leg," I yelled. J. J. tried to help, but his autonomic nervous system got the best of him, and he passed out cold. One of the male attendants grabbed hold of him before he hit the floor, and gently laid him down on the hard tile.

Flanagan and the other doctors were at her side in a flash. Jeff Kosar grabbed hold of Mary Louise's broken femur and stabilized it.

Flanagan screamed for some more Dilantin STAT, roughly grabbed the syringe containing the anti-seizure medication from an accompanying ER nurse, and pushed the liquid directly into one of Mary Louise's IV lines himself. After a few seconds of spasm, she relaxed. Fortunately, she was intubated, and after a few seconds, the portable respirator clicked back onto auto mode and unfailingly resumed breathing for her.

Flanagan pushed me aside. "C'mon, let's get her upstairs. Everybody, grab hold carefully, and let's move her off the scanning table."

Nurses, staff doctors, residents, and medical students each picked a section of underlying sheet and blanket and smoothly moved my comatose mate onto a gurney. Plastic bags attached to IV lines were hooked onto poles welded into the gurney. The Foley catheter and its receptacle was taped into position to avoid tension on the bladder and urethra during transport. Arm boards and leg splints were adjusted and secured. The endotracheal tube was detached from the automated respirator, and the faithful, ever-present respiratory tech applied the Ambu bag and started manual pulmonary inflation.

The group of medical staff, one of the finest in the country, rolled Mary Louise out of Radiology, beginning her journey to an unknown fate.

Flanagan, bringing up the rear, stopped, turned, and walked back toward me.

"It's going to be a long wait, Brady. If you're not going to be in the waiting room, give me a number where I can reach you, or your beeper number," he said to me. "I may need to get hold of you during the surgery. These cases are sometimes . . . unpredictable."

Maybe George Flanagan was expressing what had not been said aloud thus far, which was simply that Mary Louise's survival was in serious question. The oh-it's-all-so-very-clear-now message finally struck home. My esteemed colleagues, all experts in their respective fields, probably expected my wife to die.

"I'll be there. Doesn't matter what time."

"And one more thing. No matter how long you have to wait, no matter how anxious you get, do not—and I mean *do not*, under any circumstances—enter the OR. You of all people, as a physician, should know that your presence back there will destroy any confidence and sense of purpose we might have. If you feel the need, you can call the desk, talk to one of the nurses, and get an update. But stay the hell out of my operating room. That's an order, Brady."

I felt my hands slowly ball into fists, my facial muscles tighten, and my jaws clench. I gave Flanagan a hard stare, but then I let it go. I allowed him the only reasonable response a husband was able to give his wife's surgeon, given the circumstances.

"Whatever you say."

"Good," he said. "That's one less problem I have to deal with."

CHAPTER 9

HIT-AND-RUN

Wednesday, April 4, 2001

We three—Susan, J. J., and I—sat in an isolated corner of the University Hospital cafeteria. We chose a spot as far away from the front door and as close to the rear exit of the cafeteria as possible.

When Susan had tried to have a conversation with the investigating officer performing his mandatory follow-up on the accident that put my wife in her current condition, Susan had been surrounded by various news media representatives—local TV, newspaper, radio. They weren't so much interested in Mary Louise but in the postoperative status of my patient, Melvin Brown, and information regarding Meredith James's murder. Brown's was a big name in "Our Town," title of the lovely and talented Maxine Messenger's column for the *Houston Chronicle*, and I was sure it would make good copy. I could just see the headlines. Prominent Oil Man Has Bone Cancer! Daughter Murdered! Husband Suspect!

So, Susan had suggested a remote spot so we could eat but still dodge the reporters. I was not interested in sharing my grief with strangers who would have projected my private thoughts and emotions into print and taken photos of my tear-stained face with dark black circles under both eyes.

We sat in silence for a while. I looked around at my fellow diners and listened to young, vibrant nurses, male and female, full of energy, laughing and joking, recalling some now-hysterically funny problem in one of the surgical suites. I overheard something about a paperwork mix-up regarding the operative consents on two patients, one on a female having a cervical laminectomy and the other on a man who was supposed to have his prostate removed. Seems the lady discovered the mistake when she read the permit the nurses gave her. She questioned whether she actually had a prostate, and was it in the neck, because that's what she was in the hospital for: neck surgery. Fortunately, that snafu was corrected prior to any damage being done. It was funny after it happened, though.

I noticed a few families who appeared saddened, lamenting their loved one's miseries, discussing what the doctors implied but didn't say, and wishing for brighter news. Them, I could sympathize with.

When we went through the buffet line, I picked out things that looked edible. I stuck with starches, since, as a rule, they seemed less dangerous than discolored, shriveled vegetable combos. Not that I was hungry. I would have settled for coffee and a dozen cigarettes. Susan had insisted I eat something, to keep up my strength. It would be a long night, she had said.

I acquiesced, seeing as how she, as one of Mary Louise's closest friends, was acting as my wife's representative in all matters healthy. I took her advice, more out of emotional need than physical hunger.

I found myself missing Mary Louise. A deep ache throbbed in my heart, a medley of fear, sadness, and loneliness rolled into one song. Tears welled up as I tried to concentrate on cutting Wednesday's special, a gristly chicken-fried steak with french fries. I poured even more Tabasco and salsa on the meat and acted like it was the heat that made my eyes water. After all, I needed to keep up a strong front for J. J. That is the role of the father, is it not?

"So, what did he say, Susan?"

"Who?"

"You know damn good-and-well who, Susan. The police officer at the registration desk in the emergency room. He *was* looking for me. He's bound to have had some information about the accident. Isn't that why he was here?"

She nodded. "Can't it wait until we finish eating? I think you need to concentrate on keeping up your—"

"That's the third time you've said that. I want to know what he said, and I want to know now! Please!" That was about as forceful as I could be with Susan. She was like one of the family, and a great friend to all three of us. She would do just about anything for me, and vice versa.

As Susan patted her mouth daintily with her paper napkin, I appreciated how difficult it must have been for her to separate her day-to-day routine as a homicide detective from her role as a mother, wife, and friend.

She reached into an interior pocket of her beige cotton jacket and pulled out a small spiral notebook.

"You ready for this, Jim Bob?"

I nodded.

"J. J.?"

His color partially restored, J. J. nibbled at a salad that was passed off on the marquee as a Cobb, although I doubted any decent chef would have agreed. He stared into his boiled egg halves and ham and cheese slices intermingled with slightly brown lettuce and covered with a white runny goo called House Ranch, and nodded. J. J. was unusually quiet, his normally inquisitive mind a blank.

"The first officer who arrived on the scene said there was quite a crowd gathered around Mary Louise's Jeep, maybe half a dozen cars, and about ten people. The driver of the other vehicle—as yet unknown, by the way—apparently was heading east on Woodway Drive, at a fairly fast clip, when the signal at Post Oak Road turned yellow. The driver thought they—I'm using singular *they* because we don't know the sex of the offender—could beat the light and zoomed on through.

"Mary Louise was at the south corner of the intersection, apparently on her way home from Paco's Restaurant. When her light turned green, she simply pulled out and tried to turn right, the same direction the assailant was driving. Her car was hit at full force, on the driver's side. Witnesses at the scene said her car skidded into the curb, teetered, rolled onto the passenger side, then flipped onto the roof.

"A number of people stopped their cars and ran to try to rescue her from her vehicle, thinking it might catch on fire. Someone called 911 from a cellular phone to report the accident, intimated that it was a bad wreck, and suggested HPD might want to send a helicopter. That is not customary procedure. Normally, the fire department paramedics arrive first, then determine whether or not a Life Flight trip is warranted. Well, it was Mary Louise's lucky day, because the caller happened to get a rookie on the seven-to-three dispatch shift, and the operator called Life Flight.

"When the investigating officers arrived on the scene, passers-by were standing on the shoulder of Woodway, in the outlying grass, and in front of Mary Louise's passenger door. Citizens from our fair city had left their cars out in the street, so some nameless gentleman removed his jacket and was standing guard adjacent to the accident lane, and he started waving traffic over to the left. Some of the bystanders were trying to speak to Mary Louise through the windshield, which was busted out by the impact, and were talking to her, trying to see if she was all right. She had her seat belt on, so she was suspended upside down, in mid-air, her air bag discharged, like a parachutist tangled up in a tree after a bad jump.

"Everybody was afraid to do anything because of the risk of further injury. So when the paramedics arrived and Life Flight arrived, together they were able to dislodge her—with the help of several good Samaritans, I might add—load her onto the helicopter, and transport her here."

"Susan, it seems that the ER called me around three forty-five. What time did the accident occur?"

"About two thirty. By the time the paramedics arrived, dislodged her from the car, and loaded her into the helicopter, it was a little after three, which is still pretty fast. The ER staff here worked on her for thirty minutes and stabilized her as best as possible. Someone from the admitting office—there's always someone, Jim Bob, in the midst of a medical emergency, who has time to check your insurance—found her University Gold Card, recognized your name, and called the ER and told them she was your wife. That's when they called you."

"I'll be damned. I wonder why they brought her here, though? Usually a Life Flight trip from an accident that bad goes to County General. I thought maybe one of paramedics saw her Gold Card, and—"

"I know why."

I waited the required millisecond before demanding an explanation.

"She was apparently conscious for just a few minutes when the first bystanders arrived at the vehicle. Some of her words were garbled, but several motorists insisted she distinctly said the words, 'University Hospital.'"

"You're kidding me!"

"No, I'm not."

I pondered this revelation and wondered what it implied with regard to the extent of Mary Louise's brain damage and her eventual recovery. It's nothing short of a miracle that God would smile down on the kindest, gentlest person I've ever known, and decide He's going to let Mary Louise, who has to be one of His favorite children, say two words, so she can get to the best hospital facility in the world, in order to spare her life.

"What about the other car? Didn't stop, I guess?" J. J. asked, finally involving himself in the conversation.

Susan reached across the table, patted his hand. "No, sweetie. Sorry."

He put his fork down, leaned back in his chair. "Well, did anyone see anything?"

Susan folded her notebook and put it back in her coat pocket. She took a sip of coffee and stirred in more cream and sugar with a spoon.

"Susan? Did you hear J. J.?"

She stopped stirring.

"Yes, I heard him. We have very little to go on, J. J. No description of the driver and, unfortunately, no license plate numbers. Not even one. It all happened too fast, apparently. The driver never slowed down, according to witnesses.

"And what's worse, we have conflicting reports as to the make and model of the car. All I can tell you for sure is that it was black. Maybe it was a Mercedes, or maybe an Audi. But then, it could have been a Volvo, or possibly a BMW. Those are the four vehicles mentioned to the officers on the scene. Best I can do right now is tell you it was presumably a black late-model European-made vehicle. Sorry. The odds of quickly finding Mary Louise's assailant don't look promising."

About that time, I heard a commotion at the door. I spotted a portable TV camera, a photographer or two, and a local well-known reporter, Janine Carlisle, at the entrance to the cafeteria. I glanced at a nearby television set bolted to a wall adjacent to the ceiling.

"This 5:58 p.m. Channel 2 newsbreak is sponsored by your local Oldsmobile dealers, the good guys, where luxury can be yours for no down payment and sixty-month financing. Now, to Janine Carlisle."

"Good evening, ladies and gentlemen. We're here, live, at University Hospital. Channel 2 News has learned, as we reported earlier, that Meredith Brown James, wife of local neurosurgeon Dr. Frank James and daughter of prominent oil barons Melvin and Sarah Brown, was found murdered in her exclusive Memorial Bend home this afternoon. According to our crew, which reported this tragedy to you first on LIVE AT FIVE, her husband discovered the body a little after 2 p.m. Apparently, Dr. James was questioned at the scene by Houston Police Department homicide detectives but was not detained.

"It seems, folks, that this situation is further complicated by the fact that Mr. Brown underwent major surgery for bone cancer this afternoon. In a bizarre twist of fate, Mr. Brown's surgeon, Dr. James Brady, was called away to the University Hospital emergency room before the surgery was completed in order to attend to his wife, victim of a disastrous automobile collision at the corner of Woodway and Post Oak. Brady's wife's vehicle was flipped onto its roof by the impact. She reportedly was Life Flighted to University's trauma center minutes after the hit-and-run accident.

"At this time, Mr. Brown is sequestered in a private suite in an exclusive section of University Hospital reserved for VIPs and their families. We've had no comment from Mr. Brown, his wife Sarah, or Dr. Frank James. According to our sources, Mrs. Brown and Dr. James are in seclusion in Mr. Brown's hospital suite.

"We understand from our investigative staff that Dr. Brady's wife is in surgery at this time. Doctors are attempting to repair some type of brain injury, as well as multiple fractures. We have had no comment from a hospital spokesperson regarding Mrs. Brady's condition at this time, nor have we been able to locate Dr. Brady.

"That's all we have for now. We'll report more information, as we have it, on News 2. This is Janine Carlisle. We now return to our regular programming."

CHAPTER 10

HOME

Wednesday, April 4, 2001

Before they could seek me out—I was certain the news team was on a search and destroy mission—I grabbed hold of J. J., and the three of us sneaked out the back door of University Hospital's cafeteria.

After much discussion, I acquiesced to Susan's insistence that I go home, take a shower, drink some coffee, then take care of my business at the hospital. She said she would be glad to stay at the hospital and sit with J. J. in my absence to keep him company. I argued that she had a family, a husband and a young son, that she needed to be with, and she should be the one to go home, not me. But they are not in surgery, she said. They are home and healthy, and what she was offering to do was no less that what Mary Louise, her best friend, would do under similar circumstances.

Enough said, thank you very much, now hit the road, Doctor.

She was more persistent than me. I don't think I've ever won an argument with a woman who knew she was right.

I made the twenty-minute drive to our apartment in the Post Oak Tower, a forty-story residential high-rise in the west-side subdivision of Tanglewood. I felt guilty about leaving my son with Susan in the post-surgical waiting room, with Mary Louise in critical condition and in the middle of a brain operation. I also felt guilty about delaying my customary postoperative visit to Melvin and Sarah Brown's suite. I dreaded making an appearance and having to express my condolences over the tragic loss of their daughter. However, during the same visit, I would have a chance to convey my sympathies to Dr. Frank James, who would surely be with the Browns by then, and perhaps would be able to give me the details of what happened to Meredith.

I should have been up on Abercrombie Pavilion at that moment, performing my job, fulfilling the requirements of the Hippocratic oath. Instead, I continued to drive toward home, nervously lighting one cigarette after another.

I parked my truck in front of the main entrance, under the portico, and told the valet I would be down in an hour, and to leave it in front. He said he was very sorry to hear about Mrs. Brady. Her accident was all over the news, he said. And again, he was terribly sorry.

So was I.

Raj Nowarden, head of security in our building, greeted me as I entered the foyer. He pumped my hand as tears welled up—he loved Mary Louise—and also told me how dreadfully, dreadfully sorry he was. And that he was praying for her. He was from Pakistan, was grateful to be in this country, and absolutely abhorred violence of any kind. He told me the name of the Hindu god, or goddess, for that matter, since I didn't understand the name, that he was praying to. I thanked him and told him I appreciated any help Mary Louise could get. From whom, it mattered not to me.

All the lights in the apartment were off. I stepped into the foyer, closed the door, and walked into the expanse of our living room. I noticed the only light was coming from the mass of offices, fashionable retail outlets, and hotels in the Galleria complex, and from the 100-story Transco Tower. Our floor-to-ceiling windows faced due south and allowed a full view of the shopping center and high-rise office buildings. The phosphorescence from a mile south cast a bluish tint on the room.

I walked to the east, into the sunroom, and stared at the automobiles traversing the 610 Loop. I paced back to the west, into the dining room, and stared at the homeward-bound traffic on Westheimer and San Felipe Roads, driving into the fading red glow of sundown.

The apartment felt empty and cold without the warmth Mary Louise brought to the place. Sure, she'd spent a few nights away from me for one reason or another, but not under these circumstances, when the conditions of her return were uncertain. I walked into the kitchen, filled a Styrofoam cup with ice cubes, and added a diet cola. I noticed the framed photographs on the counter next to the coffee pot as I ground Seville Orange beans. There were numerous photos, remembrances of our many escapades together. I didn't want to think about those trips, but I couldn't help it. I wanted to feel sorry for myself and wallow in self-pity, so I turned on a small fluorescent counter light.

Napa Valley, California, having dinner outside at L'Auberge's restaurant, gazing down a valley at chardonnay vineyards, after my first ride in a hot-air balloon.

Sedona, Arizona, touring the Hopi Native American Reservation and Montezuma Castle.

Boca Raton, Florida, her smiling face under a huge white straw hat, sitting in the white sand, watching the clear blue water, sipping an orange drink with a small pink umbrella at the Boca Beach Club.

The two of us, dressed in our best '50s attire with his-and-her red-letter-sweater-and-white-slacks cheerleader outfits, sitting atop a customized Harley-Davidson at a charity ball, smiling and laughing through wraparound Ray-Ban sunglasses.

In Jackson Hole, at a dude ranch named Lost Creek, riding horses through the Grand Tetons. In reality, I was on a twenty-year-old bearded gelding who only knew how to trot on the way back home toward the feed trough. Mary Louise was the rider, not me.

I sipped my drink, wished for something stronger, and fought the tears. I lost. As I held my face in my hands, I felt a nudge against my leg, then a whine. In the chaos of the day, I had forgotten about my golden retriever.

I took Tip's big fat sand-colored head in both hands, kissed him on the nose, and held him tight. I retrieved a large sack of dog food from the pantry, filled his bowl, and replenished his water. As he ravished his meal, I conducted a search for signs of "Tip accidents" and only hoped that Tonita, our long-term housekeeper, had taken him for a walk before she went home. Fortunately, the apartment was, as usual, spotless.

After a hot shower, I dressed in a pair of fresh blue scrubs and grabbed a spare pack of smokes. I hadn't smoked more than five of the little devils in one day in years. That day, I found myself needing a second pack. Yet the cigarette manufacturers denied before Congress that their products were addictive.

I turned on a lamp on the nightstand by my side of the bed, sat, and struggled getting on my boots back on. My feet were swollen after fourteen hours of standing. My sneakers would be the most comfortable, but I never wore them at the hospital. Old habits die hard. I glanced at Mary Louise's picture next to the lamp in her wedding gown. Beautiful white lace dress cut low, laughing, blond hair with that windblown look, cake on her fingers and her mouth. The tears started to flow again, and I couldn't stop until Tip walked slowly into the bedroom and laid his sad head in my lap.

Tip naturally was aware something was wrong, as all intelligent canine companions did. His mistress was not there.

"I miss her too, boy," I said.

When I finally composed myself and was dressed the part of clean surgeon, I wandered through the house and checked the fax machine in my office, then hers. Mary Louise's had a continuous sheet so long that pages were piled on the floor. Mine was typically bare.

I turned on a desk lamp in each of our offices out of habit, and then one in the lengthy living room. Maybe the lights were for my own comfort when I returned, like the commercial for Motel 6: We'll Leave the Light on for You.

Mary Louise loved lights, and lots of them, so maybe they were for her, like lit candles at an altar.

Tip followed me closely and bumped into me each time I stopped.

I wandered over to the Boston baby-grand piano, sat, and played a C-seventh cord. I had spent untold hours here, playing my simple, three-cord versions of blues, country, and gospel music. I stared at my reflection in the ebony finish, patted the keyboard, and moved on.

I returned to the kitchen and poured myself a fresh cup of coffee. I sat for a moment at the breakfast table, studied the lights of the city, worked out a plan. When I got back to the hospital, I'd make a quick trip over to the Brown suite, visit with Melvin and Sarah, and make sure he was medically fit after my operation today. I'd offer my condolences to them, and to Frank James, and, in private, insist that Frank tell me Flanagan could handle the surgery he was now performing on Mary Louise. Then I'd relieve Susan and let her go home to her family, where she should have been.

I gave Tip a good pat and asked him if he wanted to go outside. When he stood on his hind legs, placed his paws on my chest, and licked my face, I took the response as a "yes."

Tip and I walked the grounds together. I drank coffee and smoked while he chased invisible alien forces through the bushes around the pool at the Post Oak Tower. Once we were back upstairs, I explained that he must sleep alone tonight, and that Tonita would feed him and walk him first thing in the morning. I hugged him goodbye and left a very sad face behind my front door.

In the truck after barely an hour respite at the apartment, on the way back to the hospital to carry out my plan, my beeper's shrill irritating sounds interrupted my gloom. Sometimes I liked to stay gloomy, wallow in it, even, and right then was one of those times. I didn't feel like being Cheery Charlie to a patient whining about a sore muscle while my beloved mate was struggling for her life.

I removed the pager from my long white coat lying on the bench seat next to me, tapped the "light" button, and looked at the green screen and the black flashing square. I pressed the "message" button, which converted the small square to a phone number, all the while trying to drive with one hand and avoid running into any of the cars speeding past me in the descending night. The LED revealed a seven-digit number with which I was all too familiar, the nursing station in the third-floor surgical suite of University's trauma center.

"Dr. Brady here. Someone call me?"

"Yes, sir. Dr. White needs to speak with you. Sorry about Mrs. Brady," said the ward clerk. "Let me get him for you. Are you okay?"

"No, but thanks for asking." I held for a moment, lighting yet another cigarette before Gary White came on.

"Jim Bob?"

"Yes?"

"Listen, I've got some bad news. Your wife's left kidney was damaged far more than the MRI showed us. Apparently, when her spleen ruptured, the kidney was traumatized as well. I have to remove the kidney. I thought I would just be able to do some ductal repair, but I was wrong. I have to remove it. I need your permission."

I couldn't speak at first.

"Jim Bob, did you hear me? I have to—"

"I heard you, Gary, loud and clear. It's not easy making decisions about your wife when she can't speak for herself. No other way?"

"No. I'm sorry. I need to know right away. I've got the procedure on hold until I have your answer."

"What do you want me to say? No, don't remove the kidney? If it's that badly damaged, she won't survive with it still in, will she?"

After a pause, he said, "No."

I choked on my words. "Then do what you have to do."

I lit yet another cigarette, cracked the window so as not to smoke myself out, and flipped on the radio. The DJ on KIKK was congratulating a young man from a small town in East Texas on the record purchase of his yearling steer at the Houston Livestock Show and Rodeo several weeks ago. Then, a Texas swing band began a country waltz, and I recognized the smooth baritone of Merle Haggard as he crooned one of his classics. Mary Louise and I loved the song, but the timing could not have been worse. I absolutely did not want her to leave me lonely.

CHAPTER 11

FRANK JAMES

Wednesday, April 4, 2001

As I stepped off the elevator onto Abercrombie Pavilion, I was reminded of an expensive Manhattan hotel, such as the St. Regis, the Carlyle, or the Ritz-Carlton. Thick, rich Oriental rugs covered large sections of the polished parquet. Ornamental mahogany tables were interspersed between lush chintz sofas and housed Tiffany lamps and Lalique figurines. Art adorned the grass-cloth covered walls, along with what maybe have been duplicates of the Old Masters' works, or possibly originals. I couldn't distinguish between a Van Gogh, a Van Cliburn, or a Van Halen.

"Sapphire Sam" Abercrombie, long deceased, had accumulated a fortune from oil and gas production, then branched out into real estate and banking. Legend has it that he tossed one-carat sapphires around to those he found favor with. Waiters, parking valets, concession vendors, and hair stylists were among the beneficiaries of his generosity. He was quite popular in his day, donating millions to the city of Houston for various philanthropic causes. Mementos of his impact on the city included Abercrombie Plaza in downtown Houston, a park-like setting with free summer concerts; Abercrombie Boulevard, a main north–south throughway; and Abercrombie Hall, where the Houston Pops Symphony performed.

Last, but certainly not least, there was Abercrombie Pavilion at University Hospital, where the rich and famous could get personalized nursing care for a mere $1000 per day, give or take a few hundred, depending on the suite size. Much of the daily fee was not covered by insurance. Sapphire Sam gave the amount of money required by University Hospital to have a wing in one's name many years ago, when, during a lengthy stay after intestinal surgery, he failed to receive the amount of personalized attention he felt he deserved. He received a seat on the board after his generous donation.

The entrance to the twelfth floor of the Smith Building, named for yet another wealthy, benevolent Houston philanthropist, was cordoned off like a funnel. After one passed through the spacious and opulent public visitation area, entry to the inner sanctum was blocked by a security desk. Admission to the patient-care area was allowed only through an electronic door, and only after security had granted clearance. While that system did provide adequate protection for the hospitalized clientele, it caused a bit of a problem in an emergency situation, like a cardiac arrest.

Fortunately, most of the temporary inhabitants on Abercrombie were not sick. They were just recovering from various and sundry operations after the critical days had been passed in the intensive care unit. Occasionally, a patient was admitted to Abercrombie for a checkup and simply needed a nice place to lay around between tests. This scenario applied primarily to foreign dignitaries, since insurance companies in this country no longer paid for in-patient testing.

"Evening," I said to a huge Black man with a shaved head in a security-blue blazer, white shirt, and red tie. "I'm here to see Melvin Brown. I'm Dr. Brady. I did his surgery today."

"ID, sir."

I handed him my badge. It resembled a credit card and displayed my name, title, and photograph. The badge also had those little lines at the bottom called a bar code, which contained the data. Supposedly, there were thousands, maybe millions of tidbits of information on those tiny vertical strands. I always wondered if security could check the card to see if my underwear and socks were clean. If so, I'm thankful I'd gone home for a shower and a change of clothes.

After swiping the card through his scanner, he took note of the information on his computer screen. He waited, then handed me back the card.

"You're clear, Dr. Brady. Sorry to hear about Mrs. Brady," he said, nodding toward a six-inch black-and-white TV screen on one side of his desk. "Been on the news. Can't believe the irony of what happened to Mrs. James and your wife. It's not going to be a pretty sight in there," he said, pointing his thumb in the direction of the patient rooms. "Good luck. Room 1224. I'll call the private-duty, tell her you're on the way back."

"Thanks," I said, as the five-second buzzer sounded. It signaled my window of opportunity to enter the patient-care area.

I slipped through the door quickly, refocused on Mary Louise since Mr. Security had said he was sorry to hear about the accident. I got so wrapped up in my thoughts of her undergoing surgery that I turned left instead of right, even though the arrows on the wall clearly pointed out that to the left were Rooms 1201 to 1220, and to the right were Rooms 1221 to 1240.

The rooms ran north to south—or possibly east to west, since I'd never figured out where that or any hospital floor was, in relationship to the sun—along an extremely long, wide corridor resembling a football field. The patient rooms were laid out in an H, so one could only get from one side to the other through the small corridor just inside the electronic door next to security. Before I realized it, I was walking down the hallway, looking for 1224, but seeing only lower numbers.

I realized my error too late. As I approached the south—or east—end of the patient rooms, I was suddenly surrounded by three burly, bald men in expensive three-piece suits. They looked to be of perhaps African or Middle Eastern descent. Each had his right hand inside the left lapel of his suit coat, and nary a one was smiling.

"Sorry, guys. Must have made a wrong turn. I'm Dr. Brady, looking for my patient."

Before I could turn around, I noticed, a few yards behind the human stone wall, two elderly men in long white robes, wearing sandals, speaking what I presumed to be Arabic.

Sheikhs, probably here at University Hospital for a medical checkup. Such men usually traveled with armed guards, not that anyone really expected a threat to erupt in Abercrombie Pavilion. It must have made the billionaires feel better, though mostly it made the administration and board members of University Hospital feel better. Our Saudi friends usually reserved three, four, or five suites when they came to town. They were good for business and were usually allowed the luxury of having private bodyguards stationed on the floor.

I casually saluted, walked back the way I came, and shuddered a little on my way toward the crossover corridor that connected the two patient wings.

I located the correct corridor, and the correct room, and rang the buzzer. The Browns' suite door was opened by a stately young redhead, a private-duty nurse, complete with a starched white uniform and an old-fashioned nurse's cap. She ushered me into the parlor, filled with plush couches, comfortable chairs, and fresh flowers on each side table. We walked through a dining room containing an oak table with eight place settings of china and crystal, past what appeared to be a guest bedroom, and into a sitting room with subdued lighting.

Frank James was sitting in a chair, his feet on an ottoman, watching a console television. He jumped to his feet when he saw me. His black hair was uncharacteristically disheveled, his white shirt wrinkled, and the Hermès tie hung loosely around his neck. We embraced and spoke softly to each other.

"Sorry about Meredith," I said.

"Sorry about Mary Louise. Wish I could have been there for her, as you know, but I just can't function. You understand?"

"Of course. How are your in-laws holding up?"

"Not good. Somehow this will all be my fault. You wait and see."

"Why? Because you've been separated? Or because you two were thinking about getting back together?"

"Take your choice, Jim. She was their only child. I can't tell you how they worshipped that girl."

The nurse left our company and entered her patient's room through a door in the far wall of the sitting room. I could hear soft crying until she shut it quietly behind her.

"Sit down, Jim. I can use the company."

"I can't stay but a minute. I wanted to come by, express my condolences to your father-in-law and Sarah, and make sure his leg is all right. I've got to get back to the waiting room and rejoin my son. Mary Louise is in surgery now, as you probably know."

"Yeah. Flanagan got the call, right?"

"Right."

"Sorry about that. I know there's some bad blood between you two. He's a competent neurosurgeon, though, Jim. Shitty bedside manner, and an asshole at heart. Probably should never have been allowed into medical school. But he's smart, and an excellent technician, which is primarily what Mary Louise needs right now. Actually, if you want to know the truth, he's a much better surgeon than I am. I have a much higher 'schmooze' factor with the patients, which gets me a lot more business. But if I had to pick the most competent doctor I know to perform delicate brain surgery on someone I cared about, like Mary Louise, I'd pick Flanagan."

"I'm glad to know that, but I don't think he's any better surgeon than you are. I've worked with both of you, remember. And I'd naturally feel better if you were in there with her instead of Flanagan, but under the circumstances . . ."

"Jim, I'd much rather be operating on Mary Louise than sitting here, bemoaning my wife's . . ." and then he broke up.

After he got control of himself, he said, "Mary Louise has other injuries, I guess."

I nodded, described them as best I could before my eyes teared and my voice cracked.

He patted me on the forearm.

"Well, she's got the best care money can buy. She'll make it, Jim."

"Thanks for saying that, Frank, even if it's bullshit."

He attempted a smile.

"Any idea on what might have happened to Meredith?" I ask.

He shook his head. "I pulled up to the security gate at our complex a little before two o'clock. That big security guard Moorehouse was on duty. I was in the Beamer, he checked my license plate number, saw the Memorial Bend sticker on the windshield above the inspection sticker, and waved me on through. I hadn't been over there since we separated, so he wrote my name on his clipboard. Guess he didn't recognize me, since I've been renting an apartment in the Ritz-Carlton for six months.

"Anyway, I parked in front of the house and sat in the Beamer for a few minutes. I kept the motor running so I could run the air conditioner. Only April, Jim, and it was already in the upper eighties this afternoon. I considered using my remote to open the garage door but decided not to push my luck. I didn't want to scare Meredith off. I decided just to be cool. Park in front, go to the front door, and ring the bell. Be polite. Act like a guest, even though I bought the damn house. But I didn't want to take any chances. I wanted the afternoon to be perfect. I wanted to move back home, you see."

He hung his head, sniffled a bit. I nodded.

"So I sat there for a few minutes and pondered the last six months of separation from Meredith. I felt a little sorry for myself, sitting there in front of my own house. I thought about all the conflicts that had punctured holes in our married bliss. My work was the main problem. You know the drill, Jim. You have to be dedicated to the patients, spend long hours at the hospital, and take care of all the emergencies. That all goes with the successful practice of a busy academic neurosurgeon. Hell, any surgeon, especially in the University Medical Center. Right?"

"Right, Frank. I know the routine, all too well. Although with Mary Louise in surgery, all that success doesn't seem so important right this minute."

"I know you've heard all the rumors, Jim, and I won't deny it. I have had affairs, and many of them. In fact, too many to count. I've never had a nurse, or a lab tech, or an X-ray tech, or a member of the house staff, or anybody else for that matter, turn me down. But that's pretty common for us docs, isn't it, especially with surgeons, for Christ's sake? C'mon, Jim, don't look at me like that. You're not telling me you've never had an indiscretion. Not even once?"

"Sorry, Frank. I'm just a boring guy."

"Well, I'm sure Meredith must have had something going on the side during our marriage, if not when we lived together, then certainly during the separation. I think she wanted to talk about that subject over lunch today, to try and put it all behind us. I had planned to fess up to all my extramarital relationships, especially those back when I was screwing everything that walked. I thought it could be a catharsis for both of us, since I don't believe that Meredith was a nun all those years. Today was to be the start of a new day. I swear all my running around was going to end. I didn't want to lose Meredith. I was coming home. For good. My life was going to change. Meredith and I were going to work out our differences.

"As I sat there in the car, I thought about her putting the finishing touches on lunch. I figured we'd have cocktails and wine, and hopefully reconcile. And then we would make mad passionate love like in the old days."

Frank leaned forward in his chair and began to whisper. "You know, Jim, I have to tell you something. I had really missed Meredith physically. She is . . . was . . . gorgeous, in great shape, and absolutely fabulous in bed. Don't get me wrong, that certainly wasn't Meredith's only redeeming quality. I missed her emotionally, as well. But in bed? My God, that woman was a hellcat. I must admit that I had become sexually desperate for her."

"Frank, I'm not sure I need to hear about Meredith and your intimacies. I mean, after all, she's dead."

"I know, Jim. Sorry, I got carried away. Once you start spilling your guts, it's hard to stop. Anyway, after a rollicking romp in the sack, I, the dutiful husband, would accompany his wife to University Hospital, where we would visit her father, who should have been in the recovery room, or maybe in this private suite, by the time we arrived. I planned to have a nice visit with the Browns and announce our reconciliation. You were supposed to come by, tell us that the old man was cured and would live to be a hundred. And, you would have a drink with us, and we'd toast the new relationship of Dr. and Mrs. Frank James. And everything would be great," Frank said, and with that, began a new round of sobbing.

After he composed himself, he continued. "So, I finally turn the engine off, get out of the Beamer, walk to the front door of the house, and ring the doorbell. And, like a proper suitor, I wait on the doorstep and avoid using my house key. I started to, but then I thought I saw Meredith walking down the stairs toward the front door to let me in. It was hard to tell, that stained glass panel is so thick. I never paid that much attention to it before, from the outside anyway.

"So, I wave. But then the strangest thing happened. Whoever it was that I saw turned the opposite direction and appeared to run out the back door, toward the pool. I waited for a minute, then tried to open the door with my key, but it didn't work. Meredith had changed the locks. So, I waited, rang the doorbell repeatedly, but she never answered the door. And then I panicked. I went back to the Beamer, called Moorehouse at the security gate, and told him to call 911. The cops came and I told them what I had seen. Before they decided to break down the door, we walked around back and found the slider to the living room ajar. They followed me upstairs and we found Meredith, murdered in her dressing room."

As he began to cry again, I couldn't help but wonder callously if I was the only pickup-truck driver who hated the word "Beamer."

"These two detectives showed up after a while and started giving me the third degree, especially this cowboy-type named Polk. There was a female detective there for a few minutes, a woman named Beeson. But then she left in a hurry, said something to the cowboy about Mary Louise. Do you two know her?"

"Yes. Susan is one of Mary Louise's best friends. I'm sure the detectives were just doing their job, Frank."

"Sure. That Beeson woman got beeped when I was on the cellular, talking to the office. She tore out of the yard like the house was on fire. It's all so incredibly ironic. I'm giving away a case in the ER to an associate because my wife has been murdered, and it turns out the patient is Mary Louise. And at the same time, you're calling an HPD detective to meet you at the ER, and she's the very same one that's investigating my wife's murder and giving me hell!"

I nodded. "Did you have any involvement in this . . . this mess with Meredith, Frank?"

He stared at me. "You mean did I kill her? Or have her killed? Is that what you're asking me, Jim?"

"I guess so."

"Not on your life. I loved that woman, more than anything. I just wish I'd been a faithful husband. Maybe this wouldn't have happened. I don't know, Jim, I just don't know."

He started sobbing again, and I just let him be. We were quiet for a time.

"Any ideas on who might have wanted to kill her, Frank?"

"No. None whatsoever. I wouldn't think she had an enemy in the world. It had to be a robbery attempt, or a rape attempt gone awry. Or maybe a pissed-off jilted lover from the past six months killed her. Who knows? She was in the wrong place at the wrong time, best I can figure."

"She was raped?"

"I don't know that yet. Those two detectives said they would have to wait for the pathologist's report before they could tell me anything."

"I'm sorry, Frank. Really."

"Me too, Jim," he said, and blew his nose.

I glanced at my watch and saw that it was almost nine o'clock. Mary Louise had been in surgery for over two hours.

"I'd better see your father-in-law, then get back to the waiting room."

"Thanks for coming," he said, as we stood and shook hands.

He walked over to the closed door that led into Melvin Brown's room, and lightly knocked. The same nurse that allowed me entry to the suite opened the door, and I stepped in to see my patient.

CHAPTER 12

THE PAVILION

Wednesday, April 4, 2001

The bedroom was huge, maybe forty by forty feet. Sarah Brown sat in a bedside chair to her husband's left, head back, bloodshot eyes open, a box of tissues in her lap. She nodded when I entered the room, but didn't stand. Her feet were curled under her, and with the oversized white terry-cloth hospital robe she wore, she looked miserably cozy.

Melvin Brown's hospital bed may have had all the bells and whistles that allowed adjustment of position—that's what a hospital bed does—but it was the nicest I had ever seen. It had a varnished oak headboard with matching footboard and was a king-sized bed, maybe even a California king. Mounted on one of the bedrails was a remote control panel with buttons to adjust bed position, room lighting, stereo, and TV functions.

I walked around the end of the bed and checked his right foot for signs of neurological or circulatory impairment. The nurse followed and gave me an update on his condition. Vital signs good, with normal temperature, pulse, and respiration. The toe circulation had been fine. He had been in a lot of pain, but the PCA pump was keeping his discomfort under control with periodic boluses of morphine.

I asked Mr. Brown if he could feel my fingers on his toes, but he didn't respond.

"He's been sedated," said a man sitting in a chair pushed up against the wall, just to the left of Melvin Brown's bed. "Too much pain, and too much grief."

He startled me, since the only room light came from the muted television, and I hadn't noticed the man when I entered the room. The nurse gave me one of those oh-no-he's-going-to-say-something looks as she rolled her eyes upward and backed away from the bedside.

The man stood, and I immediately was aware of a physical presence. He was tall and quite stocky, although athletically so. He was clean-shaven and softly handsome. But his most impressive and memorable feature was the perfect silver hair, arranged in one of those pompadour styles, with numerous waves, and stiff with holding spray. His coiffure probably wouldn't move during a hurricane. He appeared to be in his late sixties or early seventies.

"Dr. Andrew Jones. Their pastor," he said, and extended a soft, manicured hand. "And you are?"

"Dr. Brady, his orthopedic surgeon."

"A pleasure, Doctor. The surgery went well, I presume?"

"Yes, sir, very well. I just wanted to make sure he was as comfortable as possible under the circumstances."

"Yes. Well, thank you for coming by. Sarah said your nurse and a young physician-associate by the name of Dr. Long spoke to her after the surgery was completed. Do you think our man here will survive?"

"Well, sir, it's a little early to say, but the surgery went well. If the margins are clean of cancer cells, he has a great chance. We won't have the final pathology report for a week, possibly ten days."

"I see. Doctor, I want to express my condolences about the terrible tragedy that has befallen you and your family. We are sorry to hear about your wife, Mary, I believe her name is. Sarah and I saw it on the news. It accompanied the story about our Meredith."

"Thank you, Dr. Jones."

"We tried to avoid having Melvin find out about his daughter until tomorrow. Sarah and I at least wanted to get him through the first night. Although the television was on mute, he unfortunately was awake just enough to see Meredith's picture on one of those 'news-breaks' they have all the time, and he just about went into hysterics over it. That's why the nurse here had to give him additional medication.

"You know, Doctor, these times we are living in are more than we mortals can bear sometimes. We have the senseless murder of a wonderful young woman, the only daughter of two of my oldest and dearest friends. We have the hit-and-run injury to your wife, who I'm sure is a lovely woman as well. None of what has happened seems to have any rhyme or reason to it. These must be the last days we're living in, Doctor. The last days, when Almighty God shall vent his anger on the miscreants in our society."

"Yes, sir," I said. That's all I could respond with, since I was starting to become a little nervous, like I used to when I was a regular churchgoer as a child.

"Another act of fate over which we have no control. An act which only God can presume to see the logic in. Are you a religious man, Dr. Brady?"

"I don't know anymore."

"Would you like to pray with me?"

"I need to get back to the waiting room and be with my son, Dr. Jones. My wife is still in surgery. Maybe some other time."

"Fine," he said, then reached into his jacket pocket and extracted a business card. It read that he was the senior minister at Afton Oaks Baptist Church. I noted that his number was answered twenty-four hours a day. "If you need anything . . . anything at all . . . you let me know."

"Yes, sir. Thank you."

We shook hands. As I left the room, I nodded again to Sarah Brown, who sat in her chair, unmoving, distraught, with empty eyes, like a zombie in a B movie.

I waved at Frank as I exited the sitting room and observed him staring into the television. He waved but didn't speak or even look my way.

Standing back in the foyer entry to the pavilion, waiting for the elevator, I pondered what the preacher said about things we mortals couldn't comprehend. Mary Louise, victim of a horrible, possibly fatal accident, whose assailant failed to stop and render aid. Meredith James, victim of a brutal murder by an unknown intruder, in the wrong place at the wrong time, as Frank James stated. And there was no reasonable explanation for any of it.

Both events represented a tragic act of fate.

CHAPTER 13

WAITING

Wednesday, April 4, 2001

Susan and J. J. were huddled together, talking intimately, when I arrived back in the waiting room outside the operating suites where my wife was being pieced back together. They were the only two people in the vast room, which was lined with blue plastic chairs held together in groups by chrome bases. She had her arm around my son. His head was bowed.

"Time for you to go home, Susie."

"What?" she said, startled. "Jim Bob, you scared me. J. J. and I were just . . . well, just talking about his mother. And about what a great lady she is, and what strength and resilience she has, and how confident I am that she's going to pull through."

"There's not a stronger woman on the planet, if you ask me, Susan. After all, look who she's had to put up with all these past thirty years."

"That's right, and thirty years of you is enough to make anyone strong, huh, J. J.?" she said, smiling, trying to lighten his mood as best as she could. "Did the doctor get hold of you? He came out here a while back and asked to speak with you. Something about more damage to the left kidney than he anticipated?"

I nodded, and mouthed the word "Later."

J. J. continued staring at the dark-brown commercial-grade carpet, elbows on his knees, head in his hands.

"Everything will be fine. You just wait and see," Susan said, patting J. J. on the back. She stood and stretched her weary muscles.

"I guess I'd better get home, Jim Bob. Call me if you or J. J. need anything, okay?"

"Sure. I can't thank you enough for . . . for just being here. I'll never forget it."

"I wouldn't have been any place else, not with our girl in this predicament."

She walked around the end of the row of chairs, and we hugged. I felt her tremble a little and knew she wasn't nearly as positive that Mary Louise would pull through this injury as she has led J. J. to believe. But it sounded positive at the time, and I hoped it had lifted his spirits somewhat.

She wiped the tears from her cheeks, waved, and hurried off to her family.

I sat beside J. J. and asked, "Need something to eat or drink, son?"
He shook his head.

I leaned back, slouched down in the chair, crossed my legs, and put my hands behind my head.

After a time of silence, J. J. murmured something inaudible.
"What?"

"I said, do you think she's going to make it?"

I sat up and thought about how to answer.

"Well, she's young, and—"

"She's fifty-two, Dad."

"That's young enough to heal well, son. Your mother exercises every day, and she's in great health. And like Susan said, she's strong. A survivor. She has a lot going for her. She has a lot to live for."

He straightened himself and turned toward me. "You didn't answer my question, Dad. I asked if she was going to make it."

"Well, there is no way I can absolutely, positively tell you that without a doubt your mother is going to recover. She has the benefit of an incredibly talented team of doctors who will render her the best medical and surgical care available. I want you to think positively, son. I have to believe she will feel your vibrations because you two have always been not just mother and son, but intimate friends. Don't you agree?"

He stared at me for a few moments, then returned to his slumped position.

"J. J.?"

He shook his head. "I guess. It's just so hard. Mom's always been there for me, and for you too, by the way. She's always taken care of both of us. I don't think I can stand to lose her, Dad."

I saw his back tremble and shake. I laid my palm over his right shoulder, feeling the tears come to my eyes.

"Son, you're twenty-seven years old, you've graduated college, you have your own business, and you're independently successful. Fortunately, we've had very little misfortune in our lives, so, I admit, it's hard to deal with adversity. But we can get through it. We have to be strong . . . together. That's what your mother would want."

He abruptly raised his head and turned toward me. "I'm going to find whoever did this to Mom, whatever it takes, no matter how much it costs. I want retribution, Dad. I know that's wrong, but I can't help it. I've been sitting here for the last couple of hours talking to Susan. She told me a lot of stuff to try and help me, but the only thing that's keeping me from completely falling apart is the idea that I will seek out and destroy this . . . this person who has tried to destroy my mother."

"Well, J. J., I don't have any right to judge you. And right or wrong, maybe I'm taking a different approach as far as my emotions go, to help me get through this ordeal. However, whatever you require to keep your sanity, son, I'm in favor of. Okay?"

"Okay, Dad. Thanks." He stood and stretched. "You going to stay here until the surgery is over?"

"Yes. Thought I'd lay down on a couch and try to get some sleep. She's going to be in there most of the night."

"Do you mind if I take a break? I'd like to go by the office, initiate a search program, then go home and shower. I'll be back."

"Fine. What kind of search program, J. J.?

"I'm going to be accessing all the files I can get my hands on, searching for a late-model black European car. I can start with the Department of Motor Vehicles, look through licenses and registrations to start with. Then, I'll go through the dealership manifests—"

"But J. J., isn't that virtually impossible? Like looking for a needle in a haystack?"

"Yes, it is. But I already discussed it with Susan. She admitted that HPD probably doesn't have the staff to do the kind of investigative work it's going to take to find the owner of the car that hit Mom. But that's what I do for a living. Investigations. And Susan is going to give me special clearance to look at certain state and local files that would be very difficult, if not impossible, to access otherwise. By the time the forensics specialists gather clues from the scene of the accident, there should be enough information to begin a search for the vehicle. Besides, I'll be working closely with the FARTs. There are some cool guys—"

"FARTs?"

"Forensic Auto Research Technicians. It's a special branch of the Traffic Division of HPD that investigates automotive-related misdemeanors and felonies.

"Anyway, I want to start tonight. I'll be back after a while. Call me on my beeper if there's any news, good or bad. Do you have my number?"

"Yes."

"Good. See you later, Dad."

I watched J. J. walk purposefully toward the elevators, and I made a mental note that I would prefer him to be angry and motivated, rather than depressed.

I moved to, then stretched out on, a worn imitation-leather couch, a far cry from the amenities I witnessed in Abercrombie Pavilion. This spot was just an ordinary waiting room, with commercial-grade furnishings, for us ordinary folk.

I sat up and thought about Mary Louise back there in surgery. To hell with Flanagan. I wanted to check on her and see how the procedures were going. I walked toward the surgeons' entrance to the surgical suite, grabbed hold of the entry door handle, then abruptly stopped myself. I decided it was a bad idea.

I could have tried the surgeon's coffee bar, where the couches were more comfortable, but then my colleagues were probably working in shifts and would be lounging in there between operations. I'd have to listen to their conversations about how the procedures were going, and I couldn't bear the thought of hearing them speak about Mary Louise's surgeries like she was an ordinary patient. Besides, my presence might have thwarted the collaborative effort, possibly to the detriment of her care, and what would that have accomplished?

So, I returned to the waiting room, and lay down on the visitors' couch. Besides, that's all I was. A visitor. A concerned relative. Inert. Impotent. Useless.

I wasn't even able to comfort my own son adequately. Susan Beeson had to do that for me.

As I reclined, I thought of the days when J. J. and his roommate, Brad Broussard, were in their sophomore year of college in Austin, at the University of Texas. Both were computer geeks and took it upon themselves to track down the organizer of a raid on the coffers at the Alpha Tau Omega fraternity house. A rival group of hacker Sigma Alpha Epsilons had networked themselves into the computer memory banks at the ATO house and broke the bank, so to speak, by creating fake "withdrawals" from the ATO account at the Austin National Bank.

After J. J. and Brad followed a tangled paper trail and discovered the culprits, who were subsequently expelled, they developed quite a reputation around campus as first-rate CADs—computer-assisted detectives. Eventually they started a business: Setec Astronomy. From the movie *Sneakers*, it was an anagram for TOO MANY SECRETS. They took on a few projects for the bank that had sustained the monetary loss, and even did a fair amount of investigative work for the university. By the time they finished school, the boys had enough equipment and capital to start their own business in Houston, B&B Investigations.

It sounded like Susan Beeson was going to allow J. J. access to otherwise-impenetrable records, and help . . . FARTs, was it? . . . with the eventual search for his mother's assailant. Good for him. Hopefully, it would keep him from dwelling continuously on the anguish of Mary Louise's plight and her recovery. I was envious that I didn't have the capacities and abilities to keep from losing my mind over this dark period of my life.

As I settled down and my eyes got heavy, I found myself wishing I had agreed to let Reverend Dr. Jones say a little prayer for Mary Louise. But I was uncomfortable and didn't know where I stood on issues like that.

I was confused about my religious beliefs. I grew up in a conservative Methodist household in a small town in West Texas. But somewhere along the line, my faith was shaken. Maybe it was studying all that science in college, like the evolution process, the big bang theory, and archaeological data that asserted the earth is millions, maybe billions of years old. Data that has shown unequivocally that humanity is about 275,000 years old. From a purely scientific viewpoint, it's clear that our planet did not originate in 4000 BC, as Bishop Ussher postulated centuries ago.

Or maybe it was the nine years of medical school and residency training, where I spent most of my time at institutions treating people who had experienced unspeakable traumas—murder, rape, incest, mutilation, and child abuse, to name a few. Alcoholism and its complications, such as liver failure and delirium tremens, were daily problems. Drug addiction and overdoses were rampant. Dope deals gone awry produced shootings, stabbings, and the revenge mutilations, or removal, of the sexual organs of rival faction members. All that mayhem overshadowed those nice, pleasant, and quiet early years in a small town in Texas, where people were nice to each other, and everybody went to church on Sunday. I remembered back to the days when you could stop and render aid to someone whose car had broken down, without fear of being murdered. Or, if someone you weren't familiar with came knocking at your door, and it was a student selling Bibles, or the nice Fuller brush man, you didn't have to carry a weapon to greet them.

Where was God in all this? And where was He when Mary Louise was a near-fatal victim to a hit-and-run driver?

Dr. Andrew Jones of the Afton Oaks Baptist Church exhibited a demeanor that would indicate he was not confused about his religious beliefs. Maybe he ignored me and prayed for Mary Louise anyway.

I hope so. She needed all the help she could get tonight.

CHAPTER 14

SUCCESS

Thursday, April 5, 2001

It was four in the morning when I was awakened from fitful sleep by a thundering herd of blue scrubs and white coats who came to stand in front of me. J. J. appeared at my side, and we listened closely to the reports of the many surgeons, then thanked the doctors who had gathered to report on Mary Louise's current condition. Once the obligatory visit with the patient's family was complete, everyone quickly scattered to their respective homes or offices, or wherever else they might have gone that time of the morning.

"Could you get me some coffee, J. J.? There's a vending machine down on the first level by the elevators," I asked, and handed him a five-dollar bill.

"Dad, you've been a surgeon here for, what, over twenty years? Couldn't you just walk back to the doctor's lounge, or whatever you call it, and get some—"

"I'm just a husband right now, and I don't want to be a party to the medical staffs' whispered conversations about your mother's operations. Trust me, I've heard that talk most of my adult life. I don't want to know the ins and outs of her various procedures. Now, I need to make some calls. Would you mind? Getting the coffee?"

He stared at me through his thick, wireless frames, his tousled hair giving him the appearance of a twelve-year-old man-child. Then he took the money and left the waiting room, shaking his head.

"Hello?" the sleepy voice answered.

"Susan, I'm sorry to wake you, but you said to call—"

"What? Is she okay, Jim Bob?"

"They're finished. The parade of stars just came out to the waiting room en masse and woke me up. Her fractures have been repaired with plates, rods, and screws. Her spleen and left kidney had to be removed. The right kidney is fine, and the liver lacerations have been repaired. The ENT and oral surgeon were able to patch up her facial bones, remove the broken teeth, and repair the mandible. They were very happy with how it turned out. And, the ophthalmologist was able to repair the detached retina. The chances of Mary Louise losing her left eye are small, although she wouldn't make any guarantees about the quality of her vision."

"What about her head, Jim?"

"Well, Flanagan said he was able to use a new technique. I don't really understand it, but he was able to distinguish viable brain tissue from nonviable tissue with an innovative type of laser light, such that he was able to leave most of the important stuff. He said that in addition to the open head injury, she had a severe concussion. Plus, he had to drain a collection of blood from the opposite side of her head from the injury. But, he's cautiously optimistic. Those are his words, not mine."

"What about the skull fractures themselves? Was he able to repair them? Or did he leave a big dent in her head?"

"He said he patched it best he could. He was afraid to use cement because he was worried that the curing of the methyl methacrylate would produce too much heat and might damage even more tissue. He had warned me about that in the Radiology suite prior to surgery. He said it doesn't look too bad, although I think that a cosmetic defect that 'doesn't look too bad' to a neurosurgeon could be anything from a dimple to a crater the size of Mt. Vesuvius. He said he and a plastic surgeon can go in later and repair the defect if need be."

"So, overall, it sounds pretty good, huh?"

"Considering the circumstances, I'd said yes. At least she made it through ten hours of surgery."

"I told you she was strong. She's going to be all right. I can feel it. What are you going to do now?"

"Go back to the recovery room. They can't keep me out like they did in the OR, not that I really wanted to be there. Susan, I couldn't even go into the surgeon's lounge for fear of hearing something unpleasant about her. I guess I love Mary Louise too much to think of her as just another surgical specimen. Know what I mean?"

"Absolutely."

"I'm going to go back and sit with her and hold her hand. Maybe she'll know I'm there. Flanagan said that as soon as she's stable, he's having her transferred to NIC, which is Neurosurgical Intensive Care. It's in another wing of the hospital, and I want to be with her when she's in transport."

"Did you get some sleep?"

"A little."

"And J. J.?"

"Yeah. He must have returned to the waiting room after I fell asleep. I was zonked out, I guess."

Susan began to weep and could not speak.

"Susan? You okay?"

"Sure, just relieved that she made it through."

"I understand. I will probably be an emotional wreck for a while. I tried to get the tears out of my system before I called you, but . . . listen, I need to get to recovery. Thanks again for being here earlier, and sorry to wake you."

"I wouldn't have had it any other way, Jim Bob. By the way, I lit a candle and recited the Rosary for Mary Louise."

I told her about my conversation with Dr. Andrew Jones.

"I'll tell you, Susan, after reflecting on what he told me in Melvin Brown's suite, I decided to give in and whisper a prayer to the Man Upstairs myself. At least one thing is certain."

"What's that?"

"I hope there is a heaven, because whoever is there has heard about Mary Louise Brady tonight."

CHAPTER 15

NIC

Thursday, April 5, 2001

Mary Louise's head was completely bandaged in white cotton laced with tan ACE bandages. Only her right eye and cheek were visible. Even her lips were hidden by moistened flat sponges, positioned around her mouth to try and heal a deep ulcer created, I assume, when she bit down on the endotracheal tube during one of her grand mal seizures. Since patients can't tolerate an endotracheal tube for more than a few days, one of her surgeons had removed it in the operating room and, not knowing how long it would be until she could breathe on her own, replaced it with a tracheostomy. Inserted into her throat was a stainless-steel fixture that housed the plastic respirator hose. A brutal-looking steel and polyethylene outrigger, holding pins in position, covered her left jaw. Her ears were covered as well, and blood had stained the bandages over her left temple, site of the open skull fracture.

Mary Louise had the appearance of a mummy.

Her left arm was bandaged and splinted from the wrist to the elbow, and protruding from her arm below her shoulder was a massive external fixator holding her humerus fracture in place, similar to the one holding her jaw together. Her left leg below the knee was splinted as well, and just above the top of the plaster, a pin had been inserted through the lower part of her knee joint to hold her leg up in traction.

When he X-rayed her in surgery to make sure the leg fractures were well-reduced with hardware he inserted, Jeff Kosar discovered that her pelvis was broken. He said the fracture couldn't be operated on because of comminution, so traction would be required for six weeks. I knew all this, of course, since I had taken care of a number of these injuries. But now that it was my wife who had been injured, this type of routine orthopedic treatment seemed colossally barbaric and much more physically damaging than when I'd rendered the same exact treatment to someone else's wife.

The hiss of the respirator was loud during the expansion of Mary Louise's chest fifteen times per minute. The monitors above her NIC bed showed that her pulse was a decent seventy-two, her heart rate regular, with a respectable blood oxygenation level of 98 percent. Those were good signs.

I stood on her right side, with the bed rails up, and glanced around NIC. This was where the sickest of the sick went. The head cases. There were forty beds there: twenty acute beds for the critical patients whose recovery was undecided, and twenty intermediate beds for those whom the tide had turned favorably. It was the largest unit of its kind in the city. According to the flow chart on the wall behind the ward-clerk's desk, eighteen beds on the acute ward were occupied, my wife being one of those occupants.

The staff was kind enough to place Mary Louise directly in front of the nurses' station. They could keep an especially close eye on her there. Of course, monitors at each bedside were linked to monitors at the station so that if any irregularity whatsoever occurred, alarms sounded, and the nursing staff could attend to the problem immediately.

There was one nurse assigned for every three patients, a remarkably low nurse–patient ratio. And the day-shift nurse taking care of Mary Louise, Gina Genardo, was great. She had come on duty at seven o'clock this morning, about the time Mary Louise was transferred from the recovery room. Gina told me she had a master's degree, with ER, Cardiac, and Neuro certificates. She explained her credentials to me so that I would feel confident she was qualified to handle Mary Louise's post-op care. It was unnecessary but appreciated.

Gina had a warm olive complexion and stood about five foot seven, with an athletic build, long black hair done in a French braid, and dark-brown eyes. Gina was not beautiful but striking. And more importantly, she was much better informed than I was, since most of the things she told me about my wife's condition made little sense. I nodded and acted like I knew what she was saying. I'm sure she knew that orthopedic surgeons were snidely referred to by other physicians as the truck drivers of medicine. That mattered not to me at this juncture, because my role was only that of an attentive husband.

My staff had canceled my office and surgical patients for the next two days. I didn't know what to do about next week's office and surgery schedule. I felt that I probably should work, just to try and keep my mind off Mary Louise's condition, since I couldn't do much for her except sit around and wait. On the other hand, what would a dutiful husband do? Sit by her side, day in and day out, and wait?

And what would she want me to do?

Without a doubt, go to work.

I was in no shape to do that today, what with three or four hours of fitful sleep, but the issues were next week and the weeks that followed.

My partners would divide up and see my scheduled clinic patients for me and give the two patients I had scheduled for surgery Friday the option to reschedule for a later date, when I would be available, or go ahead and have one of my associates perform the surgery. My practice would have to take a backseat to the most important issue, which was the woman whose hand I was holding in NIC.

NIC was shaped like a *U*, with ten beds in front of the long ward-clerk's desk and nurses' station, and five on either side. There was a doorway on the opposite wall, past the last acute bed, that led to the Intermediate Unit. I was hopeful Mary Louise could be transferred there when her condition stabilized and her mental status improved. The pace in NIC was frenetic, with nurses running around like maniacs, checking vital signs, restarting IVs, drawing blood, pushing meds, calling codes. People in NIC were very sick, and patients there died every day.

University Hospital was a teaching institution, so there were medical students, interns, residents, and fellows constantly in and out of NIC. The Neuro teaching rounds had reached Mary Louise earlier this morning. Flanagan came through here with a pack of followers in gray and green scrubs, and short and long white coats. I heard him explaining his cases to the house staff, since the ten beds on this wall were contiguous. The "gunshot wound" this, the "subdural" that. "The meningioma is doing fine". "The glioblastoma is going down the tubes". No names. Just diagnoses.

When he came to Mary Louise's bed, he stood at the foot, picked up the chart, and thumbed through the early morning lab work and vital signs. He turned to his groupies, said something to the effect of "The head trauma case here is—" but thought better of it when he saw me, then addressed his patient as Mrs. Brady. My fists were already balled up, and I was just tired enough to recklessly go after him. He did manage, after all, to save Mary Louise's life, so I owed him a certain degree of allegiance. How much, I wasn't sure yet.

I decided that at the next meeting of the executive committee of University Hospital, of which I was a member—and had one more year on my three-year term—I was going to try to pass an addendum to the bylaws, requiring that all patients, whether conscious or not, were to be discussed by their name, not by their disease or injury.

"Coffee, Doc?"

"Huh? Oh, thanks Gina. You're too kind."

As I sipped the strong black brew, I sat down to the right of the bed in a straight-backed chair the eleven to seven nursing supervisor had provided for me when I had arrived here with my bride. The uncomfortable chair was wedged in between Mary Louise's bed and the next, occupied by a sixty-nine-year-old man who'd had a severe stroke one week ago. He was sadly still unresponsive to pin pricks and reflex hammers stimulating him every hour. On her other side there lay a woman of thirty-two, victim of the sudden blowout of an aneurysm, a small congenital defect in a cerebral artery that seemed to lie dormant until one was in the prime of life, then erupted unexpectedly. Earlier this morning, a grief-stricken young man came and stood at the bedside of the young wife and mother.

"First time here? On the inside?" Gina asked.

"No, I've been in here—Oh, you mean, as a patient? Or in this case, as the family member of a patient? Yes."

"Thought so. I told my husband Rick when he called a few minutes ago that we had a doctor sitting with his wife. I told him you looked out of place, even with the scrubs on. Been on staff long?"

"Since 1978."

She smiled. "That's a long time, Dr. Brady, to have been lucky enough to avoid 'the other side.'"

"Yes, Gina, we've been very lucky. You're married to a physician?"

"Uh-huh. Rick finished his internal medicine residency last year, then signed on for a two-year cardiology fellowship. Looks like I'll be working a while longer."

"Have any kids?"

She shook her head. "No time for that so far. Someday, I plan to be an ex-nurse, have five kids like my mother, and enjoy the lifestyle of a doctor's wife like my mother."

"Your father is a doctor?"

"Yes. He's a heart surgeon, in New Orleans. I grew up in the 'life.' You almost have to grow up in it to be able to handle this type of ICU work, what with the long hours, the patient demands, the intensity and the dying. As you might expect, the burnout rate for this type of acute-care nursing is high. Most of us can't tolerate it for more than a few years. I've done it all—CV Surgery, ER, Coronary Care—but Neuro is the worst."

She walked over to Mary Louise's right side, gently lifted her right eyelid, and shined a penlight into the pupil, checking for reflex constriction. She pulled an ophthalmoscope from her shirt pocket and evaluated the retina for swelling and hemorrhage of the optic nerve, a mini-barometer of the brain's complex status.

"So far, so good, Dr. Brady. And her vitals are good."

She went to the foot of the bed and rubbed a reflex hammer along the sole of Mary Louise's right foot.

"Negative Babinski. Cerebral function's intact, best as we can tell. Of course, I'd like to check that left foot, but with the splint and the traction . . ."

"She's had no sign of a response, though, Gina. No spontaneous respirations, no movement, that sort of thing. What do you think?"

"It's too early for a significant response. She's had a severe cerebral trauma. She could be in a coma for weeks. Didn't Dr. Flanagan tell you?"

"Yes, but I'd rather hear it from you."

She smiled. "I understand. He's a horse's ass. Cold as ice. No bedside manner whatsoever. Most of the neurosurgeons are like that, except for . . . well, except for one."

Her voice faltered a little, and she cleared her throat.

"You mean Frank James, don't you?"

She nodded her head.

"He's a good friend of mine. I called for him as soon as I got to the ER and found out that Mary Louise had a head injury. Unfortunately, he was . . . otherwise occupied."

"I know. It's been all over the news. That's the big talk around here this morning. Did he do it, or did he hire someone to do it? Personally, I don't think there's any way he could be involved with murdering his wife. He's just . . . well, he's not the type. If you know what I mean."

"Yes, I do. I've known Frank a long time. He may not have been the most faithful husband in the world, but I don't think he's capable of murder or, for that matter, of hiring someone to murder Meredith."

Gina quietly pulled out the hospital chart in the rack at the end of the bed and wrote a few comments in the nurses notes. She heaved a big sigh and put the chart back in the rack.

"His wife was a rich woman, I understand, from a prominent family."

"That's right. Her father is Melvin Brown."

"And you were operating on him yesterday when your wife was injured, right?"

"Yes. How did you know?"

"Like everyone else. The TV."

Her beeper went off, and she excused herself and walked to a glassed-in cubicle behind the nursing station.

I finished my coffee, discarded the cup, moved my chair to the opposite side of the hospital bed, sat, and carefully picked up Mary Louise's right hand. A splint supported her forearm, which housed an IV line for fluid maintenance and an arterial line for monitoring her blood's composition of oxygen and carbon dioxide.

I glanced at the elderly man next to me and watched his chest heave in and out with the pulse of the respirator. I sat up as high as I could, peered over Mary Louise's bed, and stared at the young victim of the ruptured aneurysm. Then I watched my wife's chest. In, out, in out. All three had respirators that created a disharmonious symphony . . . like a funeral dirge.

I leaned my head back and tried to dissociate myself from the pings, bells, whistles, and beeps from the life-support devices in NIC, and from the squawks of the intercom. It sounded like an amusement park, but without the fun.

CHAPTER 16

LUNCH

Thursday, April 5, 2001

It was only noon and still Thursday, although it seemed I had been in NIC for days. There were no visible signs that Mary Louise's condition had improved. There had been no spontaneous respirations and no active movement. By eight hours post-op, the anesthetic agents had been metabolized for the most part, so I had to assume that her current mental status represented the beginning of a comatose state. Her vital signs were still good, though, and her right pupil reacted quickly to light, so she was in there, but in a deep sleep. Gina continued to check the vitals every half hour, as ordered by George Flanagan.

I had studied the chart and repeatedly read the operative notes of my colleagues, Mary Louise's doctors. Out of curiosity, I had gone through the list of medications prescribed for her by the numerous doctors on the case. She was on massive doses of steroids, used to decrease brain-tissue edema, or swelling. Flanagan also had ordered a continuous mannitol drip, to also aid in the reduction of swelling. In addition, she was receiving three different antibiotics; an anti-convulsant, Dilantin, which she received in Radiology after her second seizure; and a heparin-like blood thinner to prevent clots in the legs and pulmonary emboli, which she was highly susceptible to in her state of immobility. She was also receiving medications to prevent stomach ulcers from the steroids, gastrointestinal lubricants to ward off fecal impactions, and large doses of surfactant to reduce lung burn from the respirator.

I had watched all of Mary Louise's doctors parade through NIC at various intervals this morning and systematically check her abdomen, her heart, her jaw, her Foley catheter and urine output, her reflexes, her left eye, her left arm, and her left leg, and adjust the traction. Their comments had been typical, predictable, and nearly identical:

"Looking good, Jim. I've checked her out, and she's stable." And then I would get a pat on my shoulder.

This had occurred several times this morning, with Gary White, the urologist who removed the left kidney; Mike O'Reilly, the general surgeon who repaired her liver and removed her spleen; and Joe Moore, the oral surgeon who removed her teeth and repaired her jaw. These visits were in addition to rounds by residents on the various surgical services, prodding, poking, and checking.

It seemed to me each of the doctors had removed a part of Mary Louise, but no one put anything back. It was like a surreal version of *Invasion of the Body Snatchers*, only this was called modern, superlative, tertiary medical care. I'm confident these medical experts were doing their respective best, but I felt bitterness and anger rising to the surface. I didn't like being on this side of the fence, and I didn't think the doctors were doing enough.

Then Jeff Kosar had come by. He was one of the thirty partners in the University Orthopedic Group. I was sitting behind the nursing station, in the office cubicle, drinking coffee and talking on the phone to my office staff about a problem one of my patients was having, something one of my partners couldn't deal with. Jeff waved, adding to my mental list of "The Checkers of Mary Louise," then came into the glassed-in dictation room and sat with me.

"So, how goes it?"

"Okay, Jeff. No change in her condition, though."

He nodded. "Bad injury. Real bad. It's gonna take a while, but you know that, right?"

"I guess."

I stared at Jeff. He was six three and weighed about 250 pounds. He sipped his coffee, taking care not to dribble any onto his groomed, graying beard. He crossed his legs, opened his long white coat, and reached for a cigarette.

"No smoking in here, Jeff. Oxygen."

"Close the door."

"Jeff, there'll still be oxygen in the room. You'll blow us all to hell. And, if on the chance you don't, one of these nurses will come in here and beat you about the head and face with a full bedpan. Then, I'll have to call for a 'code brown.'"

He laughed and put the cigarette away. "I miss the good old days, Jim, back when nobody knew that smoking and drinking were bad for you. And if they did, nobody cared. I used to light up wherever I wanted. These days, man, you can hardly smoke outdoors. Always some dude coming up to you, coughing, complaining about ambient air and secondhand smoke."

"I miss the good old days too, Jeff, like yesterday, when my wife was normal and healthy."

"Yeah, Jim, I know, man. Life's a bitch, and then you die. Hang in there," he said, and patted my knee and moved on.

As I thought about Jeff's philosophical comment and tried to put it into perspective, the ward clerk, Antoinette, a perky woman who I had known for years from the days when she worked in Orthopedics, called my name from her armed chair at the center of the nurses' station.

"Yes?"

"There's a woman at the visitor's desk out front who needs to speak to you. Says she's a police officer. It's not visiting hours yet, but if you want her to come back, we'll make an exception."

"That's okay. I need to stretch, maybe get a bite to eat."

"Good idea, Dr. Brady. Sitting in here all day has got to be depressing. Maybe you ought to go see some patients or something, keep your mind off things, you know?"

"Maybe, Antoinette. Be back in a while. I've got my beeper on, so . . ."

"I know what to do, Doc. Have a nice lunch."

Susan Beeson hugged me as soon as I left NIC through the sliding double doors, activated by a motion detector above an exit sign.

"How is she?"

"About the same. Still on the ventilator, still no movement."

"I figured you needed to get out of there. Buy you some lunch?"

I looked at my watch. "The cafeteria should be open."

She shook her head. "Nope. You're going to have real food. I'm taking you to the Stables. It's only two miles down South Main, and if something about Mary Louise's condition changes, I can have you back here in a flash."

"Does this mean I get to ride in the police car?"

"Yep. It's unmarked, but I'll let you play with the siren if you want."

"Goodie."

The patrons probably wondered what a doctor, dressed in scrubs and a white coat, was doing drinking a Bloody Mary at lunch on a Thursday. Normally, I would be overly concerned with my image, but that day was an exception.

I filled Susan in on the rest of the details of the surgeries, at least as much as Mary Louise's doctors had told me.

"So, what's the bottom line, Jim Bob?"

"There isn't one, yet. Wait and see, best I can tell."

She ordered a hamburger and a salad, and I got a country-fried steak and french fries, smothered in cream gravy. I topped it all off with Tabasco sauce.

"Your plate looks like a war zone."

"Thanks, Susan."

"I'd feel better if you had ordered some vegetables."

"I wouldn't."

We ate in a comfortable silence for a minute, then she asked about Dr. Frank James. "How did he seem when you went over to the Brown's suite last night?"

"Upset. Confused. Worried. Appropriate behavior for the situation, I think."

"You know he's a suspect."

"You told me yesterday afternoon. Frank seemed predictably disturbed by the whole thing, if you ask me."

"How well did you and Mary Louise know Meredith James?"

"What are you getting at, Susan?"

"I want to know what kind of woman she was. I'm going to be asking this question to a lot of people. I have to track down all her close friends, and I need to speak to her parents at some point, but I thought I would give them a day or two. My God, Mr. Brown is laying up there recovering from cancer surgery, and now this. I'm sure it's horrible for both him and his wife, but nevertheless, I need to glean critical information from them. I'll probably give it until tomorrow, though, or possibly until after the funeral. Do you know when that will be?"

"No. Can't you get that information from Frank? I hate to see Mr. and Mrs. Brown interrogated in light of all that's happened."

"I'm not going to interrogate the parents, Jim. I just want to get a list of friends and close acquaintances from them, and from Dr. James, too. Who Meredith went to lunch with, who she shopped with, who she exercised with, who she played tennis with, who she might have been dating during her separation. I'm afraid the doctor might leave out someone of interest, so it's important that I speak with the Browns."

"Who might Frank omit?"

"I don't know who. But the more people that give me names of Meredith's friends, the more complete an investigation I can carry out. That's why I'm asking how close you and Mary Louise were to her."

"We've known them for over twenty years. I see Frank several times a week at the hospital. We go to dinner together on a rare occasion, and we've been to their house a time or two for a Christmas party or New Year's celebration. But we weren't their best friends. I really know very little about Meredith, other than she was the only daughter of very wealthy people and was married to a colleague of mine. I know she worked out, and played tennis, and was active in numerous charity functions, and that she and Frank were separated for the past six months. That's about it."

Susan took a bite of her burger and chewed thoughtfully for a moment. "What about affairs Meredith or her husband might have been having?"

"What about them?"

"Well, they were separated for six months. Who was screwing who?"

"I have no idea, Susan, but I will tell you this, because you'll hear it from almost everyone you talk to. Frank fooled around a lot. Nurses, secretaries, female members of the medical staff. It's common knowledge around the hospital, but I couldn't give you a single name."

Gina Genardo crossed my mind, the way she almost choked up when she mentioned that Frank was "the only personable neurosurgeon" she knew. I thought better of mentioning her name to Susan, though. I had met the woman only once, and she was Mary Louise's nurse.

"What about Meredith's male relationships, either before or after the separation?"

"Zip, Susan."

"You're a lousy informant, Jim Bob. You don't even know if she was still seeing her own husband on occasion?"

"No. And you're right, I can barely take care of my own business, much less anyone else's. For the most part, I keep my head down, take the best care of my patients I know how to do, and try to be home for cocktail hour."

After we had eaten, and over coffee, she leaned in toward me conspiratorially. "I want to tell you something in confidence. Keep this to yourself, okay?"

"Sure."

"The reason I'm telling you is that you are a good friend, and an insider at the hospital. And this may have something to do with someone who works there, or practices there. Or it may have nothing whatsoever to do with anyone in the medical field. I just want you to keep your eyes open and your ear to the ground, so to speak. Help me out if you can."

"What are you talking about?"

"I went to Meredith James's autopsy this morning. It was routine. She was a normal, healthy, white female, except for two bullet wounds, one in the forehead, and one through the heart. The coroner found a 9-mm slug embedded in the back of her skull, same as the one the forensic technicians found buried in the carpet in her closet. From the trajectories that Ballistics at our office postulate, combined with the autopsy findings, we presume that the intruder shot her in the head first, while she was standing. Probably surprised her while she was dressing in front of the mirror.

"The second shot came, we think, when her assailant leaned over, while she was dead or dying from the head shot, and plugged her through the heart. Maybe the second shot was just to make sure."

"Isn't that like a professional hit, or something?"

"Yes, that's a typical pattern, but a non-contract hit can't be ruled out."

I sipped my coffee and picked at my Key lime pie. "But you're not ruling out the possibility that maybe someone was hired to kill her."

"Not at all. In fact, that is our working hypothesis. The doctor, of course, is the most likely suspect. The husband always is, in cases like this. But there's more to the story."

I watched her tear open a sugar substitute package, pour it into her coffee, and stir.

"Are you going to tell me, or keep me in suspense?"

She sipped her coffee and peered at me over the cup with those big brown eyes of hers, the bangs of her blond hair hanging close to her eyes, like an Old English sheepdog.

"Meredith James was six weeks pregnant."

CHAPTER 17

MUSINGS

Saturday, April 7, 2001

Saturday morning arrived, and Mary Louise's medical condition was unchanged. Her pulse and heart rate were still strong, and her right pupil reflexively constricted to light, but she had yet to trigger an unassisted respiration.

When Gina Genardo arrived at seven in the morning to begin her shift, she temporarily disconnected the automatic pilot on the ventilator and placed a T-tube over Mary Louise's tracheotomy to see if she might be able to breathe spontaneously and jump-start the machine herself. Sometimes, a patient became respirator-dependent and lost the ability or the willpower to trigger the reflex breathing mechanism. It took only about thirty seconds for the machine to produce a loud, shrill alarm signal, during which time Mary Louise's pulse elevated and her oxygen saturation declined. Gina hooked her back up on "auto" immediately.

I had gone home late both Thursday and Friday nights, long enough to shower and catch a few hours of restless sleep. I didn't leave NIC either night until after the eleven to seven crew came on, and I returned before the seven-to-three crew arrived.

Other than the two late-night trips home, and lunch with Susan Beeson at the Stables on Thursday, I hadn't left the NIC. I was afraid to. When I returned to the unit about two o'clock on Thursday after lunch, I found the bed on Mary Louise's left empty. While I was eating a steak, drinking vodka with tomato juice, and gossiping with Susan about Meredith James's pregnancy, the young wife and mother had died.

I could never forgive myself if Mary Louise did not survive and I wasn't by her side when the end came.

Susan returned for evening visitors hours both Thursday and Friday. I don't think I had ever appreciated how close she and Mary Louise were, and how much Susan loved her. Apparently, my wife had been a surrogate older sister to her friend, the police detective. Susan sobbed continuously both nights she visited Mary Louise.

Susan was still laboring intensely over the investigation of the sexual assault and murder of the twelve-year-old girl whose nude and mutilated body washed ashore on Lake Houston last week.

Susan had been working on that case day and night, trying to either solve it quickly or get enough of the preliminary work done that she could feel comfortable turning it over to one of the detectives in the Juvenile Division. She told me she was hoping to devote as much time as she possibly could to the Meredith James murder, and to the Mary Louise Brady assault, but she couldn't do that until one particular detective returned from vacation. He was a juvenile specialist, and Susan wouldn't turn over her files to anyone but him. She said it had something to do with his unusual sensitivity in dealing with the parents of murdered children. She told me that Monday would be the day she began to concentrate heavily on Meredith's and Mary Louise's cases.

She also said that she had barely seen her own son in the past few days. Her husband tried to keep Gene Jr. up until Susan got home, but at five years of age, he was usually exhausted and sleeping by 8 p.m.

J. J. had been to NIC only twice. After his fainting episode in the emergency room, he was aware of his limitations. The truth be known, I believed the real issue was that he absolutely could not bear to see his mother in this condition, even though he truly believed that Mary Louise could feel his presence, if he could just endure at the bedside long enough. So, when he had made a trip to the hospital, I generally talked to him in the waiting room and gave him an update. He had not seen his mother since the night she was injured, after her ten-hour surgery, when he walked into the recovery room with me. He nearly passed out again after seeing Mary Louise's mummified head, her multiple outriggers and splints, and her skeletal-pin traction. There was no doubt in my mind that he loved his mother more than life, so I could not fault him for his inability to see her.

J. J. had begun his work with HPD and was evaluating paint and chrome scrapings taken from the left fender and driver's door of Mary Louise's Jeep, and glass samples from what the investigators thought was part of the assaulting vehicle's headlight, found shattered at the accident scene. He told me his firm was researching various automobile manufacturers to determine which years and what models had particular kinds of paint and glass. Apparently, the crime scene investigators also found skid marks from this purported "black European sedan" that injured my wife, so J. J. was collaborating with HPD's auto techs, the FARTs, looking intensively at Mercedes-Benzes, BMWs, Audis, and Volvos, trying to identify the type of vehicle driven by his mother's assailant.

Most of the NIC nurses and technical support staff and I had become so familiar that we were on a first-name basis. Yesterday I had decided I didn't feel like being a doctor any longer, and I didn't want to look like one either, so I showed up in khakis, a flowered shirt, and Justin Ropers. I hadn't felt like shaving either, so I had a three-day stubble. The constant glare of those fluorescent lights, plus the stress of seeing my wife in a coma, had given me an unrelenting headache. The prescription sunglasses I'd been wearing since Thursday evening helped.

I looked like an aging hippie from South Florida, trying to sell tickets to Margaritaville to the hospital employees.

Mary Louise's doctors, my long-term colleagues, made rounds daily and saw me sitting behind the nurses' station, poring over Mary Louise's medical chart, or talking to Antoinette or one of the other ward clerks, drinking stale coffee from a stained Styrofoam cup. They usually stared at me for a moment, whispered among themselves, then shook their heads and moved on.

I had been in NIC so much that, for lack of anything better to do, I started helping out. I answered the phone, took messages, and entered simple data into the computer. These duties were the responsibility of the ward clerk, and by helping out, it gave Antoinette or her counterpart freedom to take a cigarette break, go to the john, or get a bite to eat. The girls started bringing me food: cookies, tacos, burgers. I took to showering in the doctor's lounge, so I wouldn't have to leave.

I had to give up on taking care of Tip. Although Tonita would feed him during the day and let him out just before she went home, it wasn't enough. When I arrived home after midnight Thursday night, I found he had done his business—number 1 *and* number 2—right by the living room door that led out onto the balcony. From the paw prints and the toenail scratches on the sliding glass door, I knew the old boy had tried to let himself out. Tip was so ashamed of himself that he hid behind the piano. I had to drag him out by the collar in order to take him downstairs for a walk. Yesterday morning, I did the unspeakable. I took him to the University Animal Clinic. I hated to do that and swore I never would again after his last stay in the kennel, when he, out of sadness and loneliness, refused to eat, and lost ten pounds in a week. However, I couldn't predict how long I would be in the current routine, and it did not seem fair to Tip to leave him cooped up all by himself for hours on end. Besides, the veterinary techs at University loved Tip, and I was confident he would be all right.

One unexpected problem developed. I not only lost the desire to *be* a doctor, I didn't even want to be *around* any doctors. I think I was mad at myself, and all physicians for that matter, although that was most irrational. So far, Mary Louise was still riding the life–death fence, and I couldn't see that this enormously expensive, state-of-the-art University Hospital medical care had done her all that much good. Her doctors, especially that prick George Flanagan, kept telling me to be patient, that there's only so much that medical science could do.

I was supposed to be at work Monday, mentally fit and ready to operate and see patients. I didn't think I could do it. Maybe my personality would undergo a miraculous transformation by then, and I would get myself together. But I wondered how in the world I could help someone else, when I couldn't help my own wife? I considered dropping out of medicine for a while, at least until Mary Louise improved. Once she got home, she would need full-time help, rehabilitation therapy, and constant care. And what better person to provide that care than me, her doctor husband, the party responsible for her presence in NIC because I was just too damn busy, and too damn important, to meet her for lunch.

And so I waited, drank coffee, went outside and smoked a cigarette now and then, and hid my constantly bloodshot, tired, and teary eyes behind my dark shades.

I didn't go to Meredith James's funeral. Frank stopped by after, I guess to pay his respects to Mary Louise. I watched him approach her bed, check her monitors, glance at the hospital chart, and pat her good right arm. I saw Nurse Gina come up beside him and stand very close. They had an intense, whispered conversation of some sort at Mary Louise's bedside. Frank stormed out immediately afterward, failing to either acknowledge me or, perhaps, recognize me in my civvies. At the time, I was sitting in the glassed-in cubicle behind the nurses' station, wearing a black tee shirt, sunglasses, and a straw cowboy hat, drinking coffee. Or maybe Frank just didn't look my way.

After he left NIC, Gina asked to be relieved for a break and left the unit crying. She didn't say much the rest of the day.

I wondered how poor Melvin Brown felt yesterday, lying in splendor at Abercrombie Pavilion but unable to attend his only daughter's funeral, seeing as how he was only a few days post-op cancer resection and knee replacement. I would bet good money that he would have traded all of his riches for a chance to go back in time and say goodbye to Meredith before she was murdered. I felt guilty that I hadn't been back to see my patient since Wednesday night, but I knew he was receiving excellent care in my absence.

I had my own cross to bear.

This morning, Gina Genardo seemed her normal, perky self, and even asked if she could buy me lunch in the cafeteria. I had become closer to her than any of the other nurses, since she was the only day-shift RN who had cared for Mary Louise since her arrival in NIC last Thursday morning. I said sure, why not. I wasn't doing anything else of significance. I was shirking my doctoral responsibilities, I had quit shaving, and that day I was wearing faded denim jeans, a Hawaiian shirt, and sunglasses in the University Hospital Neurosurgical Intensive Care Unit, where I'd been doing substitute ward-clerk work and waiting for Mary Louise to wake up from her husband-induced coma. And all the while, I was slowly being driven even crazier by the incessant cacophony of bells, sirens, beeps, and whistles, and the constant procession of people in white coats who couldn't do a damn thing for my wife.

Sure, Gina, lunch sounds good.

CHAPTER 18

GINA

Saturday, April 7, 2001

"**I** guess I should have gone to Mrs. James's funeral yesterday. Some of the other shift nurses went. What do you think, Dr. Brady?" Gina asked before she took a bite of the Saturday lunch special we both chose, an odorous and unidentifiable fish.

"Call me Jim or Jim Bob. I'm not playing the role of doctor right now. How could you, with your schedule? You work a four-day week, 7 a.m. to 7 p.m., Thursday through Sunday, don't you? Yours, by the way, is about the worst work schedule I can imagine. And besides, who would have taken care of Mary Louise and your other patients in your absence?"

"I like working a four-day week, but I didn't have enough seniority when I transferred to NIC to get the good shift, which is Monday through Thursday. And yes, I could have asked someone to cover for me for a couple of hours, but, truthfully, I didn't want to leave your wife. I know how much she means to you, and I would have felt as though I was letting you both down. You've hardly left the place since she was brought in early Thursday morning. That's three days in NIC. I hope, Dr. Bra—Jim, that someday, I find a man who loves me as much as you love your wife."

"What about Rick, your husband? He loves you, doesn't he?"

"Yes, but he's not like you. If that was me up there in a coma, he'd come by and check on me from time to time. But I can assure you, he'd spend most of his time at the hospital, making rounds, performing heart catheterizations, supervising cardiac arrests, or in the office seeing patients. He loves medicine. He eats, sleeps, and breathes it, just like my father."

"Then he's probably a better man than me. I should be taking care of my patients, instead of . . . oh, forget it. I thought you told me you were accustomed to the routine of a life in the medical profession, and that's why you felt comfortable with nursing as an occupation. And that because of your background, you were ideally suited to be the wife of a doctor."

She put her fork down, wiped her eyes with her napkin, looked into her lap. I saw big tears flowing down her cheeks.

"I'm sorry, Gina. I didn't mean to—"

"Oh, it's not that. It's just that, I don't know, I guess I've come to want more out of life than I'm getting right now. I work all day, and it's very hard and intense work, as you've seen. I'm very tired, mentally and physically, when I get home. I'd like to be able to take a hot shower, relax a while, then get dressed up and go to dinner with my husband. Or maybe take in a movie, or a play, or a concert. Or just be romantic for the evening. But no. Rick doesn't get home until nine, sometimes ten o'clock at night. By then, he's starving, and he wants his dinner immediately, which tastes lousy because it's usually cold by the time he gets there. Then, he wants me to sit with him and hear all about his day. By that time of night, I've been half-asleep on the couch for two hours. All I want Rick to do is shut up, microwave his dinner, and let me go to bed.

"And then there's the issue of children. Rick and I both come from large families. Did I tell you that my younger brother is a student at St. Mary's?"

"What's that?"

"It's a Jesuit seminary here in Houston. He's studying to be a priest. Anyway, Rick and I have twelve brothers and sisters between the two of us. I want children, but he doesn't, at least right now. He says we can't afford it. Rick wants me to keep working to help support us until he's finished with these last two years of training. He's made that very clear. And he doesn't want his children's mother to work, so, when the time comes, he wants me to stay home once I have kids, and be a mother, just like his mother. Meanwhile, my biological clock is ticking. I'm almost thirty-two years old! I don't have forever!"

I didn't quite know what to say or do. I was an emotional wreck myself, but since I was sitting directly across the table from Gina, with no exit in sight, I felt a response was required. So, I simply patted her forearm and offered her my napkin. She declined it, not that I blamed her. Cream gravy, Tabasco, and ketchup residuals, essential elements to drown otherwise inedible food, did not a pretty handkerchief make.

"But you know what's really wrong, don't you, Jim?"

I have been asked this question by a number of women in my life, Mary Louise included, and I can truthfully say that I've never, ever known the answer. I'm a good listener, but a lousy mystic.

"Frank!" she yelled, and began to sob.

By then, people around us were staring, thinking whatever strangers think when they see a man at a restaurant sitting with a woman who is crying. No one I knew was nearby, but still, it was a little embarrassing. I was in "disguise," and I didn't have on a name tag, so I doubted her outburst would affect me in the eyes of others. Besides, I looked old enough to be her father, not that it mattered. That sort of situation always implied that a man sitting with a tearful woman was responsible for her sadness.

"What do you mean, 'Frank'?"

"Frank James. We've been seeing each other . . . for quite some time," she said, trying to compose herself. "We met a couple of years ago, when I first started working in NIC. It began innocently, with a cup of coffee in the cafeteria. As our relationship progressed, we would meet for a drink, and then we started having dinner together occasionally. Then . . . well, you know what comes next. You start playing Hide the Weenie with Frank."

Hide the weenie?

"And yes," she continued, "I should have known better. I had heard all the stories, the rumors, the innuendos about Dr. Frank James, the ladies' man. But what can I say? I fell for the guy, hook, line, and sinker.

"He kept telling me over and over he was going to leave his wife. So, I kept waiting, and waiting, and hanging on, and waiting some more. Then six months ago, he and Meredith decided to separate, and Frank moved into the Ritz-Carlton. I was ecstatic because I thought we would be able to see more of each other. We'd be able to quit sneaking around to cheap motels and out-of-the-way restaurants, where none of his society friends would see us. I told him that I was willing to leave Rick, and that I wanted to either move in with him or rent an apartment nearby. But instead, we started seeing less of each other. It seemed like he was always traveling somewhere, going to some damn medical meeting. Paris, Hawaii, Bermuda. And then, a couple of weeks ago, he calls me up and says he's not going to see me again. Ever! That he was going back to his wife."

Gina started to sob again, and I kindly got up, went to the next table, and retrieved some clean napkins. Two elderly blue-haired women stared at me. One told me I should be ashamed of myself.

Gina accepted my napkin, blew her nose, and once again gathered her composure.

"Is that what that little spat, or argument, or whatever it was that happened between you and Frank yesterday, was about? When he came into NIC and visited Mary Louise after Meredith's funeral?"

"Yes. I asked him to please meet me after work and talk about our relationship. Now that Meredith was gone—don't get me wrong, I'm not happy that she's dead or anything—it's just that, well, with Meredith out of his life, we could be together."

I looked into the tearful brown eyes of this devastated young woman. There were a thousand things I wanted to tell Gina, such as how attractive she was, and how smart she was, and how much she could do with her life, given her education and experience. I could have told her how much her husband Rick probably cared for her, and that she should forget about Frank, the infidel, and make long-range plans with the man she'd chosen to spend her life with. I thought of countless other kind, caring, and empathetic words to impart to her, with which to comfort her. I had an opportunity to give her the benefit of my fifty-five years of experience, over half a century of living life to its fullest during my tour of duty on Planet Earth.

Instead, what came out?

"God, Gina, I hope to hell you aren't the one that killed her!"

CHAPTER 19

UNCHANGED

Sunday, April 8, 2001

"**N**o, Susan. I can't leave."

"Jim Bob, you can't just sit up here forever and wait. You have to work tomorrow, don't you? You've got to pull yourself together. Come with me. We'll go for a drive, get some lunch, and talk. Deal?"

It was Sunday afternoon. Loyal and persistent Lt. Susan Beeson had come to visit Mary Louise, her best friend. As we stood by her bedside together, Susan and I had held hands for a few minutes and cried together. Regretfully, my wife's condition had not changed. Her heart was still beating regularly and her blood pressure was normal, for which I was grateful, but there had been no spontaneous movement or respiration. Sustained coma, George Flanagan had called it on morning rounds. Typical for this type of head injury, he said. She could still recover satisfactorily, he lectured to his small entourage of colorful scrub outfits and white coats.

It was a little after 6 a.m. when Mary Louise's neurosurgeon came by. After his NIC rounds were complete, he pulled me aside and told me I needed to get a grip. Go home, take a hot shower, shave, clean myself up. Act like a professional, he said, before he stormed out of NIC with his Sunday followers. There were only a scant three house staff with him this morning.

Flanagan had on a double-breasted jacket and looked like he was either planning to attend an early church service, or perhaps wanted his patients to know he had an Armani suit. Most of his patients in NIC were comatose, like Mary Louise, so what was the point? Maybe church would improve his attitude, although I doubted there was enough bread and wine in the world to humble the man.

And then, Susan Beeson tried to convince me to leave Mary Louise's bedside and go wandering off for a ride in her car, so that I could allegedly relax and enjoy myself. But how could I have allowed myself that luxury while the person I cared about most in the world was lying there in a 'sustained coma'?

"No, Susan. Thanks, but you see, I really need to stay here. If anything happened while I was gone, I'd never forgive myself. When I went to lunch with you on Thursday, the woman next to Mary Louise died. I couldn't deal with that, if it . . . maybe some other time, okay?"

Susan and I were discussing the situation in the glassed-in doctor's dictation cubicle when Gina Genardo came to the door.

"I couldn't help but overhear your conversation. I think you need to go, Dr. Brady. You need to get out of here for a while. We all get stir-crazy in NIC. That's why we do three or four twelve-hour shifts a week. You can't take any more than that. It's too intense, and too depressing."

"I didn't think you were speaking to me, Gina, after my outburst at lunch yesterday."

She smiled. "Oh, that? It's forgotten. It was a ridiculous question you asked me, and it was silly of me to run off the way I did. Friends?" she asked, and extended her hand.

"Sure," I said, and returned her handshake. "You've met Susan Beeson?"

"I've seen you up here every day, visiting Mrs. Brady. I'm Gina Genardo, her day-shift nurse."

Susan stood, and the two shook hands.

"Family?"

"Excuse me?"

"Are you a member of the Brady family?" Gina asked.

"Close friend," Susan responded.

Gina leaned against the door and lingered as though she wanted to chat. "What do you do, if you don't mind me asking?"

Susan looked at me, then at Gina. "Detective, HPD."

The color drained from Gina's face. She stood erect. "Are . . . are . . . you here in an . . . an official capacity?"

"Gina, you ask too many questions. However, since my friend Dr. Brady has told me on numerous occasions that you've done a fabulous job of taking care of Mary Louise, and since you two seem to have developed somewhat of a rapport, I'll answer. Mary Louise Brady is my best friend. I love her like the sister I never had. But I have a job to do, and that includes finding whoever did this to my friend, and seeing to it that justice is done, with whatever parts and pieces of that individual that might be left after I find him. Or her," Susan said, and stared Gina down with that cop expression of hers. Susan seemed to be able to turn it on and off, like hot and cold water, and it was a scary sight indeed.

Gina brought her fingertips to her still-open mouth. She turned away to get back to her duties, stopped, and came back to the doorway.

"Do you have your beeper, Dr. Brady?"

I shook my head. "It's in my long white coat, which is at home, contemplating retirement."

She reached into the white smock she was wearing over the special turquoise scrubs assigned to NIC nurses, pulled out a beeper, and handed it to me. "You can borrow this, Dr. Brady. It's mine, so I know the number by heart. I promise you, if anything changes, even the slightest variation in Mary Louise's heart rate or urine output, I'll page you immediately."

"And as one of Houston's finest detectives, Jim Bob, I have all the up-to-date electronic equipment at my fingertips. A portable satellite phone with worldwide capabilities, a police-band radio connected directly from my car to the Southwest Substation, and, mounted on the dash, a portable computer with a direct linkup to Central Division," Susan said. "So, it will be like you've never left."

As Susan stared at me and her expression changed, she began to look cute again, with her tousled blond hair, faded jeans, a Houston Rockets tee shirt, and sneakers. She was smiling, eyebrows uplifted, very much like the look John Belushi gave Carrie Fisher in the Blues Brothers movie right before she started shooting at him with the automatic rifle she'd been carrying since he stood her up at the altar.

Gina was staring at me as well. Her black hair was pulled back in an old-fashioned ponytail, held in place with a white bow. Her minimal makeup consisted only of a little pink lipstick, but she was still a natural beauty. She began to smile a little, in spite of Susan's sharp retort, but her eyes seemed a little too wide open and bright, as though she was on alert. She seemed to be encouraging me to go with Susan, but her jaw was a little offset, like she was thinking of asking me a question. She nodded slightly.

I looked at Susan, next to me, then back at Gina, still standing in the doorway. I shook my head.

"If anything happens, I'll never forgive myself, or either one of you. I hope you know that."

Susan leaned over, wrapped her lightly freckled arm around my shoulder, and helped lift me up. She took an arm and ushered me toward the exit. I stopped, shook her loose, told her to meet me in the waiting room, and walked back over to Mary Louise's bedside. Gina followed me.

"Bye, sweetie," I said, and leaned down and kissed her bandaged forehead. I pulled her right eyelid open, and in spite of the coma and the swelling in her face from the injury, her pupil constricted fairly rapidly.

"I know you're in there. I just hope you can hear me. I'm leaving for a little while with Susan. She insists that I get out of here and go for a drive. I'm supposed to work tomorrow, but I don't think I can do it. I can barely leave your side long enough to go home and shower. I even had to put Tip in the kennel, something I said I'd never do again. But maybe if I get out of here for an hour or two, I can gather my wits about me and decide how to live my life until you get better. And you will get better, you know. It's just going to take some time."

Mary Louise had no blink reflex due to her mental state, so I gently closed her eyelid before the roughly circulating air in NIC abraded her cornea. I wanted her to be able to focus on me for a minute every so often. I felt certain she could hear me, and probably see me, but her brain wouldn't allow the motorized functions of her body to respond normally. I was certain she would confirm this when she woke up.

Although I could be delusional and completely full of bat guano.

I kissed Mary Louise again on the forehead, gently squeezed her right hand, turned to leave, and bumped right into Gina.

"That woman. She's a detective. You didn't tell her about Frank and me, did you?"

"No."

"Are you going to?"

"I don't know, Gina. Surely it will come out, sooner or later. You don't have anything to hide, do you?"

"Of course not, Dr. Brady. It's just that . . . well, I gave you that information in confidence, and I don't want my personal business made public. I wouldn't want Rick to find about my relationship with Frank."

I smiled at the young, attractive nurse, the person I felt was doing more than anyone else to help keep Mary Louise alive, and put a hand on each of her shoulders.

"Gina, Frank's wife has been murdered. The police are going to dig up every scrap of information about he and Meredith they can find. Your relationship with Frank James will become public knowledge. In fact, I'm surprised is hasn't already surfaced. It doesn't matter if I tell Susan or someone else tells some other detective involved with the case. The police will find out. In fact, the more I think about it, the better it would be for you if I told Susan myself. I can even say you asked me to tell her about your affair with Frank James. I think that if you preempted the detectives' discovery through some other source, HPD would see you in a better light as far as the murder investigation is concerned."

She hung her head and shook it to and fro. Tears started to run down her cheeks.

"You don't have anything to hide, do you, Gina?"

"No, Dr. Brady. I'm just sad."

"Okay. I'm out of here. Beep me if there is any change. Okay? Gina?"

"Sure."

As I walked toward the exit that led into the waiting room, I turned and caught Gina's eyes. She gave me a look of—perhaps anger? Or sadness? Apprehension? Relief? Or maybe just a mixed emotional bag. Her feelings were not my top priority.

PART 2

CHAPTER 20

NEW LIFE

Sunday, April 8, 2001

"**W**here you taking me?"

"For a drive. Any place in particular you'd like to go, Jim Bob?"

"Doesn't matter. Anywhere is fine. You're the driver, I'm the captive audience."

"You're not a prisoner, like most of the passengers in this vehicle, my friend. I thought it would be healthy to get you out of NIC for a while. You've been there day and night since when, Thursday? This is Sunday."

I leaned my head back, slouched down in the black leatherette seat of the city-issue Ford, and wedged myself against the passenger door. My left knee rested against a floor-mounted computer monitor with a telephone receiver attached to its left side. A CB radio sat on the dash, just to the right of the gear-shift lever, above the air conditioning vents. Susan's cellular phone rested on the seat between us. At least she had kept her word about our communication capabilities.

"What's this for?" I ask, pointing at the blank screen.

"The computer? Ah, Dr. Brady my friend, it is part of the brave new world, a world of instantaneous access. If I want to check out a license plate number or a vehicle registration number, all I have to do is access Central through the modem there, give one of the operators the info, and, presto! The subject's name, address, telephone number, and social security number appear right there on the screen. I can also pull up criminal records for the past ten years—local, state, even non-restricted federal with my password. Neat, huh?"

"Yeah. Can you punch in a few numbers and find out who tried to kill Mary Louise?"

"I wish it was that easy. I'll need some data to go on, first."

We headed south on Fannin Street, away from the University Medical Center, past the aging Astrodome, previous Eighth Wonder of the World and former home of Houston's Astros and Oilers.

Susan turned west on Loop 610 and headed around the city. It was a bright early summer day, with colorful crepe myrtle trees in full bloom. There's always greenery here in Southeast Texas, one of the positive features of living in a tropical climate. As we turned north onto the Loop and crossed over the interchange with Highway 59, known locally as the Southwest Freeway, I could see for miles in all directions. The earth was flat from this vantage point, just as the ancients suggested.

It seemed strange to be outside at all after being cooped up in University Hospital's NIC the past three days. In spite of the lush verdant foliage, everything was dull and listless to me. Unimportant. Inconsequential. Except for one issue. Mary Louise's fate.

"I have an idea, Susan."

"Good. I was beginning to think you weren't speaking to me, Jim Bob."

"Just mulling things over. There's someplace I'd like to go."

"Anywhere you want."

"You sure?"

I angled myself against the door, so I could stare at Susan. She glanced at me, then turned her head back to the highway.

"A deal's a deal, Jim."

"I've been curious about the intersection of Woodway and Post Oak, where Mary Louise was injured. I want you to take me there."

"But Jim, there's nothing to see. The debris has been cleared, and Mary Louise's car has been impounded. What do you hope to find?"

"I don't know. I just need to go there. And after that, maybe you can take me by the Memorial Bend complex, let me see where Meredith James's killer may have crossed over Buffalo Bayou. Didn't you tell me that on Wednesday, when we talked outside the ER at University Hospital, while Mary Louise was in Radiology? Or was it Frank James who gave me that piece of information? Anyway, I remember someone saying that whoever killed Meredith may have parked somewhere along Memorial Drive, crossed over Buffalo Bayou, and accessed their house through the rear gate."

"That's our hypothesis, but I don't see—"

"Susan, take me there. Please. I need to see where Mary Louise's accident occurred, although I'm not sure why. And, since I didn't make it to Meredith's funeral because I was afraid to leave the hospital at the time, I'd like to at least go by their house and, in my own way, pay my respects. You know that Meredith and Frank have been friends of ours for years. It's the least I can do. I think Mary Louise would want that."

Susan heaved a long, heavy sigh. She turned on her blinker, moved to the right lane, and took the Woodway exit off Loop 610. She traveled west and arrived at the intersection of Post Oak and Woodway. From the left lane, she turned south onto Post Oak, pulled off to the right onto a narrow spit of asphalt, then drove slowly the remaining fifty feet or so into the parking lot of Paco's Restaurant. Susan placed the vehicle in park, turned off the engine, and rolled down her window. I did the same.

It was fairly pleasant, in the low 80s with low humidity, and too early in the year for the Gulf Coast's gargantuan mosquitoes to carry off their human prey. We sat for a minute in the vacant parking area. The restaurant appeared to be closed on Sundays.

Tall pines, their bases cordoned off with creosoted railroad ties, dotted the ecologically correct asphalt and shaded most of the parking area. Oleanders lined the perimeter of the property, their bright-red offshoots signaling the rebirth of yet another growing season.

I stepped out of the car, lit a cigarette, and leaned against the trunk of the black Ford. I heard Susan's door open, then close.

"So it happened there," I said, pointing through the hedgerow toward the intersection where my wife came face-to-face with her Maker.

"Yes. Mary Louise apparently pulled out of the blacktop here, went down that little lane there that intersects with Post Oak, pulled into the street, and went up to the light, in order to turn right onto Woodway and go home. At least I assume she was going home."

"I think that was her plan. But maybe we'll never know."

Susan walked up to me and patted me on the back. "Why did you want to come here?"

I took a deep drag, inhaled until the smoke was somewhere down in my ankles, and blew it out slowly. "I'm tired of being sad. Tired of crying. Tired of sitting idly by, doing nothing about the son-of-a-bitch who did this to her—to us, in effect, although Mary Louise is the one in intensive care. I want to get mad. I want you to find out who is responsible. And I want justice. But if I can't have that, I want revenge. The hit-and-run driver's head on a silver platter will do for starters."

"And you thought that perhaps coming here would stimulate your anger? And get those murderous juices flowing?"

"Maybe."

"And what do you think you can do? You're not a vigilante. You're not a cop. You're a doctor. A doctor whose patients need him. Don't you think Mary Louise would want you to get back to work, to keep your mind focused on your practice, and let us trained profes-sionals take care of finding her assailant?"

"Hard to say what she'd want, Susan, considering her condition," I responded, as I tossed my cigarette on the ground and ground it out with the rounded tip of my Roper.

"I know how you must feel, Jim Bob, but—"

"No you don't! How could you know, Susan? You've never had . . ." As the words left my mouth, I suddenly remembered the tragedy of Susan's mother's death from ovarian cancer a few years ago. Mrs. Lombardo died a miserably painful death while Susan watched helplessly, unable to do anything to help her except administer round-the-clock narcotic pain medication.

"I'm sorry. Open mouth, insert foot, that's my motto, Susan. You *have* been there, but in a different way. Cancer is different from an assault. You can be mad at God, maybe, but there's not a particular individual you can blame. And you have time to prepare for it, and to say all those things you want to say to a loved one, things that for whatever reason you've never said before. Like you did with your mother, and I was fortunate enough to do with my father.

"But in Mary Louise's case, I haven't been able to say a simple phrase like 'I love you' or 'Goodbye' and know that she hears me. And I resent that, Susan, because there is someone out there to blame. We just have to find out who that someone is."

Susan folded her arms and stared at me with woeful eyes. "What's this 'we' stuff?"

"I want to help, to do whatever I can to find Mary Louise's assailant. I can't concentrate on my work, I think you realize. Considering the state she's in, I can't even take care of Mary Louise, the person I love the most. All I can do is just sit up there in NIC, stare at her, watch the nurses and doctors run around in circles and act like they're making her better—even though I know they're not—and try to maintain some sort of civility. I can't even take care of myself. Look at me! I haven't shaved in days. The circles and bags under my eyes make me look like I've been on a binger. So how can I take care of anyone else? How can I be a kind, compassionate, technically proficient surgeon when I'm a physical and mental wreck?"

"So, what are you saying to me, my friend?"

"What I'm saying is that I've decided to call Fran, my secretary, and have her clear my schedule for the next week or two. I want to give it at least that long, to see if I can get my shit together. If you'll have me, I'd like to follow you around while you investigate these two cases. I am willing to do anything I can to help you or anyone else that's working with you. I'll do any kind of scut work you want, as long as you'll let me help. I'll be like a Private First Class, a medical student, and a fraternity pledge during Hell Week all rolled into one. I'll sharpen your pencils, take out your trash, even go to the library and do research, as long as I'm being useful."

Susan laughed. "We don't normally do library research on murder and assault cases."

"You know what I mean, Susan. I'll do anything you ask, as long as I'm doing something to help out. I need to do this for myself, and for Mary Louise. And maybe even for Meredith James. Can you understand that?"

Susan shook her head, looked at the ground, moved a pine cone around with her worn athletic shoe.

"Are you the same guy that not thirty minutes ago was afraid to leave the hospital?"

"Yes, but coming here to the accident scene has made me realize that I need to do something besides sit in NIC or I'll go nuts, nuttier than I already am. I can't work because my work consists of making other people feel better. My job is to take care of their problems and put my own aside. I've done that for more than twenty years. This is one time I just can't do it."

Susan shook her head and looked to be thinking, I'm really hoping he isn't headed for a breakdown.

"Please? I'm begging you."

She smiled. "I hate to see a grown man beg."

"I'm not grown up yet, Susan," I said, and gave her my most illustrious smile.

"I don't know what Sam Polk will say. I think I told you that Sam has been promoted to captain and is now the chief homicide detective over our division, the Southwest. I was Sam's partner for years, and he taught me most everything I know about police work. I owe him, Jim Bob, and I do not want to get crossways with him. As for my father, who is still the chief of police, and who, I might remind you, is your patient, he will blow his stack if I let you follow me around. There is a city ordinance about that sort of thing, something to do with reckless endangerment of a citizen."

I stepped toward her, put both my arms around her, and gave her a hard squeeze. She in turn put her arms around my chest and tried to squeeze back.

"God, you're thick! My hands won't reach behind your back."

"You ought to see me snow ski. I look like a barrel on two-by-fours."

She laughed and backed away. "I'm all too familiar with your skiing techniques. That's how you came to know our mutual friend, Dr. Louis Edwards. Get in the car, Jim Bob."

"I'll meet you at the corner."

Susan moved back into her vehicle and started the engine. I lit another cigarette and wandered out of the small parking area onto the narrow asphalt driveway that spilled onto South Post Oak Road. I walked the short block, and dodged a few Sunday-go-to-meeting cars, to the intersection where Mary Louise's accident occurred.

I stood on the sidewalk adjacent to a modern service station— and I use the term "service" loosely, since the gas pumps are self-serve and the attendant sits behind bulletproof glass—and contemplated matters until Susan's horn honk signaled our departure.

I opened the passenger door and got in the car. She gunned the engine, turned left onto Woodway, and headed west. She was silent. I peered at her from time to time, waiting for some expression to indicate positive feedback about the idea of my helping her, but she said nothing.

We turned right onto Sage Road and headed north. As Sage dead-ended, she veered left onto a short street, and we stopped near a security checkpoint that separated Memorial Bend from the rest of the world.

"It's been a couple of years since I was here. Christmas party, I think it was."

"My plan today was to start from the beginning, that is, before I knew you were wanting to tag along. I've been working the Lake Houston case and I haven't paid close enough attention to the details on the Meredith James murder. I'm now assigned to this homicide and can devote more time to it since I turned the twelve-year-old's murder over to Juvenile. I want to start over and conduct my own inquiry into Meredith James's death."

"You mean, like today?"

"I arranged for Sam Polk to be at the Jameses' house this afternoon to bring me up to date on the investigation so far. I think I told you Dad ordered him here the day it happened, this being a high-profile case and all. He took over the preliminary work for me since I was tied up out at Lake Houston. Now it's time for me to go to work, do my own investigation.

"I requested Dr. Frank James's presence here this afternoon as well. I want to interview him personally, at the scene of the crime, and get a feel for his reaction to questions he's probably already been asked. But since I'm in charge of this case now, I intend to conduct the investigation my way."

"What were you planning to do with me?"

"Take you to lunch, then drop you back at the hospital."

"What am I supposed to do now, Susan?"

She stopped the car, slamming the LTD in park just before she plowed through the wrought-iron security gates. She rotated her body toward the passenger seat, glared at me, and gave me that serious "cop" look.

"Keep your eyes open, your mind alert, and your damn mouth shut."

CHAPTER 21

MEMORIAL BEND

Sunday, April 8, 2001

Having stopped the black unmarked Ford LTD at the security guard gate in front of the exclusive complex known simply as Memorial Bend, we eyed a security officer peering at us from the kiosk.

Susan extended her silver-and-gold detective's shield at arm's length outside the driver's window. A giant of a man opened the sliding glass door and pulled his sagging uniform pants up toward a distended belly, trying to get his belt as level as possible. The maneuver was a failure.

"Afternoon, ma'am," said William Moorehouse, or so the black nameplate embossed with white letters read. "May I help you?

"Yes, you may. Moorehouse, is it?"

"That's right, ma'am.

"I'm Lt. Susan Beeson, HPD," she responded. "Could you direct me to the Jameses' residence? I'm here to investigate a murder, the Meredith James case from last Wednesday. I'm meeting Capt. Sam Polk here. And by the way, we're expecting Dr. Frank James to arrive shortly."

"I see. Have some ID?"

Susan stared at the overweight security guard, who resembled an athlete gone to seed, while she was still holding her detective's shield with her left hand outside the window in plain view.

She moved her arm upward and placed the badge in Moorehouse's face, a few inches from his nose. The maneuver caused him to back up a step or two, but he held his ground.

"I don't need a pissing contest today," she said to me quietly. But she kept her cool and said nothing directly to the security guard; she just waited.

Moorehouse appeared to inspect the badge, then looked back at Susan.

"You're a little young for a detective, aren't you?"

Susan sighed, withdrew her arm from outside the window, put her badge back into a jacket pocket, and turned off the ignition of the police-issue Ford sedan. She opened the car door, bumped Moorhouse's knees, and pushed him back far enough so that she could comfortably exit. She stepped out of the car, closed the door, leaned against the vehicle, crossed her arms, and peered at the security guard. I did the smart thing, which was to remain seated in the vehicle and keep my mouth shut.

"I've had a long week, Mr. Moorehouse. I have a five-year-old at home who would like to spend some quality time with his mother on this beautiful Sunday afternoon, but duty calls. I have yet another senseless murder to investigate, and you're wasting my valuable time with this personal inquisition into my background. So, to save us both some grief, let me just say this. I'm thirty-four years old, and I've earned this badge. You remember, the one I showed you the minute I drove up? You can ask anyone on the force. I'm a good cop, and an even better homicide detective.

"And, in spite of the fact that my father is Chief of Police Stan Lombardo, I can assure you that I deserve every consideration you might reserve for, say, a male detective like Capt. Polk, who is probably already at the James residence, and who more than likely told you I was on my way here when you admitted him through this checkpoint. And I would wager the captain drove through these gates without being hassled by the likes of you.

"So, sir, unless you want to spend the rest of your day in the Central Jail, reminiscing about your being charged with obstructing a police officer in the line of duty, I'd suggest you punch whatever damn button you have in there that opens those gates in front of me, and kindly give me directions to the Jameses' home. Otherwise . . ."

"No, no, no, no. Sorry. You have your duty to do, and I have mine. Can't be too careful these days. All kinds of people, especially reporters, have been coming here these past few days with amazing tales of why they should be admitted to this complex. I'm just trying to do my job, Detective. No offense intended," he said, and oh-so-politely gave her directions as she had requested.

Susan got back in the car and fired up the engine.

"What an asshole," she said. "You've been here, right? Do you remember the way, since I was too damn mad to listen to his directions?"

"Yes."

Moorehouse activated the electronic opener and the dual wrought-iron gates slowly opened, aided by small rubberized wheels. Susan leisurely pulled into the colorful entry courtyard lined with brick planters full of numerous species of blooming flora, including irises, hibiscus, tulips, roses, and azaleas. At my direction, she turned right past a fountain, then left toward the bayou-front homes. These were the largest homes, with the best views, designed for the Rich and Famous of Houston who wanted secluded, secured privacy in the middle of this city of five million.

The fact of the matter was that Susan didn't need directions to #8 Memorial Bend. There were two blue-and-whites parked in the circular drive in front of the Jameses' home, flanked in the rear by a black LTD similar to the one we were in. Susan parked her Ford on the street, adjacent to the curb. We disembarked the vehicle and headed toward the front door via the open end of the driveway. The other end of the bricked drive was cordoned off with bright yellow tape, as was the small lawn between the drive and the curb. The tape read POLICE BUSINESS—DO NOT CROSS.

Susan flashed her detective's shield at the two uniformed officers stationed at the front door of the luxury home.

"Afternoon, Lieutenant," I heard from the two officers simultaneously. Both were smoking and were drinking what looked like extraordinarily dark coffee from stained Styrofoam cups. The cups were probably police-issue and not dissimilar to the ones stationed strategically throughout University Hospital. It looked to me like docs and cops drank the same cooked sludge.

"Gentlemen," she said, and nodded to the two men. "This is Dr. Jim Brady, a friend of mine."

One of the uniformed officers, a gray-haired patrolman appearing to be in his sixties, whose name tag read Lee Perkins, shook my hand, then opened the oak-and-glass front door for Susan, and she stepped into the foyer. The other officer was silent. I followed behind Susan. Officer Perkins accompanied us into the house and shut the door gently. He represented a stark contrast to the security guard Moorehouse who hassled Susan on our entry into Memorial Bend.

"Susan! About time. What kept you?" yelled a man I recognized as Capt.. Sam Polk, ambling over to greet us in the foyer. He took long strides from his vantage point half in and half out of a patio door that led from the two-story living room, what Meredith used to call the great room, to an outdoor redwood-and-flagstone deck.

I noticed two more uniformed police officers were outside talking to Dr. Frank James, who was sitting in a rust-colored Adirondack patio chair. He must have arrived early. It occurred to me Security Guard Moorehouse omitted that information when he spoke to Susan at the gate. Frank will be surprised that I'm here, maybe pleasantly, maybe not.

"Doctor," said Sam Polk as he shook my hand. "Sorry to hear about your wife. How are things looking?"

"Hello, Sam. About as well as could be expected, considering the situation she's in. Thanks for asking."

Sam stood about six foot four. He was lean, with prematurely gray curly hair and a handlebar salt-and-pepper mustache. He looked to be mid-to-late forties and seemed to me a handsome man, in a rugged, cowboy fashion. Susan didn't exactly cower in front of Sam, but she seemed to have adopted a different attitude. Susan had implied to me on many occasions that she looked up to Sam because he was invaluable in teaching her to be a first-rate detective, and had provided her with the opportunities she needed to gain her own respectability as an officer of the law. Something she deserved, I would think, as an exceptionally bright young detective.

He smiled and looked at Susan. "What's he doing here?" pointing a thumb in my direction.

She forced a smile, nodded, looked at her watch. She became a bit testy, either because of the Moorehouse confrontation, or because of Sam Polk's pointed question. "Sam, I don't know what to say. I took Jim Bob out for a drive, we got to talking, one thing led to another."

"And?"

"Well, I'm going to let him help me out for the next week or so, do some legwork I can't do."

"Like what?"

"I don't know yet, but I just wanted you to know that I'd like to grant him access to some of our files, and that he'll be privy to some information that—"

"Susan, you know the rules. I can't let a civilian get involved in police business. We'd have every true-crime fan in town clamoring at the substations, volunteering for duty. We've got enough trouble with the civilian telephone operators."

"Sam," Susan said insistently, "I don't have all day. Unlike you, I have another life. Surely we're not going to waste my valuable weekend time talking about how I solve my cases, are we?"

Sam shook his head and began to smile. I followed his gaze downward, where his eyes stopped and concentrated on Susan's shoes. They were tan, generic, lace-up, worn athletic shoes, which happened to have a wide, orthopedic-like toe box.

"Sam, quit looking at my damn shoes and show me the crime scene. I like to be comfortable, okay? And in spite of what you say, those cowboy boots of yours have to be killing your feet. You probably have corns and calluses on every toe."

Sam Polk had on what I would call his "uniform." When I've encountered him in the past, he's always had on the same type of outfit. He wore a white Western shirt with pearl buttons, pressed blue jeans, a tan Western-cut suede jacket, and saddle-brown ostrich boots. I had to admit, the man had great taste in footwear.

He shook his head. "I hope you weren't wearing those damn shoes during your courtship. Your husband would have to be a geek to go out with you if—"

"Sam! Cut the crap and show me the scene of the crime! All right?" Susan said, balled her right fist up, and struck him on his left shoulder.

"Fine," he said, laughing and feigning injury, and began walking up the front stairway toward the second floor. He rubbed his arm as he walked and made pitiful wounded-man sounds.

Susan shook her head and winked at me.

We followed Sam up the stairs that lead from the entry foyer to the second floor of the home. I'd seen it all before, but I couldn't help but notice Susan gazing into the enormous two-story great room as we climbed. The furnishings were contemporary and obviously expensive and included cream-colored Kreiss sofas and chairs, glass and marble coffee and end tables, and opulent multicolored glass sculptures scattered about the spacious room. She marveled at the pinpoint lighting directed at the works of colored glass art, each nestled on an individual pedestal. She stared at the plush leather chairs and the illuminated abstract art on the walls.

Beyond the main entertaining area, and from the landing halfway up the stairs, we could see onto the rear courtyard through the two-story wall of glass. We saw the sparkling blue swimming pool, many colorful potted plants, and blooming honeysuckle vines covering the cedar fence that lined the rear of the back yard. Over the eight-foot fence, we got a glimpse of the forest that lined both sides of Buffalo Bayou.

"That is the deceased's husband out on the deck?" Susan asked.

"Yep."

"I thought he was coming over later, Sam."

"He came early."

"Did you check outside?"

"If you're asking about the day of the murder, no. Nobody was in the backyard last Wednesday, Susan. It's too small to hide a child, much less an armed and dangerous assailant. Unless it was an action-figure felon," he said, laughing.

We continued to follow Sam up the second flight of stairs toward the upstairs bedrooms and the spot where Meredith James died.

Susan stopped, stepped back down to the landing, and peered at the dense foliage lining the rear of the Memorial Bend complex. She rose up on her tiptoes and turned her head from side to side.

"I mean out there, on either side of the bayou. On the day of the murder, did you send some men to check the grounds outside the fence?"

"Sure. I sent some of the crew to look around. Lee was first on the scene from the 911 dispatch. We haven't explored the area today, though."

"Lee Perkins responded to the call on Wednesday?"

Sam nodded.

"Huh. Well, it was just a thought. Never know what you might find. But, after all, I guess you're capable of covering the bases, even though you're the head of the Homicide Division and an administrator now," she said, smiling.

Standing tall above her, like a Mutt and Jeff, Sam stared down at her, curled his lower lip, sighed heavily. He squeezed around us, walked down a few steps, and leaned his head over the stairs into the living room.

"Lee Perkins? You still there?"

"Yes, sir, Captain. What can I do for you, sir?"

"Take one of the officers—leave one with the doctor, and another in front to ward off the media and curiosity seekers—and check out the grounds behind the fence. I want you to walk down to the bayou and look around. Lt. Beeson is curious, although I can't explain to you why. Don't disturb anything, though. If you find something, leave someone there, and come get me."

He looked up at Susan, now higher on the stairwell than him.

"Us," Sam rephrased.

"Yes, sir. Right away."

We watched as Officer Perkins went out the back door and gathered one of the uniformed officers standing outside with Frank James. I saw the two men remove an unfastened chain and lock from a sliding bolt that presumably secured the gate to the adjacent fence post, open the cedar gate, and walk into the lush forests surrounding Buffalo Bayou.

"That's interesting," Susan said.

She quietly crept around me and was standing on the midway landing next to Sam, watching Lee Perkins and his colleague proceed with Sam's instructions.

"What?"

"Wonder why the gate wasn't locked?"

"Mrs. James was killed on garbage day. The residents are instructed to leave their back gate open every Wednesday, or so the husband and the security people have told me. Memorial Bend employs a private refuse collection company. Guess we forgot to lock up after the forensics and coroner's crews left."

"So you think the perp came in the back way, Sam?"

"Looks that way. The sliding glass door that leads from the big room there onto the deck was ajar. There were scratches on the aluminum, and the slide bolt was bent. Looked to me like it had been jimmied. Why?"

"Well, either the intruder was well-prepared and was carrying a bolt cutter, and just happened to try the back way into this place on the day the garbage fortuitously gets picked up, or . . ."

"Or what, Susan?"

"Or maybe the killer knew that Wednesday was the right day to pick for a rear entry and a murder. Have you talked to the husband yet?"

"I talked to him for a while on Wednesday. Not much has happened since then. The chief said to back off for a few days, let the family get the Friday morning funeral over with. You know, Mrs. James's father, Melvin Brown, is a major player and philanthropist in this town, and I guess the chief wanted to show him a little respect. The chief had me pay the Browns a social call yesterday, to give them a report on what we've discovered so far. But you, my dear, have been assigned this case, so not much has happened with it. I was waiting until I could bring you up to date. That's why we're here, isn't it?"

Susan nodded.

"The reason the chief sent me over here the day of the murder was because you were tied up out at Lake Houston. He wanted a high-level representative here right away, probably for political reasons, so I came. As far as investigating the specifics of the crime, I've done only a cursory, preliminary look-see at the facts. This is your baby."

"Good. You know how I relish talking to the husbands of murdered wives."

Exit Susan Beeson, wife, mother, best friend of my beloved Mary Louise, and current caretaker of yours truly.

Enter Lt. Susan Beeson, MD—Master Detective, or, on occasion, Mad Dog.

CHAPTER 22

CRIME SCENE

Sunday, April 8, 2001

We walked up the stairs and into the master bedroom. The centerpiece of the room was an extra-wide king-sized bed, called a California king. It was a beautiful piece of furniture, with a natural wood headboard, four matching bedposts and a burgundy cotton canopy. I noticed the white carpets were dirty, probably because of all the traffic that had been in and out of the house investigating Meredith's death. A series of three large wood-paned windows provided a second-story view of the sprawling forested land surrounding Buffalo Bayou.

We walked into a massive black-and-white bath housing a large dressing table with Hollywood lights, then passed into an enormous walk-in closet. Some primal reflex caused me to stop in front of a rust-colored stain covering the white carpet in front of a full-length mirror, which I noticed held dried goo smattered about in random fashion. The unidentifiable substance appeared to have been partially wiped away, and I saw a light coating of dust on the mirror.

"It happened here," Sam said. "We presume she was standing in front of the mirror, putting on the finishing touches, getting ready to meet Dr. James for a late lunch. He told me the meeting was supposed to be an attempt at a reconciliation. Anyway, I think the intruder surprised Mrs. James, catching her totally off guard. She received a shot to the head first, then a shot to the heart for good measure. This is where Lee Perkins and the EMTs found her. Dr. James had called 911 immediately after he saw somebody run down the stairs, then exit through the back door while he was waiting on the front porch for his wife to answer the doorbell. That glass panel in the front door is leaded and is intended to be opaque, for privacy. The doctor said he couldn't see much, just a figure. We've confirmed it, at least the part about not being able to make heads or tails of someone in the foyer if you're standing on the doorstep.

"Once we had a general idea of the pattern of the shooting—it appeared there was a single shot to the forehead, followed by a single shot to the chest—the homicide technicians went ahead with their routine procedures. They dusted for prints, took photographs, and collected hair, clothing, and carpet samples. Susan, I personally watched the techs carefully bag the victim's hands to try and preserve any potential specimens from underneath those long painted nails of hers.

"The medical examiner and his technician showed up shortly after our people finished up. They completed their initial evaluation and then made arrangements for the body to be transported to the county morgue. Thursday, one of the pathologists assigned to the medical examiner's office went over the body, inside and out, with a fine-toothed comb. You were there, weren't you, Susan?"

She nodded. "Very briefly, though, so I only know a few details. Robbery wasn't a motive, in your opinion?"

"Not as far as I've been able to determine. We had Dr. James go through his possessions here and downstairs as well. He said nothing was stolen, as far as he could tell, although he couldn't be completely sure about the jewelry. He said his wife had so much, it was hard to keep track of. Seems that Meredith James had received quite a bit of jewelry over the years as gifts from her parents, plus she had her own money from blind trusts and could very well buy whatever she wanted. The doctor said he had purchased a number of pieces for her over the course of their marriage as well, and he identified as many of those as he could recall when he opened the safe for us. It was untouched as far as he could tell. However, he made it clear he couldn't vouch for jewelry she'd purchased or received in the last six months."

"And the final report from the ME's office confirmed there was no rape or signs of an assault of any kind?"

"That's right. Well, there was one thing. Did he tell you about the mark on her neck?"

Susan shook her head.

"The medical examiner noticed a line across the back of the victim's neck. It was a red mark, in a tiny depression of some sort. It extended around to the sides of her neck, then disappeared. He said it wasn't much and thought that if it hadn't been for the pooling of blood, due to the immediate circulation interruption associated with more-or-less instantaneous death, he wouldn't have noticed it."

"What did he think it was?"

"Some kind of chain, or maybe a necklace, that might have been yanked off at the time of the murder."

"I thought you said there was no sign of robbery."

"There isn't, Susan. We can't be sure that's what that mark represents. It was an educated guess on the ME's part. Besides, if it was some kind of necklace, and if it was something that she'd purchased on her own or had received as a gift in the past six months, unbeknownst to her husband, he wouldn't be able to describe it anyway. If she was wearing a piece of jewelry, maybe it looked inviting, so the murderer ripped it off on the way out."

"Anything else to show me, Sam?"

"That's about it for now. You'll have to check with Forensics, see if they can help you with the evidence evaluation. I suspect it will be clean, though. I'll bet the shooter wore gloves and, with the element of surprise, avoided any contact with the victim. I think the killer broke in the back door, sneaked up the stairs, surprised Mrs. James, plugged her, and, except for seeing Dr. James through the leaded front door glass, escaped virtually unscathed. C'mon, let's walk outside. I'll show you where we think the killer entered. Then you can have your way with the good doctor."

Sam and Susan turned to leave the dressing room, but I found myself still staring at the rust-colored stain of dried blood on the white carpet in front of Meredith's dressing mirror.

"Jim Bob? You all right?"

"What? Oh, sorry, Susan. I was just thinking about . . ."

"Mary Louise?"

"Believe it or not, no. I was considering something Sam mentioned, about Meredith being shot in the head, and then in the heart. The bullets were fired in that order?"

"Yes, why?" Sam asked.

"Right through the heart?"

"Yes."

"Then whoever did the shooting must know something about anatomy, to get a bullet right through the heart."

"Well, that's a good point, Doc," Sam stated. Except for his condolences regarding Mary Louise, it was the first time he had addressed me directly since my arrival. If asked—not that I had any intention of doing so—I'm sure he wouldn't have hesitated to render his opinion on my presence at this crime scene.

"If you'll pull up the report from Ballistics on this case, Susan," Sam continued, again addressing his former partner, "you'll find that there was essentially zero trajectory of either bullet. The head shot was fired at a slightly downward angle from only a few inches away. The chest shot, on the other hand, looks to have been fired at point blank range, with the muzzle right up against the skin. Pros in the lab say it's a 9-mm, probably a Beretta. We won't know the manufacturer positively until the microscopic evaluation is complete. Hell, it ought to be ready by now; I just haven't had the time to check it out. That's an item you'll have to check on, Suze."

"At the autopsy, the ME said that Forensics had picked up two slugs: one in a piece of the rear of the victim's skull, which had been blasted out, the other embedded in the carpet below the body. The second bullet appears to have pierced Meredith's heart on the way through her chest. The bullet wasn't visibly deformed, which means the guy's a real lucky shot," Susan responded.

"How so?" I asked.

"Well, Doc," Sam interjected, "usually a slug like that gets deflected by a rib, or the spinal column. So, it either gets stuck somewhere inside the body cavity or gets hammered by a bony structure on the way out, such that the slug is deformed. This one appeared to be clean, so it most likely went directly through her body, untouched by any bony structure. The medical examiner's final report reads like the bullet went between the ribs, directly through the heart, then out the back between the ribs. The report he faxed me also stated that from the degree of internal damage, either shot could have killed her.

"The final report states that the first slug went through the victim's frontal lobe and totally blew out the back of her skull. That's why either shot could be the 'kill' shot. Talk to the ME if you want more details, Susan. I've done enough of your work for you."

"Now you listen to me, Sam Polk. I've been working twelve hours a day on the Lake Houston murder. Between that and Mary Louise Brady's accident, I can only do so much!"

Sam feigned a wound to his heart. "Just playing with you, Detective Beeson. You getting serious on me?"

Susan just shook her head.

"By the way, there's one more item in the ME's report that I found interesting. You might want to know about it before you go out there and talk to the grieving widower."

"If you're talking about the fact that Meredith James was six weeks pregnant, I already know about it. The ME was so excited when he showed me that tiny fetus. Personally, I think he's a sick man. At any rate, that discovery changed the complexion of the crime to some degree.

"We have two victims. That makes this a double homicide."

CHAPTER 23

DETAILS

Sunday, April 8, 2001

"**S**o, Dr. James, can you give me an accounting of the circumstances that led up to you discovering your wife's body?" asked Detective Susan Beeson.

Dr. Frank James moved from the redwood Adirondack chair to a white, weather-impervious lounge chair, one of four at a glass-top patio table with a bright blue-and-white umbrella rising from an aluminum pole in its center. Sam Polk, Susan, and I sat as comfortably as possible in the other three vinyl chairs, which sat on a slate-gray flagstone deck lined in redwood, adjacent to a sparkling, immaculate pool. For whatever reason, the uniformed officer that remained with Frank while we were in the house was still standing nearby. Maybe it was protocol. Officer Lee Perkins and his cohort had not returned from their exploration of the woods behind the home.

Frank was uncharacteristically tearful, perhaps because the reality of Meredith's death had set in and this meeting was a reminder, or because he was afraid. He was, at first, shocked, dismayed even, to see me there. I explained as best I could the long-standing relationship between Susan Beeson, Mary Louise, and me. I related to Frank that Susan had forced me out of the hospital in order to provide me with a change of scenery for a few hours, and that since she would be asking him some difficult questions, she thought it might be easier for him if an old friend such as I was present. A white lie, perhaps, but at least it seemed to provide Frank comfort.

Even seated, Frank held his six-foot frame erect. He was trim, and his tailored suit revealed an athletic build. He was tanned, as usual, with an enviable full head of coal-black hair. He had to be one of those guys who got up in the morning, showered, towel-dried his hair, ran a brush through it, and looked perfect all day. His dark-brown eyes and black eyebrows gave him a Mediterranean look. He was quite a handsome figure, and I suspected even Susan felt a slight guttural rush, the way she kept clearing her throat. Frank hadn't looked so wonderful at the hospital when I saw him in the Browns' room on Wednesday. Tragedy had a way of doing that. My idea that Frank had women fawning over him constantly seemed totally plausible. Of course, he could have undergone a personality transformation, as he told me last Wednesday, and now made it his policy to reject those wayward temptations. But with Meredith dead, what would be the point?

"Doctor, I don't want you to consider me rude in this time of your incredibly disastrous trouble, but we need you to answer some questions for us," Susan said politely.

"There will be plenty of time for you to grieve, Dr. James, but, unfortunately, my time is limited today. I need you to stop crying and provide me with a brief statement so that I may begin processing my preliminary paperwork. I know you've answered these same questions before and have told this story to a number of officers, including Capt. Polk here. However, I'm playing catch-up on this case, and the more you are able to help me, the sooner I can find your wife's murderer."

Susan glanced at her watch, and I felt a little embarrassed at how calloused she had become over the last few years. She probably regretted the abrupt manner with which she was treating Frank. I could understand, though, since I hadn't been that courteous myself the last few days. Susan just didn't have the time or the patience for Frank's sniveling.

Frank James stood, removed his suit jacket, and threw it haphazardly over an adjacent redwood chair. He blew his nose into a white monogrammed handkerchief and tried to compose himself. He turned his back to the two detectives and me, looked over the eight-foot fence into the woods behind his home, then sat back down at the table.

Susan and Sam glanced at one another and waited as patiently as possible until the husband of the deceased began to speak.

"Meredith and I had a luncheon date for two o'clock last Wednesday. I arrived a few minutes early, sat in my car, and thought about things. We had been separated for six months. I'm once again telling you people that up front, so you won't have any reason to suspect me of withholding information. Okay?"

Susan and Sam eyed each other and appeared to me to be holding the same thought. I've heard Susan say it on numerous occasions. Most homicides are crimes of passion, committed by someone well-known or *related* to the victim. Both detectives nodded at Frank's comment.

"We had been trying to work things out over the telephone. You know how it is. We led separate lives for a long time, me with my medical business—I have a busy neurosurgical practice at University Hospital, as you probably know—and Meredith had her tennis, aerobics, and charity events, and her parents. She spent quite a bit of time with her mother and father. She is—was—an only child, you see. The Browns required a lot of attention, if you know what I mean."

If he was looking for a response from Detectives Beeson and Polk with that comment, none was forthcoming.

"Anyway, we sort of drifted apart. I wouldn't think that scenario all that unusual. Happens to our friends all the time."

Frank again waited for a response from the two detectives, but none was forthcoming. He looked at me and I smiled, thinking my silent thoughts. He proceeded.

"But we missed each other and desperately wanted to reconcile. So, we had been talking on the phone for a few weeks and decided to get together for lunch, see if we couldn't work things out.

"Sorry," he said, as he blew his nose loudly after another crying jag. "And then, after lunch, Meredith and I were supposed to go over to University Hospital between, oh, 4 p.m. and 5 p.m. Her father was having surgery that day by my friend Jim Brady here. We were supposed to meet Sarah, Meredith's mother, in the waiting room outside surgery, or in the suite I had arranged for them on Abercrombie Pavilion. Sarah had wanted her daughter to remain with the family all day, but Meredith had made a decision to try and work things out with me over lunch instead. That didn't make her parents very happy, but she did what was most important to her, I guess. Now I wish we had put the reunion off. If we had gone to the hospital in the morning like the Browns wanted, Meredith would still be alive, wouldn't she?"

Frank broke down again.

Susan eyed first Sam, then me. Her facial expression was blank, non-committal, like a blackjack dealer's.

My eyes wandered, first toward the numerous budding impatiens, irises, begonias, and Mexican heather in large clay pots that covered most of the flagstone deck, then back toward the house, to the dramatic two-story windows that flanked the great room. It seemed to me such a shame, in the midst of all the trappings of money, wealth, and success, that there existed this terrible tragedy. One would think that with Frank's successful career and Meredith's wealthy parents and her trust funds, the two of them should have been blissfully happy. In fact, the happy couple should be on a Seabourn cruise in the Greek isles. Meredith should not be dead, and Frank should not be answering questions as though he were a murder suspect.

Frank continued with his rendition of the events from last Wednesday. "I arrived a few minutes early, maybe five minutes until two. I sat in front of the house for a short time and tried to gather my thoughts. Meredith and I hadn't spoken during the past six months, except for the phone conversations in the last couple of weeks. And I didn't want to rush her. I tried to be exactly on time. She is—was—one for promptness. I wanted to make our meeting resemble a date. I even brought her flowers, yellow roses, her favorite." Frank's head sagged again, but he didn't cry.

"I rang the doorbell, as a proper suitor would. I didn't want to use my key because I didn't want to be presumptuous. And, as I was standing there, I believed I saw Meredith walking down the stairs to greet me. That glass is doubly thick because it's reinforced—burglar proof, you know—so all I could see was the outline of a person. So I waved. The figure waved back, or pointed at me, I couldn't really tell. Then, whoever it was turned away from the front door and went into the living room. It looked like he—"

"Are you saying it was a man?" Sam Polk inquired.

"It looked like a man, but I really can't say for sure. As I said, it's hard to see through the stained glass. Anyway, this person went over to the sliding glass door that leads to the deck, opened it, and walked outside. And then, the strangest thing happened. Whoever it was started to run along the deck and left through the back gate."

"Why does that seem strange, Doctor?" Susan asked.

"Well, at first I thought it was Meredith, and I couldn't understand why in the world she'd be going out into the back yard, much less leaving, when I'm standing there at the front door."

Frank blew his nose again and took a sip of the beer he was drinking.

"It never occurred to me that someone else would be in the house. I thought at first that maybe she'd had a friend over, and that he or she was a little late leaving. But then, you'd think whoever it was would exit through the front door. I never dreamed it could be an intruder, much less a murderer." He put his face into his hands again and wept.

"Doctor, how long did you wait on the doorstep before you tried to use your key to go inside?"

"I don't know, ma'am. Maybe five minutes. Maybe ten."

"Doctor, I don't understand why you waited so long," Susan asked. "I mean, if you thought that someone might have been in your house and might have hurt your wife, it seems to me that you wouldn't have been able to get in there fast enough."

"Well . . ."

"Well, what, Doctor?" Susan interjected.

"Well, you see, Meredith and I both had our share of sordid little affairs during the separation. That was a subject we had broached during our phone conversations the past few weeks. The thought crossed my mind that maybe she had been entertaining someone, and that person was leaving just as I arrived. I didn't quite know what to do. During our separation period, we had agreed that our private lives were off-limits to each other, which is why I rang the doorbell a few more times after I saw the unidentified person leave. When Meredith didn't answer, I tried to use my key. When the door refused to open, I realized she'd had the locks changed. So, I waited a few minutes longer, rang the doorbell a few more times, but still there was no answer. I went back to the Beamer, called the security guard, told him who I was, and that I was supposed to meet my wife at two, and asked if had he had seen her enter the complex. He said that she had, about twelve thirty or so. That's when I panicked and told him to call 911, that I thought something might have happened to Meredith. The police and the paramedics responded quickly, maybe within ten or fifteen minutes. They were talking about breaking the door down, but I suggested trying the rear entrance. We entered the house, went upstairs, and that's when we found her, in the closet . . ." Frank began crying uncontrollably and couldn't finish his sentence.

A shrill, steady beeping began. Susan, Sam, Frank, and I simultaneously reached for our respective beepers out of habit. I realized I had Gina Genardo's beeper but appreciated that it was the same model University Hospital issued to me. I depressed the green button and checked the LED. There were four black miniature stick figures, none of which were blinking, meaning each represented an inactive retained message. The sound of the beeper directed my mind back to the hospital, to NIC, and to my wife, whom I'd managed to embarrassingly forget about for the last few hours. As I clipped Gina's pager to my belt, a wave of guilt passed over me to the point of panic, creating a mild nausea.

"Shit!" Frank exclaimed. "It's a STAT call from Abercrombie Pavilion at University Hospital. God, I can't deal with this right now. Sorry, officers, but if you'll give me a minute, I need to call there. I'm sure it's Melvin or Sarah Brown trying to get hold of me. Too bad I can't get one of my partners to respond to this one!"

As Frank walked into the house, I realized how it must have happened last Wednesday that George Flanagan became Mary Louise's doctor. Frank probably couldn't deal with the STAT emergency room call he had received, since his wife has just been found murdered. So, he simply had his office staff direct one of his available partners to respond to the page.

"We have quite of bit of work to do on this one, Sam," Susan said. "We'll have to run the gamut of Mrs. James's friends, relatives, and acquaintances and interview everyone in detail. Plus, we'll have to get the names of boyfriends or other male companions she might have been with during the past six months, or prior to her separation from Dr. James, for that matter. We have to look closely at anyone that might have held a strong enough grudge to kill her. It'll get messy. At some point, we have to question the Browns, no matter how difficult that may be for them."

"Homicides like this always get messy, Susan. Question is, what do you think, old girl? Got a feel for this one yet?"

Susan shook her head. "I don't know, Sam. My suspicious nature tells me to be wary of any man as good-looking as Dr. Frank James."

Sam smiled. "It's my impression that you think I'm handsome. Does that mean I'm a suspect, too?"

"Oh, you're handsome all right, but in a rugged, Texan sort of way. Same as you, Jim Bob. But Dr. James is different. He's more movie-star handsome. A George Hamilton or Rudolph Valentino type. You know? Slick."

Sam nodded. "Oh, I know slick, all right. Slick like owl shit."

CHAPTER 24

PREGNANT

Sunday, April 8, 2001

I was continuing to feel guilty about leaving Mary Louise's side. It hadn't been that long, maybe two or three hours, but still, if anything happened . . .

I had experienced some sort of transformation since I viewed the intersection of Post Oak and Woodway, site of Mary Louise's accident. It seemed her voice had entered my head and was confirming that I should get off my lazy ass, quit feeling sorry for myself, and help out. I can almost hear her telling me that if I can assist Susan Beeson in the search for Meredith James's killer, the renewed activity would prevent me from going crazy while sitting at the hospital waiting for her to wake up. And that maybe, just maybe, that quest would somehow allow me to discover Mary Louise's assailant. How that scenario might occur, I hadn't a clue.

I excused myself from Sam and Susan's conversation about various and sundry aspects of the investigation of Meredith's murder and other ongoing cases on the homicide plate, entered the house, called the University Hospital NIC, and checked in with Gina Genardo.

What a surprise. There was no change in Mary Louise's medical condition. Gina told me she was going off shift a little early because her parents were in town, and that she would be back on duty Thursday morning and would see me then. I reminded her that I had her beeper, but she said that it wasn't a problem because she was off duty, and that I could return the pager when I next saw her. She asked if I had talked to Detective Beeson about her relationship with Frank James. I answered in the negative and told her not to worry about it, and to relax and have a great three days off. And once again, I thanked her for taking such good care of my wife.

I had picked up the first telephone I saw when I had walked into the house to call Gina. The phone resembled an ancient gramophone and rested on a laminated oak counter that fronted the walk-in bar in a corner of the great room. While I had been on hold, I had opened the built-in refrigerator, helped myself to an American beer, and took a few long swallows. I realized after my conversation with Gina, and about halfway through the beer, once the dizziness had set in, that I was starving. Susan had failed to buy me lunch, a punishment, I assumed, for my asking to accompany her here. I wandered around the first floor and looked for Frank in order to ask him if he would mind if I got something to eat, but he was nowhere to be found. The kitchen, dining room, great room, study, and powder room were empty. I figured he must have gone upstairs to speak to his in-laws on his cellular phone in private, so I wandered back outside.

"Where's Sam and the other policeman, the one that stayed out here with Frank?" I asked Susan, who was sitting alone at the patio table, watching the pool sweep make its rounds, picking up the occasional dreaded dead leaf.

"Oh, Lee Perkins came back and got him. He wanted Sam and the other uniform to see something."

"What?"

"I don't know, Jim Bob. I'd like to see for myself, but I'm waiting for the doctor to come back outside. I have a few more questions. What's keeping him?"

"I don't know. I didn't see him, so I assume he went upstairs to use the phone. Is Frank allowed to move back into his house if he wants?"

"No. No one is allowed residence during a homicide investigation. The place has been cordoned off since last Wednesday. He could stay at the Browns' house, couldn't he? I'm sure they have plenty of room. I understand they live in River Oaks, on Lazy Lane. Each of those homes has several acres of land and backs up to either Buffalo Bayou or the River Oaks Country Club. Most of them probably have guest houses as well."

"I doubt he would stay there. Knowing Frank, he'll be staying in his apartment at the Ritz-Carlton. That's where he's been living since he and Meredith separated."

"That's got to be expensive."

"Yeah, but they've got room service."

"I know you're getting antsy about getting back to the hospital. We won't be long. Can you believe the way that security guard Moorehouse hassled me when we came through the gate? I was telling Sam while you were inside that the guard must be retired military, considering the major chip on his shoulder about female police officers. Sam said I was correct, that he was a career man, in the MPs. Twenty years. Retired a master sergeant with a decent pension. Now he's a rent-a-cop. You know the type."

"Can't say that I do, Susan. I never served in the armed forces. I received deferments all through college, medical school, and internship. When I was finally reclassified 1-A and had enough surgical training to be useful, the Vietnam War abruptly ended. I must say, though, I spent almost a year during my residency on the spinal cord unit at the Veteran's Administration Hospital taking care of the interminable orthopedic problems of quadriplegics and paraplegics. I felt like I participated in the war effort because of my experience at the VA."

"When was this?"

"Oh, this was back in the mid-1970s, when the VA Hospital was full of Nam vets. You talk about a bunch of depressed human beings. We maintained a census of sixty paralyzed patients, constantly being visited by their friends who had been in and out of Southeast Asia. It must have been a nightmare over there. What was that movie? With Tom Cruise? *Born on the Fourth of July?* You mix that with scenes from *The Deer Hunter* and *Apocalypse Now*, and you have what seems to be a very accurate portrayal of how life was back then for the American soldier. I can remember the sweet smell of marijuana. It permeated the ward night and day."

"You mean they smoked grass? At the hospital?"

"Of course, Susan. The vets used a lot of drugs. Some of the ones whose arms still functioned would mainline daily. A patient would get a pass to go outside in his wheelchair and smoke with a visiting buddy but would come back to the ward higher than a kite, his head slumped against his chest, and drooling. The patients would confide in me, telling me that heroin, morphine, and opium were so cheap over in Southeast Asia that even the elementary-school kids could buy it. Life was so frustrating and so stressful back then that many of the servicemembers got hooked, and a lot of them stayed hooked. In fact, we had so many addicts on the unit that the government finally started dispensing methadone, just to prevent withdrawal symptoms during the post-op recovery from whatever procedure we might have been doing at the time. I performed countless spinal instrumentations and fusions for neck and back fractures, replaced destroyed hip and knee joints, and removed legs from infection due to ulcers that came from lack of sensation. It was a memorable year.

"So, that uniformed officer, Lee Perkins? Nice guy, huh?"

"Lee? Salt of the earth. Too nice for his own good. He's been shot twice in the line of duty. Once, he was trying to talk some punk out of shooting someone else. The second time, he got in the middle of a domestic dispute. He could have retired on a pension ten years ago, but he loves to work the streets. It is hard to believe he's still around. If I had been wounded on two occasions, I would be sitting at a desk doing an office job, pushing a pencil, at home by five every day."

"Huh. It takes some kind of man to continue working as a police officer after having survived two gunshot wounds."

"That's right. A real man, Jim Bob, and don't you forget it. A real man keeps bouncing back, adversity after compounded adversity," she said to me, staring into my face like she was delivering me some kind of message.

After a moment, she asked, "You've been to this house before, right? You and Mary Louise?"

"Yes. A few times. On a rare occasion, just the four of us, but usually for a large party. The house is wonderful. I love the 'great room,' as Meredith always called it. That glass wall gives such a fabulous view of the pool, the deck, and all those trees around the bayou. It's sad she's not going to be seeing it again. She was so proud of this place."

I had become entirely too emotional for my own good. My eyes welled up just thinking about Meredith's death and how much she loved her home.

Susan got out of her chair, put an arm around my shoulders, and gave me a hug.

"I've become a babbling idiot, Susan. Sorry. I don't guess I can really be of much help to you or anybody else right now."

"Don't worry about it. You'll get it together."

The sliding glass door to the great room opened and shut loudly, and Susan and I both turned to see Frank James walking briskly toward us.

"Lt. Beeson, unless there are more questions that need answers right away, I desperately need to get over to the hospital and see my mother-in-law. She's had some sort of fainting spell in Mr. Brown's room. I need to be as useful as I possibly can right now, so I need to get over there immediately."

"Well, Doctor, there are a number of other questions I will have to ask you, once I delve into the details of this investigation. However,

I would like you to answer this one now. Will the Browns somehow blame you for Meredith's death?"

Frank stared at Susan, then at me, as though I'd divulged a confidence to his adversary. "I love the Browns. They have been very good to me. But Meredith is—was—their only child. They knew of our separation, and I can assure you, Detective, they thought their daughter was perfect. So, if there is anyone for them to blame for anything, I can promise you, it will be me."

"If you could tell me one more thing before you leave, Doctor. Who would you say the Browns are closest to, besides their daughter? In other words, are there any other family members I can speak with?"

"Well, let me think," Dr. Frank James said, as he pondered the situation for a moment. "Both Melvin and Sarah were only children. They are religious people, I guess, and I think they're very close to Dr. Jones, the preacher over at the Afton Oaks Baptist Church. They've been members there for, I don't know, probably fifty years. They are not religious in a radical sense. I mean, Melvin likes his whiskey, and you never see him without his pipe and tobacco. And he can cuss like a sailor. But they are, you know—"

"You mean, virtuous? Moral? That sort of thing?"

"Yes. Exactly. I think Dr. Jones knows just about all there is to know about the Brown family. The old man's a piece of work, you know. You know of Melvin Brown, correct?"

"Of course. Oil man. Philanthropist. Namesake for Brown Museum, Brown Hall, and probably half a dozen other entities."

"The very one. Well, I really need to go to the hospital. You're sure it's no problem?"

"It's fine, Dr. James. Just remember that in spite of how distasteful this may seem, you are by definition a murder suspect."

Frank was highly offended by Susan's comment. "I didn't kill Meredith. I found her, remember? I'm the one that had security call 911!".

"Or so you say, Doctor. There are no witnesses, except maybe the mystery guest you allegedly saw leaving through the back door. You've seen enough movies to know that during a murder investigation, the spouse is always a suspect. My point is, stay in the area. Don't leave the city without speaking to me or Capt. Polk first. Is that clear?"

"Yes, ma'am," Frank said, suddenly frightened. "It's bad enough to find your wife murdered, but to be a suspect when you've done nothing wrong? I just want to say again, Lieutenant, that I am innocent. You make it sound like I need to get a lawyer. Do I?"

"That will be up to you, Doctor. Thank you for your cooperation."

Frank left the deck and went into the house, but then quickly returned.

"What about my moving back in here? Is the house still off-limits to me?"

"Yes. We're going to keep an officer posted outside for a few more days, just in case we want to search the house again. Just let me know where I can reach you."

Frank started to leave.

"Doctor?" Susan asked.

"Yes?" Frank answered, exasperated.

"I'm confused about one detail. You stated to us a little while ago, and to Capt. Polk last Wednesday, that once you were concerned for your wife's welfare, you called the security station at the front gate, rather than call 911 yourself. Why was that?"

Frank shook his head. "Detective, with all I've read in the newspaper and heard on radio and television, it seems that there is an abuse of 911. Too many crackpots call up and ask for emergency assistance. I thought that perhaps I'd get a quicker response if the security guard called. I thought it would be more . . . official. But, to be honest, in my panic, I couldn't remember security's number. So I drove up to the gate and had Moorehouse place the call."

Susan leaned forward in her chair. "So, you didn't actually call the security kiosk, you drove up there and told him to place the 911 call?"

"That's right."

Susan eyed me. I shrugged in response.

"One more thing, Doctor. I hate to burden you with the morbid details of your wife's autopsy, but there is an item the medical examiner found interesting. It's something you should know, or perhaps you already do."

"What, Detective?"

"Meredith was six weeks pregnant, which brings up the issue of whether or not you two had sexual relations recently."

Frank looked as though he'd been shot. His face paled, he almost stumbled, and he suddenly grabbed hold of a chair before he fell. "What?!"

Susan simply nodded. "I'm sure with all the emotional trauma you've been through, perhaps your remembrances of the last few months are a blur. So, you think about what I just asked you, and when we speak again, I'd like an answer. That will be all, sir."

Frank stared at Susan, then at me. I gave him my best quizzical look. Some supportive friend I was. He slowly shook his head, walked back toward the house, then left for good.

"I don't think Dr. James could have killed his wife, Jim," Susan said, once Frank was out of earshot. "There wasn't enough time for him to park his car in a secluded spot north of here, run through the woods, cross the bayou, break in the back gate, kill her, then return to his car and arrive at the front door of his home, fresh as a daisy, by two o'clock.

"But he could have had someone else do it. According to Sam Polk's preliminary report, Dr. James didn't have Moorehouse make the 911 call until two fifteen. Lee Perkins's report states he arrived on the scene at two thirty. The coroner's report reads that Meredith James's estimated time of death is between one forty-five and two. In case you're wondering, the ME can be that specific when a body is found shortly after its demise. If Dr. James somehow found out that his wife was pregnant, and he had not been sleeping with her for the past six months, he could have gone into a jealous rage, or hired a professional—"

"Susan, I can't imagine that Frank is responsible for Meredith's murder. I don't believe he has the stomach to do it, or to hire someone to have it done. Besides, when you told him Meredith was pregnant, his jaw dropped to his knees. He looked shocked. I don't think he had the foggiest idea."

"I would agree. I rather enjoyed watching his response, although he could be a great actor, since he resembles one. But remember, his wife comes from a very wealthy family, and he might stand to inherit a lot of money. And he may be in love with someone else, and this reconciliation attempt was simply a ruse. Trust me, Jim, you never know for sure how a murder like this will shake out in the end. I've been down this road too many times.

"This will be a high-profile case and we will definitely have to cover all our bases. The Browns will want blood for the loss of their daughter. The police commissioner will be calling the chief, the chief will be calling Sam Polk, Sam will be calling me, and I will be raising hell on down the line. Believe me, it is going to be a mess. The doctor's story about why he didn't call 911 himself bothers me. I don't know what in the world he was thinking when—"

We heard a chain rattle, turned, and saw Sam Polk, Lee Perkins, and the two uniformed officers return through the rear gate.

"So, what did you find out there?"

"Well, Susan, we combed the woods pretty good," Sam said. "No smoking guns, unfortunately. We did find one item of interest, though."

"What?"

"Well, if you walk about fifty yards east, down to the bayou, you'll find an old bridge. I can't tell if it's been used much recently, but it could explain how the perp got away. Maybe he came from somewhere over off Memorial Drive, hiked down to Buffalo Bayou, crossed the bridge, and came up the back way."

"I thought those old bridges had been torn down when this property was subdivided years ago."

"Me, too, but this one is definitely still there and usable."

"Huh. I wonder who would know about an old bridge like that, Sam? Somebody that does a lot of off-track jogging or walking for exercise? No, probably not. Most of the properties north and south of Buffalo Bayou are owned by people who can afford private security, or at least a fence that would thwart free access. Then again, maybe the shooter just got lucky or had scoped the layout ahead of time. On the other hand, maybe the bridge is simply a red herring. I'll have to think about it."

"You do that, Susan."

"Anything else?"

Sam looked at Lee Perkins and the two patrolmen, threw his head to the side, and smiled. He watched the three police officers walk slowly and dejectedly toward the house.

"What's with them?"

"Well, there was one other thing," he said, with a wry grin. "Don't think it means much, but . . ."

"Speak up, man! What is it?"

"Lee discovered an older drunk man on the north side of the bayou. We found him sleeping in a niche carved out of a tree. The men thought at first glance he had expired, but he hadn't. He was just dead drunk, two empty bottles of Thunderbird wine laying at his feet."

"Did you try to talk to him, see if he might have seen anything last Wednesday that would help us?"

"We couldn't rouse him, Susan. Like I said, he was drunker than a skunk, and he smelled to high heaven. God only knows the last time the man had a bath. Anyway, I told the boys to go back and pick him up and book him on vagrancy or public intoxication. I told them to take him to the Central Jail, put him in a holding cell by himself, get him something to eat, and clean him up. And to get him a bottle of cheap whiskey and allow the guards at the jail to give him periodic 'medicinal doses' if they have to. I don't want him going into the DTs in one of our cells. I saw a man die from that once. It's safer to feed his habit than to let him go 'cold turkey.'

"When the guy at least halfway sobers up, we'll see if he knows anything or saw anything the day of the murder that might be pertinent to our investigation, and if not, we'll let him go. You agree?"

"Yes, I do," Susan said, with a broadening smile.

"Like we always say, Suze, in a murder investigation, leave no stone unturned. No stone. Understood?"

"Absolutely. I agree, Sam. One hundred percent."

Sam sat down, rested his boots on an adjacent chair, leaned back, and smiled. So did Susan.

"Just think," she said. "Lee Perkins and his men have to travel by patrol car to the other side of the bayou and wrestle this potential witness downtown. Witness to what, we don't know. But the thought of those three officers struggling to get an odorous, belligerent drunk into the back of their police car . . ."

By then, the two of them were laughing like hyenas.

CHAPTER 25

MR. BROWN

Sunday, April 8, 2001

"**S**o, how is she, Pat?"

"No change, Dr. Brady. The day shift took her off the ventilator once, placed the T-tube over her tracheostomy, and let the oxygen flow at 100% for a minute or so. There were no spontaneous respirations. I tried it again when I first came on duty, per Dr. Flanagan's instructions, and still no response. Sorry."

Pat Gomez was an evening-shift nurse. She was short and a little stocky but had beautiful straight black hair, dark eyebrows, large friendly brown eyes, and a radiant smile. She picked up the chart at the end of Mary Louise's bed and recorded the vital signs—temperature, pulse rate, respiration rate, blood pressure, urine output.

"Any of her docs been by today, besides Flanagan? He was in early before I went out for the day."

"Not since I've been here, Dr. Brady. I noticed from the chart notes that residents from the Urology service and the General Surgery service came by on the morning shift. I'd like someone from Orthopedics to stop by. The dressings on her left leg and left arm have soaked through with blood and need to be changed. I'd be happy to do it, but I'd feel better if one of the house staff assisted me. I don't know how fragile her fractures are. Maybe I'll page someone, if that's okay with you. I mean, you don't want to help me change your wife's bandages, do you?"

"Whatever you want to do is okay with me, Pat. You have been a great help. Besides, I can't handle Mary Louise's dressing changes right now. It's just too . . . too . . ."

"I understand, Dr. Brady, don't worry about it," she said, and patted my arm. She started to walk off, then turned. "Your wife had an episode of heart block this afternoon. Gina called—"

"What?! Heart block? I called Gina earlier to check in, and she didn't mention a word of that to me! What happened?"

"Everything's fine now. She didn't want to worry you. She put in a STAT call to her husband, Rick. He's a cardiology fellow and is on duty today. He came by, gave Mary Louise a little Procardia, and reversed the EKG changes. He said he'd stop by later and check her again. It's fine," she said. "Don't worry. These things happen all the time."

Heart block. Mary Louise could have died while I was out pretending I am a detective.

I felt ridiculous standing at Mary Louise's bedside, holding her right hand with mine, and in my left, carrying a white sack whose label is a half-eaten taco wrapped in red, blue, and yellow paper. Susan had taken us to a drive-through, TACOS-TO-GO, on the way back to the hospital, since we were both starving from all that "detecting." My uneaten lunch remains were growing cold as I stood there and stared at my comatose wife, whose condition was now complicated by her heart's sudden and unpredictable failure to conduct electricity.

I pulled up a chair and sat by Mary Louise's bed. I set the fast-food sack on the less-than-sparkling tile floor, figuring I could "nuke" the tacos in the microwave the nurses use to heat their lunches, when I'm ready to complete my delectable cuisine. The taste may be improved by the microwaves.

Mary Louise's face looked very swollen. Her left eye remained bandaged, and she still wore her turban of white Kerlix topped with a brown ACE bandage. The stain on the left side of her skull, the site of the open fracture, had shrunk, due to a reduction in seepage of blood and tissue fluid. That was a good sign. But her features seemed more distorted than ever. The bruising and swelling from her cranial vault had migrated into her face, a victim of dependent drainage. The purple and red splotches were turning blue, yellow, and brown, like a bad bruise beginning to resolve. Her lips were swollen into a grimace, and her nose . . . needless to say, I won't be taking any pictures to commemorate her temporary sojourn into the spirit world. When she woke up, I would be happy to explain her temporary departure from a communicative state, but in her particular case, a picture is not going to be worth a thousand words.

I lowered the bed rail adjacent to Mary Louise's right side and, while holding her hand, told her about my day with Susan. I told her about my visit to the scene of her injury, and about the time spent at Frank and Meredith's. I told her everything: how Meredith was shot, how the intruder broke into the house, that Frank was a suspect, and that Meredith was pregnant at the time of her death. I even told her about the drunken man Sam Polk and his men found behind Memorial Bend next to the bayou. I mentioned the question of a stolen necklace, and Frank's peculiar method of calling for emergency assistance the day Meredith was murdered.

Then I decided to describe her surroundings to her. I told her about her two primary nurses, Pat Gomez on the night shift, and Gina Genardo on the day shift, and details of their general appearances, so she would feel familiar with the people who were taking care of her, just in case she could hear what was going on but could not respond. I told her how much I loved her and how much I missed her. I felt my eyes tearing up, but as I tried to wipe them, I felt Mary Louise's hand suddenly move spasmodically.

"Pat? Pat!"

She came running from the far side of the nurses' station. "What, Dr. Brady?"

"She moved! I felt her right hand move while I was holding it!"

"Let me feel, please."

She moved me out of the way and gently held Mary Louise's fingers. While she waited for a reproduction of the phenomenon, she concentrated on the overhead monitors, checking to assure herself that the blood pressure, heart rate, and oxygen saturation were still normal.

"I feel it, Dr. Brady. I'm sorry to disillusion you, but the movement represents an involuntary tremor. It's a normal occurrence in patients with prolonged coma. Nothing to be alarmed about, but then, nothing to write home about either."

"I don't know, Pat. I was telling her about my day, and about you and Gina. I went to wipe something from my eye when I felt it. I'm telling you she heard me and tried to communicate with me in the only manner she could!"

Pat employed a smile she has probably used for years on the crazy relatives of patients isolated in this unit for extended periods of time. She patted my shoulder, then started to walk away.

"Pat, Mary Louise isn't receiving any medication that can thwart or retard the awakening process, is she?"

She shook her head. "The only medication she's on that could remotely make her sleepy is Dilantin. She gets 100 milligrams, IV push, three times daily. That's the standard dose to control grand mal seizure activity, and I'm sure Dr. Flanagan will continue that for a while. Dilantin is less damaging to the sensorium than a seizure would be. Don't worry. Sit down and hold her hand some more; just don't get excited over those tonic movements."

I didn't care what she said. I believed Mary Louise heard me and that she was responding to something I said. Or maybe she was trying to tell me she loved me, too.

After a while, my arm developed a serious cramp. I let go of my heretofore unresponsive wife, except for that brief but distinct right hand movement, and sauntered back to the small office behind the nurses' station. I ate cold tacos, since I was too lazy to walk to the nurses' lounge and use the microwave, and washed them down with a cup of black crankcase oil they called coffee in NIC. Despite the coffee, I felt myself becoming drowsy.

After a time, and from a distance, I heard my name being called. "Jim Bob! Wake up, man."

"What?"

"Wake up, bud, I need to talk to you about Mary Louise."

As my eyes finally focused and I realized I had fallen sound asleep, I recognized Jeff Kosar's bulky frame standing in the doorway of what had become my second office. My left leg was asleep from supporting the weight of my right, both of which I had haphazardly propped up on the flat, two-foot extension of the wall that was referred to as a desk.

"Hey, Jeff. Pat Gomez was hoping someone would come by and change Mary Louise's bandages. I never imagined seeing a senior attending staff man on a Sunday night."

"Well, I wanted to talk to you personally. We're going to change Mary Louise's dressings in the morning down in the OR. Her tibia and femur X-rays look great, but that humerus . . . it looks like shit, if you don't mind me saying. As you know, it was so damn comminuted, I couldn't plate it, so I used an external fixator. You know how touchy those devices are. The alignment didn't look all that good on the immediate post-op films, so I've been adjusting it on rounds every day, following it up with portable X-rays. I'm still not satisfied with it. So, I want to take her downstairs, change the bandages, look at all my incisions, and play with the ex-fix. I might have to adjust a pin or two, so I want the opportunity to use a little anesthesia if necessary."

"I don't know, Jeff, I'm reluctant for her to have another anesthetic. I don't want to take a chance on suppressing any consciousness that might be trying to break through the haze of her head trauma."

"I don't know that I'll have to put her to sleep chemically, but at least I'd like to have anesthesia available. I don't want to worry about her feeling pain, for God's sake. There is no way we can know how aware she is, Jim, so I want anesthesia there, simply to cover the bases. Okay?"

"She hasn't recovered from her first anesthetic yet, Jeff. I have no idea what another one will—"

"Jim, let me be the doctor, okay? She's in a coma. It's not like she simply didn't wake up from the anesthetic. She's had a severe head injury. So, why don't you be a good boy, and let me and the anesthesiologists do our job?"

I gave him a very reluctant nod.

"Atta boy. Now go home and get some rest. You look like shit."

After a time, I decided that going home, taking a shower, and getting a decent night's sleep was too good a proposition to pass up. I kissed Mary Louise goodbye, told Pat Gomez goodnight, and made my way to the lobby outside NIC. The electronic doors to the waiting room opened just before I could push the aluminum-plate activator, and across the threshold stepped a tall, handsome young man in blue scrubs and a long white coat.

He stopped, looked at me, then smiled. "You must be Dr. Brady. I'm Rick Genardo," he said, and shook my hand.

"A pleasure, Rick. How did you know it was me?"

"Every day since your wife's been in NIC, Gina describes your unusual choice of attire, for a surgeon, anyway. Seems you don't exactly subscribe to the Hippocratic Dress Code?"

Rick Genardo appeared to be six two, with dark wavy hair and Italian features. He had an engaging smile and seemed very pleasant.

"I should thank you for rescuing my wife from yet another calamity, Rick. How do you explain her heart block?"

"I can't say for sure, Dr. Brady. Could be chemical, from an aberrant drug reaction. Dilantin can cause a slowing of the heart rate, but usually in much higher doses than the 100 milligrams three times daily she's receiving. She could have had a sternal contusion, and an associated cardiac contusion, with a delayed clinical presentation.

Or, it could be part of her traumatized cerebral function, which has caused a blowout in a tiny circuit that normally directs a rhythmic cardiac response. At least it's under control, and I don't think it's serious. If the block occurs again, I suggest we get a portable echocardiogram, and consider inserting a pacemaker."

"Good. I appreciate your concern. I must say, your wife Gina has taken superior care of Mary Louise. She's lucky to have her as a nurse."

"Yeah, Gina's a great gal, and I'm lucky to have her as a wife. Just think what great-looking kids we'll have," he said proudly. "Listen, I've got to run. After I check on your wife, I have an emergency cardiac catheterization to do. Nice meeting you, sir."

As I waited for the sole elevator operating this time of night, I considered my impression of Rick Genardo. Gina had made him sound like a heartless, controlling ogre, and a workaholic. My impression was that of a kind, caring, and dedicated young man in love with a wife he planned on having children with and on spending the rest of his life with. Perhaps first impressions can be misleading, but then again, maybe not.

My thoughts turned to Melvin and Sarah Brown—this was a very slow elevator—and I wondered how they were holding up. Guilt over not making rounds since Wednesday evening began to set in.

NIC was on the eleventh floor of the Fondren Building. Abercrombie Pavilion was on the twelfth floor of the Brown Building. The distance between the two was a one-floor ascent, and a half-block corridor walk. I glanced at the worn timepiece on my left wrist and decided that nine thirty was a perfectly acceptable hour of the evening to call on my patient.

I took the stairs and walked briskly to the security desk outside the locked entrance to Abercrombie Pavilion.

"May I help you, sir?" asked a stocky woman, dressed in a gray suit with white shirt and red tie.

"Yes. I'm Dr. Brady. I'm here to see my patient, Melvin Brown."

She peered at me from behind thick black-rimmed glasses, then stood.

"We don't get many physicians here this time of night, especially dressed in jeans, a plaid shirt, and boots. You have some ID, Doctor?"

I shook my head. "No, ma'am, I'm sorry to say that I do not. I've taken a few days off from work. My wife is in NIC recovering from a head injury and I've been camped out over there since earlier in the week. My clinic jacket's at home, and my ID badge is clipped to the collar," my pleading voice uttered. Then I gave her that irresistible look, the one that employs the wide, friendly, and compassionate West Texas smile that bonded my patients to me, their surgeon, giving them the confidence that I could take care of their particular orthopedic problem with skill and grace.

She shook her head, unsmiling. "Sorry. No ID, no entry. Those are the rules, Doctor." Then, she returned to her desk and resumed tapping on her computer keyboard.

I had no intention of giving up, and just as I leaned down, placed my size-nine hands on her desk, and started to utter totally unprofessional words that will permanently alienate me from this floor for the rich and infamous, I felt a tap on my shoulder.

"What are you doing up here this time of night, Brady? Have you finally decided to get back in the game and take care of your patients?"

George Flanagan was standing behind me, dressed in a long white coat and freshly-starched light-blue surgical scrubs.

"Evening, George. I'm trying to go visit Melvin Brown, but this young lady won't grant me admission to the floor because my ID badge is at home."

My wife's neurosurgeon removed his clip-on badge and handed it to the security attendant. She passed the barcode section of the plastic card over a red light emanating from the depths of the middle of her desk, much like the kind employed in a grocery store, glanced at her computer terminal, read what was necessary to grant Flanagan entry, and returned the card to him.

"What patient, Dr. Flanagan?"

"Mr. Thompson. 1228."

"Thank you, Doctor. You may proceed," she said, and I heard the familiar buzz that would allow Flanagan to make his way onto Abercrombie Pavilion.

He didn't move from the front of her desk.

"Ma'am, I realize Dr. Brady here appears unprofessional, but he's been under quite a bit of stress. I've recently done brain surgery on his wife, and he's having one helluva time getting back into the swing of his professional life. Now, I realize his identification badge is missing, but I can vouch for him. And besides, I'm on my way to see Gerald Thompson. In case you don't know, he's chair of the Board of Regents of University Medical Center. Now, he has what's called a berry aneurysm, a small defect in an artery in his brain. One small leak, and POOF! Thompson develops seizures, goes into a coma, and quickly dies. My job is to carefully go into his brain in the morning and surgically clip that little vessel before Mr. Thompson's brain explodes in my face."

He paused for effect, apparently enjoying the security guard's paling face, sagging jaw, and widening eyes.

"Now, when I go back there to see Mr. Thompson, I don't want to upset him. You know, ma'am, the least little rise in blood pressure could stretch that vessel, cause it to start to leak, and, well, you just never know. And, when he finds out that one of the employees of this institution is keeping Dr. Brady, one of University Hospital's orthopedic surgeons, from his appointed rounds, I can see that little vessel starting to ooze bright-red blood. Drip, drip, drip . . ."

The young woman's face was stretched in a look of horror, hand over her mouth as though that would keep her stomach contents at bay. She frantically maintained pressure on the buzzer under her desk and waved us both through.

I followed George Flanagan into the bowels of Abercrombie Pavilion. I'd have liked to have said thank you, but he walked ahead at a rapid clip, chuckling to himself. He made no attempt to converse with me after his intimidating outburst toward the security person but simply walked purposefully toward his destination. I watched after him for a moment and saw him gesture and laugh to himself. Then, oddly enough, he turned around and walked back in my direction.

"I'll be out of town beginning Tuesday night. I'll be turning my patients over to Frank James for a few days. He should be able to take care of *his* business by now, unlike some doctors I'm acquainted with. Any problems that might arise with your wife, I'm sure he'll be able to handle."

I gave him no response other than a simple nod.

"That is all right with you, Dr. Brady?"

"Yes, I'm sure Frank will take good care of her. You know, George, it was Frank I initially called the day Mary Louise was—"

"Yes, but he was . . . unavailable," he said, and marched off before I could complete my sentence.

I located Room 1224. There was no answer when I knocked on the suite's entry door, so I stepped in uninvited. There was no sign of Frank James or Sarah Brown. I made my way through the suite, tapped at the door to Melvin Brown's bedroom, then opened it, startling a young woman with short dreadlocks, large red lips, and a wide brow. The private-duty nurse was just getting my patient back into bed, apparently from a painful excursion to the john.

"Sir, visiting hours are over," she said in a clipped Caribbean accent.

"It's all right, Gwen, he's my doctor," Mr. Brown said as he settled back into bed.

Gwen fiddled with the covers, aligned his pillows, and rearranged the portable bed table holding ice, water, tissues, and a few magazines.

She stood by the bed and appeared uncomfortable by our silence. He dismissed her to the living room.

"I came by last Wednesday night, Mr. Brown, to offer my condolences about Meredith. You were still sedated from surgery, and your wife . . . well, she was . . . emotional. Anyway, I've been out of pocket for the past few days. I've been staying in NIC, in the Fondren Building, with Mary Louise, my wife. I'm sure you've heard."

He nodded.

"As a result of her accident, I'm taking this coming week off. I can't seem to think clearly or take care of myself very well, so I don't feel I'm in a position to take care of anyone else. But I did want to come by and offer my sympathies to you both."

He didn't say anything right away; he just grabbed a handful of tissues and blew his nose. He gathered his thoughts. "Sarah's taking this awfully hard. Our family doctor has her on medication round the clock. She's home now, but I'll convey your thoughts to her. Also," he sniffed, "we were equally distressed to hear about your wife. I'm sure you've got your own cross to bear right now. But I appreciate you coming by. Your young assistant, Dr. Berry, he's been here twice a day and is doing a fine job."

"Mind if I sit for a moment, Mr. Brown? I want to ask you something."

"All right," he said suspiciously. "I'm pretty tired, though."

"Yes, sir. I won't keep you but a minute."

I pulled a straight-backed chair up to his bedside. "There is a Lt. Susan Beeson who'll be coming to talk to you and Mrs. Brown soon. She's a very good friend of mine, and one of my wife Mary Louise's best friends. She is in charge of the investigation into Meredith's murder. I had the opportunity to spend the day with her, part of which we spent at Meredith and Frank's home, with a Capt. Sam Polk, who is the chief homicide detective. These people are going to be asking you and your wife a lot of questions about Meredith, about her habits, her friends, her daily routine, and anything else the detectives can think of that might help them find her murderer. Some of these questions you're going to find difficult to answer, especially the ones concerning Meredith's activities during the past six months, while she and Frank were separated."

"I believe that Polk's already been here. My days are a little fuzzy, still. I'm pretty sure he paid a social visit to Sarah and me the day after the funeral—must have been yesterday—to fill us in on the details of the murder. I couldn't go, you know. My own daughter's funeral. Sarah had to go alone. Dr. Brady, children should not die before their parents. It's not intended to be that way."

"Yes, sir."

Melvin Brown stared at the ceiling and wiped his eyes. "We're going to put up a substantial reward come Monday. That's tomorrow, isn't it? I wanted to put up more, but the mayor and the police commissioner discouraged it. Too many crackpots would be calling. But I don't think it'll do much good. It sounds like whoever killed my Meredith was, if not a professional, then a very careful individual. The policeman said they have almost nothing to go on except the caliber of bullet that killed her."

There was other information the Browns were unaware of, but I decided to leave their enlightenment of those facts to the authorities.

"Mr. Brown, do you have any ideas, anything at all, no matter how insignificant, that might give the detectives a clue as to what really happened to Meredith? Or do you know anyone that might have any information that would lead them in the right direction?"

He shook his head. "Meredith is—was—an only child. She was a loner, except for her husband and a select few close friends. I mean, she loved parties, and dancing, and tennis matches, and the country club functions, and all that, and having grown up here, and gone to school here, she knew just about everybody. But she kept to herself. Probably the closest friend she had was Myra McCann. They grew up together and were inseparable all through school. I know they saw each other a lot, since Meredith talks—talked—about her all the time. Meredith was very close to her mother and me, but she hadn't talked about her feelings, or real serious issues, for a long time, especially during the period when she and Frank were separated. But you could talk to Myra. I'm sure she'll know all there is to know about my daughter, and what was going on in her life as of late."

"Okay, I'll give Detective Beeson this information. Do you know where Myra McCann lives?"

"The Huntingdon. She and Jack bought one of those high-rise apartments a few years back. Cost him about two million bucks for three thousand square feet of floor space. Jack died last year, but Myra's still living there, as far as I know."

I rose to leave. "Well, sir, I hope you get to feeling better, physically and emotionally. I believe we cured that tumor with the surgery. I think you're going to be winning some money back from your golfing buddies before too long."

"That doesn't seem so important anymore. You know, it's pretty ironic, Doc. While you're inside this old man's leg, trying to cure him of bone cancer, his beautiful young daughter is murdered, and his doctor's wife falls victim to a hit-and-run driver. It doesn't seem like the Man Upstairs was paying much attention to his children that day, does it?"

No indeed, sir.

CHAPTER 26

CHANGES

Monday, April 9, 2001

Lt. Susan Beeson took in a deep breath and heaved out a long sigh as she and I entered the Houston Police Department's Southwest Substation on Beechnut Street. It was a little after nine on Monday morning, and the atmosphere seemed unusually quiet. Susan explained that most of the detectives had already left the office for field work, a daily necessity to investigate the incessant barrage of Houston homicides. She said the place is packed at eight o'clock every morning for the daily homicide-detectives' briefing. Most of the men and the one woman besides Susan then departed for their daily routine, which included chasing down potential witnesses to unsolved crimes, initiating investigations and gathering forensic data on recent crimes, collaborating with the district attorney's office to seek an indictment for a felony, or making an appearance in court, testifying live at trial as the investigating detective.

The Homicide Division was an open, well-lit office with numerous three-sided desk cubicles composed of transportable six-foot-high aluminum dividers lined with pale-blue cloth. There was a fresh coat of white paint on the plaster walls, and numerous windows provided a view of stately oaks and elms, giving the room a pleasant, cozy character. For the past two years, this office had been tobacco-free, as were all City of Houston and Harris County offices. The cinema image of dark, dingy, smoke-filled, yellow-walled rooms with government-issue metal desks was a thing of the past in the decentralized Houston Police Department.

Susan had made time in her hectic schedule to come to University Hospital and sit with me in the waiting room while Jeff Kosar changed Mary Louise's bandages and adjusted the steel frame holding her left arm together. Jeff seemed to be pleased with the postoperative X-rays and was able to perform the procedure with additional local anesthesia only. I spent a few minutes with Mary Louise in the recovery room, telling her I would be spending the day with Susan and to try very hard to wake up.

Susan dropped her purse on her desk and eyed pictures of her husband and Gene Jr., two people whom she had seen little of lately.

"What's that?" I asked, pointing to a map of the city.

"This red X is Memorial Bend, where Meredith James was murdered. The other red X is where Mary Louise was injured."

"Huh. The two sites seem much closer on that map of the City of Houston and Surrounding Area than they do when you're driving."

"True, Jim, but if you think about it, the locations aren't that far apart. Less than two miles."

Susan looked up, scanned the room, and waved at Capt. Sam Polk. He was at his desk in his private glassed-in cubicle, a luxury reserved for the chief detective of each division. She walked down the central aisle toward his office. I, like a small puppy, knew nothing else to do but follow her. We noticed him staring at his computer screen, punching in data with his right index finger. Although the door was open, Susan knocked.

"Morning, Sam."

"Morning, Susan," he said, without looking up from his monitor. He ignored me, and I sensed that whatever permission Susan needed to allow me to follow her around and "help" in her investigation of Meredith's murder did not include Sam's official approval.

She walked up to his desk and stood behind him, leaving me in the doorway.

"What's going on?" she asked.

"The James murder is your case now, Susan. I've been covering for you these last few days while you worked on the Smithson case and looked after your friend there. Richardson's back from vacation, so I want you to turn over your files and let Juvenile take over the Lake Houston case."

She placed a hand on his shoulder and gently asked, "Did you think about what I asked you last night? About assigning the Mary Louise Brady case to me?"

He turned around in his swivel chair and propped his boots on the desk. "Yep."

"And?"

"The techs are working on the case as we speak, just like you asked. There is not a lot of evidence to go on—not much at the scene of the accident—but what there is, they are checking into. Specifically, Forensics is looking at the skid marks, trying to get a match on the size and make of tire. There was broken glass from both cars, and paint embedded into Mrs. Brady's car from the other vehicle. Both glass and paint will have to be analyzed, and the techs will go from there. As I told you last night when you called me at home, another detective was assigned to her case last Wednesday. He's a good man, from the special crimes squad. I know the Brady woman is one of your closest friends, so the chief of that division selected one of his best people."

She smiled. "Thanks. I appreciate your promptness and diligence. However, what I wanted to talk to you about is—"

"I know what you're going to say, Suze, but Mrs. Brady is alive. And sorry, Doc, I don't mean to offend, but if you're going to be hanging around, you might as well get used to the lingo."

"That's fair," I said. Of course, if Sam Polk said something derogatory about my wife's injury, I would have to beat him to death with that bronze paperweight of a *P* resting on his desk.

Sam continued. "It's not a Homicide case. Non-fatality autos go to Special, or sometimes Traffic, but then you know that. Now, if she had—if the accident had been a fatal one, then that would be a different story. That would make it a Homicide case."

"Sam, I reviewed the department's policy manual last night. If an accident results in a severe injury, where a fatality is intended, impending, or implied, or when the outcome of the victim is undetermined, Homicide can have it. And Mary Louise Brady is . . . well, the outcome of her injury is undetermined," she said, giving me a sympathetic look. But, with her delicate hands on her hips, and that "cop" look in her eye, Susan's body language stated she was ready for a battle in order to get what she wanted.

Sam nodded and slowly smiled. "Take it easy. I know the rules, Susan, but thanks for the reminder. You have no evidence that a homicide was implied or intended. I'm labeling it a hit-and-run. The victim has survived, and probably will survive, unless I don't have all the facts, Dr. Brady," he said, addressing me for the first time.

"No one can testify as to what her mental status will be when Mary Louise exits from her coma, and she has sustained an array of other severe injuries. However, her physicians all predict she'll live, although I'm not sure I can say that a woman in an unresponsive coma is 'alive,' except from a strictly biological standpoint."

"Again, Doc, I'm sorry if my words offend you. All I'm saying, Susan," he said, turning his gaze to her, "is that you're too close to her, and it probably will affect your judgment. It is not department policy to allow a detective to investigate crimes involving close friends or relatives. One needs to be totally objective in this business, and—"

"Sam Polk, nothing will interfere with my objectivity in the investigation of Mary Louise Brady's case. I want jurisdiction transferred to

Homicide, and I want your assurance that I'm the designated detective. Right now!" she yelled.

He smiled, leaned back in his chair, put his hands behind his head. "Okay."

"That's it? Just 'Okay'?"

"What do you want, Susan, a writ of habeas corpus for her file? Or maybe an ownership title stamp? I've already talked to the chief detective in Special, and to Chief Lombardo. We are moving the Brady case to Homicide, and you are the detective of record. Happy?"

She relaxed, folded her arms. "No, I'm not particularly happy, Sam. I just want to be sure that I'm in charge of the case. Thank you."

"No problem. But you're still assigned to the James case. You were up when it was called in. I filled in for you temporarily, but I can't play favorites around here, being as you're . . . well, who you are. I didn't show you any partiality when we were partners, and I sure as hell won't do it now. But you better damn well remember that the James murder is a Priority One case. The chief has already called me."

"Dad called you? When?"

"Yes, the chief of police, Stan Lombardo, your father, called me before sunrise. He's already had a call from the commissioner this morning, who had a call from the mayor, who had a call from Melvin Brown's personal attorney, all that since 6:00 a.m."

"Huh. It's already started."

"Yep. Seems Melvin Brown's been quite a supporter of the mayor's—the maximum contributions to his campaign and re-election fund, numerous society fundraisers, and all that. He's calling in his trump cards, I guess."

"You knew this would all happen, didn't you, Sam?"

"Oh, sure, but I just didn't think it would start this quick. Hasn't even been five days since she took the hit."

"Guess I'd better get busy. I have a lot of work to do," Susan said. She turned to leave Sam's office and bumped into me at my position of door-jam supporter.

"There's one more thing, Susan."

"What's that?"

"They've put up a reward for information leading to the person or persons . . . you know the routine."

"How much?"

"They wanted to offer a million, but because of all the kooks that would attract, their lawyer advised $100,000."

"$100,000? We'll still get every weirdo in town calling here. I'll be swamped with bullshit phone calls, and I'll never be able to get anything done, Sam."

"Hold on, Susan," Sam replied. "As of this morning, Mr. Brown is providing two highly trained professionals, executive secretaries in his company, at no charge to the department, to answer specially numbered telephones in one of his offices. We'll set up a communications network, record the conversations, get everything on tape. Surely somebody will squeal for that kind of dough."

"Any problem getting a court order for the wiretap, so we don't infringe on our citizens' civil rights?"

"The request is already being processed. It will be signed by a judge this morning, a friend of Mr. Brown's, naturally. So, you'd better get to work. And Brady," Sam said, facing back toward his computer screen, "try to stay out of harm's way."

We walked back to Susan's cubicle, and she sat and flicked on her computer. "Pull up a chair, Jim Bob. God, it must be nice to be rich. Things happen much faster for the well-to-do. We've got hundreds of unsolved murder cases involving people with little or no money, situations where the family can't afford an investigator, and there's sure as hell no extra cash for a reward."

"How's that?"

"With the poor folks, it's usually a crime of passion. A fight over a wager, an argument over a woman, an altercation over an auto accident, whatever. We get skirmishes between rival factions of gang-bangers over whose turf is whose, or maybe a dope deal gone sour, or a war over one side cheating the other side out of money that was stolen from someone else to begin with. But usually it's pretty clear cut. With rich folks, though, it's a different story. There's usually a fly in the ointment. Some twist. Some weird thing involved that's not obvious."

"Like what?"

"Like there's always some aspect of the case we don't know about, something that's not overtly apparent. And rich people can afford to decoy, so their tracks are usually covered better. It's never quite clear what actually happened, because the water is too muddied. You understand what I mean?"

"You mean like the Joan Hill case? Where a physician husband allegedly murdered his wife by serving her bacteria-contaminated pastries, but escaped conviction? And then her father allegedly hired a hit man to murder the husband, but there was a mistrial on questionable grounds, and the father died, and nobody could prove any of it?"

"Yes. And then the novelists, the screenwriters, and the TV and movie producers get rich portraying the story, but nothing is ever solved."

"I hope this case doesn't become just another Texas saga, Susan."

"Me, too, Jim Bob, me too."

The intercom on Susan's desk phone buzzed. She punched a button to activate the speakerphone. "Yes?"

"Hey, Suze?"

"What, Sam?"

"Our friend's awake and talking this morning."

"What are you talking about?" she said.

"The drunk man Lee Perkins found sleeping behind Memorial Bend yesterday."

"Oh, him. Sure. Is he still in a holding cell at Central Jail? Does he know anything? Did he see anything?"

"Don't know, Suze. He apparently slept all night. The jailer just called me. He is awake and alert. You'd better get down there."

She shook her head, rolled her eyes in exasperation. "So what are we waiting for?"

"We? This is your case. I have work to do in preparation for our eleven o'clock meeting with the chief."

"What meeting?"

"Oh, I must have forgotten to tell you. Chief wants to see us this morning and go over the James case. I'm sure I told you, Susan."

"You damn sure did not, Sam Polk. But that's an even better reason for you to come downtown with me, since the Central Jail and Dad's office are in the same building. Besides, aren't you curious? As the chief homicide detective of this—I want to say 'precinct,' since it sounds more substantial—substation? I mean, you have to answer to the brass, not me. I might forget to tell you something important," she said, and smiled and winked at me.

"You're impossible."

"Yes I am, but I'm damn good at this job. Now if you don't mind, would you get your arse in gear? Let's find out what he has to say."

"You know, Susan, I wouldn't mind so much being seen out in public with you if you owned a decent pair of shoes."

Susan disconnected the intercom system after a brief, but loud, slap of the palm of her hand on the speaker.

CHAPTER 27

COOT

Monday, April 9, 2001

"**Y**our name, sir, is Coot Atkinson?" Capt. Sam Polk asked, after he and Lt. Susan Beeson introduced themselves.

"Charles is my given name, guvnor. I've been known as 'Coot' for quite some time now."

The three of us had ridden together in Sam Polk's city-issued black Ford LTD from HPD's Southwest Substation to the Central Substation in downtown Houston, on Reisner Street. An elevator carried us to the ninth floor of Houston Police Department's headquarters, the location of the Central Jail, a three-story modern structure atop the Central Substation. Susan explained to me on the way downtown that this structure housed the short-termers, such as convicted felons awaiting transfer to the overcrowded state penitentiary in Huntsville, persons charged with a crime who await trial and are unable to make bail, persons convicted of a misdemeanor who are serving a thirty- to ninety-day sentence, and a bevy of drying-out intoxicated people charged with vagrancy, like Coot Atkinson.

The two detectives questioned Coot in one of several interrogation rooms located between the first two of three electronically operated solid-steel doors, each with vertical steel bars at eye level serving as a small window. I watched and listened from behind a two-way mirror, in a tiny room with three desks not unlike ones I used in elementary school. The room, as was the interrogation room, was windowless, lit only by bright fluorescent ceiling lights. Being alone, I chose to turn the overheads off, since there was adequate light emanating through the glass from the adjacent room. The cubbyhole I was in felt airless and quickly reduced me to a state of sweat-induced dehydration. Unfortunately, I was unable to locate a taxpayer-funded, Evian-filled refrigerator.

"You were picked up for vagrancy yesterday, just north of Buffalo Bayou, behind a private residential enclave known as Memorial Bend. Do you remember that, sir?"

"That I do, guvnor. I believe I gave the three Keystones a little run for their money when they unjustly accosted me. They were a tad sloppy, I might add," he said, smiling.

Coot had to be in his sixties, although appearances of those in the homeless life could probably be deceiving. He had a ruddy complexion with broken spider veins across his nose and cheeks, a full head of recently washed and still-wet gray hair, an untamed beard, and bushy gray eyebrows. His orange jumpsuit, which read Property of Houston Central Jail, brightened his alcoholic flush. Scattered upper and lower front teeth were missing, and the ones that he still possessed appeared brown and crumbly. His features were clearly visible from my vantage point, approximately fifteen feet away, through the two-way mirror.

"Where are you from, Coot?" Susan asked.

"From everywhere, m'lady."

"Originally?"

"Liverpool, England, home of John, Paul, George, and Ringo. Heard them play many times in the local pubs when I was a lad."

"That means you're how old?"

"Fifty-two. Perhaps you might think I look a bit older, lassie, but it's been a hard go these past few years."

Coot sat at a small table, seated directly across from Susan and Sam. A guard, armed with a short-barreled 12-gauge Commander shotgun, stood at the door and watched the prisoner.

"If you would, Coot, tell us what you were doing in those woods, back along Buffalo Bayou," Sam said.

"Well, guvnor, I was having myself a spot of rest after lunch, such as it was. Just taking a little nap, when the three bobbies roused me from my reverie."

"Do you remember what you had for lunch?"

"Oh, quite, sir. Two bottles of fine wine."

"That's all. No food?" Susan asked.

"I only eat once a day, usually in the evenings, when I can scour a bite from one of the receptacles in the neighborhood. Unless, of course, I enjoy a bit of luck and perhaps find I haven't spent my last shilling on Mr. Thunderbird, or perhaps some kindly chap tosses a little change my way. Other than that, it's me and the old Browning-Ferris."

Sam wrinkled his eyes. "Like BFI, the dumpster company?"

"Waste management company, young man. Often, there are quite a bit of delectable remains—I prefer to think of them as leftovers—in the receptacles that I take advantage of. And there are especially wonderful discards in one of the two large containers behind Memorial Bend."

"And you have no income?" Susan asked.

"Oh, dearie, I have a pittance from unemployment—actually, social security now, but that barely covers my expenses for the grape. I have been on the dole, so to speak, for some years now. I was laid off in the early 80s, during the oil boom decline. Not many positions for a British geologist these days, are there now?"

"Now what is the story, Coot? Did you, or did you not, see anything unusual last Wednesday? The jailer had instructions to prepare you for this question."

"Well, guvnor, on the news this morning, I saw a tidbit about young Mrs. James being murdered. I was relaxing in the rec room after breakfast. Shot with a pistol, I hear. And it seems to me, that perhaps you are wondering if the—what are they calling him? The intruder, that's it—if the intruder perhaps came up the back way, across the old bridge. Is that the sum of it?"

"Yes, sir, that's what we'd like to find out," Sam replied.

"Well, you understand that I'd finished my lunch by then. I'm sure I had the usual that day, two bottles of aged Chablis, bottled the previous week, I think," Coot said, and laughed heartily before erupting into a severe coughing spasm. Susan instructed the guard to provide the prisoner with a glass of water, which he did.

"So," Coot continued, once his throat was clear, "I might have been a little fuzzy. However, the pedestrian traffic along that part of the bayou is scarce, so I distinctly remember the jogger."

Susan and Sam leaned forward. "What jogger?" she asked.

"A jogger in a white suit. You know, baggy pants gathered at the ankles, blousy zip-up top, with a baseball cap and sunglasses."

"Man or woman?" Sam asked.

"Well, guvnor, I can't rightly tell you. Could have been a man with longish hair, or a woman with shortish hair. The uh . . . the chest didn't have a much of a bounce to it, so if it was a woman, she was, shall we say . . . underdeveloped. But then, the top was baggy, so I can't say for sure."

"Any facial hair, Coot?"

"Nay, lassie. Clean as a whistle."

"Was there a pattern to the running? I mean, was he, or she, running along the bayou, or through the woods, or what?" Sam questioned.

"Well, sir, there was a pattern. I saw the jogger come from the north, the Memorial Drive area, come through the woods, stop and check the old wrist watch, like the runner was timing or pacing his- or herself, then cross the old bridge over the bayou, and head toward those delightful homes on the south side at the Memorial Bend complex. Then, after a time—I cannot say how long it was, since I was dozing—the jogger comes charging back through the woods, making a God-awful racket. Woke me up, it did."

"Where did the jogger go, Coot?"

"Headed back off in the direction from whence he came, dearie."

"You said he, Coot?"

"Oh? Figure of speech, my dear."

"And you didn't see a vehicle?" asked Sam.

"No transportation in sight, sire."

"And where were you all this time, Coot?"

"Sleeping under my favorite giant oak, guvnor. Incredible amounts of shade, with a small niche in the trunk, perfect for my back and head. Ah, to be nestled in the brush right now, sipping—"

"Any possibility you could identify this jogger, Coot? What if we showed you some pictures?" Susan asked.

Coot shook his head. "I wasn't that close. Sorry."

They rose to leave. Susan reached over, shook Coot's hand, said, "Thank you for your help."

"See ya, Coot. You are free to go. Vagrancy charges have been dropped," Sam said.

Coot looked a little forlorn. "Oh, too bad. I was rather hoping for a longer respite from the torments of the world. Quite enjoyed the fried chicken last evening. And that bourbon. Nectar of the gods."

"Sorry, Coot. The department is on a tight budget."

When I saw Sam and Susan exit the room in front of the armed guard, I took my leave from the kindergarten desk. I observed Coot being escorted through the second set of electronic barred doors, as the next jailer took him by the arm and led him back toward his cell. Sam and Susan joined me in the drab hallway, then the three of us exited through the massive steel door at the jail entrance and returned to the elevators.

"What is this about fried chicken and bourbon, Mr. Sam 'Don't-Get-So-Involved' Polk? Is a gourmet dinner and whiskey for our less fortunate citizens on the city budget? I understand the whiskey, since you were worried he would go into the DTs, but fried chicken?"

We stepped into the elevator, and Sam punched the button for the third floor. "That's right. But I paid for dinner and the booze out of my own pocket."

"You? Really? Maybe I've been wrong about you all this time. Maybe you do have a compassionate side."

"Could be. Just don't tell anyone. Wouldn't want to ruin my image."

CHAPTER 28

THE CHIEF

Monday, April 9, 2001

"**M**orning, Lottie," Susan said to the woman at a desk in the outer office of Major Stan Lombardo, Chief of the Houston Police Department.

Lottie Malcomb looked up admiringly and waved, continuing to talk into an operator's headset connected to a twelve-line telephone, and entered a message for her boss on her computer's display of the chief's daily schedule.

"Yes, I promise he'll call you back within the hour, Commissioner," she said. "No problem. Thank you, sir." The chief's administrative assistant shook her head, disconnected the line, picked up another blinking line, and asked the party to Hold, Please.

"Politicians. How are you, Susan?" Lottie said, stood, and hugged the boss's daughter.

"Good, Lottie. You know Dr. Jim Brady?"

She shook my hand. "I've talked to you on the telephone several times, Doctor, usually when His Highness's hip is hurting. Nice to meet you."

"Likewise," I said.

"Sam."

"Lottie."

"What a day," she said, picked up the blinking phone line, recorded another appointment into the computer, and logged it onto the chief's schedule. "Everybody wants to see him, and it has to be today or tomorrow. Good thing it's close to lunch time, since I'm already beat."

"Always the way it is, Lottie. Feast or famine," Sam Polk responded.

"You're looking dapper today, Sam," Lottie said, as she scanned his lanky frame, from his brown slacks, to his white, long-sleeved Western shirt, up to the tan Stetson he was holding. She leaned over the desk, looked at his boots. "Lizard?"

"Yep."

"Matches your hat, too."

"Always try, Lottie. The chief's expecting us at eleven. Sorry if we're a tad late."

"He stepped out but should be back any minute. Go in and have a seat. Y'all want some coffee?"

We all did.

Lottie Malcomb looked to be in her late forties, early fifties, maybe a little heavy for Cosmopolitan, but a strong, full-figured Texas kind of woman. Her hair was dyed—faint dark roots were visible—and piled on her head in a swirl. Her hips swayed as she walked, causing the tight blue dress to rotate slowly and sensually. Her calves contracted artfully in those three-inch black pumps. On her way to the kitchen adjacent to her office, she glanced back in Sam's direction and smiled.

Coffee in hand, we stepped across the threshold into the inner office. Sam placed his hat on a mahogany table by the door and sat in one of the two leather chairs opposite the chief's large mahogany desk. Susan took the other.

The emotions I felt, hanging behind Lt. Beeson and Capt. Polk, were not unlike those from twenty-five years ago as a medical student, when I followed attending staff doctors around for four years. You were not supposed to ask or answer questions unless you were instructed to do so, sort of like the adage, which no longer seems applicable in our modern society, children are to be seen and not heard. Learning in med school occurred by observation and independent study, and while there was nothing wrong with that, it was a bit more difficult at halfway through my fifties than it was in my early twenties.

So, I sat quietly on a couch off to the side, peered at two large Navajo rugs depicting pueblo scenes on the dark plank floor, and admired Chief Stan Lombardo's collection of kachina dolls, locked behind the glass of a mahogany bookcase, highlighted by pinpoint accent lighting. Bright daylight from the morning sun spilled into the room and cast jagged shadows across the Native American figurines. And for some inexplicable reason, the Navajo artful weave, portraying town life as they once knew it, caused me to sadly reflect on Mary Louise's plight.

"So, how's the James investigation going?" Lottie asked, as she distributed freshly brewed coffee.

"We just started, Lottie. Susan and I are trying to piece it together best we can. Not much to go on yet," Sam replied.

"That's why he wanted to see you two," Lottie said, and patted Sam on the shoulder before turning to me.

"I'm very sorry to hear about Mrs. Brady," Lottie said to me. "How is she?"

I cleared my throat. "Mary Louise is still in a coma, but her fractures seem to be aligned well, after some adjustment, and the ophthalmologist doesn't think she's going to lose her left eye. Otherwise, her vital signs are stable, and she seems to be holding on."

"That's good. I wish her the best."

Suddenly, I heard the outer door slam, and the familiar three-point walk.

"Morning, Chief," Sam said, standing.

"Morning, Daddy," Susan said, and threw her arms around her father, who stood rather stiffly and stared at me over his daughter's shoulder.

"Morning, Stan," I said, smiling.

Houston's chief of police limped into the room, supported by his ever-present ebony cane with a mallard-head handle. He had on his dress blues, complete with epaulets and medals. He slipped off his jacket, loosened his tie, sat in his brown leather desk chair, and reclined.

He was about sixty years old and had tousled gray hair and bushy gray mustache. He was five ten or so, and heavy—around 250 pounds—but tough as hell.

"How's the hip, Stan?"

"Hurts all the damn time. Should have sued you, Brady."

I couldn't help but smile as I recalled hearing about the annual Houston Police Department deer hunting trip some years before, when Stan Lombardo fell out of his elevated deer blind and broke his hip. He claimed a defect in the ladder that led to the stand, minimizing the fact that he had Bloody Marys and not coffee in his insulated thermos. The hip had deteriorated from arthritis after the break was repaired, and he had required a hip replacement. I had done both procedures. His hip was much better but would never be as useful as it was as before the fracture.

"Tell me what you have on the James case, Sam."

Sam sighed. "This is Susan's case, Chief. I've just been helping out for—"

"I just asked the chief homicide detective from the Southwest about a case. Can I get an answer?" he said insistently.

"Sure, Chief. We have a forty-five-year-old doctor's wife, daughter of a prominent Houston family, murdered in her closet while getting all dressed up for a rendezvous with her husband, from whom she'd been separated for six months. There were two gunshot wounds, both 9-mm, fired from the same gun, one to the head, the other to the heart. Coroner says either wound would have been fatal.

"Looks like a rear entry to the home from the patio," Sam continued. "A sliding glass door was jimmied, but otherwise there was no destruction of personal property, no signs of theft, no signs of rape or molestation of the victim. There were no signs of a struggle on the part of Mrs. James, so the attacker appears to have caught her totally off guard. Her fingernails were clean as a whistle, no hairs or skin remnants to suggest she tried to ward off her assailant. Initial print studies from the interior of the house are unremarkable. Her prints are, of course, everywhere, as are the maid's and the husband's, even though he supposedly hasn't lived there for six months. All the other prints we found do not match any known offender, at least as far as local and state records are concerned. We haven't checked federal yet, but I think that'll turn up negative, too. My guess is the shooter was skilled enough to wear gloves and avoid leaving any prints. And from the looks of the stairs, which, according to the maid, who went home at noon that day, were vacuumed right before she left, the killer probably had sense enough to remove their shoes.

"Wednesday is garbage day at Memorial Bend, and the back gate to each home is always left open. Apparently, the perp came across Buffalo Bayou on an old bridge and went in the back way. Probably came from somewhere to the north, might have parked a vehicle off Memorial Drive somewhere. We have a witness, if you want to call him that, who saw a jogger coming and going through the woods about the time of the murder. I would assume that if this jogger was wearing athletic shoes and wore them into the house, the techs would have found some evidence, at least on the stairs, or on that white carpet in the victim's bedroom. A speck of dirt, or mud, or grass, or a leaf, or even an imprint from the sole of the shoe. But there was nothing found.

"The only two other clues we have are that the ME found a shallow depression on the back of Mrs. James's neck that could represent the imprint of a necklace, or a chain, that might have been forcibly removed from the victim, probably after the murder. Also, according to the medical examiner, the deceased was six weeks pregnant. We don't know what to make of that yet. We asked the husband, Dr. Frank James, about it, and he seemed . . . surprised."

"I see. This 'witness' you found, is he reliable?"

Sam shook his head. "Intoxicated ex-geologist who lives in the bayou area under a tree and eats out of the BFI dumpsters in the neighborhood. Couldn't ID the sex of the person he saw running, so who's to say what he actually saw."

Stan Lombardo rubbed his hairy hands over his face and sighed. "What's your next move, Sam?"

"Well, we have a lot of checking to do, Chief. We have to question the deceased's friends, acquaintances, and parents, although I've moved slowly with the Browns, what with the funeral and his recent surgery. I stopped by Mr. Brown's suite at University Hospital on Saturday, but I had little to report at the time, and he wasn't up to answering questions. We need to compile a list of as many names as we can, systematically go through it, and simply start asking questions. We do know that Meredith James worked out at Body Rock on Kirby every day, so I thought we would start there. Of course, the doctor is still my number-one suspect, since it looks very much like a professional hit to me. I have no idea what the motive might have been, other than money or another woman."

"What about the pregnancy? How do you see that fitting in?"

"Don't know, Chief. Could have been she was still sleeping with her husband, and for whatever reason, he doesn't want us to know. She could have been sleeping around and was very unlucky. Her husband didn't act like he knew anything about the pregnancy, so I thought we'd try and find out who her doctor was, go see them, and review the deceased's medical records. The coroner is doing a blood type and DNA analysis on the fetus. The next logical step would be to take a blood sample from Dr. James and see if he's a compatible father. Regardless of whether the baby was his or not, though, I still think he's a reasonable suspect.

"Also, I thought we would take a look at the records from the security gate at Memorial Bend. The guard on duty records entries of nonresidents: name, make of car, and license number. Those records may give us a clue as to who Mrs. James was seeing in the last six months. We'll also check out her phone bills, try to coordinate the entry logs and her telephone conversations, see what we can come up with."

"It's going to get complicated, Sam, with Melvin and Sarah Brown for parents. Big reward, $100,000. Of course, the setup Mr. Brown is paying for will reduce our staffing requirements, but you and Susan are still going to need a number of extra detectives as well as uniformed officers to assist you in the investigation."

"Yes, sir, that would be helpful. I know you want us to try and solve this murder quickly, but from the looks of things, I don't know if we'll be able to oblige you."

"I know you'll do your best," Stan said. He turned his chair and looked out his window at the massive downtown interchange between Interstate 45 and Interstate 59. "What do you think, Susan?"

"Sir?" seemingly surprised that her father had spoken to her.

"About the vehicular assault of Mary Louise Brady?"

"Well, sir, Sam's assigned me to both cases."

"And what does that mean you're going to do, Susan?"

She paused for a moment, perhaps organizing her spur-of-the-moment thoughts. "Sam has brought you up to date on the James case. With respect to the Brady case, witnesses at the scene could not identify a single license plate number or letter of the vehicle that sped away from the hit-and-run. And from the report I read, and my discussion with the investigating officer, there is confusion as to the make of the car. About all I can tell you is that it was a black European sedan. Could be a Mercedes, Volvo, BMW, or an Audi. Those were the names mentioned by the citizens that were kind enough to stop and try to render Mary Louise aid.

"So, I have the guys in Auto scraping Mary Louise's Jeep. They're looking for samples from the assailant's vehicle, paint samples from the fender, embedded glass from a headlight, maybe a fleck from a chrome bumper. It is possible we'll be able to obtain certain data from a microscopic study that will allow one of the manufacturers to help us identify the car. If we get lucky and figure out the make of car, then we'll have to start searching in registrations and titles and comb the local dealerships for sales records. We have to look at state title-transfer records for resale information. Then we have to search the DPS records. You know, Dad, we'll have to ride the paper trail, and maybe we'll find something, maybe we won't. I personally think it's a longshot, but I don't know what else to do. I've contracted with J. J. Brady's investigative agency to help us track down the vehicle, so he'll be networking closely with the techs in Auto."

The chief smiled and affirmed Susan's plan with a slight nod. "I've got a lot of pressure from above, you two, mostly on the James woman's murder, of course. But we don't want the citizens of Houston to think the police department is going to ignore the fact that a physician's wife—hell, anybody's wife, for that matter—can be run down in our streets and left for dead while we sit idly by on our thumbs, concentrating our all our efforts on a society woman's murder."

"Yes, sir, I'm glad you brought that up," Sam interjected. "How quickly we solve these crimes is based a great deal on our staffing capabilities."

"I'll give you the people you need, Sam."

"Thanks, Chief."

"Anything else, Susan?"

"Yes, sir. In pursuing the hit-and-run of Mary Louise Brady, we must assume that whoever hit her Jeep sustained damage to their automobile. Unless the assailant has mechanical and body-repair skills, the car is going to have to be repaired commercially. So, once we determine the make and model of vehicle that hit her—I should say, 'if' we can, because I still think it's a long shot—we'll need to comb the dealerships for recent repair jobs of those types of vehicles. Plus, there must be hundreds of independent auto repair contractors, unauthorized by the respective factories, who do body work, especially for cash.

"Of course, then we should assume that if the hit-and-run driver took the vehicle in for repairs, they would probably need a rental, unless the perp has the luxury of having more than one vehicle. But if you assume that the hit-and-run driver is a local, and they took the assaulting vehicle in for repairs *and* rented a car, maybe we can cross-check dealership and body-shop records against rental-car records. It'll be a logistical nightmare and will take a large number of investigators to accomplish the task. But we might get lucky."

"Yes, Susan, it will be difficult, but any job worth doing is worth doing well. Work hard, and good luck," he said, and he stood and extended a hand to Sam Polk.

"Thanks again for the promotion, Chief. I appreciate it, and I can assure you that I won't let you down."

Stan Lombardo nodded, then turned to me.

"My hip is still sore as hell, Brady, but I'm going to go easy on you today, since you're going through a difficult time in your life. But after that wonderful wife of yours wakes up—and she will, because I know good and well that God surely wouldn't take her away and leave the likes of *you* around—and after we catch the son-of-a-bitch responsible for her current condition, I'm going to come down to your office and get an X-ray. I swear you put this artificial hip in backward."

CHAPTER 29

MOOREHOUSE

Monday, April 9, 2001

After the meeting in Chief Lombardo's office, Sam Polk, Susan Beeson, and I experienced a silent drive back to the Southwest Substation. The pressure to solve the Meredith James murder case was heightening, and the two detectives lost themselves in private concentration. The ride back to Beechnut Street was a blur for me, as the weight of Mary Louise's assault dragged me into a depressive state.

Upon our arrival at the Southwest, Susan immediately returned to her desk in Homicide and put in a call to Dr. Frank James's office. She used her speaker phone, apparently a perpetual habit, but one which freed her hands for a search she initiated on her computer terminal.

"That's all right, ma'am. He gave me his beeper number yesterday so that I could reach him quickly if necessary and avoid inherent delays through the answering service. I'll page him myself, thank you," she said, and abruptly disconnected. She punched Frank's beeper number into the touch-tone phone, and when the shrill receiving tone was heard, she tapped in the number of her direct line and followed it with the "star" key.

Frank quickly returned her call.

"Morning, Dr. James, this is Lt. Susan Beeson. Where are you?"

"I'm at the Marriott Hotel on Fannin, adjacent to University Hospital. Why?"

"You're not working today?"

"I had one surgical case early this morning. I decided to come back to my room and rest before my clinic this afternoon. With the events of the past week, I am tired and worn out, Detective. I can't seem to get enough sleep."

"I see. I thought you were staying at an apartment at the Ritz-Carlton Hotel, your place of residence for the last six months."

"No. Well, yes, I am. But the Marriott is interconnected with the hospital, and I've been so busy running back and forth between my office and Melvin and Sarah's suite, taking care of . . . anyway, I rented a room here last Wednesday night, and except for picking up fresh clothes, I haven't spent much time at my apartment. Is that a problem, Detective?"

"Not as long as I am able to get in touch with you on a moment's notice, Doctor. The reason I called is this. I need to speak with you in person. When is a convenient time?"

"Well, Detective, it's what, twelve thirty? I see office patients beginning at two o'clock. Then, I have a meeting—"

"Let's say one o'clock. My office?"

"Where's your office?"

"Southwest Substation, on Beechnut Street."

"Oh, God. You're not going to make me come out there, are you?"

"Yes, sir, I am."

"Lieutenant, it will be difficult to get there by one and get back here to the office in order to see patients on time. Couldn't we—"

"See you at one o'clock. Sharp."

Susan clicked off the speakerphone and stared at me. "You know, after all these years on the police force, I still get pangs of regret when I make demands on people, especially in a case like this. Dr. James is a prominent surgeon, a friend of yours, and seems truly disheartened over the fact his wealthy society wife has been brutally murdered. On the other side of the coin, Jim Bob, we don't know but what he didn't kill her himself. He really has no alibi, other than that stupid security guard Moorehouse's confirmation of the doctor's story.

"When Officer Lee Perkins and Sam Polk interviewed the doctor the day of the murder, Dr. James told them that he had operated at University Hospital that morning, made rounds, walked to his office in University Tower and cleaned up his desk, made a few phone calls, then went to his apartment at the Ritz-Carlton to shower and change. Moorehouse confirmed to Lee Perkins that Dr. James arrived at Memorial Bend a few minutes before 2:00 p.m., then went to the house to meet his wife for lunch. According to the log book, which I haven't seen yet, but which you and I will pick up today, the doctor returned to the security gate at two fifteen, told Moorehouse he thought there was a problem at his home, and had the security guard call 911.

"Unless the ME is incorrect about the time of death, which I doubt, there just isn't enough of a time window to allow Dr. James to run that route across the bayou and show up at the gate at two o'clock. I want to go over those entry logs with a fine-toothed—"

The phone on Susan's desk rang before she could complete her sentence. "Dad! What a surprise. Did you forget to tell me something at the meeting we just had?" she said, laughingly.

Stan Lombardo's booming bass voice was clearly heard through the speakerphone. "Well, I don't like to fraternize with my daughter at work, especially in front of Sam Polk. So, how's my grandson?"

"Good, although I haven't seen much of him in the last few days. You're welcome to come over one night this week and have dinner. Of course, Gene is driving up to Dallas today for a meeting. He is staying with his parents, and he's taking the baby along with him for a visit. So, maybe we can have dinner together, just the two of us. You up for it?"

There was a pause, then, "When will Gene Jr. be back home?"

"Friday."

"Friday sounds good. I'll check my calendar," he said, and chuckled.

"Oh, thanks a lot, Dad. If you change your mind and want to come over and have a quiet dinner alone with your daughter, you're always welcome. Remember, though, that I'm supposed to meet the security people at Memorial Bend around four o'clock today and pick up those entry and exit logs they use to record nonresident visits. I'm going to ferret out the visitors to Meredith Brown's home in the last six months. There will be a ton of paperwork associated with those records, so I'll be at home every night, plowing through names and license numbers. Just give me a little notice if you want dinner, okay?"

"Sure."

"Fine, Dad. Thanks for calling."

There was a long silence on the other end of the line. Susan looked at me and shrugged.

"What, Dad?"

"I told Sam Polk I'd assign some uniforms and two or three other detectives to help you with this case. I told him to devote as much personal attention to it as he can. There's a lot of pressure of me from upstairs, but I guess I told you that."

"Yes, you did. But thanks for the additional personnel. We need all the help we can get."

He hesitated again. "So, what are you going to do with Dr. Brady, besides babysit him?"

Susan rolled her eyes. "Well, there's going to be a tremendous amount of paperwork to get through once we get our hands on those logs. Jim Bob can spend whatever free time he creates for himself away from the hospital helping me do that. You know, Dad, this is a transition week for him, because next week, he has to get back to the normal grind of being an orthopedic surgeon. I'm giving him something to do to try and keep his mind off Mary Louise's situation.

I can't just let him sit up there in NIC and watch his mind wither away. Mary Louise would never forgive me if I didn't do something to help her husband keep his sanity. Besides, he's no dummy. He might figure out some obscure detail and break the case for us. You said we need all the help we can get."

"I see. Of course, I'm sure a smart young policewoman like you is aware of the fact that it takes many years to become a good detective. Don't get me wrong, Susan; I'm glad the department is able to assist Dr. Brady in maintaining a healthy mental outlook in his time of trouble, but don't expect much from him. He can't seem to do his *real* job all that well."

Susan tapped her fingers on her desk, and contorted her face into an irritated look. "Jim Bob is sitting right here beside me, Dad, and since I'm on speakerphone, is there anything you'd like to say to him?"

"What?!"

"Thanks for the vote of confidence, Stan," I said.

We heard the chief's end of the line disconnect.

Susan Beeson pulled the black unmarked Ford into the entry drive of Memorial Bend. She parked off to the side, out of the way of entry traffic, got out, and walked toward the security kiosk for her meeting with William Moorehouse, the security guard on duty the day of Meredith James's murder. I, the allegiant pup, moved out of the shotgun seat and followed in her stride, like an overgrown wayward child.

Moorehouse stepped out of the air-conditioned comfort of his guardhouse and greeted Susan just in front of the retractable gate.

"Detective," he said.

"Mr. Moorehouse," Susan replied. "You remember Dr. Brady?"

"I do. Doctor," he said. "This is Terry Lewis. He's my partner on the day shift."

Susan nodded to the thin man as he stepped to the doorway of the kiosk. He smiled, waved, said nothing. Not much taller than Susan, he had short-cropped hair and a pencil-thin mustache, and pearly-white teeth.

Both security guards were dressed in identical uniforms, consisting of blue pants with a darker blue stripe down the side, white short-sleeved shirt, and black tie. The upper-left shoulder patch read A-1 Security Services. Each wore a large leather belt housing a walkie-talkie, a flashlight, and a large can of Mace. My recollection was that gun permits were rarely granted to private security personnel in Houston, but that soon could change.

"What can I do for you, Lieutenant? I'm due to be off just about now," Moorehouse said, glancing at his watch. From his ruddy face and overgrown midriff, I suspected Mr. Moorehouse was already starting to salivate over the thought of his first beer.

"I understand you keep entry and exit logs for all nonresident visits?"

"Entry only, Detective. We got too many people coming in and out of here to log both. You got your delivery people from the grocery stores, like Randall's, Kroger, and Rice Epicurean. You got your laundry people, at last count, about twenty different ones. You got tons of florists—these people here get a lot of flowers. You got your Chinese places that deliver, like Hunan and Shanghai River—they're always over here. And then that . . . what's it called, Terry?"

"Takeout Taxi."

"Yeah. They bring food from restaurants all over town. Then you got your service people—electricians, plumbers, gardeners, pool service, telephone repair, cable repair, appliance repair. And everybody has at least one maid. Hell, some of these people have three different kinds of house help. Then you got your social calls, lunches, dinners, all kinds of parties. You wouldn't believe the number of people come in and out of this—"

"Okay, Mr. Moorehouse. I get the point. But you do keep entry logs, right?"

"Right."

"How are they organized? By the day, the week, the month, what?"

"Weekly. There's a book for every week, with a log for each day."

"Is it divided into deliveries by recipient address, or what?"

"Nope. Just a log, kept according to time. Lists the name of the person making the delivery, the company if applicable, the make and license plate of the vehicle, and the destination."

"Good. May I see them, please?"

"Which ones?"

"Each log for the past six months, including last Wednesday, the day Meredith James was murdered."

"What? Why, that's, that's—"

"Twenty-four books, give or take."

"I'm not sure I can give them to you, Detective. They may be property of A-1. Or they might belong to the residents here. There could be some confidential information in the logs. Could be privileged, for all I know. I'll have to check with the office. I'm sure there's no problem in your looking at them here, but—"

"You do just that, Moorehouse. You call your supervisors from the kiosk while I wait. But please keep in mind that my request for those logs is part of an official investigation of a homicide, one, I might add, that was committed on your shift. And maybe, just maybe, there is a clue in those records that will lead us to the person or persons who killed Meredith James. Now, I want those logs. We can do it the easy way, and you can simply hand them over, or I can get a subpoena and have you bring them to my office, where you will sit your butt down and watch me research them for the next several days. Which will it be?"

"You don't need to threaten me, Lieutenant. I'm very familiar with police procedure. I just want to clear it with my supervisor at the main office."

"I understood that you are in charge of security here at Memorial Bend."

Moorehouse became a little red-faced, appearing to lose a handle on his superior attitude. "I usually work the day shift, Detective. Occasionally, I'll pull a double, or a weekend—"

"I called your office before I came here. The company supervisor told me you're the director of security for the complex. Your responsibilities include the various shift schedules, resident complaints, and generally ensuring that the level of security your company provides is what the owners are paying for. And I must say, he is upset, and rightfully so, that a homicide occurred here, in broad daylight, on your shift. Do I make myself clear, Mr. Moorehouse?"

By that time, Susan's neck veins were visibly distended. Out of the corner of my eye, I watched Security Guard Lewis creep back into the kiosk.

"What are you implying, Detective? Surely you don't think I somehow shirked my duty the day the James woman was murdered. I'll have you know I spent twenty years in the United States Army in the military police, and I have my stripes to prove it. I can assure you that no one got past me here at the gate. I saw nothing suspicious that day, I heard no shots, and I saw no irregularities or disturbances of any kind. There was nothing I could have done to prevent—"

"That's all well and good, Moorehouse. But while I'm looking over those logs to see if I can find a clue to Meredith James's murder, you might be thinking about an answer to these two questions. One, why is it that since last Thursday, you've insisted A-1 hire additional security guards in order to place two men on each shift during the week at Memorial Bend, when you've always insisted that one was more than adequate coverage? Secondly, and I really want you to think hard about this one, sir, what individuals might possibly be aware of the fact that the foolish director of security of this complex instructed the homeowners to leave their back gates open every Wednesday for the purpose of refuse disposal, knowing full well that the only security guard on the premises would be at this front gate?"

CHAPTER 30

THE LOGS

Thursday, April 12, 2001

On Tuesday, I had established a routine for myself in an attempt to maintain my mental health and avoid the obsession of constantly simply sitting at NIC.

I would arise in my empty apartment at the Post Oak Tower at 5 a.m. and perform menial exercises that would keep my heart going for a couple of extra months. A few sit-ups and push-ups and some jumping jacks, although it's more difficult than one might think in cowboy boots. After a shower, I would go to the hospital, review the recent nurses' and doctors' progress notes in Mary Louise's chart, and sit with her for a while. Most of her treating physicians made rounds early, between six and eight in the morning. Between their comments and the chart notes, I attempted to keep abreast of her bladder, bowels, heart, liver, and lungs, as well as the status of her multiple fractures. And, most importantly, I observed notations about her mental status and performed a daily cursory neurological examination myself, just in case any of the so-called experts missed any slight sign that would indicate Mary Louise was emerging from her coma.

Much to my chagrin, there had been essentially no change in her medical condition. Her pulse remained regular, her blood pressure continued to be stable, her temperature was normal, and her urine output was adequate. These were all good signs, to be sure. Mary Louise's internal operating systems were in fine shape and were serving her well.

All except one. Her cerebral function. The one that provided her smile, her laugh, her insight, and her warm and caring personality. The primary bodily function that provided those aspects of her being and persona that enticed me to love her, and to care for her, did not work. Mary Louise's mind was the most important segment of her anatomy, the part that produced her magnetic aura which, like an ancient siren, drew me to the chair by her bedside day after day. That pulled my hand into hers and kept me waiting for an undeniable sign that she in fact knew I was with her.

As of yet, my affections for her had been physiologically unrequited.

Gina Genardo came on duty early Thursday, having been off for the past three days. She was more quiet than usual. I didn't know if that's because she was more rested after some well-deserved time off, or if there was trouble in paradise—assuming that would adequately describe her home life—or if she was hesitant to express her feelings to me after her encounter last Sunday with Susan Beeson.

I wanted to ask Gina about Frank James and determine if she had seen him, but I decided to let her warm back up to me a bit first. Our relationship may have no longer been as spontaneous as it was when Mary Louise first arrived in NIC a week ago, now that Gina knew that Mary Louise's best friend was the homicide detective assigned to investigate the murder of Gina's former lover's wife. But I wanted to know how my friend Frank was handling the burden of being a murder suspect, and I was curious if Gina could shed light on the subject.

When I arrived in NIC on this day, Thursday, and encountered Gina, she was adamant about my returning her beeper, the one she loaned me last Sunday before I left to spend the day with Susan Beeson, the one I had forgotten to bring with me today. She insisted

I bring it back to NIC this evening if my return occurred prior to the shift change. If not, she instructed me to, without fail, return it to her first thing Friday morning. Her paranoia over a simple pager piqued my natural curiosity and almost commanded me to pull up those four retained messages I noted on Sunday, sitting in Frank's backyard, and jot down the designated telephone numbers.

Frank had shown up for his meeting at Susan's office on Monday afternoon, the purpose of which was to obtain a blood sample to ascertain the identity of the father of Meredith's unborn child. Susan told me last evening that the preliminary blood tests indicated that Frank's blood type was *not* compatible with the six-week fetus found inside Meredith James. That fact would be consistent with Frank's story, which continued to be that he and Meredith had not enjoyed a sexual relationship since their separation. Whether or not this revelation made Frank a better or a worse suspect, I did not know. That would depend on whether or not he had known she had been intimate with someone else, and what his response to that discovery would be. Capt. Sam Polk called it the *J* factor: jealousy, and all that the concept implied.

As far as my schedule was concerned, I tried to assist with Susan's investigation into Meredith James's murder with an intense study of the entry logs from Memorial Bend. That had turned out to be a major project, filling the days between my morning and evening visits to the hospital.

There were over 18,000 entries in the myriad logs dating back over the past six months. This number represented an average of five entries per day for each of the twenty residents. That was almost 100 per day, 3000 per month, and so on. Much of the writing was scribbled in security-guard hieroglyphic, so it had taken quite a bit of time to decipher the name of a particular visitor, the representative company when applicable, the make and model of vehicle, and the license plate number. I had carefully and systematically made a separate list of the entries to the Jameses' home as I went along, so that eventually, once I entered that data into a computer, anyone who was interested could go back through the list and try to make some sense of it. The job was, however, tedious and time consuming.

I believed this work was important for two reasons. One, it kept my mind somewhat focused on a problem besides my comatose wife, for whom I had been able to do absolutely nothing. And two, it freed up Susan and the two additional detectives Sam Polk assigned to the case to check out other leads, although they seemed to be scant at that time except for the typical crackpot calls induced by the $100,000 reward offering that had been splattered about the newspaper and television. Unfortunately, the HPD professionals had other cases on their respective dockets, so not a single detective could focus all of their valuable time on the James case alone.

My own apartment had become too depressing in Mary Louise's absence, so I opted to work at Susan's West University home. Gene, her husband, wasn't due back until late Friday. He had been in Dallas for the week at an accounting seminar, learning new IRS rules. Better him than me.

So, Susan gave me a key to come and go as I pleased. The logs I was working on were far too bulky to haul around town, and I didn't want to think about the repercussions I might have faced if they were misplaced. So, all in all, it was safer, easier, and more reliable to review them at the Beeson house.

Gene Beeson was a good man and a good provider. He worked as an in-house accountant for Coastal States Gas and Pipeline Corporation. Some years prior, he decided to go to school at night and on the weekends, and after two years, he finally obtained his MBA from the University of Houston. The CFO at Coastal made Gene senior accountant soon after he received the advanced degree and, from what Susan told me, was grooming Gene to replace him in a couple of years.

The fact that Susan also earned an ample income as a detective lieutenant with the Houston Police Department allowed them to buy a nicely refurbished home in West University Place, an incorporated community within the city limits of Houston. It was convenient to downtown and the University Medical Center, close to her office in the Southwest part of town, and only ten minutes from Gene's office in a high-rise building in Greenway Plaza adjacent to the Summit, home of the NBA Champions two years running, the Houston Rockets. Sure, it had been a few years since then, but we hadn't forgotten.

West U was full of restored and new two-story homes on small lots and was chock full of children. The community boasted excellent neighborhood schools, convenient shopping centers, and a reliable police force. The Beesons probably could have afforded a much larger house in the suburbs, but living in the center of this sprawling city of five million was well worth sacrificing a thousand or so square feet of living space, or so Susan told me.

Gene Jr. was also out of town this week, visiting his father's parents in Dallas. My decision to work at the Beeson home was also influenced by the two-year-old's absence.

It took me almost three full days, from Monday evening to Thursday afternoon, to generate a list of entries to Frank and Meredith James's home over the past six months. The list was staggering, even with the other nineteen residences eliminated. I had been working in Susan's study and it was a wreck, resembling the aftermath of a paper hurricane, with debris scattered helter-skelter. My plan was to enter all the data into Susan's computer, make a hard copy, then activate the modem and transfer the information to her office computer so that she, Sam Polk, and the other detectives assigned to the case could access this data from the Southwest Substation.

Over 750 entries were logged in for the James residence since Meredith and Frank separated in October of last year. I divided them as best I could into logical groupings. There were over 150 deliveries associated with sustenance, including restaurants, grocery stores, and liquor stores. Meredith had over 180 service calls. These included weekly landscape maintenance and pool service company visits, Houston Lighting and Power, Entex Gas Company, Warner Cable, Southwestern Bell, Action Alarm, Cody's Appliances, and Denny's Electric, just to name a few. Of course, Susan and her colleagues would have to check to see if the individuals representing those various companies were actually who they said they were. That alone would be a monumental task.

The largest segment of entries appeared, at least on the surface, to be social calls. There were 358 of those, an average of two a day. Looking at the times the visits were logged in, there seemed to be a pattern. Meredith usually had a visitor in the afternoon, and another in the evening. Afternoon visits were usually associated with a female name, evening visits with a male name. There were exceptions, of course, but that was the trend. And there were repetitive callers, such as Myra McCann, who, according to Melvin Brown, was Meredith's best friend. She had been out of town since the funeral and unavailable for questioning. According to her housekeeper, Mrs. McCann was due back Thursday evening. Susan had given me the dubious assignment of talking to Mrs. McCann in order to glean the name of the man most likely to have fertilized Meredith's egg. I had no idea what my qualifications for this job were, other than I was available.

As I was sitting there in Susan's study, trying to stretch a cramp out of my lower back, typing as detailed a list as I could into Susan's Mac, I was frustrated by a few entries where the name, car make, or model was undecipherable. Also, a series of entries struck me as odd. I didn't notice it the first time through, since I was too busy trying to decipher the entries and ferret out the callers to the James house. I realized there was a pattern for floral deliveries, which I then listed as a separate category. Meredith averaged one delivery per week during October, November, and December, which seemed logical to me. Having fresh flowers delivered weekly was, I thought, a luxury, but an event I expected a woman would enjoy. Mary Louise had done that for years, and I had come to enjoy fresh sprays as much as she.

And although there was a smattering of increased entries for floral deliveries in late December, that would correspond to the Christmas season, a time when, again, I would expect an increase in household flora. Holiday wreaths, evergreens, holly, poinsettias, mistletoe, and the like for the festive season.

But in January and February, I noticed a daily entry into Memorial Bend for Chic Stems, an upscale plant house in the River Oaks area. Most of the sixty entries listed the same driver, and for two months, Monday through Saturday, Meredith James had flowers delivered. That implied some type of meaningful relationship to me. I inserted an asterisk next to these entries and made a note for Susan to check out Chic Stems and find out who had been sending those flowers to Meredith.

As I looked back at the long list of visits I had labeled as "social calls," I saw that I had enumerated about a dozen female names. Myra McCann was the most prominent of these as far as frequency. Female visits occurred mostly during the day and only occasionally at night. Usually, when there was an evening entry associated with a female name, there were several others as well. Logically, this could have represented a dinner party or a fundraiser of some sort. I didn't remember if Meredith played bridge, but I wasn't sure the issue was all that important.

It seemed to me—and this was surprising, although it probably shouldn't have been—that Meredith had more than her fair share of male callers. In October, November, December, and March, on the average of three or four per week. There were numerous names, thirty or so, but none ever appeared more than two or three times. She apparently was being escorted out on the town frequently, which, for a relatively young, wealthy, and beautiful single Houston woman, would be normal.

However, the January and February logs revealed a different story. One man's name appeared almost exclusively during those two months, and on numerous occasions. In fact, he visited daily, usually in the evening, but occasionally in the late afternoon. This definitely appeared to be some sort of relationship to me, and the man's frequent visits appeared to coincide with the daily floral deliveries. I highlighted the name, the license plate number, and the make of car.

He drove a Mercedes, or at least I assumed so, since the make of car was abbreviated to "Merz" by the various security guards that granted him entry. The logs listed the man's name as Foster Grant.

The name seemed very familiar to me, until I realized that the moniker was also a brand of fashion eyewear, sunglasses in fact. The name struck me as odd, but then, Jim Bob might be considered an unusual name by folks who lived north.

I couldn't help but feel some sadness over the last entry in the log book. Meredith's final visitor was her husband, Dr. Frank James, who entered Memorial Bend at 1:55 p.m. on Wednesday of last week. His entry was logged in by Security Guard William Moorehouse, who dutifully wrote down Frank's auto's make and model— a 733i BMW, Frank's precious "Beamer"—but in the column for the license plate number, a line was drawn; he did not record the license plate number. This probably represented a meaningless omission, but I highlighted it for Susan anyway.

One never knows, does one?

CHAPTER 31

MYRA

Thursday, April 12, 2001

It was a little after 5 p.m. on Thursday afternoon when I pulled into the cobblestoned drive outside the front entrance to the Huntingdon, a luxury high-rise condominium on Kirby Drive, in the heart of River Oaks. The uniformed valet waved me under the elaborately appointed portico, opened the door to my sleek black Chevrolet Silverado, and asked me to check in with security in the lobby.

Another uniformed man at a large semicircular security desk asked me my business and invited me to sit while he called upstairs to the residence of Ms. Myra McCann. I made myself comfortable in the spacious lobby by sitting on a soft, bulky orange-and-yellow chintz sofa, staring at the frescoed twenty-foot-high ceiling, and admiring the thick, convoluted moldings that embellished each doorway.

After a few moments, the host—this place was more like a hotel than an apartment building—accompanied me to the elevator bank. Once the faux-wood door opened, he inserted a silver key into a slot adjacent to the thirty-second floor button and bid me a good day.

I was somewhat surprised when the elevator door opened directly into the foyer of a beautifully appointed apartment. A gorgeous woman was standing in the entry as I stepped off the elevator.

"Dr. Brady, I presume," she said, extending her hand.

"Yes. Pleasure to meet you," I responded, my voice cracking.

"The pleasure is mine, Doctor. Come this way."

Myra McCann was a tall woman, about five foot nine. Her skin was pale, not particularly unhealthy but a distinct alabaster shade. She had long, thin fingers with immaculate French-manicured nails. She was dressed in black. Black silk slacks and black three-inch spike heels, with a touch of bare white skin showing beneath her tailored pants. She had on a halter top, cut low, with cleavage that looked to have been artfully constructed with plastic surgery. Around her neck was a thick hammered gold choker, probably 18 karat. Her hair was platinum blond, coiffured into a teased configuration that Rod Stewart would be proud to wear.

I followed her into her living room and couldn't help but notice her hips, buttocks, and legs as she sashayed in front of me. She walked with a fluid motion, practiced and artful. Seductive. Sensual. Powerful. Her lower extremities remind me of ZZ Top's song "Legs."

I felt an urge to run like hell in the opposite direction.

"Cocktail?" she said, glancing at her Rolex watch, complete with diamond face and bezel and a diamond-studded band.

I looked at my sport watch with the worn leather band and clasped my hands behind my back. "Sure. Scotch?"

"You look like a single-malt man. I have the Glens—Glenlivet, Glenfiddich, Glenmorangie—and some stellar Macallan. How about a twenty-five year?"

"Sounds great."

A woman with a figure like Myra's and a bar stocked with twenty-five-year-old single-malt Macallan scotch should have to wear a warning sign, such as THIS WOMAN MAY BE HAZARDOUS TO YOUR HEALTH.

"Please, have a seat. I'll bring your drink to you."

I left her standing at the mahogany walk-in bar, which was covered with crystal decanters of all shapes and sizes, and moved into the main seating area. I walked over to the center wall, composed of floor-to-ceiling windows and revealing a spectacular view of downtown Houston. I headed to an unusual brown-and-white cowhide chair whose arms and legs were formed from Texas longhorns, and sat. It was extraordinarily comfortable.

In the background, I recognized the jazz piano wizardry of Alex Bugnon. There was a fine G. Harvey painting on the wall opposite the chair I was sitting in. I stood and walked over to looked at the brass plate on the lower half of the frame. The oil was entitled *Men of the American West* and appeared to be an original. On my way back to sit on Bevo's grandpa, Bevo being the University of Texas longhorn steer mascot, I noted a number of Oriental vases and Waterford crystal pieces scattered about on various pedestals and polished wooden tables. From the comment that Melvin Brown made to me on Sunday about this place costing two million dollars, and from the looks of the artwork and accessories, it appeared that Ms. McCann was quite well-to-do.

"You single-malt scotch drinkers normally like it on the rocks. I hope that's okay," she said, and handed me a deep amber liquid in a heavy crystal old-fashioned glass.

"Perfect. Thanks again."

She settled down into an adjacent chair, one of beige leather with wooden feet shaped like tiger's paws. She was drinking a clear liquid on the rocks, vodka I presumed, in a stem glass with crushed ice.

"Nice place, Myra. Have you lived here long?" I asked, trying to make small talk before the nature of my mission became apparent.

"Three years. Jack—he was my husband but died of heart trouble last year—bought this place so that I would feel safe in the city. He traveled quite a bit in his business. Oil and gas. He didn't want to worry about me coming and going from a house alone, with all the risks that implies, when he was out of town. So, he bought this place for me soon after we married, which was less than four years ago. It was his second marriage, my third."

Myra seemed to have little trouble opening up to strangers.

She sipped her drink and stared at me. "You know, when you called and left that message on my answering machine, I thought about ignoring it. I mean, I don't know you from Adam, and I can't possibly imagine why you would like to talk to me about Meredith. I know your wife—at least I've met her—and I've heard Meredith and Frank mention your name, but other than that, I don't know anything about you. And by the way, I was very sorry to hear about Mary Louise. How is she?"

"About the same. Still in the coma. It's been seven days now. She was injured last Wednesday, the same day Meredith was murdered. She seems to be recovering from her other injuries, but, well, she had quite a bit of damage to her brain in the accident. The neurosurgeon that operated on her will not give me much of a prognosis. He's promoting a wait-and-see attitude."

"Who was it? The surgeon, I mean?"

"George Flanagan."

She shook her head. "One of Frank's partners. It's all so tragic, Meredith's murder and your wife's accident, all in the same day."

"Yes, it is."

"So, Dr. Brady—or is it all right if I call you James?"

"Jim is fine."

"Okay, Jim. So why did you want to see me? You mentioned something about Meredith on the phone?"

"Yes. To make a long story short, I have taken this past week off. My wife's accident has put me in a frame of mind that is not conducive to taking care of patients. One of Mary Louise's best friends is Lt. Susan Beeson, a detective with HPD. She is the officer who is spearheading the investigation into both Meredith's murder and my wife's accident. She's taken me under her wing for the week, which keeps me occupied, and at the same time allows me to do some leg work for her. The department is very shorthanded, you know."

"So, you're sort of playing detective?"

"Well, not really. Let's just say I'm helping the detectives out. Your name came up when I talked to Meredith's father about her close friends, so Susan Beeson asked if I would mind coming over and talking to you about Meredith's activities in the past six months."

She smiled, then laughed. "Want another drink?"

"No, I'm still nursing this one. Great scotch."

"Should be, for $195 a bottle," she said, as she stood and slithered to the bar to freshen her glass.

"So, what do you want to know?" she asked from across the room.

"Was she seeing anyone in particular during the past six months?"

"She saw a lot of people. You mean, like men?"

"Yes," I smiled.

"You think a former or current lover might have killed her?"

"I don't know, Myra. That's for the police to determine. I'm just checking out some names the police have gathered, and I thought you might be able to shed some light on these people."

"What *people?*" she replied, and accentuated the word, almost to the point of making it an expletive.

"Well, I don't pretend to know all the men she was seeing, but I have at least a partial list." She returned to her chair, so I handed her a chronological listing of the men whose names appeared as visitors to the James residence in the entry logs from Memorial Bend over the past six months.

She scanned the list, nodded occasionally. She made an awful face. "He was a creep. Number eight. Rustin. What are these numbers out to the side?"

"The number of times that they called on Meredith at her home."

"I see. Rustin has a 'one' by his name. Thought it might be a ranking of some sort. A 'one out of ten' would fit Rustin perfectly."

"Anything you can tell me about these individuals would be helpful. The detectives assigned to the case will be talking to each and every one, I'm sure. I'm just asking you to render a personal opinion."

"This list looks long. Our little Meredith was busy, wasn't she? Must be thirty names here."

"Twenty-nine, I believe."

"I don't know all these guys, but the ones I do, I'll put little notes by their name. 'Creep' for Rustin. Let's see, 'Hunk' for Bowers. 'Great fuck' by Stone." She looked up at me, I guess to check out my reaction. "I dated him, too. That's personal knowledge, Jim. I fixed her up with Stone. At the time, I thought she needed a little . . . diversion, if you know what I mean?"

I nodded, gave her a polite smile. "Any names you can help with will be appreciated."

She continued down the list, smiling at some names, laughing at others. At one point she looked up at me, stuck her Montblanc pen partway into her open mouth. I expected that 'Regurgitate' would go by that man's name.

As she neared the bottom of the list, she stopped, stared, and gave me a questioning look. "Foster Grant? Is that a joke?"

"That's the most prominent name on the list, in terms of sheer numbers."

"Sixty-two visits? That's how many times he came over to her house?" she asked incredulously.

"Yep. According to the security records. Why, do you know him?"

"No. Meredith kept him a secret. At first, I thought she just wanted him all to herself and was afraid that once he laid eyes on me . . . well, you know how it is."

"Not really. I've been married to the same woman for thirty years."

"Well, Jim, fact of the matter is that there are few good men out there, so we girls have to share them from time to time, if you get my drift. But if one of us finds a man that might be a keeper, we sequester him off to ourselves, to keep our friends' hands off until he's bitten the hook and can't shake loose."

She had an animated look and a sparkle in her bright blue eyes.

"Sounds sort of like fishing."

"Exactly, Jim. Us single girls are out there trolling constantly, throwing out different kinds of bait, seeing who will bite what. I suspect our girl Meredith was either throwing out some heavy bait, keeping the man sequestered, or . . ."

"Or what?"

"Or he was married, in which case the happy couple couldn't be seen in public. I mean, Meredith and Frank were formally separated, so it was no big deal for her to be seen about town. However, if this man, this Mr. Grant, was still married, and not formally separated, he would more than likely want to play 'Slam-the-Salami' in private. You get my drift?"

That was the second time in a week I had heard a Houston woman relate sexual play to processed porcine meat. Gina was the other, when she referred to her affair with Frank James, and termed it playing "Hide the Weenie." Maybe pigs were a horny lot.

"So, as good of friends as you two were, you never even met the man?"

"No. I knew she was seeing someone, but she was very discreet about it. I caught a glimpse of him once, in the Galleria area, on Westheimer, I think. I saw Meredith's car, and I pulled up beside her to wave—she was driving—and I saw this man in her passenger seat. Meredith waved and sped ahead, so I couldn't tell you what he looked like. Tinted windows, you know," she said, and shrugged.

"From what I've learned from the logs, Myra, it seems that she saw this man intensely for two months, in January and February, and then it was over. By March, and during the beginning of April, she was dating other people again."

"I'd say that's about right. When she quit seeing the guy, she still wouldn't tell me about him. It was a big mystery. I will tell you one thing, though. This name? Foster Grant? That is a brand name for sunglasses. I doubt very seriously that's his real name, which makes me think that he was probably married, which would explain all the secrecy."

"And that maybe after a two-month fling, he decided to go back to his wife?"

"You bet, Jim. Most men do. No matter how hot the sex is, no matter how exciting it is to fuck around on the old lady, most men go back to the safe environment. Dinner at six, helping kids with their homework, and no blow jobs. Go figure."

I nodded as though I understood what she had just told me. "One more thing I'd like to ask, Myra. When Meredith's autopsy was performed, the pathologist discovered a six-week fetus. Did you know anything about that?"

Myra's mouth fell open. Her look of shock gave me my answer.

"I can't believe it. She's always been so careful. I wonder . . ."

"Wonder what?"

"Well, Frank and Meredith never had any children. They went through fertility studies, hormone therapy, the whole ball of wax. Frank checked out okay, so they always thought it was Meredith's problem. She even had several unsuccessful attempts at in vitro fertilization. Looks like they were wrong, which makes me think . . ." she said, then stood abruptly, and went back to the bar. Being a gentleman, I followed.

"What?"

"Don't you see? If she gets pregnant, that's good for her marriage. Maybe Meredith thought that if she played her cards right, she and Frank could get back together, and he would never be the wiser about the pregnancy. She was so excited about that lunch date with Frank last week. I'll bet she was going to get him in the sack, effect a reconciliation, then pretend he was the father when she started to show. The baby might be a few weeks early, but it happens all the time. I'll be damned," she said, and gulped a fresh drink, sans ice.

"I don't imagine you'd know what doctor she was seeing, would you?"

"Hell, yes, I know. We've been going to the same man for, I don't know, twenty years. Dr. Leon Weekley at Women's Hospital."

I jotted the name down. "Well, you've been very helpful Myra. I'd better go."

"You don't want to stay and have another drink with me?" she purred.

"Sorry. I need to get up to the hospital, see how Mary Louise is," I muttered, and quickly swallowed the last few drops of my delectable scotch. I set my glass down on the counter and turned to leave, when Myra came from behind the bar in a flash and wedged her spike heels between my boots. Her breath was hot and close and smelled of alcohol. Her mouth parted slightly, and she slowly licked her lips. And, if I had been of a mind to, I'm sure she would have taken me in her arms and given me a ride for my life.

"Myra, I—"

She put her arms around my neck. "Jim, your wife has been in a coma for a week now. You are a healthy, virile man, and I know you have feelings. Strong feelings. Feelings you should not keep to yourself. It's not good for you to be all . . . pent up."

She gently thrust her pelvis against me and moved it from side to side. I tried to think of horrible and painful personal tragedies, like maybe a sharp stick in my eye, or a compound thumb fracture, or a hemorrhoid operation, but Mr. Happy had a mind of his own. I felt him engorge with blood, despite the fact I was yelling to him silently to mind his own damn business. This was the wrong woman, don't you know that, you idiot?

"See? You like me, don't you?" she whispered, pulled me to her harder, and enveloped my closed mouth with her large, pouting, red lips.

I grasped her shoulders and literally had to shove her away. "Please, Myra."

She looked hurt, then angry, then laughed. "Never hurts to try, Brady," she said, and she straightened her trousers and walked toward the foyer.

We waited in silence at the elevator. When the door opened, I stepped in and turned around to face her.

"Thanks again for your help."

"No problem. And if you change your mind, give me a call," she said, and winked.

As the elevator door closed, I saw her delicate fingers catch the rubber matting, and the door sprung back open.

"What?" I said, fearing she would attack me in the elevator, knowing as she did that my resistance was already down.

"The guy you're interested in? Foster Grant? I'm just drunk enough to tell you that I know his real name, but not drunk enough to tell you what it is. Now, if you want to hang around, or come back and visit me some other time, maybe I'll share it with you. Until then, you and your detective friends will just have to figure it out some other way."

She smiled, laughed, and waved as the elevator door closed in my face.

I had no intention of going back there, so some other way it would have to be.

PART 3

CHAPTER 32

THEORIES

Thursday, April 12, 2001

As I sped away from Myra McCann's, I phoned Lt. Susan Beeson on her cellular. For some reason she was unavailable, according to the computerized voice, which I found puzzling, since the portable phone was with her at all times. I then called her home and left a message that I had completed the entry log analysis and had seen the McCann woman, and I asked if she would like to discuss some most interesting information over dinner.

I then called J. J., who had been silent for days. I had left messages at his office and at his apartment but had yet to receive a return phone call. According to Susan, he had been working feverishly with HPD's auto techs, trying to trace paint, chrome, and glass residues from the assailant's vehicle that were scraped from his mother's Jeep or retrieved from the scene of the accident. He was indefatigable with respect to his investigative work, but on occasion, when he homed in on a particularly intriguing subject, for whatever reason, he lost all track of time and space. I suspected this was one of those times. I left another a message for him, this time at his apartment, since it was close to six thirty in the evening. I told him I would like to hear an update on his progress and that he could probably find me at the

Beeson home later in the evening, and I invited him to join Susan and me for a late supper.

I parked the truck in my assigned spot in the subbasement parking garage of University Tower. I had paid for this space for over twenty years, but it seemed alien to me. I took the elevator up to the second-floor sky bridge, a fancy name for a covered crosswalk that provided access to University's medical school, three office towers, and five hospitals. After an almost three-block walk, I weaved my way into the Fondren Building, whose Neurosensory Center housed NIC on the eleventh floor. While I was waiting for the interminably slow elevator to arrive, I overheard a heated conversation between two people, a man and a woman. Being the naturally curious sort, I stepped to the end of the elevator bank and peered around the corner into an alcove with public restrooms, telephones, and a water fountain.

Nurse Gina Genardo and Dr. Frank James seemed oblivious to the presence of visitors and hospital staff until they caught me staring at them from the elevator lobby. As they cut their eyes toward me simultaneously, I noticed that Gina was crying, her black ponytail in disarray, and that Frank was red-faced and angry. They both stared at me for a moment, each of us thinking our private thoughts. Gina was wearing scrubs, as usual, but carried her purse and a lightweight jacket on one arm. I assumed she was off duty and headed home. As she wiped her eyes with a tissue and turned back to Frank, the bright fluorescent lights in the nook caught the glint of a stone at base of her throat, a diamond the size of Rhode Island.

Fortunately, the elevator car arrived before Gina could once again harass me about the borrowed beeper, which remained at my apartment. I boarded my ride and wondered if she was still in love with Frank and was trying to entice him to start seeing her again. I was also curious about the necklace Gina wore, whether it was a gift from Frank or perhaps a birthday or graduation gift from her heart-surgeon father. One thing I was sure about was that her humble cardiologist-in-training husband could not have afforded such an item.

Once I arrived in NIC, I placed my chair in its usual position by Mary Louise's bedside. Visiting hours hadn't begun yet, so the place was quiet. The bed adjacent to Mary Louise's right was empty once again, which allowed me more room than normal. To her left was an elderly woman with IV lines in both arms, on a respirator, with a white blood-stained turban around her head. My guess was that the new admission had a brain tumor removed, and I hoped for her sake the lesion was benign.

I told Mary Louise about my discovery of Meredith's presumed suitor, Foster Grant, and included a brief summary of my encounter with Myra McCann. In my wife's normal state, she might have gone ballistic over my description of an event such as the one I experienced this afternoon. In her current state, though, it didn't seem to bother her at all. She seemed happy just to hear my voice.

I sat patiently with Mary Louise for the next hour and a half, talking softly to her while I held her hand, until a major wave of visitors invaded what I had come to consider my space. I kissed her chapped lips gently and told her goodbye. There had been no noticeable repetition of the hand movement I felt the previous Sunday. I sadly left the unit, disappointed yet again that her mental status remained the same. She continued to be in a coma, despite my efforts to arouse her conversational instincts. I wondered how long she would remain in the vegetative state.

"Thanks for picking up dinner from the Grotto, Jim Bob. I was about to pass out from hunger."

"Starvation is an ugly way to die, Susan. I called the maître d' and occasional chef, Reuben, from the car and told him that you and

I would be researching Mary Louise's accident tonight. He loves her dearly and said that preparing dinner for the detective working on her case was the least he could do. Reuben would not let me pay for dinner. He even threw in this bottle of Pinot Grigio. He said the wine will relax you and allow your mind to think more clearly."

Susan smiled. "It's wonderful."

We were sitting in Susan's dining room across from each other at an antique table that seated ten. Aluminum tins of fresh Italian cuisine were scattered on the ancient oak surface and included Veal Milanese, linguine with clam sauce, Sicilian salad with artichokes, thick-crusted Italian bread soaked in a light olive oil, and fresh cannoli for dessert. Reuben made the best cannoli I had ever tasted. In fact, it was so delicious that he often wouldn't sell the pastries and kept them for himself. I was sure his need for a size 50 belt represented an endocrine aberration and had nothing to do with a predilection for his own desserts.

Susan stared to the side of me, chewing an artichoke silently. I turned around and saw pictures of her immediate family on a sideboard table.

"Miss them?"

"Yes, mostly when I'm in bed. I never thought I would say this, but I miss the noise. Gene sleeps facing me, with his mouth open, and snores constantly. He could sleep through a hurricane. We start out with Gene Jr. in his bed, but during the night he gets scared, starts crying, and I go get him. He usually ends up lying between us, sprawled all over his dad. When I wake up, he usually has his arms around Gene's head, and a foot over his back, almost to the point of smothering his father, much like a cat might suck the breath out of a child in a fairy tale. He is only five years old, and he's already starting to snore like his father. But I must love it, because I miss them both terribly. I can't imagine the loss you're feeling, Jim Bob. I know, God willing, that my husband and son will be safely home tomorrow. But with Mary Louise . . . I guess the waiting, and the uncertainty of it all, is the worst part."

I felt my eyes start to tear. I excused myself, walked outside, lit a cigarette, and glided to and fro on a wooden swing on the front porch. It was a pleasant night, with the temperature in the low 70s and a clear, unpolluted sky.

After a while I heard the screen door open and watched Susan pad onto the porch in fuzzy pink rabbit-ear house shoes and a thick pink terry-cloth robe.

"Sorry, but I needed to get comfortable. I'm glad Sam Polk isn't here to see these shoes," she said, and she sat down and handed me a cup of steaming black coffee.

We rocked back and forth in silence, watching as neighbors strolled their dogs for the last outing of the night. It was after nine and a school night, so the neighborhood, normally bustling with kid activity, was relatively quiet. The scene caused me to reminisce about Tip and our bedtime walks. I experienced a stab of guilt over my placement of him into a kennel, more than likely filled with ordinary, unintelligent canine companions. When Tip returned home, we would read some Shakespeare together.

"I didn't mean to hurt your feelings earlier, when I made that comment about Mary Louise."

"You didn't, Susan. What you said was true, it just reminded me of my . . . my feeling of . . . of being incomplete."

"Let's change the subject. We don't need to get morbid. Tell me about those entry logs from Memorial Bend. Did you finish the project?"

"Yes, finally. I've never seen service calls, deliveries, social calls, and the like documented on a list before, so maybe all households are subject to that volume of entries and exits. I entered the data relative to the James household into your Mac and printed you a hard copy. I intended to transfer the data to your office computer via modem, but I wasn't familiar enough with the process to do it quickly, and I ran out of time. Myra McCann insisted I be at her apartment no later than 5 p.m."

"I really appreciate your efforts. It saved me, what, three days?"

"Probably. I've worked on this list since Monday evening. There is an item I think you'll find interesting. I know it's late, but do you want to see it?"

"Yes, please," Susan responded, and took a sip of her coffee.

I went inside, gathered up the twenty-eight-page sheaf of papers from Susan's study, brought it back out to the porch, and gave her a brief rundown of the 750-odd entries listed as visiting Meredith James's home beginning the previous October, up to the last entry, that being Frank James's afternoon visit in the BMW the day of Meredith's murder.

Susan thumbed through the myriad of service calls, deliveries, and social visits, and looked at me with wonder in her eyes. "This is a staggering piece of work, Jim Bob. I can't believe the amount of time—"

"Don't worry about all those extraneous entries. It will take weeks, maybe months for your people to check out all the names on the list, and make sure people are who they said they were. I want you to look at the last few pages, where I've enumerated the male callers to Meredith's home. And pay particularly close attention to the intensity of Foster Grant's visits in January and February."

"Sixty-two visits?"

"That's right. And if you'll look back a few pages, under Floral Deliveries, you'll see that Chic Stems delivered flowers every day except Sunday during that two-month period he was seeing Meredith. I definitely think it represents an intense relationship between the two of them."

Susan flipped back and forth and saw the pattern that intrigued me when I compiled the data. "Foster Grant. The name sounds familiar. Who is he?"

"That was my initial reaction. I thought he was perhaps a local athlete, or a 'bold-faced type' from the gossip columns. But then it came to me. It's a brand name for fashion sunglasses."

"So, perhaps it's an alias? Or maybe a cruel parental joke?"

"My thoughts exactly, until my encounter with Meredith's friend Myra McCann at her apartment at the Huntingdon this afternoon. She was coy with me for a while, even 'rated' Meredith's suitors, as you can see on that separate list I had her review. Before I left, though, she as much as said that the name Foster Grant is an alias."

"Does she know his real name?"

"I couldn't tell for sure." And I honestly could not. Maybe Myra wanted to use me for her own private purposes, then discard me like a well-read newspaper and deny she knew anything about Foster Grant after all. I wasn't about to find out.

Susan didn't say much, except she started to shiver while she perused my list.

"Myra appeared to be surprised about Meredith's pregnancy and seemed to think that perhaps that was Meredith's compelling reason to reunite with her husband. Seems Meredith's inability to conceive was a point of contention in her and Frank's marriage for quite some time, could have still been, for all I know. Myra was able to give me Meredith's doctor's name, since they shared the same physician. He is Dr. Leon Weekley at Women's Hospital."

Susan was cold, so we moved inside, poured more coffee, then settled into the living room. She curled up on a thick-cushioned sofa in Zuni reds and blues—seemed both father and daughter had a penchant for Native American artifacts—put her feet under a throw pillow, and sipped her coffee. I chose a leather La-Z-Boy recliner, propped my size-12 lizards up on the elevated footrest, and relaxed.

"You want me to start a fire for you, Susan?"

She shook her head. "I'm going to have to go to bed before too long, and I don't like embers burning while I sleep."

I watched Susan set her coffee down, pull a wrinkled tissue from her robe pocket, and dab at her eyes. I wanted to tell her about Gina Genardo's affair with Frank James, which I had known about since Gina broke down in the University cafeteria during lunch last week on Friday, or maybe Saturday—those days were a blur—but I did not know if their relationship was relevant to the investigation of Meredith's murder. I probably should have allowed Susan to make that determination.

"Susan, are you all right?"

"Sorry. It's just that I have an oppressively large case load. The department is shorthanded, we have new assignments every day, and right now it's just too much. My first priority, professionally, is the Meredith James murder. It is, as you've heard all too often, a high-profile case. A prominent Houston citizen's only daughter is shot professional-style, in her own home. How did the shooter know to gain entry through the unlocked rear gate? Did the intruder know the victim? Was it personal? Was it revenge? Was it perhaps a hired hit? Or was it a robbery/rape gone sour?

"I've looked at this case intensely since Monday, and I'm going nowhere. The house was undisturbed, and there were no visible signs of assault, sexual or otherwise, on the victim. Thus far, we do not have a damn clue. Not a fingerprint, not a sprig of hair, not an article of clothing, not a footprint. Nothing. None of the neighbors saw anything, the few that were home that time of day. And that obnoxious security guard Moorehouse has been virtually worthless.

"We need a break in the case, and the only piece of worthwhile information available to the department thus far is what you have found in the entry logs, this Foster Grant person. And if that name is an alias, which presumably it is, and if this investigation continues in the same vein it has for the past week, we won't be able to discover his identity. First thing in the morning, I'll run his license plate number from off your list and see what I come up with. If the name Foster Grant is an alias, then the plate number is possibly bogus as well. Then, I'll have to go see Moorehouse again, try to get a physical description, and see how that pans out.

"And if all that isn't enough, there's the issue of Mary Louise and her assailant, my personal priority," she said. "We have been unable to come up with any worthwhile evidence that might lead us to the person or persons responsible for Mary Louise's injuries. It is one issue, Jim Bob, to run a yellow light and accidentally hit someone. That I could understand, forgive, even. But to leave the scene of an accident when you know you've hit someone hard enough to flip their car? Whoever it was should rot in hell, and I will do everything in my power to see that happens. But so far, even with our lab technicians and B&B Investigation's staff working round the clock, searching every database known to humanity, we don't have a damn thing."

Susan was angered by her rendition of this complicated scenario and pounded a fist on the lacquered pine coffee table in front of her.

She got up, retrieved another cup of coffee for herself, and sat back down. She immediately stood up and started to exit the room.

"Come into the study, Jim Bob. I want to show you something. I've got this crazy idea, and I need to share it with someone."

"I'm sorry about the mess in there. I didn't have a chance to clean—"

"Don't worry about it," she said, as she began rifling through the lap drawer of the desk I had used the past three days to analyze the Memorial Bend entry logs.

She unfolded an oversized map of the city of Houston and thumbtacked it to the only blank wall in the room.

"Meredith James's murder occurred here, at Memorial Bend, where Sage Road dead-ends, around two o'clock in the afternoon," she said, and she drew a big "2:00" and a red circle around it. "Mary Louise is run down here, at the intersection of Woodway and Post Oak Road, around two thirty," and drew a big "2:30" with a red circle around it as well.

I stared at the proximity of the two numbers. Susan stood in front of the map, red pen in hand, like a third-grade teacher. "Meredith James's murder occurred here," she said, and pointed at the "2" on Bayou Lane, a one-block street just west of Sage Road's dead-end into Buffalo Bayou, and about a mile north of Woodway. "Let's assume Meredith James's killer escaped detection by leaving the property through the backyard. We know for a fact that the back gate is always left open on Wednesday for refuse pickup. There is nothing behind Memorial Bend except woods and Buffalo Bayou. If the shooter was on foot but had a car someplace, where would it be? Close enough to run to, but in an out-of-the-way spot where it wouldn't draw attention, like maybe in a parking lot or something. And what's on the other side of the bayou? Memorial Drive. It flanks the bayou on the north and runs parallel to Woodway.

"Now, Mary Louise is injured here, at the corner of Woodway and Post Oak," she said, and pointed to the "2:30." "According to eye-witnesses, her assailant was heading due east on Woodway in a big hurry. That means the driver of the assaulting vehicle was coming from the west. But from where?"

Using the red pen, she traced a path starting at Memorial Bend, moved south along Sage Road until the pen came to Woodway. She then traced a line along Woodway, and went east, right to the "2:30," the intersection where Mary Louise's car was violently rammed and flipped onto the roof.

"Do you see what I'm getting at, Jim?"

"Yes, I think so. Your assumption here is that whoever killed Meredith James may have also run into Mary Louise's car?"

"Exactly."

"Huh. Like the preacher, Dr. Jones, said: an act of fate."

"What?"

"Never mind, Susan, I was just thinking out loud. You know, I can't decide if that's a ridiculous idea that defies logic, or if it's so simple that we're stupid not to have thought of it before."

"My sentiments exactly. But there is a fly in the ointment. There is approximately a thirty-minute time differential between the murder and Mary Louise's accident. It would only take a few minutes—five at the most, even in traffic—to drive the short distance between the two crime scenes. So how does one explain that?"

Before I could answer, she rifled through the desk again and came up with a ruler. She checked the mileage-per-inch scale on the map, then measured the distance between the two crime scenes in question.

"About 1.5 miles, via the most direct route. See the problem with timing?"

"Yes, but—"

"But now look at this," she said, and illustrated the pertinent streets with her red marker. "The only way to get to Woodway from Memorial Drive, in the vicinity of the Memorial Bend complex, is either Chimney Rock Road to the west, or Post Oak Road to the east. There are no other through streets running north to south in the vicinity, and Post Oak happens to be disjointed, and only a two-lane street in that neighborhood. Besides, the assaulting vehicle was coming from the west, on Woodway, and not south, down that narrow part of Post Oak. Of course, the 610 Loop is only another mile or so to the east, and you can get anywhere in the world from the Loop, since it goes all the way around the city. Now, if I had just killed someone, and I was in a big hurry, that would be the fastest exit off Memorial Drive. And I've thought to myself, time and time again, that this would have to have been the logical escape route. Of course, the killer could have gone west on Memorial Drive, wandered around the Memorial Villages, eventually connected with Interstate-10, and ended up in San Antonio.

"But if you think about it, my theory represents a reasonable assumption. A murder, a speeding getaway vehicle, and a hit-and-run accident. Two crime scenes, only 1.5 miles apart. But the timing is bad."

She chewed on the end of her pen and free associated.

"Unless . . . could it somehow take thirty minutes to get from Memorial Bend to the corner of Woodway and Post Oak? I think so. You have to figure the killer was on foot. After he kills Meredith, he runs out the back way, crosses the bayou, locates his car—which has to be far enough away not to arouse suspicion—travels west on Memorial to the first intersection, heads south on Chimney Rock, then back east on Woodway, runs the light at the corner of Post Oak, and plows right into Mary Louise."

She shook her head. "But then, I have a problem with my own theory, because that route would be unlikely, since I'm postulating the assailant made a complete circle before leaving the neighborhood. And that' a ridiculous concept."

A silence ensued. Then, it struck me. "Unless . . ."

"Unless what, Jim Bob?"

"That stretch of Memorial that corresponds to Memorial Bend's location, can you remember what's there, between, say, Chimney Rock Road and the 610 Loop?"

"Not offhand. Why?"

"You'll have to drive over there and see, because to take the route you've outlined, the killer would have had to park on the north side of Memorial Drive, head west, decide for some reason to turn south onto Chimney Rock, then turn east onto Woodway. If the car that hit Mary Louise had been parked on the south side of Memorial, the logical route would be to head east, and hit the 610 Loop, in which case Meredith's killer would have been nowhere near the corner of Woodway and Post Oak."

"Regardless of these various route theories, do you realize the implications here, Jim Bob? If Meredith's killer and Mary Louise's assailant could be one and the same, a whole new avenue of investigation is open to us. If our lab boys, with the help of J. J., can come up with a vehicle type based on those paint, chrome, and glass samples, then we may be able to work backward and retrieve a list of local owners of that make and model. If we then assume that the assailant's car sustained enough damage to require repair, and that the driver might have rented a car, we can possibly cross-check body shops and rental-car establishments with known local owners of the potential vehicle in question. And, if we get lucky, we might be able to take the information you've gleaned from the entry logs, combine that with clues Dr. Weekley and the management of Chic Stems may provide us, collate it with the vehicle type and corresponding body-shop and rental-car info, and possibly come up with a suspect. I have a feeling deep in the pit of my stomach that we're on to something, and I need to talk with Sam about it. Are you staying or going?"

"No way I'm leaving. All these assumptions, potentials, and possibilities are upsetting me to the point of indigestion. I think a cannoli might help, don't you?"

SAM POLK

Thursday, April 12, 2001

olk."

"Evening, Sam. I hope it's not too late to be calling."

"Susan?"

"Yes. Am I interrupting something?"

"I wish. Do you have me on speaker phone?"

"Yes. Jim Brady's here with me. We have some things to share with you, and I want him to be able to speak freely and hear what you have to say. Okay?"

"Sure. Let me get a beer," Sam said, as the receiver on his end clunked onto a hard surface.

"I hope we're not interrupting anything important," I said to Susan.

"I seriously doubt it. Sam is a forty-nine-year-old divorcé with three children, and he's a career police officer. He could have remarried, but he's reserving his devotion exclusively for his kids and the job.

"For the most part, Sam enjoys his freedom, the ability to come and go as he pleases, though he rarely exercises it. As far as sex is concerned, I doubt that's ever really been a problem for a man like him since his divorce. There should be plenty of women in this town who are attracted to tall, rugged cowboy versions of Dirty Harry."

"I hope he can't hear you, Susan."

"I'm not telling you anything I haven't said to Sam's face. Besides, there's so much racket in the background he probably couldn't hear a tornado blow through."

She took a sip of freshly brewed coffee. We moved back to the dining room table in order to spread out our reference material. At one end of the antique table was my compilation of the Memorial Bend entry log data, and at the other, the map of Houston illustrating the proximity of the two crime scenes in question. Susan's ubiquitous speakerphone lay between us.

"I'm sure he's saved quite a bit of money. His three-bedroom ranch-style house in the Sharpstown subdivision is probably paid for, and his tastes are moderate. His only real vice is Western boots, especially the exotic skins—lizard, anteater, crocodile, alligator. I don't know how many boots he has, but he wears a different pair almost every day. His favorite saying is, 'If I was married, I'd have two pair of bull hides, and she'd have jewelry and a Saks Fifth Avenue charge card.'"

"What's so damn important to call me at eleven o'clock at night?" Capt. Sam Polk thundered through the speaker.

"Sam, I can hardly hear you. What's that racket in the background?"

"ESPN. A rerun of the Daytona 500. Want me to shut it off?"

"Please," she said, and after a few seconds, the connection was clear.

"Better, Suze?"

"Yes, thank you. Listen, I've been ruminating these past few days about a possible connection between Meredith James's murder and Mary Louise Brady's accident. I've gone through my proposed scenario with Jim Bob, and he thinks it's logical and reasonable. Now I want to run it past you. What if—and just suppose, Sam, for the purposes of intelligent interchange—that whoever murdered Meredith James also ran down Mary Louise Brady's car?"

The phone was quiet for a few moments. "Now what in the world ever gave you that idea, Susan? Sounds far-fetched to me. Of course, maybe the good doctor there knows more about detective work than I do," he said, sarcastically.

I rolled my eyes, and Susan winked.

"Just listen for a minute, Sam. I've studied a map of the city repeatedly, and I think this is a reasonable possibility, at least one we need to check out. Look at a map, so you can follow my line of reasoning."

"Susan, I've been a cop in Houston for almost thirty years. I grew up in this town, and I know these city streets like the back of my hand. I can picture the layout of the city grids with my eyes closed. Now what's your point?"

Susan gave Sam Polk the scenario she had carefully worked out and shared with me, and explained to him in detail her reasoning for suspecting that Meredith James's murderer was also responsible for Mary Louise's hit-and-run.

"So, what do you think?"

I heard a long sigh through the slightly tinny speaker. "Tell you what, Suze, let me mull it over. We'll talk at the station house in the morning, say seven or seven-thirty. Bring the map you've been working on, if it will make you happy, we'll go over it together, and I'll let you know what I think. How's that?"

"That's fine, but I have more, and I want you to consider what I think might be the big picture. Jim Bob's spent the past three days going over these entry logs from A-1 Security, the ones for—"

"I know what he's been doing, Suze," he said, injecting a subtle amount of venom into his voice. "So?"

"Well, he's isolated the entries to Meredith James's home. Believe it or not, they amount to over 750 visits in the past six months."

"What?! That's close to, maybe five a day?"

"Yes, but it's typical for the complex. Some residents had more, if you can imagine that. When is the last time you received that many non-business phone calls in a day, much less five visits to your home?"

Sam was silent, so Susan continued. "Anyway, we'll have to waste an incredible amount of time checking into these various delivery and service people, making sure they are who they said they were, you know?"

"Yep. Happens every time we have a murder investigation."

"The most important point of all this, in my opinion, is that during January and February, Meredith James received flowers. A lot of flowers. Every day except Sunday, in fact. And during the same time frame, the same man's name recurs on the entry log, usually in the evening, but occasionally during the day, over sixty times."

"So? She had a boyfriend. She was a good-looking woman, Suze. Hell, I'd drive over there every day to see a face like that. Her corpse looked better than most of my dates."

Susan was unsuccessful in stifling a laugh. "Sam, you're a piece of work. Look, I'm not saying it's unusual for her to have a boyfriend. What is interesting is that the man's name is Foster Grant. Now, as the result of a conversation Jim Bob Brady had this afternoon with the deceased's best friend, a Ms. Myra McCann, we believe the man used an alias, but that's irrelevant in terms of this discussion. According to the entry logs at Memorial Bend, this man drives a Mercedes. There's no mention of color, of course, but we do have a license plate number on all the vehicles, including his."

"C'mon, Suze, it's late. Is there a point to all this gibberish?"

"The car that hit Mary Louise Brady was a black European sedan, type unknown. If my theory is correct, and the two crimes are linked, like I think they are, Foster Grant could be our first suspect."

"Good God, Susan, have you been drinking? Or has hanging out with Brady ruined your acumen for quality detective work? Meredith James was having an affair. So what? Interesting, but it doesn't prove anything. She was separated, you remember. And I'm sure if you start listing all the guys in town who could afford to take her out, you're going find a helluva lot of Mercedes, BMWs, all kinds of luxury cars, some of which will be black."

"I know, Sam. But don't you think it's strange? A suitor of Meredith James uses an alias, drives a Mercedes, which could possibly be black, sends flowers and visits Meredith James every day for two months. Then, the bouquets and the social calls abruptly stop, and less than six weeks later, Meredith James is murdered. If you combine those facts with reports of eyewitnesses at the scene of Mary Louise Brady's accident, who saw a black European car of some sort, and the geographical proximity of the crimes, I think we have a reasonable link. We could have our first suspect."

"Susan, maybe the guy is married and went back to his wife. Or maybe he simply tired of sweet little Meredith. Or maybe Mrs. James threw him out for some reason or another. Happens all the time, an intense romance, followed ultimately by intense hate. That's the classic definition of a marriage, in my opinion. Besides, how do you know it was Grant that sent those flowers?"

"I don't, Sam, but it's a reasonable assumption, since the deliveries occurred during the time when he was visiting daily."

"Did security at Memorial Bend note that Grant's Benz was black?"

She hesitates. "No, but it could be the car—"

"C'mon, Suze, that would be way too easy. The only man on the list that appears to have been having a prolonged affair with Meredith James decides to kill her, and on the way out of the neighborhood, runs into Brady's wife. You don't know what kind of vehicle hit Mrs. Brady, you don't know what color of Mercedes this Grant fellow had, hell, you don't even know the man's real name, or so you said. This isn't a daytime soap opera. Solving a murder just doesn't happen that way."

"Well, you're probably right. Anyway, I thought I would get Grant's address from the DMV—assuming we have the correct license plate number—go talk to him, get a feel for his story, maybe ask to see his car. It certainly can't hurt anything. Besides, as far as I know, it's the first potential break in the case. What do you think?"

"Fine. But even if you're lucky enough to find this Grant person, he probably won't let you look at his car, so you'll need a search warrant. To get one you'll have to show probable cause, and I personally think the DA will laugh in your face. I mean, really, what do you have to go on, other than the fact that he may have dated Meredith James for a couple of months, possibly sent her flowers, and drives a Mercedes? It sounds to me like you'll be wasting valuable time on a wild goose chase, and still be obliged to check out every name on that damn list. All 750 of them. And if you stop and think, Susan, and try to be objective, who's to say the shooter had ever been to the house before? From my vantage point, it looks like a professional hit. I still vote for the husband."

Susan was silent for a moment, then heaved a long sigh. "Leave no stone unturned, you always say, and you're the Homicide chief, so you must be the smart one," she said.

"Yeah, I'm a real smart dude. That's why I'm sitting here drinking beer alone on a Thursday night, talking to you. I'll see you tomorrow," he said, and hung up.

We stared at the silent phone for a moment.

"He didn't sound too excited, Susan. Maybe your theory is—"

"Far-fetched? What about bullshit? Or would absurd be a better description? I don't know for sure, but I'll say this. Denial is Sam Polk's initial reaction to any potential clue to a crime. If I know Sam, he'll ponder it for a couple of hours, startle himself out of a deep sleep several times during the night dreaming about it, awaken all fired up about it, and come into the office and somehow think it was his idea. Regardless, maybe we'll have our first potential lead."

Susan stood, stretched, and yawned. "I want you to go home and get some rest. Tomorrow, I want you to pay a visit to the proprietor of Chic Stems and try and wrangle the name of the guy who sent all those flowers to Meredith James. And if you have time, make an appointment with that gynecologist, Dr. Weekley, and see if you can glean any information about Meredith's pregnancy."

"Those are tasks for a detective, Susan. Don't you think—"

"We're extremely short of personnel, Jim Bob. You've been to florist shops before, and you know how to ask questions, so I don't see that you'll have a problem. If the management of Chic Stems gives you any trouble, call me. As far as the gynecologist is concerned, you're a doctor and a friend of the deceased, so there's no reason why he shouldn't talk to you. Don't worry, it'll be a breeze."

"I'm not so sure, but I'll do my best."

"And if you complete those two tasks and have any extra time, why don't you cruise the area of Memorial Drive along Buffalo Bayou, opposite the Memorial Bend complex, and search for a logical place for Meredith James's assailant to have parked a car. I'll do the same, and we'll compare notes later in the day."

"Okay. Listen, by any chance did J. J. call here and leave a message before I arrived?"

"No, why?"

"Oh, he hasn't returned my phone calls this week, so I'm a little worried. I invited him here tonight to share a Grotto dinner with us, thinking that would get a response out of him. I guess my feelings are hurt."

"He's been very busy, Jim, working around the clock with the lab techs in Auto, trying to identify the car that hit his mother. He's on a quest, just like you. Now you go home and get some rest. J. J. may have left a message on your recorder at home. Who knows, maybe you can talk him into going with you tomorrow while you check out leads for me."

Susan walked me to the front porch and hugged me goodbye. I hesitated at the head of the sidewalk.

"What?" she asked.

"There is something I've known for a week or so but haven't told you. It probably has nothing to do with Meredith's murder or Mary Louise's accident, but . . ."

"Jim Bob, I am so tired, I might just fall asleep against this column. If whatever you want to tell me has nothing to do with these two cases, it can wait until tomorrow. Call me after scoping out the flower shop and the doctor's office. Good night," she said, turned, and went inside.

At least I felt better, my guilty conscience for withholding potentially vital information quieted. If, when I finally got around to telling Susan about the love affair between Gina Genardo and Frank James, she became angry, I would simply dodge her bullets by reminding her that I tried to tell her several times but she was too tired or too busy.

I didn't like it when things were my fault.

CHAPTER 34

CHIC STEMS

Friday, April 13, 2001

"**S**o, where have you been all week, and why haven't you returned my calls?"

"Sorry, Dad. I've been completely immersed, working with HPD. You know how it is when I get started on an investigation."

"Your mother's still in ICU, J. J. I can't believe you haven't been to see her, as close as you two are."

"Dad! I just couldn't, okay? I can't stand seeing her like that. I'm not like you. I'm not used to blood and guts and that awful hospital smell. That's why I never had any interest in medicine. It's not my thing. And I especially couldn't stand to see Mom lying up there with that tube coming out of her throat and IV lines everywhere. I cannot think of her in that way. She's always been so beautiful, and kind, and smart. Seeing her lying there in a coma, it's just too much for me. Besides, nothing has changed since I was up there a week ago, or you would have told me. She doesn't even know you're there, Dad."

"You don't know that, J. J. She might be aware of her surroundings but unable to respond. You never can tell about coma patients. That's why I go there every morning and every evening, sit with her, hold her hand, and tell her about my day. Your mom knows all there is to know about the investigation of Meredith James's murder and her own assault, that's for sure. Besides, you told me yourself the day she was injured that you wanted to see her, that she would recognize your presence, even if she was unable to respond. Do you remember that conversation?"

"Yes, Dad, but I was wrong. And so are you."

"I may be, J. J., but I'd rather err on the side of too much visitation rather than too little, just in case."

My son and I were supposed to meet at NIC at University Hospital at eight o'clock in the morning. He finally returned my dinner-invitation phone message late last night and had agreed to spend the day with me. I suspected that after I left her house, Susan Beeson had called J. J. and encouraged him to accompany me on the day's scheduled rounds. My guess is that he had acquiesced primarily at her behest, rather than from an intense desire to spend time with his father.

I had spent my usual two hours or so with Mary Louise, from six to eight this morning, before visiting hours began. My son had agreed to join me, visit with his mother for a short time, and then spend the day with me. He was a no-show. Well, not really a no-show. When I came out of the NIC and passed through the waiting room on the way to the elevator, there he was.

In his defense, J. J. had always had a serious aversion to unpleasant situations involving the sick and dying, and especially the deceased. He had been to one funeral in his life, that of his favorite grandparent, and subsequently had refused to attend the memorial services of any of our relatives. He avoided funeral homes and hospitals at all costs, so his inability to visit his mother in her current state was understandable. My concern was that Mary Louise would think he didn't care about her, especially if her subconscious was more active than her comatose state would imply. But then, maybe I was way off base.

I made a special effort to write a note last night to remind myself to take Gina Genardo's beeper to NIC so she would quit hounding me. As luck would have it, she had called NIC early in the morning and told the nursing supervisor that she had to drive her Jesuit seminarian brother to the airport and wouldn't be in until eight thirty, thirty minutes after my departure. I considered leaving the beeper with Antoinette, the ward clerk, but thought better of it and, out of habit, clipped it to my belt. I did not want to be responsible for losing her pager. Why she was so intent on repossessing it, I could not figure out, especially since it's one of thousands issued by the hospital at no charge to either house staff or employees.

"What's our game plan, Dad? I mean, do you really need me today? There is a ton of work I could be doing at the office. The efforts of my firm are concentrated on finding Mom's assailant. Between my people and HPD's people, we've managed to retrieve some reasonably conclusive data, but at some point I need to assimilate the information and generate a report. I believe we're close to a breakthrough in the identification of the hit-and-run vehicle."

"Well, J. J., your presence with me is not absolutely necessary. I haven't seen you or talked to you in almost a week. I thought it would be nice if we could spend some time together. You know, like father and son?"

J. J. looked disheveled in his wrinkled khakis and a worn white cotton shirt with the sleeves rolled up, and, in his lap, a denim jacket. His blond hair was in its typical disarray, and one of his hiking boots was untied.

"Some quality time, huh, Dad?"

"If you want to call it that."

He hung his head. "It's hard to spend 'real' quality time with anyone right now, considering the condition Mom's in. You understand, don't you?"

"Yes. Look at me. I haven't been able to work at all this week, although, like it or not, I have to start back seeing patients and doing surgery on Monday, if I want to feed and clothe myself. I do understand. So," I said enthusiastically, "tell me about this potential breakthrough in your mother's case."

J. J. heaved an exasperated sigh. "I have a meeting with Susan later. I'd like to discuss our discoveries with her first."

I looked over at my son, at the set of his jaw and his pursed lips, and realized the futility of further attempts at conversation.

"Fine."

From University Hospital we wound past the Rice University campus and traveled north on Kirby to West Alabama, where we dined on taquitos stuffed with potatoes and cheese, omelets with chorizo, and flour tortillas laced with ranchero and green chili sauce at the Cortes Deli. Once sated, we washed that mixture down with diet sodas and continued our day of Quality Time and Togetherness. I wasn't exactly looking forward to spending the day cooped up in my pickup truck with a cranky twenty-seven-year-old kid who had his own successful business, drove a Porsche, and had the correct answer for every question.

My first stop was Chic Stems, a floral design and delivery establishment at the corner of Buffalo Speedway and Westheimer Road, in the heart of River Oaks, the most exclusive neighborhood in Houston. As I parked my truck in front of an enormous greenhouse adjacent to the main entrance, I was struck by the beauty and vibrant color of a sea of fresh flora. The impatiens were so bright, they appeared painted. The hibiscus were in full bloom, in deep shades of red, orange, and yellow. Purple and blue Mexican heather, huge budding yucca, and flowering cacti were abundant in large clay pots. How plants that needed a lot of water could flourish with desert shrubs and flowers under the same greenhouse roof was a mystery to me. That's why I was a surgeon and not a horticulturist.

"I'm going to talk to the proprietor about a former customer. You want to listen in, J. J., maybe learn the art of productive interrogation?" I said, with what I considered a good W. C. Fields imitation.

He shook his head. "I'd rather look at the plants," he said, and wandered off.

So much for Quality Time.

I strolled casually up to the central counter and waited behind a lady carrying calla lilies in green florist's paper. I waited until she was finished paying her bill, then I stepped forward.

"Morning. I'm Dr. Jim Brady. I need to check on some flowers that were delivered daily back in January and February of this year."

"Excuse, me, sir?" asked the light-brown-skinned man standing behind the counter. His name tag read Mohammed Akhbar. His nails were immaculate and manicured, and his white shirt was pristine. He was freshly shaven—I could smell the strong scent of a pungent aftershave—and had dark eyebrows and a black mustache.

"I'm sorry to bother you, but my cousin, Foster Grant, who lives in Santa Barbara, California, has a problem with his bill from your place of business, and he hasn't been able to call about it. Since I live here in Houston, he asked me to come by and check it out. You see, he stayed with me for a couple of months, met this woman, and started sending her flowers. And, well, you know, one thing led to another," I said, leaned forward, rested my elbows on the counter, and used a quiet, conspiratorial tone with Mohammed.

I smiled, tilted my head, raised my hands in a question.

Mr. Akhbar nodded, stared for a moment, then his face brightened. "Oh. A woman. A very special woman, I presume."

"Yes, indeed. He was extremely happy with your services and has no complaints whatsoever about any of the flower arrangements your firm prepared. In fact, he said your work is far superior to the average Southern California florist. He told me he paid all the bills, but he continues getting invoices at his home address in California, where his wife lives. You see the problem?"

Mohammed's face brightened with his recognition of the delicate situation.

"So, my cousin asked me to come by and check on his account for him. Can you help me?"

Mohammed relaxed, readied himself to solve this dilemma. "Sure. No problem, sir. What was the name again?"

"Foster Grant. He sent flowers to #8 Memorial Bend just about every day in—"

"Oh! Mr. Grant! I remember him! A wonderful man, simply marvelous, with an exquisite taste in flowers. That's odd," he said, and punched information into the keyboard of his computer. "I thought Mr. Grant had settled his bill."

He continued to enter data, letters, maybe numbers, since I couldn't tell from my side of the counter.

"I didn't know your cousin was from California."

I nodded in the affirmative.

After a moment, he stopped with the punching, stared at the screen. "I'm sorry, sir, but your cousin is receiving a bill incorrectly. In fact, I don't see how it's possible."

"What do you mean?"

"Well, look at this," he said, and turned the computer screen toward me. "He made his first order on January 3rd. He listed his address as Houston, Texas, and paid cash for the flowers. They were sent to, as you said, #8 Memorial Bend. No name was given as to whom the flowers were being sent, just that they were to be delivered the following day between ten and twelve, and then each and every day after for the next week. Except Sunday. Do you see?"

"Yes."

"Then, look here. Mr. Grant came in next on January 9, placed another order for various custom arrangements to be delivered daily for the week following. And he continued that until February 27, which was the last time he was in. So, he should not be receiving a bill. He paid cash, in advance, every week for two months. I cannot believe he is receiving a bill, because his address is not listed. If someone is paying with cash, we do not require an address. Privacy, you see, is very important in our business."

"Huh. That is very strange. I wonder why he's receiving those statements."

"Doctor . . . Brady, was it? I am here every day, rain or shine, just like the mail carrier, and I think I assisted Mr. Grant each time he visited our store. He was such a good customer, I often gave him a long-stemmed yellow or red rose as a gift for doing business with us. There is simply no way he can be receiving a bill. I am sorry he has returned to California. I would love to have him as a customer on a regular basis."

"Well, I'll give him that information. By the way, we are talking about the same Foster Grant, aren't we? I mean you don't have two in that computer, do you?"

He rechecked his screen, punched in more letters.

"Other Grants, Doctor, but only one Foster."

"Huh. You sure? About this tall," I said, and pointed about two inches above my head, "with black hair and a black mustache?"

"Of course not, sir. Mr. Grant is about this tall," he said, and leveled a hand at his shoulder level. "With red hair. And very muscular, sir. You should know that, if he is in fact your cousin."

Mohammed looked to be five foot ten, which would make Foster Grant a well-built, red-headed male, between five foot six and five foot eight inches tall.

A mental image appeared immediately of a man who only last night I saw with tight blue form-fitting scrubs, a long white coat, and slicked-back red hair. Foster Grant's description matches that of Dr. George Flanagan, the neurosurgeon who, only one week ago, sliced open my wife's skull. Surely he and Foster Grant were not one and the same. There must have been hundreds of short, red-haired, Houston males who . . .

Foster Grant. George Flanagan. Same initials but reversed. Both he and Frank James were neurosurgeons in the same group, so their wives would be participants in periodic medical functions. Could the Jameses and the Flanagans have been social friends? Flanagan worked out vehemently, and so did Meredith. I wonder if the similarities warranted—

"Sir? How can this be your cousin if . . ."

I nodded to Mr. Akhbar. "You know, maybe I have the wrong store. Thanks for your help."

CHAPTER 35

DR. WEEKLEY

Friday, April 13, 2001

"**W**here were you when I needed you?"

"For what, Dad?"

"To help me find out who was paying for flowers to be delivered to Meredith James's home in January and February."

J. J. looked at me from the passenger seat and stared forlornly. "Looking around. They had some nice bromeliads. They're Mom's favorite, you know."

I heaved a long sigh and shook my head. "You really are in the ozone layer, aren't you?"

He smiled, J. J.'s only sign of jocularity in the past week.

"If you don't feel your mother can hear you or comprehend your presence in the ICU, why would you be thinking about taking her flowers?"

He shrugged. "I have no intention of taking Mom flowers. I was just thinking about how your apartment is always full of fresh plants and blooming flowers. The place always smells so good. I miss that."

"It's really your mother's scent we miss, J. J. Her perfume, hair spray, and cosmetics, mixed in with her orchids and geraniums, and all those herbs she likes to grow—parsley, rosemary, thyme. She is responsible for everything: the fresh flowers, dinners with family and friends, trips to exotic places. We miss her presence because she makes life worth living."

J. J. sniffed and wiped his eyes with a wrinkled sleeve layered with caked dried matter.

I drove, in silence, south on Buffalo Speedway, past Holcombe Boulevard, back east on South Braeswood, and wound around until I located the Women's Hospital on Fannin Street, south of the University Medical Center. It was a squat, white, unremarkable three-story building housing the largest and most renowned group of obstetricians and gynecologists in Houston.

I pulled a parking stub from the automatic vendor, located a parking place, and led J. J. by his elbow into the functional, unobtrusive lobby. I located the office of Dr. Leon Weekley on the marquee, took the elevator, and wandered with my son through the maze of cubicles and waiting rooms until I found the doctor's receptionist on the third floor.

"Hello," I said to an attractive young woman with a name plate that read Margarita. "I'm Dr. Jim Brady, and this is my son, J. J. I have an appointment to see Dr. Weekley."

"Okay, surprise me. Which one of you is pregnant?"

"Excuse me?" I asked, somewhat incredulous. I was aware of non-traditional relationships, but . . .

"C'mon, guys. I saw that movie with DeVito and Schwarzenegger. It can happen. So fess up, which one of you is it? I bet it's you!" she said in J. J.'s direction.

He was smiling broadly by then, an even more welcome change, maybe at the joke, or maybe at Margarita on general principles. She was buxom and had long thick brown hair and a spray-on white receptionist's uniform. She stood, winked at my son, strolled toward a glass partition, and disappeared.

"Boy, is she a looker, Pop."

"With a sense of humor, I might add. Her hair will gray, her neck will wrinkle, and her abdomen will sag after a few babies, but she will always have her personality. I've told you time and again, don't—"

"I know, I know. Don't marry a woman for her beauty, marry her for her laugh. Growing up, I must have heard that stupid poem of yours a hundred times. How did it go? Let's see . . .

"Roses are red, violets are blue,
Good-lookin' girls, become wrinkled and gray, too.
They get fat, and bald, and bloated with gas,
But the one you'll love anyway, is the one who can laugh.

"That's probably why I'm still single, Dad. Every time I see a woman like the receptionist there, with beautiful brown hair, big brown eyes, and lips to get lost in, I think about that damn rhyme and wonder if she has a sense of humor. You have ruined me, but you know that, don't you? I can't admire a woman with stellar physical features for very long because I begin to picture her in a muumuu, with an almost bald head and false teeth, and wonder if we will be able to make each other laugh when we're old folks. And I want to point out to you, Dad, that Mom is an absolutely gorgeous woman. Or at least she was, before her accident. Now I ask you, after all these years, why in the world did you recite that ridiculous poem repetitively, when you in fact married a beauty queen?"

"Your mother has a great sense of humor. She made me laugh from the first time I met her. Back when I was a med student, I went into a department store she was managing, asked to see something for my mother for Mother's Day, and—"

"I know that story, too. She sold you something you couldn't possibly afford, and she asked you if you were spending your Health Professions Student Loan money on a gift. And if you were, how could you possibly afford to eat? And she presumed that you would have to dine on beanie-weenies for the next month, and how could a nice girl from Dallas let that happen, and would you like to have dinner sometime? Is that about the gist of it?"

"Close, J. J."

"Close, huh? What did I leave out?"

"Actually, I told HER I was spending my med school loan money on my mother's gift, and that I'd have to eat beanie-weenies for a month, and wouldn't she like to take a poor, starving med student out for dinner? And she said, Sure, maybe in the next lifetime. After I called her every day for a month, she finally agreed to go out with me, and even then it was just to try and stop me from bothering her any further. But, lucky for me, we went to a hotel bar after dinner. When the piano player went on break, I asked him if I could "pitch a little woo" to my date, and he said yes. By the time I finished 'It Had To Be You' and 'Unforgettable,' she was mine."

"That's not how Mom tells it."

"I married Mary Louise for her sense of humor, J. J., in spite of her periodically flawed memory. The fact she is beautiful was simply icing on the German chocolate."

We waited in Dr. Weekley's cubbyhole of an office for about thirty minutes before a bald, bespectacled man in his early fifties breezed in, dressed in surgical greens with fresh reddish-brown spots, operating cap and mask—neither of which is ever allowed to be removed from the surgical suite after use—and a long, wrinkled white coat stained black in various areas. The doctor reminded me of obstetrical sights long forgotten, like placenta previa, meconium-stained amniotic fluid, and breech births, three superb reasons I stayed as far away from OB-GYN as possible.

"Sorry I'm late. Tough delivery. Leon Weekley," he said, and extended his hand to J. J. and me.

"No problem. I understand about being held up in surgery."

"Sit, sit. You're an orthopedist?"

"Right. At University."

"And you?" he asked J. J.

"I have a small investigative agency here in town. We do discreet inquiries, that sort of thing."

"You're not the type, at least the kind I'm familiar with in the movies and on TV. You don't have that Philip Marlowe look."

"We're into computers. Saves on the feet."

He nodded and laughed at J. J.'s comment "So, what can I do for you, Brady?"

"You had a long-term patient by the name of Meredith James. She was a very good friend of my wife's and mine, and unfortunately is deceased, as you probably know."

"Sure, it's been all over the radio and TV broadcasts and in the newspaper. The byline is that she was brutally murdered by an unknown intruder. She was a patient of mine for years and an absolutely great gal. What about her?"

"She was six weeks pregnant, or so the attending pathologist said when he autopsied her. A friend of mine, a detective in the Homicide Division of HPD, told me that when she questioned Frank James about it, he seemed surprised, shocked even. And when Forensics at HPD analyzed the DNA on the fetus and compared it with sample strands from Frank James, they said that in all probability, he could not have been the father. I guess my question is this: can you enlighten me as to whom the father of Meredith's child might have been?"

Dr. Weekley stared at me, and his face seemed to lose its color. He opened his mouth to speak, then gazed out his tiny window into the noontime haze. After a moment, he asked, "What's your interest in this, Brady?"

"Well, these are simply routine questions that the police are going to eventually ask you anyway. As you may know, my wife was injured in a hit-and-run accident the same day Meredith James was murdered. There is evidence that the two crimes may in some way be related, that perhaps Meredith's killer, in a hurry to flee the scene of the crime, possibly ran headlong into my wife's car. HPD has no proof of that; it's merely an unfounded supposition of one of the detectives. So, I'm asking you, as a favor, do you have any ideas about the nature of Meredith's pregnancy? I don't know if this information will help HPD solve either crime, but it certainly can't hurt."

He sighed. "She came in, concerned that she might be pregnant. She presented with all the classic early pregnancy symptoms: morning nausea and vomiting, hyperphagia, swelling, mood irritability. I wasn't only Meredith's OB, I functioned as her family doctor as well. I treated her for the usual maladies—coughs, colds, flu, diarrhea, whatever. So, when she came to see me, I examined her, drew some blood work, took a urine sample, checked her vital signs. You know, the usual, assuming she had a flu syndrome. And, by God, I couldn't believe it, but she was pregnant! When I first told her, she became hysterical and left the office in tears. I mean, look at it from her angle, Brady. She was forty-five years old and separated from her husband. Her reaction was, I think . . . expected. Before she left, she questioned me about the possibility of . . . a termination.

"Then, a few days later, she called me up and came in for another consultation. This time, she was euphoric. Said she wanted to have the baby and asked me all those typical questions an 'older' mother should ask. How to take the best possible care of herself, the complication rate of older pregnancies, the incidence of Down syndrome, that sort of thing. That was the last time I saw her."

"She had tried to have children before, right?"

"Yes," he answered hesitatingly. "Normally, that would be confidential information, but since Meredith is dead, I guess I can discuss it with you. Both she and Frank went through fertility testing many years ago, when the techniques had not been as nearly perfected as they are now. As I remember, Frank's sperm count was a little low, but the primary problem lay with Meredith. She suffered from blocked fallopian tubes from an old ovarian infection in her college days. We didn't have the sophisticated laparoscopic procedures that we do now. Back then, we were still trying to open up the tubes. Now, we just harvest an egg from the uterine wall during ovulation, mix it with sperm from the male in a petri dish, and reinsert the fertilized ovum into the uterus. Fifteen years ago, our rate of success was small, so Frank and Meredith eventually gave up."

"I see. Do you have her chart handy?"

"Yes, why?"

"I'd like to know the last two dates she was in the office, if you don't mind."

Dr. Weekley pushed his gold-rimmed glasses onto the end of his nose, opened a thick manila folder, leafed through numerous pages, then pointed a finger to her most recent visits. "March 23 was the date of her pregnancy test. Her last visit was March 27."

"And she was killed on April 4, a week or so later."

Dr. Leon Weekley then shared his thoughts with me. "Meredith was adamant about keeping the pregnancy test results from Frank and told me repeatedly she wanted it to be a surprise. I didn't think that was an unusual request, since the two of them were separated, and she was probably wrestling with the decision of whether or not to have the child. But then, I just assumed she and Frank were still sleeping together and were working out their marital problems from separate residences. I never thought they would get a divorce, and I certainly never considered Meredith could be pregnant by another man, which is why I was so surprised to hear your comment about the DNA testing of Frank and the fetus.

"Unfortunately I'm a little old-fashioned, and maybe I shouldn't have been so adamant that Frank should know about the pregnancy as soon as possible. I've been down this path on numerous occasions in my practice and I felt there was a fifty–fifty chance Meredith would change her mind again and try to terminate the pregnancy. Many women at her age go back and forth between euphoria and depression, trying to decide whether to have the child or not.

"I'm insistent that the decision on whether or not to terminate a pregnancy should be shared between the two people that created the baby, and, if the couple decides to terminate, that it should be done at the soonest possible date. I personally believe in the sanctity of life at conception, and I could not morally agree with Meredith's decision, if she happened to choose termination, and I told her so. Meredith assured me she would tell Frank at her earliest convenience. I've been down this road many times, and I was simply trying to anticipate Meredith's mood swings by insisting that Frank be informed. To think that she was pregnant by another man . . ."

"I have no idea if Frank and Meredith were still intimate physically, Leon, and I'm certainly no DNA expert in matters regarding paternity. I'm simply repeating what I was told by one of the detectives. I was present for Frank's questioning by the police last Sunday, and he seemed very surprised to learn about Meredith's pregnancy, which would tend to substantiate the fact that he was not the father." There was no reason to share with Meredith's former obstetrician Myra McCann's opinions about Meredith's unexpected pregnancy as a motivation for reconciliation with Frank.

"Well, I just assumed . . ." Dr. Weekley said, hesitated, looked at his watch, and stood. "Listen, I have to get back to the delivery room. I've got four of them in labor. When it rains, it pours."

"Leon, you've been very helpful. Thank you for your time," I said, and shook his hand.

J. J. and I followed Dr. Leon Weekley out of his office, through the reception area, and to the elevators. He opened a stairwell door adjacent to the elevator bank and turned to me before he took the stairs down to the operating room.

"You know, it's too bad, Brady. Meredith finally got the one thing all her money couldn't buy, and she loses her life before she can enjoy it. That's a cruel twist of fate, don't you think?"

Yes, I did.

CHAPTER 36

J. J.

Friday, April 13, 2001

Memorial Drive was a major six-lane, east–west Houston thoroughfare that began in downtown and wove its way for miles into the hinterlands near Katy, Texas, home of Clint Black. At Susan's behest, I cruised the north side of Memorial Drive, headed in a westerly direction, and peered into driveways of office buildings, apartments, schools, retail outlets, and private residences, looking for potential obscure parking places that Meredith James's killer might have employed the day of the murder.

My efforts were concentrated on the four-mile span between Loop 610 and Fountain View Drive. The Memorial Bend complex was situated at the end of Sage Road, which would have bisected the four-mile distance if it had not dead-ended into Buffalo Bayou. I was unable to see Memorial Bend from my vantage point, since it was separated from Memorial Drive by a half-mile of dense woods surrounding Buffalo Bayou.

I made a U-turn at Fountain View and headed back east on the south side of Memorial Drive. Since Susan's single-assailant theory was dependent on a westerly exit on Memorial—an easterly exit would have put Meredith's murderer and Mary Louise's assailant nowhere near the vicinity of my wife's accident—I paid little attention to driveways and other potential parking spots on the south side of Memorial Drive. To pass the time, before maneuvering yet another illegal U-turn at the 610 Loop, I tried to make idle conversation with my son.

"Why can't you tell me what you've learned about the vehicle that may have hit your mother?"

"I'll wait until after the meeting with Susan Beeson."

"She didn't mention a meeting to me, and I was at her house until almost midnight."

His response was a careless shrug.

Having made that illegal U-turn at the 610 Loop, I slowly drove west again on Memorial Drive, much to the dismay of the honking horns of busy Houstonians with places to go and people to see. I wasn't very good at surveillance stuff. My general impression was that Meredith's murderer could have parked anywhere along the four-mile stretch and gone undetected by the 50,000 or so people who have passed me at breakneck speed in the last fifteen minutes.

J. J. was a quiet companion during our lunch at America's restaurant, where we dined on plantains with green chili sauce and a platter of chicken, beef, and shrimp fajitas. At the time, I passed his unusual silence off as hunger, but something was eating at him.

J. J. had always been an introvert, the opposite of his mother and me. I suspected it was difficult to be an extrovert when both parents exhibited that type of personality. But he'd been much less communicative than normal the past week, and today, he had said very little. He wandered off aimlessly during my conversation with Mohammed of Chic Stems fame, and he sat listlessly in Dr. Leon Weekley's office, almost to the point of rudeness, choosing to stare out the tiny window adjacent to the doctor's desk.

"You don't want to talk about it?"

"No."

"C'mon, son, why are you shutting me out? With your mother in the condition she's in, well, it's just you and me."

He was silent as I once again stopped at the red light at Chimney Rock. I glanced at him and noticed he had a scowl on his face.

"You and I have never been that close, Dad. But Mom and I have always been best friends, and I miss her. She has always been an expert at filling in the silences between you and me. I talk to Mom, you talk to Mom. You and I rarely talk to each other in her absence. I sometimes don't know what to say to you. I'm sorry if that offends you, Dad, but it's just the way I feel."

J. J. may be correct in his assessment of our relationship, but I couldn't help but be offended by his words. But he and his mother were close, and perhaps Mary Louise had always been the intervener between my son and me.

"Listen, why don't we put the intricacies of our relationship aside and try to focus on pinpointing potential parking spots Meredith James's killer might have employed in order to cross Buffalo Bayou and access her home. Okay?"

"Look, Dad. This is a joke! You are not a cop! You're an orthopedic surgeon, for God's sake. You don't know a damn thing about a homicide investigation. By giving you these little errands to run, Susan Beeson is just humoring you in order to keep you from wasting twenty-four hours a day sitting up in NIC, waiting for Mom to wake up. And I'm sure she'd like to avoid, if at all possible, having you call her every five minutes to see if she's found a clue as to the identity of Mom's assailant. She's allowing you to 'help' her for Mom's sake, not yours! Don't you see that? She's throwing the dog a bone, to keep him busy and out of her hair."

"I don't think Susan sees my interaction with her department like that at all. Look, I spent last Sunday and Monday with her, Capt. Sam Polk, and Chief Stan Lombardo, learning the facts of the case. Then, I spent almost three days going over the visitors' logs from Memorial Bend, categorizing the entries for the Jameses' home. It was me who found the name Foster Grant on the daily log sheet sixty-two times. And today, if you had paid even the slightest bit of attention to my conversation with the manager of Chic Stems, you would have learned that this Grant person, who sent daily fresh floral arrangements to Meredith James during their two-month relationship, is around five feet eight inches tall, is well-built and muscular, and has red hair. And for your information, Mr. Smart Ass, that description happens to fit someone I know.

"And now I've learned from Dr. Leon Weekley—and you would have too, had you not been rudely staring out the window—that Meredith James discovered she was pregnant less than two weeks before she was killed, and that she was insistent during her last office visit that her husband not be told. I think this is all reasonably vital information that can perhaps help Susan solve Meredith's murder."

J. J. had no response but chose to sit there with his arms folded, in a self-righteous pose. I felt my face begin to warm, and my foot got a little heavy on the accelerator.

"You do understand, young man, that the reason I wanted to get involved with this case in the first place is because I'm too distraught over your mother's injury to perform my real job? I wanted to do something, anything, that might keep my mind off Mary Louise's medical condition. And secondly, you should know, if you talked to Susan last night, which I assume you did, since you have graced me with your presence today, that there is a reasonably good chance that whoever killed Meredith James also ran Mary Louise down on their way out of this area, which is why we're driving around in circles here on Memorial Drive. So it seems to me, Your Highness, that if I can help Susan determine the logistics of how the assaulting vehicle got from somewhere here on Memorial Drive to Meredith's home, then to the intersection where your mother's car was rammed, next to Paco's Restaurant, then I've made a significant contribution to the police investigation.

"And, just for the record, speaking of who's doing what to help find your mother's assailant, just what the hell have you been doing the past week? Huh? Have you been down at your office, exploring your cybernetic contacts and trying to identify the type of car that hit her? Trying to match paint and chrome samples, or glass fragments, or tire tracks, anything at all that might determine just exactly what kind of 'black European car' injured her? Or have you been sitting on your ass in your apartment, feeling sorry for yourself, and sulking, which is why you can't answer my question about the progress of your work?"

By then I was red-faced, my carotid pulse was pounding in my ears, and my blood pressure was probably pushing 180 systolic. My breathing was labored, and my vision blurred with tears. I was so angry at my son that I could have smashed his face with my bare hands. I made a squealing U-turn at Fountain View with the left turn signal bright red.

J. J. didn't comment but remained indignant, with that angry, flushed, holier-than-thou, pursed-lip look he gets. Although there is probably no greater human love than a parent's love for a child, the look on his face made me, on occasion, want to slap the shit out of my offspring.

"I've been working diligently, Dad, as have the people at my agency. And we have gathered a great deal information, with the help of HPD's computer systems. Maybe it will help Susan solve the case, and maybe it won't. I have been busy doing all that I can do, but, unlike you, I've done it behind the scenes. I haven't shirked my other obligations, like you have. I have many clients, all of whom are very demanding and who expect me to carry out the work they have hired me for, because to them, their particular problem is the only one that matters. I can't just drop everything like you have and sashay around town acting like, I don't know, Doctor Detective, playing a role for which you haven't had a minute's worth of training.

"You know, Dad, I've worked with HPD before. I know my place in their organization. I know my limitations. I never try to play the role of a law enforcement officer. I do adjunct work for them, on a fee-for-service basis. I use my computers and my contacts all over the country to gather information on behalf of the department. Sometimes I can help them, sometimes I can't. But I never overstep my boundaries. I talk to the techs in Forensics every day, and we compare notes about, like, what years did Porsche manufacture and use heat-resistant, tint #4 glass in the E38963 series? And in what models did they use that glass? Or, for example, what years did the various European auto makers use Michelin SRT-17s as the manufacturer's standard tire? In the Mercedes 500 series, or in the 300 series? Or was it the BMW 535i series, or the 733i series? How about the Porsche 930, or the 935, or maybe the 911? That's the kind of stuff I do. I'm not a cop, and I don't pretend to be a cop.

"You, on the other hand, go around like . . . like Spenser, or Travis McGee, or Kinsey Millhone, but with no experience whatsoever. It's a joke, and the guys say something about it every damn day!"

"What guys?"

"HPD's forensic guys. 'Say, Brady, we hear your old man is playing Philip Marlowe again, har-de-fuckin'-har-de-har-har.' And I'm sick of listening to it. I just wish you'd go back to doing what you do best and stay out of the professionals' way. Quite frankly, you're an embarrassment!"

As the light at Chimney Rock colored to red, I slammed on the brakes. Were it not for the seat belt, one or both of us would have had a concussion, and one at a time per family is plenty. I was so mad and frustrated that I was unable to control the well of water beginning to flow from my eyes, and I began to scream.

"DO YOU THINK YOU CAN GET IT THROUGH THAT SHAGGY-HEADED THICK SKULL OF YOURS THAT YOU ARE RIGHT? I DON'T HAVE THE FOGGIEST IDEA WHAT THE HELL I'M DOING! BUT AT LEAST I'M DOING SOMETHING, AND THAT I'M DOING IT FOR YOUR MOTHER? THAT I'M TRYING TO MAKE UP FOR THE FACT I WAS TOO DAMN BUSY TO SHOW UP FOR LUNCH LAST WEDNESDAY, AND THAT IT'S MY FAULT SHE'S UP THERE AT THE HOSPITAL IN

A COMA? DON'T YOU KNOW THAT BY NOW? DON'T YOU REALIZE THAT I'M DOING ALL THIS BECAUSE HER INJURY IS TOTALLY MY FAULT? CAN'T YOU SEE THAT? DOES THE FACT THAT I'M TRYING TO REDEEM MYSELF FOR FAILING YOUR MOTHER IN HER TIME OF NEED NOT MEAN ANYTHING TO YOU?!"

Tears were streaming down my face to the point that my vision was blurred. Once the light turned green, I sped forward, pulled into the first driveway I saw, slammed the gear-shift lever into park, and turned off my engine. I hung my head and sobbed.

J. J. slid over to my side of the truck cab, put his arm around my neck, and sobbed along with me.

CHAPTER 37

ST. MARY'S

Friday, April 13, 2001

My son and I held each other closely, sharing our despair over the woman that meant more than life itself to each of us. We apologized to each other, and, like an abrupt rainstorm that obliterates a humid, smog-laden day, our animosity ended. Our most hateful conflict, and its quick resolution, reminded me of the proverbial family reunion during holiday season.

Once my eyes cleared, I realized I had parked at the entrance to the visitor's lot of St. Mary's Seminary. A placard below the name identified St. Mary's as a Jesuit graduate school for those devout souls preparing for the priesthood. After a moment, I realized this was the school where Gina Genardo's brother was enrolled in his theological quest.

The campus looked to encompass a large wooded area of ten or twenty acres. It appeared from the entrance that the Jesuits' property ran south, toward Buffalo Bayou. As if on command from some deep, inner source, I reignited the engine and drove along the well-kept asphalt road lined with immaculately trimmed oleanders. I drove along the entry path and stopped at a small guard house, although I saw no gate that might preclude a spontaneous entry.

A wizened silver-haired man in mismatched slacks and sport coat, with a white shirt and bright yellow tie with tiny crosses on it, looked up from his reading material. It appeared he was studying the most recent quarterly missal.

"Can I help you, son?" he asked.

"Well, I'm looking to visit young Father Genardo. He's a seminary student."

"Veer to the right and park anywhere you want. Go inside and talk to Father O'Brien and find out where *Mister* Genardo's current class is," he said, correcting me, then peering at his watch, bringing it up close to his bifocaled eyes. "Although, this time of day on Friday, most of the students are preparing for weekend services. The Jesuits of St. Mary's provide a good deal of community service, assisting at mass at various churches serviced only by an itinerant priest. We have quite a shortage of men of God these days, as you might have heard. The young seminarians play an essential role in the Church's ability to continue feeding the flock."

He gave me a wave, then returned to his perusal of sacred literature.

Large clay pots full of bright-red hibiscus lined the walkway to the entrance of the administration building. J. J. and I avoided the opportunity to meet with Father O'Brien and walked in a southerly direction toward Buffalo Bayou. I already knew Gina Genardo's brother had left town for the weekend, since she was late for work this morning in order to drop him at the airport, and I preferred not to be asked any penetrating Jesuit questions. Security appeared to be nonexistent at St. Mary's. In fact, the entry kiosk looked to be more of an information booth. As we began to stroll the grounds, I hoped, in order to avoid curiosity seekers, that my son and I appeared to be inspecting the facility where J. J. was considering spending the next six years in order to become a man of the cloth. That would be the byline, if asked.

"What are we doing here?"

"Looking around, J. J. I pulled into the driveway here purely by accident, because I couldn't see. But it appears from this vantage point that the Jesuits own quite a bit of land around the seminary. Their property could run east to west, and it's possible it could run all the way down to Buffalo Bayou. I thought we would explore the area and see if we can cross the bayou and access Memorial Bend from here. Don't ask me why, because I can't give you a reason."

"But didn't Susan say that in order for Mom's car to be hit by Meredith James's killer, the driver would most likely have to have been traveling west on Memorial, and then for some unknown reason, turned back south onto Chimney Rock in order to head back east on Woodway and be able to run into Mom at Post Oak?"

"That's correct."

"But if the killer parked here, at St. Mary's, on the south side of Memorial Drive, the logical direction to drive upon exiting this facility would be directly east, toward the Loop, and in the opposite direction from the corner of Post Oak and Woodway. Right?"

"Right. If you look at the map," I said, and picked up a small oak tree limb for a pointer and drew a faint imprint in the St. Augustine grass—appropriate for a seminary, I bemused.

"Woodway runs east to west, and so does Memorial Drive. The two streets are separated by Buffalo Bayou. Chimney Rock makes the west end of the box, and, if you look closely at the map, the only logical east end of the box is Loop 610. Neither Sage Road, which abuts Memorial Bend, nor Post Oak Road, where your mother was injured, are through streets. This means that the intersection at Post Oak and Woodway, adjacent to Paco's Restaurant, represents the middle of the south end of the 'box' and is accessible only via this 'rectangle' I've drawn, except through small side streets that aren't appropriate for this discussion. Buffalo Bayou runs parallel to Woodway and Memorial, between the two streets, in the middle of the box, which is the forest in which we're standing. And this is where I would like to look."

"But I don't understand . . ."

"Just walk with me, okay?"

And so we began to wander through the oak, elm, maple, and cypress trees on the south end of the land of the Jesuits and headed in the general direction of Buffalo Bayou. After walking for ten or fifteen minutes, we appreciated a rivulet's clearing in the forest. It was hard to comprehend that the old bayou, which began in downtown Houston as the massive Houston Ship Channel and Turning Basin at the Port of Houston, then courses west through the city, was but a trickle of water.

We walked along the banks of the murky flow, looking for some sign that we were nearing the Memorial Bend complex, such as an ancient rickety bridge. J. J. spotted it first and headed down the bank toward the old wooden crossing. I followed but heard a rustling to my right and stopped. I walked a few yards west and saw a dirty brown wool blanket on the ground in front of a notched oak tree, and a half-empty bottle of Thunderbird wine laying on its side.

As I reflexively reached out to halt the flow of cheap wine into the earth—why, I have no idea—a hairy, liver-spotted paw reached from behind the thick base of the tree and slapped my hand out of the way.

"That's me private property, guvnor. Hands off, unless ye might share a shilling or two with an old bloke who's down on his luck."

The face was familiar, ruddy, with broken spider veins across the cheeks and a bulbous nose that would be diagnosed as rhinophyma in the dermatology clinic. He wore a tattered topcoat and a worn and faded blue watch cap and was sitting on the other side of the tree, dazed and confused.

I knew this man. His name is Coot Atkinson.

"Hello, Coot. Remember me?"

He looked at my face carefully, squinted, shook his head. "Can't say that I do, guvnor. Have we met?"

"Yes. At the police station last Monday, the morning after you spent the night in jail? Remember?"

"Can't say as I do. I remember a pretty young thing and a cowboy, although with your blue jeans and white shirt, there is a vague similarity. But you are not him. I have a keen memory for arresting officers," he said, started to laugh, then coughed violently.

Coot had a better memory than I did. I had been behind the two-way mirror during his interview, so he was correct. We had not met.

"I thought you lived on the south side of the bayou, over by Memorial Bend, closer to the BFI dumpsters. What are you doing on this side?"

"You are mistaken, guvnor. This has been my home for quite some time now. The good fathers here at St. Mary's often help me out, on occasion give me a hot meal or perhaps a new blanket. When the weather gets nasty, sometimes one of the Jesuit brothers sneaks me into the dormitory. I've discovered that although leftovers are bountiful at the Memorial Bend dumpsters, I'd rather be closer to God than the rich folks."

"Hey, Dad!" J. J. yelled, as he ran up the incline from Buffalo Bayou. "That old bridge takes you right up to—who's this?" he said, stopping in his tracks about ten feet from Coot.

"Coot Atkinson, meet J. J. Brady, my son. By the way, I'm Dr. Jim Brady. We haven't been officially introduced, although I saw you Monday at the Central Jail."

J. J. kept his distance, partly from fear and indecision, partly from the smell. Coot had clearly lost whatever cleanliness he might have gained from his overnight stay at Central Jail.

"So, might you have a shilling, or perhaps a pound, for the likes of an old salt like me, good doctor?"

"Coot, I'd like to ask you a question or two, and I promise I'll make it worth your while. But first, I'd like to walk along the bayou with my son here, cross the bridge, and see how far it is over to the Memorial Bend complex. Will you be here when I return?"

He smiled, showed his brown gum lines and diseased teeth. "Certainly, guvnor. Me plane to Heathrow doesn't leave for two hours," he said, started to laugh again, then began a spasmodic choking. I stood there for a minute, making sure he didn't go into cardiac arrest, then walked with J. J. down the hill toward the bayou.

"Who in the hell is that?"

"That, J. J., may be the only witness to the person who ran through the woods here last Wednesday and killed Meredith James. He was of no help at all to Susan Beeson and Sam Polk on Monday. Coot said he saw a jogger running from this direction toward Memorial Bend. Then later, he saw the same jogger running back, toward Memorial Drive. He could not describe the person, couldn't even say whether it was a male or a female. Of course, he'd had his typical lunch. Two bottles of Thunderbird wine."

"So, what good is he as a witness if he didn't see anyone except this jogger, and can't even identify the sex?"

I shrugged. "Never hurts to ask."

We walked across the short, rickety old bridge that, in the old days, connected the mansions of the wealthy on the north side of Buffalo Bayou to their servants' quarters on the south side. In those days, the bayou was much larger and probably required a bridge. These days it would be a soggy six-foot walk, but certainly feasible.

J. J. and I wandered further south and slightly west and arrived at a clearing just behind the Memorial Bend complex. We walked up to the paved foot path installed by the residents to allow BFI easy access to the garbage bins at the rear of the houses, went to the eighth gate, and stopped. It was locked, but between two warped slats of the wooden, ten-foot-high fence, I could see the Jameses' backyard with its immaculate landscaping and sparkling pool.

And I wished at that moment to be a kid again, at a baseball game, watching the old New York Yankees through a knothole in the fence at Yankee Stadium. I could still remember names from the starting lineup in 1965: Richardson, Tresh, Mantle, and Maris. I was participating in Little League baseball back then, and it was my dream to see my beloved Yankees play ball. I never made it, other than in those imaginary series between the Yankees and the Dodgers played in my backyard with a baseball bat and smooth, round river rocks. Those were the good old days. I just wish I had known it at the time.

"C'mon, let's go, J. J., before Coot gets scared and runs away."

We made it back across the bridge and easily located Coot, asleep within his tree. I had to shake him to rouse him.

"Coot, it's Dr. Brady again. Coot? Coot!"

"Wha . . . what?" he said. He rubbed sleep from his eyes and tried to sit up straight.

I pulled out my money clip, removed a $100 bill, and waved it in front of this unfortunate intoxicated man. His eyes suddenly brightened as he struggled to his feet. He had to hold onto his tree house to balance himself, still wobbly from his alcoholic haze.

"This bill is yours if you can tell me the answer to my question. Are you listening?"

"Aye, sire," he said, bowed slightly, still holding onto the tree with one shaky palm.

"You remember you told the two detectives on Monday at the jail about the jogger running through here on Wednesday of last week, the day the woman was killed over at Memorial Bend?"

He nodded.

"And when they asked you if you could tell anything about the person's face, you said you could not. You said you couldn't even identify the sex of the individual, remember that?"

"Aye, guvnor."

"So my question is, why?"

"Why what, sire?"

"Why couldn't you tell the sex of the person you saw running through the woods?"

"Well, guvnor, whoever it was had on a loose jogging suit and wore sunglasses and a cap. The jogging suit was bulky, and I couldn't see an outline of the figure all that well."

"But what about the hair, Coot? Didn't the hair give you a clue? As I remember, you said the person you saw had long hair."

He nodded slightly, grew a smirk. "That's the magic question, isn't it, guvnor? Man or woman?"

"Your answer could be helpful in finding the James woman's killer."

Coot scratched his scraggly beard, musing over his answer. "You see, when I left England, it was the '60s. New music and a new breed of young people. They had different ways of dressing and wearing their hair. Now, in my day, we always cut it short, but then, well, the kids started a new trend. The boys had hair as long as the girls. And then I come here to the States in the late '60s and everybody's a—what did you call them? A hippie? Hair down to their knees, men and women alike."

I waited for more, but he was silent. "So what's the point, Coot?"

"They asked me if the jogger was male or female. I couldn't tell honestly, because, well . . ."

"Because why?" I said, and waved the $100 bill in front of his face. God forgive me, because I knew he'd go out and buy more cheap rot-gut wine with it, but, for Mary Louise's sake, I needed an answer.

"Sometimes young men, even in these modern times, still wear their hair in a ponytail, don't they? So how could I be sure?"

CHAPTER 38

FARTS

Friday, April 13, 2001

Due to breakfast at Cortes Deli, my stops at Chic Stems and Dr. Leon Weekley's office, lunch at America's, the protracted argument during passes along Memorial Drive, the tour of the St. Mary's Seminary grounds, and the conversation with Coot Atkinson, I had caused J. J. to be late for his meeting with the forensics people in HPD's Auto Division, Det. Lt. Susan Beeson, and Capt. Sam Polk. I offered to drive him directly to the Southwest Substation to avoid his being even later by stopping at University Hospital's parking garage so he could get his own car. Truth of the matter was that I wanted to talk to Susan and share with her the information I had gleaned from the day's sojourn. It was also time to buck up and share the Frank James–Gina Genardo liaison with her. Coot's reappraisal of the situation, and his mention of a jogger with a ponytail, might shed new light on the murder of Meredith James. I was no detective, but for what it was worth, I felt the need to come clean with Susan about the surreptitious affair.

J. J. was angry again, at being late for the meeting, at being driven by his father in a pickup truck, or at whatever the stress surges of a twenty-seven-year-old young man might have created as a target. So I used the silent drive into Southwest Houston to reflect on what I considered vital information with regard to the Meredith James murder and the Mary Louise Brady assault.

Meredith had what I presumed was a torrid love affair in January and February with a man whose description matched Mary Louise's neurosurgeon, Dr. George Flanagan. He was one of Frank James's clinic partners, so George would have had ample opportunity to get to know Meredith over the years through holiday parties, clinic retreats, and University faculty–spouse events. I believed their relationship to be feasible, at least as a starting point for inquiry. In addition, considering George's physique and the knowledge that Meredith worked out daily at a place called Body Rock, as I vaguely remembered from a conversation I'd had with Susan Beeson, perhaps the two struck up a more intimate relationship and began exercising an additional set of . . . muscles. Of course, that could have been done at Body Rock or some more private place, but which muscle groups the two used, and where, did not concern me.

The alleged affair between George and Meredith had ended, for whatever reason. Meredith discovered she was pregnant on March 23, three weeks after their two-month relationship ended, and was at first devastated by the news. Then, when she returned to see Dr. Leon Weekley on March 27, Meredith was almost euphoric but insistently informed the doctor that Frank was not to learn of their great fortune at that time. Why? Perhaps because, as Myra McCann suggested, the pregnancy gave Meredith the opportunity to retrieve her husband from divorce court by bestowing upon him the one gift she had been unable to give him during their lengthy marriage. Meredith more than likely assumed that Dr. Weekley would not suspect her fertilization to have come from someone other than her husband, a fact that he confirmed to me earlier in the day.

Meredith's tragic and brutal murder occurred on Wednesday, April 4. Who had a motive to kill her? Presuming Dr. George Flanagan was mystery man Foster Grant, and he was Meredith's lover, why would he kill her? Because she dumped him? Because she was pregnant? I doubted that George, assuming he was the hidden lover, even knew Meredith was pregnant when the affair ended on or about March 1. And if her lover was in fact George Flanagan, maybe he simply went home to the security of his wife, as Myra McCann suggested.

So, who else might have wanted Meredith dead? Frank? What would he have to gain? A relationship with Gina or some other woman? Doubtful, since he could have had Gina regardless, or any other woman, for that matter. Money? Frank had plenty of money from his successful practice as a neurosurgeon, so would the lure of inheriting Meredith's massive wealth have been a significant motive for murder? Or could he somehow have learned of Meredith's pregnancy, didn't want the public embarrassment of divorcing a woman with child, and killed her? Doubtful. I don't think Frank would have the stomach for it. But could he have hired it done, with or without the knowledge of Meredith's pregnancy? The possibility seemed remote.

And what about Dr. Leon Weekley? He seemed nervous, agitated even, when discussing his insistence about Meredith informing Frank of her pregnancy as soon as possible. Could he have called Frank and told him the news personally, on the chance Meredith would not tell him? If so, then why did Frank act so surprised last Sunday when Susan mentioned it to him?

All these ponderings reminded me of a friend's saying:

Everything changes, and there are no answers.

Although there were probably untold players in the game, many of whom I didn't know yet, one name began to stand out in the forefront of my mind. I felt a little queasy as I drove and tried to shake off an undeniable sense of foreboding. Although Gina Genardo was a wonderful nurse and had taken expert care of Mary Louise, I could not deny that she had been having an affair with Frank James until he supposedly broke it off during his separation from Meredith. What would be Gina's motive? Love? Money? Revenge? A presumed higher standard of living? And what evidence existed for Gina's murder of Meredith James? Well, for one thing, she had been sleeping with Frank James, but according to rumor, Frank's sexual partners had included half the hospital community at one time or another. What else? The fact that Gina's brother attended St. Mary's Seminary, a ten-minute walk from Memorial Bend, did not make her a murderess. From the looks of the place, anyone could walk, or drive, right in. So, what was bugging me about Gina? She was off the day of the murder—her shift was Thursday through Sunday—but so what? Could the word of a homeless alcoholic like Coot Atkinson be taken seriously? Could his description of a jogger with a "ponytail" be accurate? Could Gina Genardo have loved, or hated, Frank James enough to kill his wife? And if Susan Beeson's single-assailant theory was correct, and Gina killed Meredith James and subjected Mary Louise to near-fatal injuries in the hit-and-run accident, how could she possibly take such good care of her in NIC? And if, in fact, Gina was the assailant, would she even have known who it was she had run down?

There had to be something else . . .

"I scheduled this meeting so that I can personally give Chief Lombardo an update before his four o'clock meeting with the mayor and the police commissioner. I'm surprised to see you here, Brady, but it seems these days that you just pop up all over the place unexpectedly, don't you? So, who wants to go first?" said Capt. Sam Polk.

Five of us were crammed in his small private glassed-in office. Homicide detectives in HPD's Southwest Substation scurried about outside the relatively soundproof confines of Sam's office, chasing paper trails, looking for the city's most wanted. Lt. Susan Beeson, dressed in tan slacks and a light-blue cotton pullover sweater, sat directly in front of Sam's desk in a faux-leather chair with arm rests. Next to her, in an armless worn vinyl chair, was a young man named

Kevin. He looked a little older than J. J. but just as disheveled, with tousled hair and even thicker coke-bottle lenses housed in thin wire frames and perched on the bridge of his nose. His glasses kept falling over the nasal bump so many plastic surgeons were fond of removing, such that his right hand was in perpetual motion, constantly pushing the nose piece back up in order to allow his eyes to focus. When he was introduced to me a few minutes ago, Sam Polk laughingly said Kevin was in charge of HPD's FARTs: Forensics Auto Research Technicians. Apparently, Kevin sat in a cubicle all day, played with a computer, and, using modern technology, reconstructed crime scenes that could in any way be related to a vehicular-associated felony. That would include shootings, robberies, drug deals, and motor vehicle assaults of any kind, such as auto–pedestrian accidents and hit-and-runs.

"Kevin?"

"Uh, sir?"

"Tell us what you have, son."

Kevin looked toward the worn, stained couch where J. J. and I were sitting. J. J. gave him a barely perceptible nod and a smile of close friendship. I wondered at what age a child's peers became cool, smart, and trustworthy, and a father became stupid, incompetent, and inarticulate. And did the process ever reverse itself?

"Well, Capt. Polk, Lt. Beeson gave me a project toward the end of last week. As you know, an unidentified vehicle struck Mary Louise Brady in her vehicle in the middle of the intersection of Woodway and Post Oak Road. Mrs. Brady was apparently returning home from Paco's Restaurant, which sits on the south side of that intersection. When she pulled into the intersection and was attempting to turn east—to the right, sir—a vehicle struck her on the driver's side of the car. The impact was severe enough to completely flip Mrs. Brady's 1998 Jeep Cherokee onto its roof. When passers-by stopped to render her aid and to call 911 for assistance, the first onlookers found her suspended by her seat belt.

"As you know, Mrs. Brady has survived the crash but is still in a coma at University Hospital," he said, and he briefly glanced toward J. J. and gave him a nod of condolence.

"Now, Lt. Beeson was not at the crime scene initially. Her involvement came a few days later. Fortunately, the technicians that arrived on the premises shortly after the accident were quite thorough. There was a good bit of debris in the street, such as broken glass, splinters from a fender, and pieces of a bumper. There were also a number of skid marks, primarily from the assailant's vehicle, since we assume when Mrs. Brady was hit, she was almost totally unaware of what she was about to experience and was therefore unable to apply her brakes.

"So, during the past week, I've been involved in trying to determine the type of vehicle that injured Mrs. Brady, with the help of J. J. Brady, who, I must say, Captain, has been of irreplaceable benefit in this investigation. Without his sources on the internet, I doubt we could have gleaned the information we will present to you today. You know, these days, automotive manufacturers are reluctant to speak with law enforcement agencies. Seems they are always afraid of products liability, since the police don't usually call unless there's been some sort of crime committed. So, I don't think I could be—"

"Kevin," Sam interrupted, looked at his watch, "could you please get to the point. I have another meeting in less than an hour."

"Sorry, sir. Anyway, using glass samples from what we assume is the right front headlight of the assaulting vehicle, and from paint samples embedded in the driver's door of Mrs. Brady's Cherokee, from chrome debris in the street, and from the fresh tire-track skid marks found at the scene caused by the driver's attempt to swerve into the left lane and avoid colliding with Mrs. Brady, we have come up with a vehicle. Not THE vehicle, sir, but a vehicle type. As you know, witnesses described a black European sedan. We started our search with Mercedes-Benz USA, shifted to Bavarian Motor Works, then to Porsche in Stuttgart, and finally to Volvo through our Stockholm connections. We even made contact with the people at Ferrari, who enlightened us with certain specifications in their line of Italian sports cars and who also put us in contact with a man who had knowledge of the particulars of Lamborghinis and Maseratis.

"But, sir, all that aside, J. J. and I are fairly confident—roughly 98.5 percent on the chi-square reliability test—that the vehicle in question was a BMW, 700i series, manufactured between 1989 and 1993. Those are the only years in which all the parameters fit, down to the original Michelin radials."

With that, he closed his notebook and looked at Capt. Sam Polk.

Sam leaned forward in his chair and slowly nodded his head. "Excellent work, Kevin, I'm sure. But, as I remember, Susan, your primary suspect is . . . what's his name?"

"Foster Grant."

"Right. I could have sworn you told me he was listed in those entry logs as having driven a black Mercedes. I don't understand how—"

Susan raised her hand, stopping him mid-sentence. "I called the DMV and the DPS this morning. Foster Grant does not exist, and the license plate number he used at Memorial Bend does not exist. So, maybe he didn't drive a Mercedes after all. Just listen, Sam. We're not finished."

He stared at Susan. "What else is there?"

"A search of current local owners of a black–actually, midnight ebony, it's called–700i series BMW, model years 1989 through 1993. J. J.?"

I turned to look at J. J. He reached for the inside of his faded, wrinkled denim jacket, opened it, and pulled out a folded sheaf of papers. As he opened them, I recognized computer printer paper, the old type with alternating green and white spaces and evenly-spaced holes punched along each vertical edge.

"Captain, Susan asked me to work with Kevin on the project. As you might expect, since my mother was involved in this accident, I was eager to help. I've had my staff on it day and night for the past week or so," he said, and glanced at me. "Kevin and I were able to collaborate in determining make and model of the vehicle in question, and, with further study, have developed a list of current owners. It wasn't so hard to come up with a list of owners, provided the vehicles were purchased in Texas and were still owned by the party who initially purchased the vehicle. Once we had the type of vehicle and the model number, Kevin and I were able to obtain serial numbers for all 700i series BMWs manufactured during those years that were shipped into this country.

"We then developed a software program that enabled us to search the United States Department of Transportation for those serial numbers. BMWs are, of course, imports, so the DOT keeps immaculate records regarding their distribution. We then—"

"That's a federal institution, J. J. How did you get their cooperation? I don't remember getting a call for Authorization of Assistance. Did you, Suze?"

She shook her head.

"Well, then?"

"I've been doing this for a while, Captain, and I have my sources."

Sam Polk stared at my son, seemed to decide that the less he knew, the better, and motioned for J. J. to continue.

"So, we then got online with the Texas Department of Public Safety and the Division of Motor Vehicles, traced those vehicles registered with DOT, and cross-checked them with DPS and DMV records. Of course, some of the cars whose original manifest said they were going to Texas did not, for whatever reason. Sometimes an individual orders a car, then changes their mind. Or if an individual in Colorado, for instance, wants a specific amenity on a vehicle and they don't have it in Denver but they have it in Houston or Dallas, and the customer is willing to pay for transport charges, they can get that particular car in a few days and avoid waiting for another shipment from European operations.

"Anyway, I don't want to bore you with the details, even though Kevin and I adhere to the creed espoused by Frank Lloyd Wright that God is in the details. I'm assuming what you need, Captain, is this alphabetical list, which represents, as best as Kevin and I can determine, current Houston owners of 1989 to 1993 700i series BMWs, each of which is compatible with the vehicle that injured my mother."

He handed the crinkled set of papers to Sam Polk. Sam carefully unfolded them and looked up at Susan. "Have you seen this?"

She nodded.

"Any hunches?"

"Yes. I've marked what I think is the most important name on the list."

Sam put on his ten-dollar drugstore reading glasses and started to scan the list. "These are all currently registered in Harris County?"

"Yes," J. J. said.

Sam continued reading, then stopped about halfway down. He looked up at Susan, nodded, then continued reading. After he flipped through several pages of computer paper, he again looked at Susan. "There must of hundreds of vehicles listed here, but I assume you've drawn my attention to one particular BMW, the one with a big red circle drawn around it."

Susan nodded yet again.

When he finished, he placed the papers on the desk and looked around the room. "You boys have done some excellent work. I'd like to talk to my lieutenant alone now, if you don't mind."

J. J. and I rose from the couch. Kevin slinked out of his chair. I wanted to tell him that he was brilliant, to hold his shoulders up, be proud, and to stop slouching around like he's some pimply junior-high-school kid in trouble for throwing spit wads. But I stifled my fatherly self.

"Brady, you can stay," Sam Polk said.

I sat back down and, through the office's glass door and windows, watched J. J. and Kevin stroll through the Homicide squad room and give each other a high-five.

"Can I see the list?" I asked.

Sam Polk handed me the wrinkled sheet of paper that contained a large red mark encircling the name of an owner of the type of BMW that had changed my and Mary Louise's lives. I read the name, then reread it, and suddenly felt the majority of the blood circulating in my veins divert itself from my brain. I got dizzy and tried to lean forward and put my head between my legs, but I felt myself start to pass out in spite of it all.

Somewhere in the distance, I heard a man and a woman call my name, and then I sensed blackness overwhelming me.

CHAPTER 39

THE BEEPER

Friday, April 13, 2001

"Jim Bob? Jim Bob! Can you hear me?"

I slowly weaved my mental way out of a dazed and confused state and began to detect the pungent aroma of smelling salts. My head jerked involuntarily away from the foul scent, and I pushed a soft hand from my field of slowly refocusing vision.

"Are you all right?" Susan Beeson asked.

"I think so. What happened?"

"You passed out. Are you sure you're okay?"

I nodded, embarrassed. "Sam, I'm sorry—"

"He left. Had to go downtown to Central for a meeting with Dad. The police commissioner and the mayor want an update on the James murder, so Sam will be briefing the chief on the current status of the case."

I struggled to sit up from my supine position on the floor and leaned my head between my legs. Susan handed me a cold soft drink, which I sipped slowly to settle my stomach.

"Susan, I've never passed out in my entire life. I've done a thousand gross, bloody operations with never so much as a wave of nausea. But when I saw Frank James's name circled on that list—"

"Don't worry about it. It happens to everybody once in a while. I'm surprised you've held up as well as you have, considering all this stress with Mary Louise's injuries. But before you get too bent out of shape about Dr. James's being on that list, let me remind you of a few facts.

"Based on the coroner's estimated time of death between one thirty and one forty-five, which he believes to accurate, it seems to me logistically impossible that Frank James could jog across the bayou, kill his wife, and then arrive at Memorial Bend dressed in a suit at one fifty-five, according to Security Guard Moorehouse and the entry logs. And do not forget, he had Moorehouse call 911 at two fifteen. The timing's all wrong, much to Sam Polk's dismay. He has been trying to somehow pin this murder on Dr. James from day one.

"In addition, the doctor couldn't have been Mary Louise's assailant. Her car was hit at two thirty or so, and even though Dr. James's BMW is on that list of compatible vehicles, he physically could not have been at the site of her hit-and-run accident. He was questioned at his wife's murder scene for about two hours, long after Mary Louise had been injured and had been Life Flighted to University Hospital."

"What was the name of the initial investigating officer at the murder scene?"

"Lee Perkins."

"Right. Did you ask Lee and Sam about the condition of Frank's car the day of the murder, just to be sure?"

"Yes. Sam said that when he pulled up into the Jameses' circular drive, he pulled in behind two blue-and-whites and a fire department ambulance. He did not notice a civilian vehicle. I called Lee Perkins while you were passed out. He was the first in the procession to the Jameses' home, and he insists there was no vehicle parked in the driveway when he arrived. Dr. James was standing in the driveway, in a state of panic. I can't believe that neither an experienced patrolman nor the captain of detectives thought to look at Dr. James's car that day. Of course, at the time, neither officer was aware of Mary Louise's accident, nor could they know of the possibility that Mary Louise had been injured by a car driven by the murderer of Meredith James.

"Point is, Jim Bob, Frank James's car is only 'compatible' with the BMW that hit Mary Louise, since it is well-documented that he was at Memorial Bend at the time of her injury, and in his BMW. Don't you remember that we read on the entry log from Memorial Bend that Dr. James's vehicle was the last visitor entered as having access to Meredith's home? And that it was logged in as a BMW?"

"That's true, and I understand what you're saying, Susan, but are you telling me that no one actually saw Frank James's BMW at his home on the day of the murder?"

"That's exactly what I'm telling you. Of course, since his BMW is one of hundreds of vehicles on that list that FARTs compiled, we'll have to check each and every one. But I can assure you, the car that ran into Mary Louise, if it's still around, will be pristine. It's been ten days since the murder, so I'm sure the vehicle's owner, unless they are without a single brain cell, will have had the car repaired by now. I think the trail is cold, and that we're a day late and a dollar short.

"And I'll tell you what I told Sam before he left. Give up on trying to pin this crime on Dr. James. His alibi seems airtight."

"So, what's Sam going to tell your dad?"

"Not much, other than we have leads, and we're working on Mrs. James's murder twenty-four hours a day."

"Is he going to relate to him your theory about one assailant for both crimes?"

"Yes, because at least with that approach, we can continue to concentrate on Mary Louise's case in tandem with the James case. However, this list the boys compiled makes my theory a bit shaky, unless we can somehow correlate those BMW owners with visitors to Memorial Bend using those entry logs. Right now, I think the mysterious Mr. Foster Grant is still our best suspect. But without an accurate name and a valid license plate number, it's going to be difficult to track him down. Our only hope in finding Grant is to go back and see Moorehouse, try to get a description of the man, and see if he can give me some kind of clue as to the man's identity. I have my doubts, though."

I stood, walked around the room, saw several jovial detectives point my way, and laugh. Of all the places to experience syncope for the first time in my life, it would have to be at the police station.

"Susan, I'm glad Sam isn't here, because there's something I have to tell you. I should have told you before, but the timing was not right. I tried to tell you last night before I left your house, but you were too tired and sent me home before I could—"

"What? What is it?"

"Gina Genardo, the NIC nurse taking care of Mary Louise . . ."

"Yes?"

I hung my head. "She has assured me that their relationship is a thing of the past, which is why she's been so upset with her life, but the truth is, Gina was having an affair with Frank James."

After Susan finished yelling and screaming at me for withholding information and possibly altering the complexion of a murder investigation because of my personal fondness for the nurse who has taken stellar care of my injured wife, she sat down, exhausted, and listened to my rendition of the facts I'd gleaned from the day's activities.

I related to Susan the substance of my conversations with Mohammed Akhbar of Chic Stems, Dr. Leon Weekley, and Coot Atkinson. I told her that Dr. George Flanagan fit the description of Foster Grant, and that perhaps he was Meredith's January–February lover and the father of her child. I relayed Coot's use of the word "ponytail" in connection with the jogger he saw, and I described the proximity of St. Mary's Seminary, Gina's brother's current residence, to Memorial Bend.

"None of this may mean a damn thing, Susan, if I understand the logistical problem in your single-assailant theory. If Meredith's killer parked the vehicle on the south side of Memorial Drive, at a place such as St. Mary's, it would have been too easy simply to turn right and head east, toward Loop 610, and get on the freeway, rather than drive west on Memorial, cut south on Chimney Rock, then double back and turn east on Woodway and create Mary Louise's accident. Or am I missing something?"

"Yes, you are, Jim Bob, but that's beside the point. And I hope you've enjoyed yourself this week, because once Sam Polk gets wind of the Gina Genardo–Frank James link, you are history with this department, whether or not it has anything to do with solving these two crimes or not. I guess you know that."

"I can understand, Susan, and I'm very sorry. I guess that's what you get for trying to help me out. As the old saying goes, 'No good deed goes unpunished.'"

Susan finally cracked a smile, which made me feel slightly better. "You've helped us out a lot, Jim Bob, and you have my thanks for that. I just cannot believe you didn't tell me sooner. You know, we stress this type of issue to our incoming recruits. It is departmental policy not to allow our uniformed officers or our detectives to become involved in investigating crimes against relatives, or even close friends. One tends to get too emotional, and it colors logical thinking. If one of our people gets involved in a case that is too close for comfort and doesn't relinquish it, they are subject to dismissal. This is a classic example."

I nodded. "It's a good thing I don't work for HPD, huh. I'd be living with Coot Atkinson."

She started to laugh. "Anyway, I'll share some information with you that I gleaned today, which adds credence to the theory that Meredith James's killer and Mary Louise's assailant were one and the same.

"I called the City of Houston's Department of Public Works this morning. On Wednesday of last week, work was scheduled to be done on the south lane of Memorial Drive. According to the supervisor I spoke to, Memorial Drive eastbound, between Chimney Rock and the 610 Loop, was reduced from three lanes of traffic to only one. If you happen to be correct and the killer parked at St. Mary's Seminary, then the quickest way to exit would have been to snake through the snarled traffic in the south lane, cross over to the north lane, and head west. That would explain my theory of how the vehicle in question could have made almost a complete circle before leaving the area. The BMW in question could have been at Post Oak and Woodway through that circuitous path, because on that day, it was the quickest route to Loop 610. Also, the timing fits. It would take a jogger about fifteen minutes to run across Buffalo Bayou after killing Meredith James, and another fifteen to fight the traffic across Memorial Drive and arrive at the intersection where Mary Louise was injured."

"You're kidding me."

"Nope. So, you just might be right about where the killer's car was parked during the crime. The only problem is that we do not have a suspect, unless you want to call the ubiquitous but as yet unknown Foster Grant a suspect. I believe Frank James has been eliminated as a suspect for either crime, although Sam Polk still maintains he is somehow responsible for his wife's death. I think he's grasping at straws."

"Susan, what if Foster Grant is actually George Flanagan, and he drives a BMW, and not a Mercedes as the logs state? He could be the assailant responsible for both crimes."

"True, Jim Bob, but why would the security guards as a group falsify the logs? Grant entered the complex at all hours of the day and night, and no one individual security guard could have been present for every visit.

"Can you at least get a picture of Dr. Flanagan from a medical roster? I want to show it to the manager of the Body Rock, the work-out studio, and to the man you talked to at Chic Stems. At least we may be able to confirm the identity of Foster Grant. If Flanagan turns out to be Foster Grant, then we'll pull his DMV records, see what kind of car he drives, and check out the license plate. It could be a dead-end, but . . .

"Why are you just sitting there, Jim Bob?" she yelled.

"I thought I was dismissed from the investigation."

"Shut up and get me that picture!"

I used Sam Polk's phone to call Fran at my office. I asked her to open the current Harris County Medical Society Pictorial Roster and fax me, as it turned out, page 216. I waited in anticipatory silence as the fairly clear copy of that particular page came through Capt. Polk's fax machine. Susan had purposefully returned to her desk to check for messages and to confirm her appointment with the Body Rock manager. I looked at the likeness of Dr. George Flanagan and decided it was adequate for Susan's purposes. I borrowed an empty manila folder from Sam's file cabinet and carefully placed the unfolded fax into it.

I returned to the couch, laid my head back, and thought. I closed my eyes, drifted off for a few seconds, then heard a distant beeping sound. At first, I thought it must be a detective's pager signaling from the squad room, but when I opened my eyes, I realized it was coming from my belt. I unclipped Gina Genardo's beeper, pressed the green button that stopped the irritating signal, and pressed it again to call up messages on the "clipboard." I centered the indicator over the blinking stick figure, which represented the active window message, and tapped the green button again. The message read:

April 13--3:20 PM--863-9593

The message was from the current date and time. I wondered who was calling her. I tapped the green button again, to return to the screen. There were four saved messages, the same ones that I noticed last Sunday when I sat on Frank James's patio and listened to him answer Susan's questions. I click the most recently saved message.

April 12--6:12 PM--863-9593

That was from yesterday, Thursday. Where would Gina have been at 6:12 in the evening? Still on her shift at NIC, normally, although I saw she and Frank in the telephone alcove at the second-floor elevator bank at about that time.

I returned to the screen and clicked the third saved message.

April 4-2:28 PM--863-9593

My heart started to race when I realized that April 4 at 2:28 PM was the day Meredith James was killed, and roughly the time when Mary Louise's car was struck.

"What are you doing? Did you get the picture of Dr. Flanagan?" Susan asked.

"What? Oh, yeah, I got the picture. It's in the folder."

"What are you—did the hospital call you? My God, it's not bad news about Mary Louise, is it?"

I shook my head. "Remember last Sunday, when you came up to NIC and took me out for a drive?"

"Yes?"

"Well, remember that Gina Genardo let me borrow her beeper?"

"So?"

"This is it. She has been trying to get it back, but we've missed each other this week for one reason or another. The pager went off a few minutes ago, and I was curious to see who had called her. This is interesting. Can you get me a piece of paper?"

"Listen, Jim Bob, I have an appointment—"

"Please, Susan?"

She begrudgingly handed me a sheet of Sam's office stationery, and I wrote down the three most recent dates, times, and phone numbers. I brought the next-to-the-earliest saved message to the screen.

April 4--1:10 PM--863-9593

Susan watched at first with disinterest, but her anticipation grew as I wrote down the day, time, and calling number.

"Are you telling me that you've had Gina Genardo's beeper since last Sunday, and that these phone calls you're writing down occurred on the day of the murder?"

"I guess so."

She shook her head. "And that they were saved in her pager, and you didn't tell me?"

"Looks that way, Susan. I'm sorry, I didn't know."

"How many more are there?"

"One."

"Pull it up, dammit."

I did, and it read:

April 4-9:22 AM--863-9592

"Is that a 2 at the end, not a 3?"

"Seems to be, Susan, but it's probably an error."

"Do you realize what this means? Someone called your nurse friend three times the day of the murder. The first call was in the morning, about four hours before Meredith was killed. The second call was only thirty to forty-five minutes before the murder. The last was thirty to forty-five minutes after the murder, and about the time Mary Louise's car was sideswiped."

She walked over to Sam's desk and picked up the phone. "Give me the number."

"Which one?"

"The one with four pages."

"8-6-3-9-5-9-3."

She punched in the numbers, waited for a few moments, then hung up and redialed.

"What are you doing, Susan?"

"I'm calling the second number, the one with the 2 at the end. I got one of those messages that said 'the party to whom you wish to speak is either unavailable or out of range' for the first—Shit! I'm getting the same message on this number."

"Susan, surely you don't think that George Flanagan and Gina . . ."

"C'mon, let's get in the car!"

CHAPTER 40

DILANTIN

Friday, April 13, 2001

Susan and I climbed into her unmarked LTD, with me in the shotgun seat. She flipped the switch on her portable flashing red light, set in on the roof, sans siren. From Beechnut Street, I assumed she would connect onto the Southwest Freeway, exit at Kirby, and travel north to Body Rock.

"I normally do this myself, but I'm in too big of a hurry to stop and fiddle with the computer. So, I need your help. Pull out the tray that houses the keyboard. No there, under the monitor."

I did as Susan instructed me and tilted the computer screen toward me.

"Turn on the screen with the top right key. Good. Now, after it warms up, you'll get the Menu screen. See it?"

"Yes."

"Now, using the track ball, bring the pointer to the line where it says 'Central,' and click the mouse. The computer is now calling Central dispatch. When one of the operators picks up the call, they will know it's my system trying to log in. You will see something cute on the screen if they're not too busy, or if they are, all you'll see will be a message for my code number. What do you see?"

"It reads, 'Code, please.'"

"Must be a payday Friday afternoon in Houston. Type in 'BeeGees.'"

I turned to look at her. "What?"

"C'mon, Jim Bob, just type it in. I know it's a little corny, but you know, we're the Beesons, and I have two 'Genes.'"

I did as instructed.

"Now what does the screen read?"

"It reads, 'What do you need, Susan?'"

"Good. Now, type in a message saying that I want a trace on both those phone numbers from Gina Genardo's beeper. Do you remember them?"

"I wrote them down."

"Good. Type in the two numbers and tell the operator that I want an ID on the caller. Then, type in that I'll be out of the car for five minutes but instruct her to stay on the line."

I completed the task like an efficient executive secretary. "Now what?"

"Now we wait. I'll leave the motor running. Lock your door. I have a spare key."

We had arrived at Body Rock. Susan jumped out of the car with me in tow, blustered into the lobby, walked rapidly to the first-floor information desk, and showed her badge to the svelte young blond woman with hair teased so high that she could attract lightning. She was likely in her early twenties, and she stood and took a step back, which gave us a full view of her figure, the bright Day-Glo orange leotard leaving little to the imagination.

"I'm here to see Manny!" Susan yelled. The receptionist leaned against a purple wall behind the waist-high desk and pointed to a stairway off to the left. Susan and I passed several youthful bodies, each dressed in a form-fitting workout suit, bicycle pants, or unitard. I suddenly felt out of shape and tried to suck in my stomach as I played follow-the-leader and took the stairs two steps at a time.

The mirrored staircase emptied into a mammoth warehouse-like exercise room. It was filled with every imaginable type of exercise bike, stair machine, and cardiovascular equipment known to humanity. Floor-to-ceiling mirrors lined the four walls. In the back, I noticed a separate large weight room, closed on three sides, but open to the Great Exercise Hall. Susan and I walked past sweating bodies of all shapes and sizes trying to sweat off a week's worth of alcohol and high-cholesterol lunches in a single Friday afternoon.

Most of the participants were women, and the ones in the best shape were scantily clad. Try as I might, I was unable to keep my "eyes front" as we walked toward the weight room.

Manny Bachrach appeared to be of Polynesian descent. He was a massively muscular man, a conditioned version of a Sumo wrestler, with tight, gnarled rectus abdominis muscles. He was in the supine position, on a weight bench, his head precariously resting underneath a barbell chock full of weights. I estimated he was bench-pressing around 400 pounds.

"Manny? Remember me?"

Manny opened his eyes and lifted the sagging barbell to its housing above his bald, shiny head. He smiled, jumped from the bench, and bowed graciously. His five foot ten body glistened with sweat. His biceps, triceps, pectoral and latissimus dorsi muscles were still bulging despite the fact he had dropped the weights. His quadriceps and gastrocnemius muscles were enormous, and it occurred to me that if he just stood behind the line of scrimmage with his arms out in the middle linebacker's position, the Houston Oilers might win the AFC championship.

"Mrs. Beeson. It is so good to see you again. Are you here to reconsider my offer?"

Susan blushed. "No, Manny, I'm not quite ready for the 'Try It You'll Like It' membership yet. I am considering hiring you as a masseuse, though, but I'll have to let you know."

"I will be happy to be of service, at your convenience," he said, and bowed again.

"By the way, this is Dr. Jim Brady. Manny B."

"Manny."

"Doctor," he said, bowed again, and gently shook my hand.

Susan opened her folder. "When I was here the other day and asked you about anyone that seemed to be close to Meredith James when she worked out, you mentioned that there was one particular man you remembered. It was a few months ago, and they were here together quite a bit."

"Of course. My muscles may be large, but the circulation to my brain is still quite functional. The man's name is Grant. He is a relatively new member here."

"That's not his real name, Manny, but that's not important right now. I'd like to know if this picture is a good likeness of him."

Susan showed him the faxed copy of page 216 of the Harris County Medical Directory and pointed to the photograph with a red circle around it. Manny studied it closely, then picked it up with his thick, muscular fingers.

"This is Mr. Grant, no question about it. But it says here his name is—"

"That's not important now, Manny. Thanks. You've been very helpful."

We turned to leave when Manny addressed me. "I will be happy to help you as well, Doctor. Looks like you could use some conditioning," he said, smiling.

I smiled back. "I'll call you, Manny."

"Very good, sir. I'll be expecting you." And he bowed yet again.

Susan trotted through the exercise space, down the stairs, and into the afternoon sun. There was a gentle breeze wafting across Kirby Drive, and the temperature was beginning to cool.

When we got back into the car, I saw there was a message waiting on the screen.

"Now what, Susan?"

"What does the monitor say?"

"'I'm waiting.'"

"Good. Punch the F5 key there on the top row, then read me what's on the screen."

"It reads, 'Both numbers assigned to Frank James, MD.'"

Susan revved up the engine, kept her left hand on the steering wheel, turned toward me, leaned over, and rested her right elbow on the seat between us. "Tilt the monitor a little this way."

I twisted the ten-inch screen in her direction and watched her expression. "You know what this means, Jim Bob?"

"It looks like Frank James called Gina Genardo's beeper three times the day of the murder. If you suspect that George Flanagan is somehow in collusion with Gina, I wonder why Frank would be calling her, especially the day his wife was murdered?"

Susan screwed her face up into a frown and seemed to be thinking intensely. She started to smile. "I wonder . . ."

"What?"

She sat erect, leaned back into the driver's seat, and put the car into reverse.

"Type in a message, something to the effect that I want an ID on the site of origination of those two phone numbers. Home, office, car, cellular, whatever. ASAP."

I typed in her request. "Is that all?"

"Also key in that I want a current address and phone number on Dr. George Flanagan, and list any vehicles registered to the man."

I did as told. "Now what?"

"That'll take some time, so relax."

"Susan, I can't relax. I'm getting antsy about getting back to the hospital. I have this eerie, sort of sick feeling in my gut, such that I can hardly stand riding in the car. I know what we're doing here is important, but . . ."

"I have only one more scheduled stop to make, and that's at Chic Stems, just to confirm from a second source that Foster Grant is George Flanagan. Then, I can take you back to your car, or we can go up to NIC together."

"I'd like to be there before visitor's hours start, so I can enjoy our quiet time together. And I want to check Mary Louise's chart. I'm worried."

She reached over, patted my knee. "No problem."

Susan turned west onto Westheimer, sped down to Buffalo Speedway, turned into Chic Stems's parking lot, and again left her motor running. As we entered and walked up to the central counter, Mohammed spotted me and immediately picked up the telephone.

"I'm calling the police," he yelled to me. "You have no business interfering with the privacy of our clientele," he said angrily, and he dialed the number of River Oaks Patrol, glued to the base of the phone on a yellow label.

Susan reached over the counter, pushed the button on the contoured white princess phone, and cut the connection.

"What the—"

Susan pulled the leather case containing her detective's shield from her purse, opened it, and stuck it in her host's face. "The police are here. Put the phone down, sir."

Mohammed did as she asked and stared blankly at her, then at me, then back toward Susan.

She opened the manila folder, removed the highlighted picture, and showed it to the proprietor of Chic Stems.

"Is this Foster Grant, the man who came in here every week during January and February and paid cash in advance to have flowers delivered to Meredith James?"

He leaned down and looked closely at the black-and-white, two-inch by two-inch photo.

"I never knew the name of the person to whom the flowers were sent. Only an address, as I told this man earlier. Besides, the picture is very small, very small, indeed. There is a likeness certainly, but—"

"I'm involved in a murder investigation, sir. If I find you have been untruthful with me for whatever reason, and your lack of candor results in any delay whatsoever in my ability to solve this case, I will arrest you and book you for aiding and abetting a fugitive."

Somehow, Mohammed's memory bank was jarred free. "Yes, officer. That is Foster Grant. There is no doubt in it."

Susan and I got back in the car, rolled the windows down while I nervously smoked, and waited for a response from Central on the site of origination of Frank James's two phone numbers.

"I'm curious about why you want to know the origin of Frank's three calls to Gina Genardo the day of the murder. I mean, what does a phone call prove?"

"I have a hunch, Jim Bob. Let's wait and see what the operator types in."

"But I'm confused. We now know that Foster Grant is really Dr. George Flanagan, former lover and probable father of Meredith James's unborn child. You can prove that with DNA testing, right?"

"Yes, we can, within a 99% probability factor."

"So, if you can prove that he owns a BMW, then isn't he still your best suspect? You can prove he had a relationship with Meredith, which would lend support to your single-assailant theory. Besides, didn't you tell me not thirty minutes ago that Frank James was no longer a suspect?"

Susan shrugged. "Why would Flanagan kill her? Because she was pregnant? Because he was pissed that Meredith ended the affair? From what Myra McCann said, and from what you told me Dr. Weekley said, Meredith wanted to keep the child, and apparently wanted to reconcile with her husband, and perhaps convince him the baby was his. I do not see an obvious motive with Flanagan. And, as I remember from perusing that computer printout J .J. and Kevin generated, he doesn't own a BMW. There was no Foster Grant or George Flanagan on the list."

"There was no Gina Genardo listed as owning a compatible BMW either, Susan. I must admit, the three phone calls on her pager are peculiar, but I'm sure there is a reasonable explanation for them.

In addition, Dr. Weekley wasn't sure that Meredith really wanted to keep her baby. Remember, he was insistent that she tell Frank as soon as—"

"Quiet! We've got an answer."

The light-blue background on the monitor sizzled for a moment, then printed out the terse message:

George Flanagan, MD--DMV reg. 1994 Merz. 560 SEL

Numbers req. as follows:
863-9592--assig. F. James, MD--1993 BMW 733i
863-9593--assig. F. James, MD--1995 Porsche 930

"Anything else, Susan?" the computer read.

"I knew it! I just knew it!" Susan yelled, and slapped me on the back. "That lying son-of-a-bitch Frank James has two cars! He beeped his girlfriend three times the day of the murder. The first call came from his BMW, the next two from his Porsche! My next step will be to check the cellular phone records for both those numbers, to see if telephone conversations were transpiring between his two vehicles that day during the time of Meredith's murder and Mary Louise's assault. I'll bet you any amount of money that Dr. James was in the Porsche that day when he went to Memorial Bend for the lunch date with his wife. He probably parked it on the street instead of in the circular drive, to avoid attention. Both Sam Polk and Lee Perkins would have remembered a Porsche. And that's probably why James had Moorehouse call 911. There would be a record of that call, and the originating phone number would be on file with the fire department. So, my best guess is that someone else had access to his BMW, meaning it could be the vehicle that Meredith James's killer drove, and the same vehicle that assaulted Mary Louise. I think it's all been a setup!"

"But Susan, you and I both have talked to Frank, and we both looked at the entry logs. In his conversations, he used the word 'Beamer' repeatedly. And in that last entry, when he went to meet Meredith for lunch, Moorehouse wrote down that he was driving a BMW."

"Moorehouse penciled in 'BMW' for Dr. James's car, but if you remember, he omitted the license plate number on the entry log that day. What if the doctor was in his Porsche when he came to see his wife, and, for some unknown reason, Moorehouse falsified the entry logs?"

"But for what possible reason? And if so, then who was driving Frank's BMW?"

"The good doctor won't tell me the truth, so there's only one way to find out," she said, and started the engine, turned on her official light, and sped out of the parking lot.

"Where are we going, Susan?"

"To Memorial Bend. I want to talk to Moorehouse."

As Susan drove like a bat out of hell toward the Memorial Bend complex, I picked up her cellular phone from the seat between us dialed in the number of NIC.

"What are you doing?"

"I feel that queasy sensation coming on again, the one I got before I passed out in Sam's office. It's like I'm going to be sick, but it's an emotional thing. I have this eerie sense of . . ."

"Foreboding? Does that describe it?"

"Maybe. It's hard to say, Susan—Hello, Antoinette? Dr. Brady. How's my wife? . . . What kind of arrhythmia? . . . A bundle branch block of some sort? That's what she had last weekend, isn't it? Is one of the cardiologists there? . . . Good. So she's stable, and . . . Okay. Listen, I'll be up there in a little while to check on the details, but I'd like you to do me a favor. I want you to call the lab and have a tech come upstairs and draw a STAT Dilantin blood level on Mary Louise . . . I know I'm not her treating physician, but I'm a doctor, and she's my wife, and it's critical information . . . Understand, Antoinette, I do not want you to tell a single nurse on the floor that I've ordered this test . . . No, not even Gina. Now, will you do it? . . . Good. STAT, remember? . . . Okay, thanks. Oh, one more thing, I need to talk to someone in the pharmacy, the specific one that services NIC. Get me the number, please . . ."

Susan gave me a what-in-the-hell-are-you-doing look.

"Yeah, I've got a pen . . . Thanks. Oh, and Antoinette? As soon as you have the Dilantin levels, call me at this number . . ."

I asked Susan for the cellular phone number, relayed it to Antoinette, clicked off, and dialed the pharmacy.

The line was answered on the second ring by Kelvin, who identified himself as a pharmacist.

"This is Dr. Jim Brady. Are you the pharmacist in charge of NIC?"

The man spoke in a clear Caribbean-influenced voice. "Yes, sir. What may I do for you?

"I need ask you some questions about my wife's medication, particularly Dilantin . . . Yes, Mrs. Brady was admitted to NIC last Thursday morning. Do you have her file handy? . . . Good. I'd like you to go through it and tell me the status of her Dilantin dosage. In other words, has it been the same since she's been there, or has it been changed? . . . Yes, I'll wait."

I covered the mouthpiece and said to Susan, "Of all the times not to have a speaker phone. I want you to hear this conversation, just in case."

"Why didn't you say so? Hang up, call him back on the modem. It has a built-in speaker."

"You've got to be kidding me."

"Tell him you'll call him right back."

When the pharmacist returned to the line, I told him to stay put, then called him back on Susan's modem line, and once I was connected with the pharmacist, Susan punched a button and hung up the phone.

"Are you there, Dr. Brady? The connection sounds . . . distant."

"Yes, I'm here. We're on a speakerphone in the car. I can hear you fine. Go ahead, please. What is your name?"

"Kelvin. Listen, the initial order sheet copy we received, on Thursday, April 5, which is always the yellow copy, showed that Dr. George Flanagan ordered the patient to have Dilantin 100 milligrams intravenously three times a day. On Friday, April 6 we received a second order sheet, increasing the dose to 400 milligrams three times a day. I was off for the weekend, and the pharmacist on duty thought this was a terribly high dose, even approaching a toxic dose, in fact, but before he had a chance to call the floor to get confirmation, he received a call from one of the nurses explaining the dosage change. Gina Genardo RN is listed in our records as having stated that the patient was still seizing on the current dose, and that Dr. Flanagan had ordered the increase."

"Hang on a second," I said. "Mary Louise wasn't having seizures, as far as I know."

To Susan, I whispered, "That's all bullshit."

"Let him finish," she answered quietly.

"Sorry, go ahead, Kelvin."

"Yes, sir. The elevated dose was maintained on Saturday and Sunday. Then, on Monday, I was back on duty and received a yellow pharmacy sheet that read the dose was to be 100 milligrams three times a day. That being the standard dose for seizure control, I did not question it. The standard dose was continued on Tuesday and Wednesday.

"Then, this week, on Thursday, which was yesterday, I received an amended order sheet copy, once again increasing the dose of Dilantin to 400 milligrams three times per day. And once again, a nurse called, again Gina Genardo RN, explaining the failure of the lower dose to control the patient's seizures. I made a note that the patient was still having grand mal episodes on the lower dose of Dilantin to justify the distribution of that much Dilantin to a single patient.

"But I must tell you, Dr. Brady, that a dosage that high bothered me, and I felt compelled to speak to a physician about it. I called Doctor Flanagan's office but was told he was out of town this week, and that Dr. James was taking his calls. I spoke to Dr. James personally yesterday afternoon, and he assured me that the prescribed dose of Dilantin was to be 400 milligrams, given intravenously, three times daily. So, I authorized it. Is there a problem?"

"Kelvin, this is very important. I want you to go up to NIC and somehow retrieve the chart on my wife, get it out of there, and take it to your pharmacy. If you get any flak from anyone, talk to Antoinette, the ward clerk, and tell her you are doing something for me. She won't ask any questions, but she'll figure out a way to get you that chart. Then, I want you to carefully go through the doctor's orders, the doctor's progress notes, and the nurses' notes, and see if you can substantiate those dosage changes. I have looked at that chart every day, and I'll swear to you there's been no such amendment to her original orders. I'll call you back in exactly thirty minutes."

"Are you telling me, Dr. Brady, that your wife's initial dosage of 100 milligrams three times daily has never been officially changed?"

"That is my opinion, but I want you to check it out. And hurry."

"But Dr. Brady, how—"

"Kelvin, this may be a matter of life or death. Do it, and I'll call you back!"

Susan disconnected the modem phone, then asked, "Jim Bob, when did Flanagan turn Mary Louise's care over to Frank James?"

"As I remember, when I saw Flanagan up on the Abercrombie Pavilion last Sunday night, after I returned from spending my day with you, he told me he was leaving town on Tuesday, and that Frank would be in charge of his patients. I forgot about it until Kelvin mentioned it."

We were both quiet for a moment, and I sensed a palpable panic burgeoning within the confines of Susan's police car.

"Jim Bob, what are Gina Genardo's on-duty days in NIC?"

I hung my head, exasperated. "Thursday through Sunday."

"And those are the days the pharmacy received notification of the increased dose of seizure medication?"

"Yes."

"If Mary Louise is being overdosed on this drug Dilantin, and the excessive dose was confirmed by both Gina Genardo and Frank James on separate occasions, then that could imply that their relationship is not over after all. In fact, if the pharmacist confirms your suspicions, and Gina is responsible for falsifying the medical records, then there is a very good chance that we'll know who the driver of Frank James's BMW was the day Meredith was murdered."

"Susan, I just cannot believe that—"

"Listen, you better take Gina Genardo off that white horse of hers! If the lovesick Gina, for whatever reason, murdered Meredith James and used Frank James's BMW as her transportation that day, and accidentally rammed Mary Louise's car during my proposed circuitous escape route, and is now attempting to keep your wife in a coma using excessive doses of medication authorized by Frank James himself, then there's a chance Mary Louise might have seen her face right before impact."

"And you know, Susan, this could all be a fairy tale," I angrily responded. "Gina is a nurse, a quality health professional. As far as I'm concerned, she's kept Mary Louise's complications to a minimum. And maybe Flanagan did change Mary Louise's dose of Dilantin, and I just missed it. What you are proposing seems circumstantial, at best."

"True. But if you are totally convinced of what you're telling me, why did you call up to NIC and ask for a Dilantin blood level? And why did you want to speak to the pharmacist? And why did you ask him to retrieve the chart? You must have doubts, too."

"I regretfully admit that you're correct. I've been concerned that Mary Louise is showing no signs of waking up. Then, when she had symptoms of heart block last Sunday, I—"

"You didn't tell me about that!"

"No, I didn't. Gina's husband Rick came up to NIC and saw Mary Louise. He seemed very much in love with his wife, by the way. I decided to read about the side effects of Dilantin this week, and two of the most prominent are the induction of a coma-like state, and heart block, which is failure of the heart to conduct regular beats. Those complications occur especially in a patient who's receiving an overdose of the medication. As a result, I've been suspicious these past few days. Now, with those phone calls from Frank on Gina's beeper the day of Meredith's murder, and with Frank James owning two cars, and with Frank approving the elevated Dilantin dose, I don't know what to think."

"Sort of depends on what Moorehouse has to say about Frank James and George Flanagan, and also what that pharmacist comes back with, doesn't it?"

"I guess. It is very difficult for me to believe that a nice girl like Gina, daughter of a doctor, wife of a doctor, and sister of a priest-to-be, could be responsible for these terrible acts. She looked so pitiful yesterday, when I saw her talking to Frank, all teary-cycd, her hair—oh my God."

Susan put on the brakes and looked in her side mirrors and her rearview mirror. "What's wrong?"

"I knew there was something else bothering me, and now I realize what it is. I should have told you before."

"What else is new, Jim Bob? You need to come clean, before it's too late. What is it?"

"Well, when I arrived at the hospital yesterday, I told you I saw Frank and Gina talking in the alcove by the elevator bank, and that Gina was crying."

"So?"

"Well, she was wearing this necklace . . ."

CHAPTER 41

GRIFFIN'S

Friday, April 13, 2001

It was a thick, rowdy, Friday-afternoon, Happy-Hour, honkytonk crowd at Griffin's Shillelagh Inn and Irish Bar. A Hank Williams, Jr. song about partying hard tonight was blaring over the sound system, and the heavy bass beat was encouraging the patrons to take Hank's words seriously.

Security Officer William Moorehouse seemed oblivious to the surrounding activity. He was obviously off duty but still in uniform, sitting at the bar, drinking, and smoking an unfiltered cigarette.

Susan had sped to the Memorial Bend security office after we left Chic Stems and was told by the man on duty that Moorehouse got off around 4 p.m., but that she could probably find him at Griffin's. That was his favorite watering hole, and according to the man we talked to, Moorehouse went there every afternoon after work.

Susan and I walked in unnoticed. This was not the kind of bar where only folks from the neighborhood patronized the place, and where everybody knows everyone else's name. We initially stopped at the close end of the bar, adjacent to the front door, and ordered a beer from the bartender, whose name plate stated MIKEY. Once we had been served, Susan showed Mikey her badge and asked him if Moorehouse was here and what kind of shape he was in.

After Susan's brief conversation with the bartender, who looked to have played defensive line for a professional football team, we approached Moorehouse, who sat at the other end of the bar and was now, according to Mikey, a servant to his fourth boilermaker. He appeared drunk, and he hovered in front of a sweating longneck beer and an empty shot glass. He didn't seem to notice Susan, nor me, nor his blitzed barstool neighbors. He just continued to drink and smoke, silent in his thoughts.

The crowd standing at the bar was three deep, but with the onset of Vince Gill's "I Believe in You," the dance floor flooded, allowing Susan and I to step forward and stand behind Moorehouse. He took a long draw from his unfiltered cigarette, blew the smoke out through pursed lips, and spat out the residual tobacco. He stared toward a familiar, pleasant-looking woman on a TV set, which sat high above the bar and was bolted down.

Moorehouse craned his neck to hear the news, but he blinked his eyes slowly, as though his concentration faded in and out as his blood-alcohol level ascended into what Mikey called his customer's nightly state, somewhere between bulletproof and invisible. I turned my eyes in the direction Moorehouse was concentrating and recognized the personality on the television as Janine Carlisle, telecasting the last "Live at Five" spot prior to the *Six O'Clock News*. Only last Wednesday, which to me seemed a lifetime ago, she brought the news-breaking story of Meredith James's murder and Mary Louise Brady's near-fatal accident to tuned-in Houstonians. Ironically, she was providing an update on that same story. Over the din of laughter, clinking glasses, cracking pool cues, and music to cry in your beer by, she reported that the authorities were shocked that no worthwhile leads had been forthcoming from the $100,000 reward put up by Melvin and Sarah Brown on behalf of their murdered daughter. As a closing statement, Carlisle reported that Mary Louise Brady, injured the same day that Meredith James was murdered, is, sadly, still in a coma.

I whispered, "Not for long," if my theory panned out.

Susan and I continued to watch but said nothing as Moorehouse pushed his huge belly closer against the scarred oak bar, turned his head toward Mikey, and waved at the bartender for another round.

When Mikey's response was not as quick as Moorehouse anticipated, he battered the bar with both hands, in Khrushchev style, and shouted, "Mikey! Mikey! Mikey!"

"Knock it off, Billy," said Mikey, as he slammed down a fresh beer and a fresh shot glass full of amber liquid. "Keep it down, or I'm gonna throw your fat ass outta here!"

"Ha! You and what fuckin' army?"

"An army *ant* could knock you off that stool right about now, Bubba."

Mikey wiped the bar in front of Moorehouse. "Say, Billy, don't you work over at that place? Where they found that doctor's wife murdered last week?"

"Yeah. What about it?"

"You were on duty, weren't you, when she got bumped?"

"So?"

"I heard the lady reporter, Janine, talking about it just now. No clues yet, man. Cops ain't got shit. You didn't see nothing that day?"

"Not a fucking thing, Mikey. Nobody got past me. Not that day, not ever. I was an MP for—"

"I've heard the story, Billy, about a thousand times. What happened over there? Any idea?" Mikey said as he looked over Moorehouse's thick shoulder and shot a conspiratorial glance at Susan.

Moorehouse leaned forward, whispering his reply as if the drunks flanking him on each side of his barstool cared. "Hear tell the perp came in the back way, over the bayou, somehow. Least that's what the boys in blue been telling me."

"Huh. All that dough, all that security, and for what? If somebody wants to nail you, they can get to you. Man, if a guy really wants to do somebody in, there is no stopping him. Where there's a will, there's a way. Right, Billy? Billy?"

But Moorehouse seemed to be off in la-la land again and ignored the question. He dropped his whiskey into the beer mug, shot glass and all, downed the mixture in one long continuous gulp, and motioned for another boilermaker.

Susan tapped Moorehouse on the shoulder. He slowly turned around on the bar stool and stared first at her, then at me. There was no recognition in his face for a moment, then a light clicked on somewhere, and he attempted a smile at Susan.

"Detective? What are you doing down here? Can I buy you a drink? Hey, Mikey, bring a—what are you drinking, sweetheart?"

Susan shook her head and set her untouched beer on the bar next to the security guard's empty mug. "I'm not your sweetheart. I'm here to ask you some questions. You remember Dr. Jim Brady?"

He looked at me, then shook his head.

"We can't talk in here. Come outside," Susan said.

"Let me get another drink first, baby."

"No more drinks, Moorehouse. And I'm not your 'baby.' I'm a police officer, this visit is official business, and I want you outside. Now!"

Moorehouse slid off his stool and stood erect. He was a large man, well over six feet, and weighed close to 300 pounds. He glared down at Susan's five-foot-five frame and scrunched up his face like he wanted to take her by the neck and toss her into the crowd. He puffed out his chest and started to pull his right arm back as though he was going to hit her. She quickly backed away, drew her service revolver from her satchel-purse, and aimed it at his chest. At the same instant, Mikey the lineman-cum-barkeep grabbed Moorehouse's right arm with his, and with his left, put a hammer lock on the security guard's head.

Deftly and with experience, Mikey walked slowly down the bar, Moorehouse in tow across the counter, knocking patrons off their stools as he walked. Highball glasses, full beer mugs, and unconsumed shot glasses came crashing along the bar and onto the floor, spilling wet, sticky alcohol mixtures onto surprised and angry patrons leaping off their barstools to avoid injury.

Mikey swung around the end of the bar, kicked open the front door, and released a befuddled and outmaneuvered Moorehouse onto the gravel parking lot. Susan and I followed, she with her gun hanging at her side, and watched as Mikey got a water hose from around the corner of the clapboard nightclub, turned it on full force, and drenched Moorehouse from head to toe with cold water.

"I think you're going to drown him, Mikey. That's enough," Susan said.

Mikey dropped the hose, walked around to the side of the building, and turned the water off. "Anything else I can do for you, ma'am?"

"No, thanks. I'll take it from here."

"Happy to be of service to a local law enforcement officer. I run a clean operation here. And I was tired of that loud-mouthed son-of-a-bitch anyway. Guess I better go back inside, make sure they're not stealing all my beer," he said, and returned to the bar.

William Moorehouse, the confident and overbearing uniformed security guard on duty last Wednesday afternoon at Memorial Bend, sat in a mesh of water and mud and wiped his face with his bulky forearms. He bent his legs upward, rested his elbows on his knees, and placed his chin on his linked hands.

Susan squatted down, opened her folder, and showed him the faxed photo of Dr. George Flanagan. "Moorehouse, you may lose your job over this, but if you tell me the truth, I don't think you'll go to jail. Of course, I can't promise that, but if you'll cooperate with me, the district attorney might go easy on you. Are you sober enough to talk?"

"Yeah."

"This is a photo of the man who frequented Memorial Bend almost every day back in January and February, bound for Meredith James's home. Do you recognize him?"

He took the photo with wet hands and peered at it. There were spotlights on the front and sides of Griffin's that lit the parking area brightly, a precaution designed to limit the club's liability over the typical violent mishaps that occurred nightly outside Houston establishments such as this. I had no doubt that Moorehouse could see clearly.

"Before you answer," Susan said, "you should know that this man has been positively identified by two *reliable* witnesses already, so be very sure of yourself before you answer."

As Moorehouse stared at the photo, water dripped from his hands, his hair, and his face onto the fax. The fax paper quickly became damp and limp in the security guard's hand.

"That's him."

"That's the man known to you as Foster Grant?"

"Yep."

Susan took the wet page and placed it carefully back in her manila folder. "And I don't guess it would surprise you to learn that his name is not really Foster Grant?"

He shook his head.

"Do you know his real name?"

He nodded.

"And?"

He heaved a sigh, dropped his head onto his thick wrists, and mumbled.

"I couldn't hear you, Moorehouse."

"Flanagan. Dr. George Flanagan."

"Very good. We are on the right track. How much did he pay you and your colleagues to write down an incorrect name and license plate number on the entry logs? Surely you, as an ex-army MP, had to realize that eventually we would run the license plate. And when the Department of Public Safety would tell the Houston Police Department that it was a nonexistent number, did it ever occur to you that we detectives might figure out that there was a reason why Dr. Flanagan didn't want an accurate record of his visits to Meredith

James's apartment? And didn't you realize that eventually, even us local idiot city cops would figure out that, in order to falsify a license plate number, somebody would have to get paid off? In fact, several somebodies? I mean, after all, you couldn't be there each and every time he showed up at Meredith James's house. You had to pay off your buds, so they would follow in your example, and put down the same alias and incorrect license number. How much?"

Moorehouse continued to sit, shook his head.

"C'mon, this is your one chance to come clean with me. What's it going to be? Cooperation, and possible leniency, or ten to twenty years in the slammer on a conspiracy-to-murder rap?"

"Man, I'm not guilty of murder! I had nothing to do with the James's woman's killing. I took a grand and I split it between the guys. But I did it as a favor to the Doc. I mean, he told me he was married, and was sneaking off for a little 'strange.' What harm could it do? Everybody does it. And if he wanted to pay me for it, what the hell?"

"One thousand dollars. Unbelievable. Just to try and eliminate the possibility of Flanagan's being found out as an adulterer. First of all, Moorehouse, I don't believe everyone does it, and I don't believe for a minute that you split that money evenly, but that's neither here nor there. And just for your information, we do not care that much about Dr. George Flanagan, alias Foster Grant, right now. The fact that he was cheating on his wife and sleeping with one of his partners' wives is not so important compared to what happened to Meredith James, and subsequently to Mary Louise Brady. Surely you know that's why Dr. Brady and I are here. Don't you?"

He shrugged his shoulders.

"We know that you lied to the investigating officer the day Meredith James was murdered. We know you falsified the entry logs, something you've probably become adept at over the years. There's nothing wrong with getting a little extra 'pay' now and again, is there? Well, is there?!"

By now, Susan was red-faced and screaming at Moorehouse. His body seemed to sag and collapse, and the ex-MP security guard resembled a whipped dog. Then, he started to cry.

"So, what happened that day, you sorry sack of shit?" Susan asked, still holding her pistol at her side, but with such a menacing look, I feared she would use it on him.

He wiped his eyes and began to speak slowly.

"I never lied to anybody. I swear to God, no one ever asked me what kind of car Dr. James was driving that day. No one!"

"So, you didn't falsify the entry logs?"

"I didn't say that."

"Tell me your story, Moorehouse. Right now!"

"I walked out of my kiosk that day, like always, and saw this expensive car pulling into the drive. I didn't recognize it, but I saw the "MB" tag on the lower left windshield, above the state inspection sticker. The windows were tinted real dark, and I couldn't see in. Then, the driver's window came down, and I saw that it was Dr. James. Every vehicle owned by a resident must have a sticker, to allow them easy entry and exit. I have been working there since the development opened five years ago, and it's a policy I started. I was there when Dr. and Mrs. James moved in. But for the last six months, the doctor's car had not been through the security station, as far as I knew. I wondered if maybe I somehow had just missed seeing him, or if Dr. James wasn't living there. And I figured that was probably the case, considering the number of male callers Mrs. James had been having, especially people like Grant . . . Flanagan . . . whoever. Course, there weren't so many male callers on my shift, but there were quite a few coming in on the three to eleven shift, and quite a few going out on the eleven to seven. You know what I mean. Or at least that's what my men would tell me when I relieved them in the morning.

"Anyway, I thought I'd play it cool. I talked to Dr. James for a minute, asked him how he'd been, acted like I was glad to see him. I don't really give a shit who comes and goes into the complex, as long as I do the job I'm paid to do."

"And no matter who pays you, or what they pay you for, either," Susan angrily said. "Go on, before you make me throw up."

He hung his head lower. "So, I asked Dr. James if this is a new car, and he says yes. And I ask him, since I haven't seen him around, how he got the 'MB' sticker. He said he got it from the management of the complex, that the car was a surprise gift for his wife. That they were meeting up for lunch, and that it was kind of a . . . what did he call it? A reunion surprise. That he and Mrs. James had been separated, but that they were getting back together. And, just in case he and his wife's wires got crossed, in order to not screw up the surprise, could I just put down that he was driving the BMW, and enter the old license plate number on the entry log. And he handed me a C-note."

"A hundred dollar bill?"

"Yeah."

"Your thirty pieces of silver, huh?"

"Listen, lady. What harm could it do? The guy owned a house in the complex, his car had a resident sticker, he said he was going to see his wife, and he told me the car was a gift for her. What the hell was I supposed to do?"

"Just finish the story. I really feel sick now. So, you, the dutiful security guard that you are, wrote down Dr. Frank James's entry into Memorial Bend about five minutes until two o'clock last Wednesday and logged him in as driving a BMW 733i. But you screwed up. You couldn't remember the license plate number, could you? Could you?" Susan screamed.

"No, there's just too many cars going through there to—"

"And in your superior wisdom, rather than look the number up, to complete the lie, you simply and lazily drew a line through the space for a license plate number, didn't you, Moorehouse?"

He nodded.

"But that's not what the doctor was driving, was it?"

"No."

"Did you see Dr. James's BMW at all that day?"

He shook his head.

"Why don't you tell Dr. Brady and I what kind of car Dr. James was driving last Wednesday, the day his wife was murdered, the same day Dr. Brady's wife fell victim to a hit-and-run driver."

The security guard hung his head even further, shook it to and fro, and said, "A sweet refurbished red Porsche 930 Turbo, with a spoiler on the rear, with . . . with . . ."

"With what?!" Susan screamed, and leveled her snub-nosed .38 police special at the downtrodden security guard's head. "Tell me why you couldn't write down the license plate number on the new car, for no other reason than to fill in the blank space on the page!"

"Don't shoot me, please! The Porsche still had those—those temporary cardboard tags."

CHAPTER 42

THE RACE

Friday, April 13, 2001

"**I** was worried you were going to shoot him, Susan."

"I could have, I was so mad. Dr. Frank James, the poor, pitiful, grieving husband, wasn't driving his BMW the day his wife was killed, and Moorehouse, the stupid fool, lied for him for a measly hundred dollars. Compared to what Flanagan paid him, Mr. Security Guard sold out cheap. Don't you see? It all fits! Someone else could have been driving James's BMW that day! Whoever it was could have parked at St. Mary's Seminary, jogged across Buffalo Bayou, passed Coot Atkinson unknowingly, sneaked in the back door of the Jameses' home, murdered Meredith, jogged back to the car, and sped away. The fact that roadwork was being done on Memorial Drive eastbound could explain the circuitous route the driver took. And, in the panic from the horror of the moment, or because of preoccupation with talking on the phone—remember, that third call came about thirty minutes after the murder, and about the time of Mary Louise's accident—the driver could have rammed Mary Louise's car.

"Jim Bob, my guess is that at some time during their relationship, Dr. Frank James convinced his nurse-lover to kill his wife and to use his car during the mission. If you look at those three calls from April 4 on Gina Genardo's pager, it is apparent that Frank James made the first call of the morning to Gina from his BMW. The next call came from the doctor's Porsche, so he had obviously switched cars prior to the murder. The third call, which came after the murder, was probably to confirm that the deed had been accomplished. In addition to these incriminating phone calls on Gina's pager, Coot Atkinson remembered a ponytail on the jogger. And now you've witnessed Gina wearing a necklace that could be the one ripped off Meredith's dead body by her killer. As far as I'm concerned, Dr. James outright lied about any jewelry that might have been stolen from the premises the day of the murder. As I remember, he searched Meredith's safe and said he found nothing missing, although he couldn't account for any items purchased in the past six months during their separation.

"So, we can prove Frank James wasn't in his BMW at the time Meredith was killed. If we subpoena records from Houston Cellular, and they show that he and Gina were making calls to each other between his Porsche and his BMW, which I believe she was driving, before and after his wife's murder, then we've got 'em. And, if we can prove that Dr. James bought his wife that necklace you saw Gina wearing—"

Before Susan could complete her thought, the cellular phone rang.

"Hello? . . . Yes, Antoinette . . . I know, I was away for a few minutes . . . That was quick. What's the number? . . . Did you say 60 micrograms? What's normal? . . . No, I don't know either, but I can speak to someone who does. Thanks for calling. Oh, by the way, is Gina still there? . . . Is she getting off at seven tonight, as usual? . . . Why? . . . One more thing, at what time of the day does Mary Louise normally get her Dilantin, and can you check the medications record and see at what times her Dilantin was administered today? . . . All right, I'm on my way. Thanks again."

"What was that all about?"

"I have no idea what the normal, therapeutic blood level of Dilantin is. I'll have to ask Kelvin, the pharmacist."

"Why were you asking about Gina Genardo's schedule?"

"She came in late this morning because she said she had to take her brother to the airport. Antoinette said that Gina's staying past her shift to get her twelve hours in and to help out, because they're so busy in NIC."

"Why did you ask about the times of day Mary Louise receives her medication?"

"Something you said keeps bothering me. That was the purpose of my call to the pharmacist in the first place. Let's suppose that Gina was the driver of the BMW that hit Mary Louise, and in the split second before impact, Mary Louise might have seen the driver of the vehicle, as you suggested earlier.

"Remember, when Life Flight arrived on the scene, the paramedics found Mary Louise hanging upside down, suspended by her seat belt. She told the good Samaritans, or the EMTs, I forget which, to take her to University Hospital. So, presume that Gina was the driver of the assaulting car and thinks the woman she injured at Woodway and Post Oak saw her face. And suppose this woman turns up as a patient at the hospital where the hit-and-run driver works, on the same floor, in the same unit, even. And suppose Gina figures out that Mary Louise was her victim. Would you want the person you left for dead in a hit-and-run accident, while exiting the scene of a crime where you had just killed someone, to recognize you? Maybe that's what Mary Louise was trying to tell me last Sunday night, when I was giving her a description of the personnel in NIC, and her hand started to shake. Pat Gomez said it was a 'normal tremor of deep coma,' but I never believed it."

Susan nodded. "It all fits, doesn't it?"

"I think it all depends on what Kelvin has found in the hospital chart, and what the standard blood level of Dilantin should be. I'll tell you, though, what is absolutely unnerving me at the moment is that when Gina called in to the NIC this morning and said she'd be late, she told the shift supervisor that she would administer her patients' routine meds when she arrived, and that she didn't want to burden her coworkers; the medications could revert to their normal schedule after that. Antoinette said that, as a result, Mary Louise's first dose of Dilantin would be two hours late. Now I'm worried that . . ."

Using the modem speaker phone once again, I rang the Neurosensory Pharmacy and asked to speak to Kelvin.

"Kelvin, Dr. Brady here. What do you have for me?"

"Well, Dr. Brady, I'm afraid we have a problem. Dr. Flanagan's original orders for Dilantin 100 milligrams three times daily have never been changed. Apparently, the yellow copy we received in the pharmacy was some sort of duplicate, altered to justify an increase in the Dilantin dose to 400 milligrams three times daily. It looks as though the *1* was converted to a *4* on the yellow copy we received, but not on the original. I don't remember this sort of thing ever happening before, Dr. Brady, and I'm very upset. I intend to call an administrative inquiry into the matter as soon as—"

"Don't do anything yet, Kelvin. Let me get this straight. My wife got the normal dose of Dilantin on Thursday of last week, and the increased dose Friday, Saturday, and Sunday. Then, on Monday, she began receiving the standard dose again, which was continued Tuesday and Wednesday, but started receiving the quadruple dose yesterday. If that's accurate, what would be the effect on her mental status?"

"Well, Dr. Brady, Dilantin, while designed to control seizure activity, is not intended to interfere with the brain's normal recovery from trauma, as long as it's given in a therapeutic dose, and the patient maintains a therapeutic blood level. So, a quadrupling of the dose would cause extreme drowsiness, somnolence, respiratory depression—"

"In other words, it could induce or maintain a comatose state?"

"Possibly, but she would have to have blood levels in the, oh, the 60 to 80 microgram range."

"Kelvin, I just had a STAT Dilantin blood level run on my wife. It's 60 micrograms! Is that high enough to keep her in a coma, and possibly do further irreversible brain damage?"

"Yes, it's possible, but I'm no neurologist. You'd have to ask—"

"But what if the medication is reduced immediately, and she's kept on a physiologic dose. What happens then?"

"Let's see, the half-life of Dilantin can be as short as twenty-four hours, or as long as four days. Today is Friday. Maybe on Monday, or possibly Tuesday, with the standard dose of Dilantin, Mrs. Brady may start to wake up. Unless of course, she would remain in a coma as a result of her head injury, something the medication given in a physiological dose would not alter."

"I see. Thank you very much. I'll be at the hospital as soon as I can. Keep this information between you and me until you see the whites of my eyes. Meet me in NIC."

I clicked the phone off and felt my panic reach a boiling point.

"Does this mean what I think it does, Jim Bob?"

"Yes, Susan, and you'd better step on it. Mary Louise's Dilantin is normally administered intravenously three times daily, at 7 a.m., 1 p.m., and 7 p.m. Her next dose of medication is due in fifteen minutes. Gina normally gets off at seven but she's staying late to make up for being tardy, and allegedly to help out, since Antoinette said they're swamped up there. As bad as I hate to admit it, it looks like Gina Genardo may be trying to kill someone that she thinks can link her to the murder of Meredith James. And that someone happens to be Mary Louise!"

Griffin's is located in the Lower Heights, on a side street in a decaying neighborhood in transition to an industrial complex. Only fifteen minutes south is the Museum District, which, with its expensive eclectic restaurants, the Contemporary Arts Museum, the Museum of Fine Arts, and upscale shopping plazas, represents a distinct contrast to its northerly neighbors. The University Medical Center is normally about a fifteen-minute drive further south from the Museum District.

Susan and I peeled out of Griffin's parking lot at six forty-five and were a good thirty-minute drive away from University Hospital, a place I needed to be in ten to fifteen minutes if I intended to save my wife's life.

As Susan sped down Montrose Boulevard, red light flashing and siren blaring, she used her CB radio to call for two backup police cars to meet her in the Neurosurgical Intensive Care Unit at University Hospital.

A light rain was falling, and the flashing red light atop the black unmarked Ford reflected off the black asphalt like a Christmas tree with blinking lights. We were doing over 60 mph when we caught a red light at the South Main intersection. Susan slammed on the brakes, skidded for a moment, then sat on the horn and weaved her way through the thick southbound traffic headed for a peaceful weekend at home or at Galveston beach. We crossed over to Fannin and turned south toward University Hospital. By the time she reached Hermann Park Drive, we were doing 70.

She made an illegal U-turn in the middle of Fannin Street, jumped the curb, and sped toward the University Hospital emergency entrance. Susan stopped her car in the middle of the restricted parking zone and left the engine running. Both front doors flew open, and we hit the ER automatic doors in a dead run.

"What the hell is—" I heard the security guard stationed just outside the emergency room say as we ran past.

"Move my car!" Susan yelled to him as we flew down the corridor, past the waiting throng of sick and injured people and their families, most of whom were veering out of the way, looking shocked and scared as we ran past. I was in the lead, and I wondered if Susan had drawn her gun again, but I didn't want to stop and take the time to look back. I bounded up the stairwell door adjacent to the ER, taking two steps at a time, and pulled open the entry door that led to the second-floor sky bridge.

I hit the enclosed sky bridge in a dead run. About the only pedestrian traffic at seven o'clock on a Friday night in a major teaching institution is house staff on weekend duty, night shift employees, and hospital visitors here to see infirm friends and family.

"Get out of my way!" I yelled, as I ran past Dunn Tower, past the Brown Building and on past the Fondren Building, housing the plush Abercrombie Pavilion. Through some reflex adrenaline surge, I streaked even faster when I hit the relatively empty second leg of the sky bridge that led into the Neurosensory Center. On the way, I thought briefly of Melvin and Sarah Brown and wanted to stop and tell them that I was doing this for them too. And I transiently wondered if perhaps they would forgive me for being such a shitty doctor the past nine days. However, paying the Browns an apologetic postoperative visit was not on my list of priorities at that moment.

The elevator button was heat-activated and lit up quickly when I tapped it. The wait seemed interminable but was just enough for Susan to catch up with me. She was heaving and sweating, and she rested by placing her hands on her knees. Her gun was not exposed, fortunately, seeing as how there were at least half a dozen other people waiting in the elevator lobby.

The door opened with a ping, and Susan pushed other folks waiting for the car out of the way, flashed her badge, and said simply, "Police business." The elevator door closed on angry and cursing faces and whisked us directly to the eleventh floor.

We flew through the NIC waiting room full of anxious family and friends about to be admitted to the intensive care unit to visit with loved ones between seven and nine o'clock.

As I hit the aluminum plate adjacent to the two automatic doors, I saw Susan stop, and heard, much to the dismay of the visitors who were patiently waiting, her fading words as I ran toward Mary Louise's bed:

"Ladies and gentlemen, I want to apologize for any inconvenience this may cause you, but you will not be able to enter the Neurosurgical Intensive Care Unit at this time. Thank you for your patience."

I was certain there would be much grumbling, complaining, and desperate pleas from family members who were there to perhaps see a loved one for the last time. I was sorry for their pain and their anguish and could, after having spent over a week up here myself, understand their plight. At that point, however, my only real concern was the health and survival of one Mary Louise Brady.

As I turned the corner toward the NIC nurses' station, I noticed the nurses were hovered over charts and paperwork, preparing for the shift change. I glanced to their immediate right and saw that Mary Louise's bed was empty.

"Where's my wife?!" I screamed as I looked at the hospital-issue clock over the nursing station and saw that it was 6:59.

Employees gathered at the desk turned their heads in my direction and looked puzzled. I didn't see Gina Genardo, but in the blur, I spotted the friendly face of Pat Gomez, ready to take on her evening shift.

"Pat! Where is Mary Louise? Where did you put her?"

The other nurses backed away. My white shirt was drenched with sweat, and its tail had come loose from inside my jeans. Beads of sweat were rolling down my face, into my eyes, over my glasses. My hair was probably askew, and I was sure these employees thought I had finally lost my mind and were probably considering calling the Psych Ward for two technicians and a straitjacket.

Fortunately, Susan Beeson ran up behind me, badge in an outstretched arm, and screamed right next to my ear. "Where's Mary Louise Brady?!"

A startled Pat Gomez spoke with a trembling voice. "We moved her to the Intermediate Unit across the hall. She is not what we consider 'critical' anymore, Dr. Brady. We've had so many emergency admissions today that—"

"Where is she?!"

"Just down the hall, through the south end of NIC. Go through the sliding—"

I didn't hear the end of it as Susan and I ran past nurses trying to take vital signs and push IV meds, aides trying to empty Foley catheter bags, and other technicians attempting to draw blood and run EEGs at the bedsides in the wake of our storm. The automatic sliding doors weren't quite fast enough for me. The one on the right side bent and broke off its hinges as I hit it. I tripped over the aluminum door but managed to quickly regain my balance before I fell and broke my wrist.

The central nursing station in the intermediate NIC was also crowded with staff readying themselves for the shift change. I scanned the twenty-bed unit as I ran, looking for—

And there she was, her back to me, standing at a patient's bedside, which was off to the side, mostly out of the field of vision of the Intermediate Unit nurses' watchful eyes from their central nursing station. As I ran, I saw Gina pick up her patient's IV tubing and glance over her right shoulder. She did a double-take when she saw me, and she quickly turned back to the patient, who happened to be in skeletal traction, with a cast on the left arm and the left leg and was hooked to a respirator. Mary Louise.

"Gina! Do not move another muscle! Stop immediately!" I screamed from across the unit.

Gina's position with respect to Mary Louise did not change. She nervously glanced in my direction as I ran toward her but continued working with the IV.

I hit her full force from the rear, knocking her completely off her feet and onto Mary Louise, whose bed rail was down in order for Gina to push the IV drugs that I suspected could end my wife's life.

I grabbed Gina by the collar, lifted her off Mary Louise's fractured body, and threw her down onto the tiled floor. Susan ran up behind Gina with her police revolver drawn.

"Get up! Get up!" Susan ordered.

"What in the world is going on, Dr. Brady? I'm just trying to give your wife her seizure meds."

And there, in the rubberized medication receptacle, in the middle of the IV tubing, was the syringe. The needle was in the tubing, the near-full plunger hanging loosely, innocuously, like a trout caught on a fly line. I gently grabbed hold of the syringe and carefully extracted the needle without a drop entering Mary Louise's vein.

"Where's the cap, Gina?"

"What?"

"The needle cover? Where the hell is it?"

"It was in my mouth. It must have fallen out when you hit me. What is going on, Dr. Brady? You can't just come in here and—"

"Shut the fuck up, Gina," I said angrily. I opened the medication cart, pulled out a sterile 21-gauge needle, removed the cover, and put it over the needle with Mary Louise's 7:00 p.m. dose of seizure medication. I dropped the other needle in the red biohazard box resting on the drug cart.

By then, nurses from both sides of NIC had gathered around the scene, whispering amongst themselves, but no one addressed either Susan or me directly.

"Get up, Mrs. Genardo," Susan ordered, and pulled the nurse up by her left elbow. She kept her revolver pointed in Gina's direction.

"Pat Gomez, are you here?" I asked.

The small sea of white uniforms parted, and Pat hesitantly walked through the crowd.

"Yes, sir?" she said, with a quivering voice.

"See if Kelvin, the pharmacist on duty, is in the unit yet. If not, get him up here right away, Pat. I want this syringe analyzed to see how much Dilantin it contains."

Pat just stared at me but didn't move.

"Now, Pat!"

She moved back through the throng of white uniforms toward the nurses' station.

Susan took over. "Okay, everybody out of the way. Get back to your business, and give us some room here," she said, holding on to a sobbing Gina Genardo.

A large woman in a freshly-starched uniform stepped forward. "Now see here, young lady! This is a hospital, and I'm the nursing supervisor. I demand to know what is going on here! Why have you disrupted our patient care? These people are sick, and I don't appreciate—"

"I'm a police officer, and I'm here on official business. If you're in charge, then clear the area and shut up!"

The woman was taken aback. "I'm calling security."

"You can call whoever you like as long as you stay out of my way," Susan yelled. She turned to Gina. "Come along," she said, and pulled Gina into a small alcove adjacent to the end of the Intermediate Care nurses' station, about fifteen feet away from Mary Louise's hospital bed. Susan pulled up a chair, her gun still aimed at Gina's chest, and roughly sat her suspect down.

Gina Genardo sat in an orange vinyl straight-backed chair, head in her hands, and sobbed. A coworker brought her a white hospital blanket and wrapped it around her shoulders. Gina's makeup had run down her cheeks, and mascara oozed between her manicured fingers. I noticed the same glint on her neck I saw yesterday, and now that she was closer to me, I appreciated a thick gold chain housing what looked to be a three-carat solitaire diamond. The bright fluorescence of the NIC overhead lighting caused the stone to sparkle and rays of reflected light shoot between Gina's steady stream of tears, like a rainbow.

"I'm going to read you your rights, Mrs. Genardo," Susan said. "You have the right to remain silent . . ."

I walked over to Mary Louise's bed, pulled up a visitor's chair next to her, sat quietly, and tried to take a few deep cleansing breaths. I realized that I was winded and hypoxic. Holding Mary Louise's hand, I began to explain to her the discoveries of the day and the presumed mechanism by which Gina Genardo had been keeping her in a coma.

In a few minutes, four uniformed officers arrived, pistols drawn, further frightening members of the NIC staff as nurses and aides screamed and dove for cover. Once the policemen saw that Susan had the situation under control, they holstered their respective weapons and listened with interest as Lt. Beeson related to them her version of the events that led up to our presence in NIC on an emergent basis.

"I'm waiting on the pharmacist to bring Dr. Brady the results of some tests before you take the nurse into custody," I overheard Susan say to her fellow officers.

I tuned out the police officers' conversation and turned back to the one and only true love of my life, gently massaged her right arm and hand, and repeated for the hundredth time that she was going to wake up and be fine. For the first time since Mary Louise's injury, I was sincere in my convictions.

After about fifteen minutes, a young man dressed in white shirt, brown slacks, athletic shoes, and a light-blue smock walked into the Intermediate Unit of NIC.

"Dr. Brady?" he said, in his familiar Caribbean lilt.

"Yes. You must be Kelvin," I responded, and I stood and shook his hand. "That is Lt. Susan Beeson of the Houston Police Department," who continued to stand over a sobbing Gina Genardo. "What's the verdict, Kelvin?"

He shook his head. "Well, Dr. Brady, a nurse was attempting to administer this medication to a patient? Your wife?"

"Yes, Gina Genardo, the same nurse that authorized the increased Dilantin dose on two occasions."

"Well, sir, I've analyzed the medication in the syringe Mrs. Gomez gave me, and I'm sorry to say, there's nearly 1200 milligrams of Dilantin in the tube. Looking at the chart, and at the pharmacy record, that's the total amount of seizure medication the pharmacy has issued in Mrs. Brady's name today. And, as you and I discussed earlier, that dose of 1200 milligrams per day, spread over three injections, is still four times the normal amount of 300 milligrams per day."

"Kelvin, just give us the bottom line," Susan interjected.

"Yes, ma'am. I don't believe Nurse Genardo gave Mrs. Brady either her morning dosage of 400 milligrams, or her midday dose of 400 milligrams. We guard these medications very closely. I believe that this syringe represents three doses, totaling 1200 milligrams."

"Kelvin," I asked, "what would be the effect of a 1200 milligrams bolus of Dilantin to a patient who is *not* in the middle of a grand mal seizure?"

"I can't say for sure, Dr. Brady, considering your wife is on a ventilator. However, that kind of dose in a non-respirator patient would result in a respiratory shutdown."

"You mean that the patient would quit breathing?" asked Susan.

"Yes, Officer."

"And die?"

Kelvin hesitated a moment. "As I told Dr. Brady on the phone, I'm no neurologist, but I believe, based on my training and experience, a single dosage of Dilantin in that magnitude would be lethal."

Susan lifted Gina Genardo by the elbow and turned toward the four assisting officers. "I want her cuffed, taken downtown, and booked."

"What are the charges, Lieutenant?" asked one of the men.

"I am arresting little Florence Nightingale here for the murder of Meredith James and her unborn child and the attempted murder of Mary Louise Brady!"

Gina suddenly bolted from her chair and attempted to make a break from captivity. Susan and her four colleagues quickly subdued the prisoner and cuffed Gina's hands behind her back.

Gina cried uncontrollably and yelled for help at the top of her lungs as she was led away from NIC. As she vainly struggled to release herself from the four burly police officers, she suddenly dropped to the floor, kicking and screaming like a two-year-old in the midst of a temper tantrum. One of the officers cuffed her ankles, and the four carried her through the unit like a squirming sack of potatoes.

Susan and I heard her parting words as she repeatedly screamed them at the top of her lungs:

"Frank never told me she was pregnant!"

MARY LOUISE

Tuesday, April 17, 2001

To say that the next few days brought a media circus to the University Medical Center would be an understatement. Once the radio, television, and newspaper people got wind of the arrest of Dr. Frank James as an accomplice in the murder of his wife, a crime allegedly committed by a nurse with whom he'd been having an affair, all hell broke loose.

Det. Lt. Susan Beeson had been deservedly credited with solving the heinous crime, and she made several public statements about the extensive behind-the-scenes investigation carried out on behalf of Meredith Brown James and Mary Louise Brady. Susan received a citation from the Houston Police Department for her brilliant piece of detective work in formulating her theory of a single assailant in the James and Brady cases.

My son, J. J., and his firm, B&B Investigations, were credited with invaluable assistance to the Houston Police Department in the determination of the type of vehicle that struck Mary Louise, and in developing an ownership list of compatible BMWs. Fortunately, at my request, the name of Dr. James Brady was omitted as part of the investigative team. My role in this tragic case of murder and mayhem was simply that of the grieving husband, whose wife just happened to be in the wrong place at the wrong time when Gina Genardo came barreling through the yellow light at Post Oak and Woodway in her attempt to flee the scene of Meredith James's murder.

Further review of the Memorial Bend entry logs did reveal a Tiffany delivery to Meredith James's home several weeks prior to the murder. A sales associate identified the necklace worn by Gina Genardo at the time of her arrest as the exact one purchased by Dr. Frank James. The clerk located a delivery receipt from the store, confirming that the package had been sent to #8 Memorial Bend, destined for Meredith James.

Dr. Leon Weekley was the benefactor of more incriminating evidence when, after reading a newspaper article about Dr. Frank James's arrest, he called HPD, talked to Susan Beeson, and revealed that he had personally called Frank after Meredith's visit to him on April 4. He was worried that Meredith might do something rash, and he thought that her husband should be informed of the situation. He explained that he was simply doing his job and protecting an unborn life. The Texas Medical Board is looking into the matter.

The bottom line? Frank James knew Meredith was pregnant one week prior to her murder.

Dr. George Flanagan was confirmed as the DNA father of Meredith James's unborn fetus with a 99% probability, and no criminal charges were filed against him for falsifying his name and license plate number with Memorial Bend security. Speculation existed, however, that divorce proceedings might be forthcoming.

Susan made quite a hit on the local news and was special guest on a morning talk show originating in Houston yesterday. She told me last night, when she came up to visit Mary Louise, that she was scheduled for an appearance on *Oprah!* about profiling men who had murdered their wives. She was adjusting well to her new-found fame as a local celebrity and had already been approached about possibly writing a book about the crime, as well as acting as a consultant for a potential *Movie of the Week.*

The two conspiring lovers, Gina and Frank, were at odds with each other, according to news reports. It seemed that several prominent criminal defense attorneys had come to Gina's rescue and were suggesting that Nurse Genardo was temporarily insane, blinded by love for Frank James, and, like Meredith, merely a victim of the devious plot to have his wife murdered. Word by way of Susan Beeson was that the district attorney's office was considering a lesser charge against Gina in exchange for her turning state's evidence against Dr. Frank James, a man responsible for murdering not only his wife but his unborn child as well. Public sympathy for Frank was nil.

Susan Beeson was, naturally, opposed to the DA's office cutting a deal with Gina and thought that both Gina and Frank should enjoy the benefits of living in a state that had reinstated the death penalty. Susan maintained that Meredith's murder was well-planned and expertly executed, and nobody made Gina pull the trigger on Wednesday, April 4. As far as Gina's attempted murder of Mary Louise was concerned, there was no irrefutable proof that she was driving Frank James's BMW that day. No one could deny, however, that she was caught red-handed in NIC with that syringe full of a lethal dose of Dilantin, obtained through the falsification of hospital documents.

My position in this matter? I think the Old Testament says it best. An eye for an eye . . .

Melvin Brown left University Hospital, his knee wound healing well. He and Sarah were in seclusion in their River Oaks home and refused interviews with any of the media services. Mr. Brown called me yesterday and asked if I would mind coming by the house to remove his stitches, since reporters and cameramen continued to loiter outside his home and watch his every move. He thanked me for the role I played in the discovery of his daughter's killer, information revealed to him in confidence in a meeting with Chief Stan Lombardo and the mayor of Houston. It would seem to me more appropriate for Lt. Susan Beeson to have relayed the solution of Meredith's murder to her parents, but then, rank has its privileges.

And lastly, Capt. Sam Polk's words to Susan, his former partner and student, regarding Dr. Frank James's arrest? "I told you so."

I picked up Tip on Saturday morning, who, by his actions, must have thought I had put him up for adoption. Except for my morning and evening sojourns in NIC with Mary Louise, I spent the weekend with Tip. We walked, we played ball, we chased squirrels—well, him mostly—and I fed him nothing but his favorite treats, medium-rare sirloin and vanilla ice cream.

J. J. apologized repeatedly for his behavior, feeling himself a victim of a week's worth of intense stress and no sleep. He joined in the Tip festivities over the weekend, uplifted by my continued insistence that his mother was going to wake up soon. I forgave him for isolating himself the previous week and for the statements he made to me last Thursday. The words were said in anger and desperation, and I was sure he would take them all back if he could. Besides, he was my son, and I loved him in spite of his occasionally aberrant behavior. That was one's parental duty, was it not?

It was late Tuesday afternoon, and I had struggled through my first day back in the office seeing patients. My last, an elderly lady from Brazil with arthritis of her left hip, had tried all the standard anti-inflammatory medications, had undergone three cortisone injections with only short-term relief, and had been using a cane for two years. But she didn't want a hip replacement.

"There's nothing else I can do, Mrs. Diaz. You have only two choices. Live with your pain or have an operation."

"I can't believe it. I come all this way, to the specialist in Houston, and what does he tell me? Live with this pain. It is not possible, doctore!"

"I didn't say you had to live with it. I said I could fix it. With surgery, by replacing your hip."

"Ah, madre de Dios! I no want this surgery! Do something else! What can you do?"

I shook my head. "I'm not Oral Roberts, ma'am."

"Who is this? This Oral Roberts? You think I should see him, then?"

Just before I lost my patience with this woman and said something I'd regret later, Fran, my secretary, knocked and simultaneously opened the exam room door.

"Pat Gomez called. From NIC. She wants you over there right away!"

"Shit!"

I left Mrs. Diaz, and, for the second time in the past four days, made the trip to the Neurosensory tower in a dead run. My under-exercised muscles were still sore from Friday's jaunt. Unfortunately, without Lt. Susan Beeson, I had to ride in a crowded elevator, which, naturally, stopped on four floors before I reached the eleventh. By the time I got to Mary Louise's bedside, I was breathless.

Pat was smiling. "You didn't have to hurry. It isn't an emergency. In fact, it's nothing bad at all. It's great!"

I sat in my customary position, the one I'd occupied for almost two weeks. I held Mary Louise's right hand, looked at her pale face, at her casts, her stocking cap, her . . .

"You've got her on the T-tube! For how long?"

"Over an hour. She's been breathing on her own for one hour! Are you excited, or what?"

I was so thrilled, so elated, so beside myself with joy that I could not speak. I held onto Mary Louise's thin hand and patted it gently as the tears rolled down my cheeks. I tried to tell Pat that I was grateful, anything whatsoever that would be complimentary, but the words would not come. Antoinette, the ward clerk, and several of the other nurses who had cared for Mary Louise stopped by, patted me on the arm and on the back, and before long, everybody was crying.

As I was trying to compose myself and brush away the tears from my eyes and face with my left hand, I felt pressure in my right palm. It was faint, but steady. I glanced at Mary Louise's right hand and watched as her fingers straightened, then flexed. Then, I felt a stronger squeeze. I noticed her right leg stir, first a gentle flexing of the knee, then a stiffening of her quadriceps muscles. She took a deep breath and heaved a big sigh.

I leaned into her face and kissed her dry, cracked lips.

"Can you hear me?"

Her right eyelid moved—her left was still bandaged—ever so slightly, then her head nodded.

"It's me. Do you know that?"

Mary Louise nodded again and squeezed my hand harder. Her lips moved and began to part. She tried to speak, but she had a tracheotomy, which prevented the vocal cords from working. In order to allow her to make an audible sound, I would have to detach the T-tube and cover the airway in the small metal and plastic tube that protruded from her throat.

"She's trying to talk, Pat. What should I do?"

"Well, it's much too soon to discontinue the T-tube, but it might be all right to slip it off for a second, plug the trach, and hear what she has to say. You want to try it?"

By then, nearly the entire team of NIC nurses, ward clerks, and technicians that were not involved in emergency care of other patients were gathered around Mary Louise's bed. Some were smiling, some laughing, and all were crying tears of joy.

I leaned down into my wife's face. "You need the oxygen, but I'm going to remove it for just a second and arrange it so you can talk. Okay? But just for a second. Do you understand?"

She nodded, still struggling with that right eyelid. It was like a war going on behind there. I gently lifted the right lid. Her pupil constricted immediately due to the bright light. She shut it immediately, probably out of pain from light exposure.

I turned toward the opposite side of the bed. "Okay, Pat, go ahead. But stay close, just in case."

Pat Gomez, bless her heart, detached the T-tube and held a gloved finger over Mary Louise's tracheotomy apparatus. I leaned down and put my left ear over her mouth. Her voice was raspy, and she struggled with her speech. She had been in a coma for close to two weeks and she was weak and dehydrated, recovering from multiple fractures and internal injuries. But in spite of her condition, she was able to whisper words that made the hours spent at her side worthwhile.

She spoke slowly, but the words were clear. "Thanks . . . for . . . holding . . . my . . . hand."

I lifted my head, and Pat reattached the T-tube. By then, my tears were flowing uncontrollably, and my vision was blurred. I looked at the entourage surrounding Mary Louise's bed, witnessing their expressions of unconcealed anticipation.

"What did she say?" I heard from too many voices to ignore.

"She thanked me for holding her hand."

Pat and all the dedicated folks in NIC nodded in collective agreement at Mary Louise's statement, affirming their conviction that comatose patients absorb mental and physical stimuli, whether they can respond to it or not.

I had to ask Mary Louise a question, to see if Gina Genardo's futile attempt to end my wife's life was even necessary. I leaned down and asked her if she saw the face of the driver that hit her.

She shook her head, mouthed the word "No."

No. Gina, I hope you rot in hell.

It was clear that Mary Louise had more to say, so once again, Pat detached the T-tube. Mary Louise struggled with the next few words, but they indicated to me that she was going to be all right, and that, most importantly, regardless of whatever scars or residual deformities she might have retained as a result of her injuries, she hadn't lost her sense of humor.

Mary Louise said this:

"The . . . next . . . time . . . I . . . invite . . . you . . . to . . . lunch . . . don't . . . stand . . . me . . . up."

And then she gently put her weakened right arm around my neck and kissed my cheek.

READ ON FOR A SNEAK PEEK

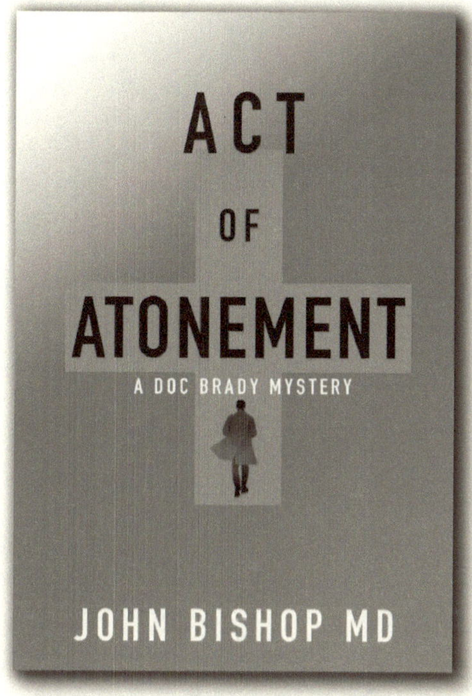

I hope you have enjoyed *Act of Fate*, the fifth book in the Doc Brady Mystery series. I'm pleased to present you with a sneak peek of *Act of Atonement*, the sixth book.

Please visit **JohnBishopAuthor.com** to learn more.

PREACHER AND BULL

Sometime in the 70s

The day began with such promise. Two friends, and very unlikely ones at that, making a trip south and east just to eat at Kitty's Purple Cow in Surfside Beach, Texas. Kitty's had the best burgers in those parts—double meat, double cheese, with bacon and jalapeños, served on a toasted sesame-seed bun, slathered with butter and Kitty's own brand of homemade aioli sauce. You could sit outside at a redwood or concrete table under a palm-thatch umbrella and enjoy the sounds of the beach near the confluence of the Gulf of Mexico and Galveston Bay. Or so Bull had said, since he was the experienced diner at Kitty's.

As far as Preacher knew, Bull had no other name. Of course, Bull had a first and last name, but Preacher didn't know what they were and really didn't care. Preacher had so few friends in his crazy, mixed-up life, he was happy as a clam to just have Bull as his traveling buddy.

Bull and Preacher were hobos. The word "hobo" sometimes had a negative connotation, implying "bum" or "tramp" or just about any word that would describe someone who doesn't work and more likely than not was also a "wino." But Bull and Preacher took great offense at being called any one of these other names because, in their respective minds, a hobo was simply a traveling worker. A bum did not work at all. A tramp worked only when forced to. But a hobo, well, he was gainfully employed but didn't have enough money or social skills to have his own transportation, and definitely did not fit into one of the molds you're supposed to fit into to be a so-called "standard" member of the work force.

Preacher and Bull liked their wine, there was no denying that. Thunderbird, Night Train, Wild Irish Rose, all favorites. These wines were "fortified" and, through some process of fermentation that they didn't understand, ended up being around 20 percent alcohol. This amount of alcohol packed a wallop, both while you were drinking it, and most certainly when the morning hangover arrived, accompanied by the sledgehammer that pounded your head until the cure arrived, which was more fortified wine. An endless cycle, for sure, but that was their life. Not that they would turn down beer or cheap whiskey, but wine seemed to be the cheapest and most accessible alcohol available, and certainly had the most predictable outcome.

The other fact of their respective lives that embodied nonconformity was their mode of transportation: riding the rails. That, in train lingo, was the epitome of being a hobo, at least in the mind of the railroad employees, who spent many a dollar trying to rid the freight trains of the scourge. Although there were many trains to choose from, Bull and Preacher loved the Katy, short for the Missouri-Kansas-Texas Railroad company. Say M-K-T a bunch of times in succession, and you get Katy, for short. The Katy's tracks ran from Kansas City all the way to Galveston, Texas.

The Katy was the most liberal in allowing "traveling workers" to board their freight trains without paying. Of course, the tricky part was running alongside the tracks, grabbing a ladder that was welded to each boxcar, and hoisting yourself up without getting run over by the rail wheels. Bull and Preacher had seen their share of men literally cut in half while trying to board a train illegally; it happened when getting off the train, too, although it much less common.

The Katy used "yard bulls," essentially railroad cops, to police the train stations and railroad yards. Their job was to secure the rail yards and prevent theft from or damage to railroad property. So, men who were riding the rails were on constant lookout for the bulls, whose job was to keep the boxcars clear of hobos and the like. But you couldn't watch everybody all the time, and usually, eventually, men like Preacher and Bull were able to board a train illegally and head out for their destination.

This was how Preacher and Bull met. Bull was himself a yard bull based in Oklahoma City, a Katy terminal. And Preacher lived in Oklahoma City, that is, when he was sober and had gainful employment. Preacher's skills ran along the line of sales. He had worked for many door-to-door sales companies, including Fuller Brush, Encyclopedia Britannica, and Sunbeam vacuum cleaners. But his specialty was selling the New King James Bible. Man, he could sell those Bibles. Problem for Preacher was that selling anything involved cold calling on households, and back in those days, for the most part, the men went to work, the kids went to school, and the wives stayed home alone. And with his good looks, that afforded all sorts of opportunities to get himself into trouble.

Bull, back in the days of his employment with M-K-T Railroad, had thrown Preacher out of an empty boxcar so many times, he couldn't remember. Over time, they would have conversations about life (which were usually enhanced by fortified wine). They eventually struck up an odd friendship and started traveling together. Bull was able to maintain his job as a railroad bull via a special dispensation from the Katy bosses, so he was able to ply his trade in the various cities along the Katy routes—Omaha, Kansas City, St. Louis, Oklahoma City, Dallas, Ft. Worth, all the way south to Houston and Galveston. And Preacher did whatever Preacher did to eke out a living.

And so it was, on that warm evening in July, that Preacher and Bull deboarded the Katy in Galveston, Texas, and by some small miracle were able to hitch a ride in the back of a pickup the forty miles to Kitty's Purple Cow. Preacher had a bottle of Night Train left over from the ride down from Oklahoma City, and while Bull ordered their burgers, Preacher staked out an outside table and listened to the surf.

Bull brought out a tray stacked with the burgers, fries, onion rings, and two tall glasses of iced tea. While they enjoyed their meal, they noticed a good-looking young woman giving Preacher "the eye." Or at least Bull assumed she was looking at Preacher. After all, Bull was over six feet tall, heavy, and nearly bald, and he had a mug on him with all sorts of distortions from multiple fights. Preacher, on the other hand, was five feet eight inches or so and a lean 140 pounds, with a full head of black, slicked-back hair and a smile that showed his pearly whites in all their glory. And the more the young woman stared, the madder Bull became.

Preacher tried to defuse the situation, having been in this position before, but to no avail. Bull had killed most of the bottle of wine by himself, and he wasn't a pleasant drunk. All of a sudden he stood up, yelled something to the effect that he was sick and tired of Preacher having all the fun, and pulled out a pistol. It looked to Preacher to be a .25 caliber, which was a pea shooter, but a gun was a gun and capable of killing when aimed at the proper body part.

Preacher stood and tried to wrestle the weapon away, meanwhile hearing screams from the folks eating their dinner and trying to clear a getaway path to safety. The two struggled, and with Bull being the much larger man, he was able to gain dominance with the gun. But it seemed to Preacher that maybe the wine had weakened his friend, and suddenly he felt he was gaining control of the situation, when the weapon discharged. There was silence for a moment, and then Bull began to fall. Blood began to stain Bull's chest. Preacher felt the weapon slip from his friend's hand and used that moment to look around his torso to make sure he wasn't the one that was hit. No, clearly Bull had taken the round and was falling fast. Preacher screamed for help and tried to use napkins to stem the flow of blood from what was now an obvious entry wound in Bull's chest. All he could hear in the background was "call the police" and "there's been a shooting" and "there's a murderer at Kitty's." As Bull fell, Preacher fell with him, and he saw the light beginning to leave his friend's eyes. Bull wasn't going to make it, and there Preacher was, holding a gun, and about to be the obvious choice of whom to blame. Fear took over, and he lit out.

ABOUT THE AUTHOR

Dr. John Bishop has led a triple life. This orthopedic surgeon and keyboard musician has combined two of his talents into a third, as the author of the beloved Doc Brady mystery series. Beyond applying his medical expertise at a relatable and comprehensible level, Dr. Bishop, through his fictional counterpart Doc Brady, also infuses his books with his love of not only Houston and Galveston, Texas, but especially with his love for his adored wife. Bishop's talented Doc Brady is confident yet humble; brilliant, yet a genuinely nice and funny guy who happens to have a knack for solving medical mysteries. Above all, he is the doctor who will cure you of your blues and boredom. Step into his world with the first five books of the series, and you'll be clamoring for more.